David Colgrove

Six P.M. Sunday

A Novel

yonek enterprises

Published by:
Yonek Enterprises, LLC.
PO Box 7267
Redlands, Ca. 92375
Contact publisher@
The Sandborg Literary Agency
309.343.6822

First Yonek Enterprises, LLC. Hardcover printing: May 2006

ISBN: 0-9778376-0-2
LCCN: 2006923994

Cover design: 1106 Design

For Stephanie and Jason, my precious children,
to whom I owe everything.
For opening my cynical eyes
to the possibility of miracles.

I work in the busiest Trauma Center

in Orange County, California.

Fifty thousand patients a year busy.

Ten major traumas a day busy.

Gunshot wounds and stab-wounds

rolling in around the clock.

Home base for what we like to call

The Orange County Knife and Gun Club.

Part 1

*"Life is what happens to you
while you're making other plans."*
—John Lennon
9/October/1940–8/December/1980

I've saved hundreds of lives, delivered fifty-two babies in my forty months as a resident physician at UC Irvine Medical Center. I've cracked eighty-seven chests, massaged eighty-seven traumatized, bloodless hearts back to life.

I've been threatened, mauled, and berated by out-of-control individuals. Some of whom were my patients, the majority of whom were my bosses, the Emergency Department attending physicians.

I've faced death every day and night since my internship began on July first three and a half years ago. I lost so much rest during my first year on the job that I slept through an entire week's vacation. But I wouldn't have it any other way. For two reasons. I absolutely love my job. For a long time, it was the *only* good thing in my life. More importantly, that's the way it has to be in the crucible that is medical training. We suffer and sacrifice, evaluate ourselves constantly, while working under impossible conditions so that we can function at peak efficiency under the worst stress imaginable. The Attendings work us like dogs so we can pull your feet out of the fire, should our paths cross on a rainy Tuesday at three in the morning.

But my narrative doesn't focus solely on life and death in the ER. This is primarily a story of life with my lover, Natalie. We had it all, intelligence, strong personalities, fascinating jobs, and undeniably powerful chemistry. We had a relationship forged under intense pressure. A bond that seemed unshakable. We cared so much for each other that we staked our love on the illusory promise of a perfect marriage.

But we all know about the quest for perfection in the real world. We all know about relationships built upon a foundation of sexual chemistry.

I'm Steven Adler, and this is my story.

Chapter 1

I can sum up my life in a few sentences. I'm twenty-eight years old, have three hundred bucks in the bank but don't owe a cent to anyone. I've never been married, live in a crappy one-bedroom apartment in the city of Orange, and practically live in the Emergency Room. But I don't feel sorry for myself. Not at all. I have lots of friends, have actually been in lust a time or two, and I drive a great car, a ten-year-old Guards Red Porsche 911. What more could a Southern California native ask for?

The most important thing in my life, though, is my career. I love my job; love the adrenaline spike of a bad radio call, the satisfaction of pulling off a great save. I have nine months to go in my four-year residency and it seems as if I've only been here a couple of weeks. My days are filled with the aches and pains of the walking wounded. But I live for my nights in the Department. Everything happens at night. All the Hell-raisers are out and about. All the crazies come in, and Lord do we love the crazies in the ER.

But that wasn't happening this particular evening. Thursday, ten o'clock, September fifth, the slowest night in the last few months. Our census was down forty percent from a year ago. *The Orange County Register* had just run a series of articles about a newly forged truce in the Santa Ana gang wars. Great for the community. A real relief, as everybody wanted to put a stop to the killing. But from a strictly selfish perspective, peace in the barrio was bad for our business.

I'd done all my stupid paperwork, finalized the schedule through the rest of the year; everything I could think of to keep busy, everything but rotating the tires on my car. I was seriously bored, bogged down by lassitude, so I decided to walk around, just to keep from falling asleep.

I prowled through the unit, checked and rechecked the defibrillators, made sure the carts were stacked, even went into our holding cell, affectionately known as Drunk and Disorderly, confirmed that the wrestling mats we used to protect the drug-addled were neat and tidy. Our chief of security, George "The Mangler" Gomez, was in there, practicing takedowns with a burly third-year student. George was my best friend in the department. He stood five-eight, weighed two-thirty and moonlighted as a pro wrestler. He was featured every Wednesday night on Channel Five and had a huge following in the Barrio. He'd comped me a couple of tickets to the Olympic in LA three months ago and I was blown away. He'd beaten the world champ, a guy named Hulk something-or-other, and proved to be a tremendous crowd favorite. He told me the following week that it was all scripted. Said he was supposed to lose his next match. I was shocked and heartbroken.

I stood and watched them grunting and huffing like a couple of bulls. Must have watched them the better part of ten minutes. Bored out of my skull. Would have killed to do a fecal impaction case. Wait, strike that; I'd never be that apathetic as long as I lived.

Amy Tran, our new night nurse supervisor, passed me in the hall, stifling a yawn as she pushed up the ramp toward the cafeteria. She stopped opposite me in the hallway, back against the drunk-tank doorway. Her yawn was contagious. I suppressed one of my own as I greeted her. "Anything cooking, Amy?"

8

She rubbed her eyes, looked ready for a four-hour nap. "Nope. The radio's dead, haven't heard anything from the medics in more than an hour." She shook her head. "Weird. The waiting room's empty. I haven't been down here that long, but I've never seen it like this."

I took a peek at my watch. More than two hours to go. Only two major cases all night; the worst one had come in at six. A drunk driver had hit a family headed to a tee ball game over in Tustin. The drunk came in without a scratch. The family he hit? They had it much worse. The mom was in the ICU with a concussion; rule out subdural hematoma. The kids were okay, thankfully, but the dad was in surgery with a lacerated liver. Made me mad enough to chew nails, but I'd seen it my whole career. The fucking drunks came through without messing up their hair; the people they hit were mangled for life. If they even made it out of here alive. Somebody had to do something about this: Judges? Legislators? *Anybody?* It made us crazy in the ER.

Overall, the skimpy caseload had made for the longest shift of my career. I nodded sympathetically, my thoughts on the same track. "I know, Amy. I'd give anything for an interesting case."

She grabbed my arm, eyes wide. I'd just done it. My stupid, unbelievably naïve fate—tempting words were sure to unleash The Curse. ER's everywhere were ruled by superstitions: *Never* complain about being slow, lest jerks, morons, and mayhem inundate you immediately. Full moons flushed out the crazies. Rookie interns brought bad luck; carried their own personal black clouds into the department. And never, ever wear white shoes, lest you be showered with blood from an unexpected source: a chest tube in a bad gunshot patient, a GI bleeder who's vomiting all over the room or . . .

"Ectopic. Incoming. Trauma One. BP sixty over palp. Three minutes out." The radio nurse, Sharon McDonald, was leaning into the hallway, headset around her neck, screaming up and down the hall to alert the troops.

Ectopic pregnancies, which occurred when the fetus implanted inside or even occasionally outside the confines of the fallopian

9

tube instead of in the wall of the uterus, were potentially one of the worst cases we saw. Treacherous and stealthy, ectopics caught even the best physicians off guard occasionally. The women typically came in with vague abdominal pain; most, if not all, were unaware of being pregnant. The usual patient came in, was worked up as an appendicitis or even a gallbladder attack, put in one of the back rooms awaiting labs and occasionally, after a few hours of waiting, out of nowhere, all hell would break loose. The abnormal implantation of the fetus would sometimes erode through an artery, causing uncontrolled intra-abdominal bleeding and lead, in the worst case, to . . .

"Full arrest. One minute out." Amy and I were already setting up in Trauma One. My resident had the cut-down tray ready to go in case we needed to access a large vein in a hurry to replace her blood. Respiratory was in place, the lab was here for the cross match, orderlies for patient transfer. Everybody present and accounted for. Almost everybody, I realized with a sickening jolt of terror. I took another headcount to confirm my fear and cursed under my breath; shot out into the hall.

"Where's OB? They call back?" I was met with a blank stare from the teenaged ward clerk. Shit! I *knew* it. Nobody called. Bad as it was, I knew I needed to stay calm, no matter what. The troops took their cues from their leader; for better or worse, and I *absolutely* couldn't afford a panic situation.

I took a second to compose myself, boiling inside, shot a look at the idiot clerk. "Patty, you need to put in a stat page to the senior OB resident." She nodded blankly, went back to her phone call.

I'd had it with her. Couldn't afford to be polite anymore. I ran the two steps to the nurse's station, slammed the phone into its cradle and snarled, "Now, Patty. Do it now."

Mad as I'd been in years, churning with adrenaline, I turned back toward the Trauma Room and nearly collided with the medics.

They rushed through the door, an ashen-faced young woman strapped to the gurney, still as a corpse. I shoved to the head of the table and listened to their hurried report. "Intubated en route from Tustin-South Coast. Sixteen gauge, left antecubital. In full arrest a minute ago. Bolused her with a liter of saline, shocked her twice." They stopped the gurney parallel with the table. "Got her into sinus. Rate of ninety-five. Fully diaphoretic. BP forty over zip."

We quickly unhooked the restraints and hoisted her onto the table. The crew chief read from his clipboard. "ER doc at Tustin did a tap after the HCG came back positive. Frank blood." That meant the diagnosis of a ruptured ectopic pregnancy was confirmed. A positive pregnancy test and an aspiration of the abdominal cavity that returned pure blood left no doubt.

Respiratory hooked the endotracheal tube to the ventilator and I took a quick listen to her chest. Breath sounds bilaterally. The tube the Tustin ER doc put in was in proper position. A break for us.

The fire chief helped put her in Trendelenberg, a head-down positioning maneuver we used to help maintain a patient's blood pressure; a last-ditch, low-tech procedure to stave off cardiogenic shock. He continued his report as he cranked the bed into position. "Tustin transferred when she started to crump. Couldn't get an OR crew in fast enough." I looked at the patient's pretty face, smooth brown complexion a washed-out shade of tan from her acute loss of blood. A halo of unkempt hair and a cheap blue plastic necklace nested between her breasts. She looked about sixteen.

The nurses cut off her worn, freshly laundered clothes and I instantly guessed the truth. This patient had been "dumped." She was clearly poor, probably had no insurance, no job, no money. Tustin worked her up, met the minimum standard required by law, and then did a "wallet biopsy," which she'd failed. They must have taken their time after the financial check, judging by her grave condition, probably gave priority to the paying clientele, I thought bitterly. The rest was painfully obvious: Her BP began to fall and they called the medics in a panic. Got on the radio and dumped her over here, sent the poor girl on her way, circling the drain, half dead. We saw it all the time

Made us livid. They should just send them to us from the jump. We're prepared for everything and we don't give a rat's ass about the patient's wallet. This is what we do.

I took a quick look at the IV in her left arm and made a vow to take this one up with Administration in the morning.

Trauma One was set up exactly like the OR suites upstairs, right down to the anesthesia machine, dedicated wall suction, and operating lights. Behind my left shoulder stood a bank of cabinets filled with sterile abdominal and chest trays. We drilled for this constantly, could crack a chest in less than five minutes, surgically expose an arm vein for fluid or blood replacement access, and massage blood into the bloodstream by manually pumping on injured, failing hearts. We could even . . .

"Open her here, Adler. She won't make it upstairs." Natalie Bogner came rushing in; hair haphazardly stuffed into a bonnet, scrub top untucked, surgical mask already tied in place. She cut her eyes from the patient to the monitors, took in the grave situation at a glance, and began barking out orders.

Looked at Amy first. "Prep her. Just splash on the Betadine." Natalie shoved her hands into a pair of sterile six-and-a-halves and waved a hand over the patient's trunk. "Chest to pubes."

Carol Vigner, one of the staff nurses, broke open the major abdominal pack, quickly spread it over a large Mayo stand and walked toward Natalie, surgical gown open in her outstretched arms. She shook her off. "No time, Carol. We'll do this without."

She grabbed a number ten scalpel and gave me an expectant look. "Just gonna' stand there, Adler?" She gestured to the pale belly framed by blue sterile towels before us. "I need another pair of hands." I ran to the sink, grabbed a pair of seven-and-a-halves and hustled back to the left side of the table.

"What about anesthesia?" I took a quick look around the room. Nobody had arrived from upstairs yet and Natalie was clearly ready to cut. Amy's thirty-second prep was done, the patient had a good IV line, and her pressure was stable, albeit gut-wrenchingly low, at forty over zero. We had everything we needed except that critical member of the team.

"Can't wait. On the way." Natalie made a quick transverse incision from one side of the patient's pelvis to the other. Dark blood immediately welled up behind her scalpel stroke. "Besides. She's not going to feel this." She was right; the unconscious woman never flinched.

I blotted a stream of dark blood trickling from the incision, looked up; tried to meet her eyes. They were still trained on the incision. I spoke to the top of her blue-paper bonnet. "Where's your attending, Natalie?"

She didn't look up. Another swipe of the scalpel and she was through the thin layer of yellow subcutaneous fat and on top of the fascia, a shiny, transparent layer of tissue surrounding the abdominal muscles. "Up in OB, doing a crash C section."

She shoved my suction into the wound, caught a bleeder with an expert flick of her mosquito clamp, and said, "It's just us." Grabbed the other end of the bleeder and the blood stopped flowing. "Three-O silk." I reached over to the Mayo stand, but Amy was faster. She was gowned and gloved, a large retractor called an Army/Navy in one hand, an eighteen-inch strand of silk suture in the other. Natalie's voice was tight, her words clipped; her hands, however, never wavered. She guided my left hand closer. "Suck here, Steven. Can't see." Bad as it seemed at first, Natalie had the bleeding controlled in ten seconds.

She grabbed the retractor, motioned for me to do the same. We tugged against the muscles, fought a virtual brick wall of resistance. The patient's abdominal muscles, amongst the strongest in the body, were still rigid because the patient was not properly anesthetized. Surgical patients typically got a dose of a muscle relaxant, actually a paralytic agent like . . .

"Sux. Give me a hundred and fifty milligrams of succinylcholine." Alan Nachman, third-year anesthesia resident, and one of my best friends, blew into the room. A wiry marathon runner at five-five, tireless worker, competent as most of his attendings, he was clearly what we needed for this horrendioma of a case. He took a loaded, labeled syringe from Carol Vigner, pinched the IV line, and quickly administered the paralytic agent. Took a peek down toward the belly. "That should help a bit. Get you past the abs anyhow."

Nachman dialed in the ventilator settings, checked the IV placement, and grabbed the lab tech standing a few feet away, leaning stoically against the wall, clip board in hand. "Type and cross her for six. Need it yesterday." He adjusted the IV rate wide-open, checked the anesthesia gauges, and swore under his breath. "Anybody bother to get some fucking O-Neg?" He was calling for fresh blood from so-called universal donors, an urgent replacement source when there was no time for an adequate cross-match.

"Five minutes away," Carol Vigner shouted from the hallway as she jotted a progress note, phone handset balanced on her shoulder.

"Fuck it." Nachman squeezed the IV fluid bag between his hands in a desperate attempt to push fluids into the patient's veins; support her falling blood pressure. He yelled out to Carol, "Get me five units FFP, then." It was a smart move on his part, one I'd used dozens of times. He was ordering fresh frozen plasma. A "quick and dirty" way to increase fluid volume. Fresh frozen plasma didn't have the oxygen carrying capacity of blood but was quicker to get and would tide us over for a few precious minutes.

Natalie shoved the retractor through the muscle plain. I did the same. Noticed immediately it was much easier this time with the Sux on board. She directed my Army/Navy retractor across the patient's belly until we were through the first layer of muscles, then up toward the patient's head to spread the last layer, adjusted the pitch of my retractor so she could see deeper into the wound. "Good, Steven. Now, hold this while I enter." She handed her retractor to me, directed me to spread harder as she made a quick slice through the peritoneum.

She wiggled a few fingers into a space the size of her fist and used her left hand under the thick, translucent membrane as a guard as she cut along the full length of the skin incision, taking care to avoid cutting the intestines that rested just beneath the millimeter-thick peritoneal layer.

There was a rush of bright red blood and sticky clots the size of baseballs as soon as Natalie entered the abdominal cavity. My suction was quickly overwhelmed. Natalie shoved her arms into the belly, began scooping out the clots with both hands. I was amazed, hadn't seen this much blood since my last gunshot-wound to the belly. Natalie's frantic voice interrupted my musings. "Amy. Hook up another suction for Dr. Adler."

She directed my metal Yankaur deeper into the abdomen while she felt for the dome of the uterus and the attached fallopian tubes. Head bent in concentration; Natalie was up to her elbows in blood, her eyes never leaving the abdomen, voice muffled by her mask. "Use one of Dr. Nachman's if you need to." She nodded toward the anesthesia cart, aware that there was always a spare suction setup there. The nurse quickly powered up the anesthesia suction and handed me another Yankaur, which Natalie promptly positioned directly under her fingers. She took a moment to meet my eyes. "Good, Steven. Now maybe I can catch the artery."

She felt her way around the bloody cavity, guided my hand deeper, along the dome of the uterus as she shot a question toward the head of the bed. "Alan, what's her pressure doing?" Natalie held my suction in place against the artery, grabbed a lap sponge, a cotton gauze about eight inches square, and packed it against the right side of the uterus; directed her voice once again in Nachman's direction. "I can probably get a handle on her bleeding, but she's about bled out, the vessels are flaccid as *hell* in here."

"I know that, Natalie." His voice was on the edge of panic. Nachman was squeezing in the last bag of Fresh Frozen Plasma as fast as the IV tubing would allow. "Be nice if we had some fucking blood."

Carol Vigner rushed into the room a second later, cradling six one-liter bags of blood in her arms. "Here you are, Dr. Nachman."

She set the blood on his machine and quickly began helping him with the infusion.

I took a second's break as Natalie packed the wound. Looked across the table at my resident. "Martin. Do a cut down. Dr. Nachman's going to need access." Randy Martin was one of my best second-years. He knew the drill and could easily do a cut down on his own. As we say in residency training, *see one, do one, teach one.*

I watched over the drapes. He cut through the skin and sub-cutaneous tissue on the inside of the elbow looking for a large vein. Found the antecubital and spread the soft tissue away from the vessel, just as I'd taught him. I silently ticked off the steps and watched him perform to perfection; clamp the upper part of the vessel, make a horizontal slit in the front wall of the vein, grab the pediatric feeding tube, about ten times the diameter of an IV catheter, slide it in, and remove the clamp. Now slip a tie around the tubing and secure it to the vein. I smiled with pride under my mask as he slipped the tube home, a perfect job. Done in less than two minutes.

Nachman hooked up the blood bag to the plastic hub of the feeding tube and squeezed in a unit in less than ninety seconds. He changed out the bag and had two more units in, five minutes later. Took a satisfied look at the monitors, caught my eye. "Good, Adler, now I can do something for you." He took a peek around the drapes. "How we doing with the bleeding, Natalie?"

Natalie was a picture of total concentration. "Found it. The damned ovarian artery's pumping like a motherfucker." She removed the sodden lap sponge and drew my sucker into the cavity. "Carefully, Steven. I need to get a tie . . ." She moved my hand a millimeter to the left, slipped a mosquito clamp around the ruptured artery and locked it down. The sense of relief in the room was palpable as the hemorrhage slowed.

She nodded toward the Mayo stand. "Give me a Two-O silk." I handed her a suture with a shaking left hand, the sudden spill-off of adrenaline showing in my tremor. She grabbed it deftly with another mosquito, wound it around the tip of the clamp and threw her knots.

Nachman leaned over the anesthesia drapes and whistled. "Nice job, Natalie. Only took fifteen minutes." He turned and adjusted the IV rates, slowing the flow of blood to avoid fluid overload.

Natalie never broke stride; hands busily mopping up, her head practically in the abdomen. "We're not done, yet. Still have to do a salpingectomy." She swept a clot away from the destroyed fallopian tube with another fresh sponge. "Her right tube's shot. Be lucky if I can save her ovary."

"Her BP's eighty over fifty, rate's down to one-ten, so we're okay up here." Nachman plopped down in his chair for the first time since coming in. A sure sign the crisis had passed.

The next half-hour passed quickly as I helped Natalie resect the damaged tube. She was able to spare the ovary. A definite break for the patient. I admired her dexterity and sound operative judgment. She never hesitated, never wavered while taking out the vital fallopian tube. Like all good surgeons, she lived by the credo that if it was causing a problem, and was damaged beyond repair it had to go, no matter what.

I'd known Natalie Bogner for nearly eight years, since our first day in Gross Anatomy at UCLA. Four years later, she'd ranked number five in our class of one hundred forty, the highest-finishing female graduate in our school's history. She'd been accepted to every OB residency program on her list, including Brigham's back East at Mass General. I was surprised to see her at UCI, frankly. Not that our training was second-rate, it just didn't measure up to Harvard's. She'd stayed in Orange County for her husband, Henry Marx, the Porsche Guy, owner of Newport Motors, a sawed-off, bald multimillionaire and overall arrogant prick. Okay, that's my opinion. I'd seen him once, at their wedding, and hated him on sight. Was I giving him the benefit of the doubt? Had I spent enough time with him to form such a harsh opinion? No and emphatically no.

You've probably guessed by now that I had, and still have, a major thing for Natalie. Every male with a pulse as well as more than a few females in our class did. Natalie Bogner-Marx won the DNA trifecta: she's gorgeous, highly intelligent, and talented, a combination that's as rare in medicine as it is in any other highly competitive field. She carries maybe a hundred fifteen well-toned pounds on a five-eight frame. Keeps her long black hair expensively coiffed, eyes the color of acid-washed denim, and a smile that works better and faster than Viagra. Then there's her voice. Think of Kathleen Turner driving William Hurt insane in *Body Heat.*

Our relationship thus far has been the epitome of unrequited lust; I had it in spades, she couldn't care less. I was always relegated to the dreaded, just-a-friend hell. I admit that I'm not the most confident guy in California when it comes to women, but I did give it a try. More than once. Over the years at UCLA, we'd gone out for coffee, studied Anatomy late into the night, gone to a few Bruin basketball games, the usual subterfuge that we pathetic male creatures practice like hungry rats running a maze. Big surprise, we'll do anything to get into a woman's panties. Even endure Friend's Hell. Predictably, I'd gone home every night alone, with bruised pride and Big Bruin-Blue Balls.

Nachman's voice, barking an order to the charge nurse, brought me up short. Natalie was almost finished. As a surgeon, she was fast and good. Way better than a lot of the OB attendings I'd seen upstairs during my internship. Fifteen minutes after the salpingectomy, she had checked for recurrent bleeding, irrigated the belly, and closed the three major internal layers.

A minute later, she took a deep breath, stretched her back and sighed deeply. She caught me staring at her nipples, straining against her thin scrub-top. Lord have mercy. She shook her head. Gave me a sly smile. "Have your resident and the student close for me, Steven. I'm going to dictate."

Our eyes met and I smiled under the mask. She remained impassive; exhausted, no doubt, by the stress. I was exhilarated by the harried save, high on the adrenaline spike I'd needed like cocaine. "No problem. We can handle it."

She bumped gloved fists with me and nodded. "Thanks, Steven. Good job."

"Right back at you. Fastest I've ever seen."

She stripped off her blood-soaked gloves. Blue eyes intently on mine. "I'm fast *and* good, Adler." She wiped away the wet talc from her hands with a dry sterile towel. "Any hack can be fast."

Typical surgeon, I thought with a laugh. Arrogant because they *are* perfect. Don't believe it? Just ask them.

I helped transfer the patient to the floor, supervised the ICU nurses, and was in the elevator five minutes later. Looked down at my brand-new kicks. Snow-white Nikes. The one with the blue swoosh. Fifty-five bucks at Sport Chalet. Spotted all across both tongues and toes with fresh blood and congealed clot, the leather soaked, laces a disgusting shade of pink. I cursed my own stupidity all the way down to the locker room. Here I was, nearly an attending, bemoaning our slow night, practically begging The Curse to pay us a visit, and now this—a brand new pair of white Nikes shot to hell. I felt like a dumb-ass rookie.

Chapter 2

Alone in the locker room a few minutes later, I stuffed my bloodied, sweat-stained scrubs in a hamper, stripped out of my boxers and bloody socks and headed for the shower. I stopped in front of the mirror outside the row of stalls, caught a glimpse, and took a quick inventory. My six-three, swimmer's body was in good shape, thanks to frequent workouts at the Jack LaLanne across Chapman Avenue from my apartment. I still had all of my light brown hair and decent enough features: prominent nose, strong chin, and a good smile, thanks to three years of expert orthodontia. I was nobody's idea of a leading man, just an interesting-looking, halfway attractive guy. I ranked myself about a seven on a scale of a hundred. But I'd been told that I'm better than average looking. Hell, I'd settle for that in a heartbeat.

I chose the shower stall closest to the back wall, cranked the hot water all the way to the maximum setting. Ten minutes of running water and I felt like I'd had an hour's sleep. My muscles began to relax; I could feel my toes and fingers for the first time in what felt like days, even started to lose my tension headache.

I soaped up, turned my back to the water, closed my eyes, and slumped forward, alone with my thoughts.

Steam billowed toward the open archway; the overhead lights shone opaque; the life-and-death sounds of the ER were muffled, far away as in a half-forgotten dream.

A minute or two later, I heard a shuffling noise to my left, near the open archway; must be another resident getting off shift, I thought. I closed my eyes tighter, wanted to stay lost in my warm cocoon.

A form appeared out of the gloom. I tried to focus through the steam, nodded distractedly, got no response, and wondered, what the fuck? What kind of creep sneaks around like that? Didn't they see me here?

The person approached without a word. Kept coming, water splashing gently on my ankles a few moments later. Two more steps, a few inches from my face, features obscured by the steam. I tried again to see through the billowing cloud, caught a few details: athletic body; long straight hair, a slim, black, vertical strip standing in stark relief against white skin framed by flared hips. Long, sculpted thighs.

She came into my arms, cloaked in mist, glossy, wet, black hair brushing her shoulders. Kissed me full on the lips.

Strong tapered fingers tight around me, gentle at first, then firm, hurried. Insistent. I was hard before she broke our embrace a moment or an hour later.

She bent and brushed an urgent kiss all the way down my belly. Took me in her mouth and I was near release in seconds.

Gently moved her head, her chin in my palm. Right thumb brushing her lips.

Eyes closed, her hand on me again, frantic now. My fingers trailing up her thigh in the dark.

Fingers sliding inside her in the mist. Whispered begging. Over and over again. *Make me come.*

No sounds now except hissing water. Hearts pounding though our chests. Excitement to last a lifetime. Emotion impossible to sustain beyond the next hurried breath.

Whispers on my neck. "Please, Steven. *Please.*"

Kissed her with eight years of pent-up need. Hands on her ass.

Spun her around, arched back up against the tile.

Lips tight on mine. She moaned deeply. I inhaled her passion, endless craving firing my cells as she opened to me.

Held our kiss. Breathing forgotten as she urged me in.

Harder than I'd ever thought possible. Tighter than I thought I could stand.

Desperate embrace.

Time completely lost in an ancient rhythm.

Fists hammering my ribs.

Scream in her throat. Nails on my back. "Steven, Steven, Steven. Oh, *God,* Steven."

She held me tighter still. Urged me to release.

Kissed me harder.

"Oh, *Jesus.* Natalie." Impossibly tight now. "God, you feel so good, Natalie."

Moved her hips faster with each breath.

Hands on my shoulders and a heartbeat later she was cradled in my lap.

Long legs tight around my waist.

A mingled scream and we came as one.

A long moment later, I stood under the stream, Natalie in my arms, close as only a man and woman could be. Head on my shoulder, lips at my ear. "Thank you, Steven." She brushed her lips against mine, tasted of sex. "You don't know how much I needed that." She wiggled in my lap, had me ready to come again in a few short seconds. I tried to hold back. A slow, circular move I'd never experienced before made it even worse for me as she kissed me long and hard on my neck.

She pulled slightly away and looked down, her voice a mixture of detached professionalism and debauchery. "Why, Doctor Adler. Judging from what's going on down there, I'd say I wasn't the only one needing some special attention tonight."

She kissed me quickly on the lips, braced her hands on my shoulders, and gave a little hop. Looked down. Smiled sadly, gave me a light caress, and was gone.

Her voice carried from the locker room, over the hissing shower. "I hope you know how long I've wanted that, Steven."

That just shows you about life, I thought, as I stared down at my wilting erection. Eight years of blue balls and she's the one who's been waiting. Go figure.

I grabbed a towel from the cabinet and sang for the first time since junior high, all the way to my locker. "Doctor, Doctor, give me the cure. I got a bad case of loving you." Grabbed a fresh pair of scrubs, combed fingers through my hair, and laughed to myself. You mean lust, Doctor, Doctor Adler. You've got a bad case of lust. Lust is good, though. Sometimes even leads to love, I reminded myself with an idiotic smile.

As exciting as this turn of events was, I tried to make sense of it. Maybe that's Natalie's way of relieving stress after a bad case, I thought. She's been through a lot lately; I'd heard rumors for months about her marriage breaking up, the hellish pressure of residency, the anxiety we all faced about getting a job. God knows I'd fantasized about that exact scenario hundreds of times. With an interchangeable cast: Amy Tran, my charge nurse, Barbara Manning, Jane Quon, the beautiful Internal Medicine resident I'd spent entire nights drooling over. Natalie a few times a week, as well. Would I have acted out my fantasies with the other women? I'm sure I would have. Eventually. Not with Natalie, though. Always thought she was out of reach, even before she married The Porsche Guy. Never saw my chances as anything but the old slim and none.

Goes to show you about life, I thought. Not one bit of action since I broke up with my last girlfriend, Elaine Liu, the X-Ray tech, and now the woman of my dreams practically attacks me in the shower.

I stuffed the towel into the hamper, dumped my dirty Nikes in the trash, and grabbed an ancient, emergency pair from the

24

top shelf. As my arm cleared the locker, shoes in hand, a folded square of paper hit the floor near my feet.

A common enough site around here, I thought, as I stared at the floor and the lined yellow progress note lying next to my foot. I opened it up; read the words in Natalie's firm and feminine hand: "Check your look in the mirror, gorgeous. *Before* you go back out."

I palmed the note and ran to the sinks. Expecting what? A newfound confidence? No question about that. Better features? No fucking way. Lurid fantasies-come-true only took a person so far. Checked my face, nothing. Pulled my shirt up, nothing. I moved closer, leaned over the sink. My eye caught something low down on my neck, on the right side. Pulled the shirt down over my clavicles and there it was. Natalie's lips imprinted for all to see. Believe it or not, my first hickey. Nearly thirty, an attending next July, and I looked like a sexed-up teenager, sneaking back home from his first serious date.

I shook my head, headed down the ramp for the inevitable jokes and whispers, wishing like hell that I'd worn my turtleneck tee. Unfolded the note once again. Noticed for the first time the postscript, tiny and nearly hidden at the bottom of the note. "You made me come, Steven. Three times. I love the way you do it. I got tired of waiting for you to make the first move. Sorry if I stepped on you toes, Nat."

I liked that last part. She's been the object of my desire for eight years and I'd never had the guts to make a serious play. I had a good laugh all the way back to the Department, found myself humming like a dolt. Step all you want, Natalie.

Looking back, I realized my life changed forever that night in September. Of course we're never aware of life's transitions, monumental or trivial, positive or negative; not while we're still fighting our way through the journey. No doubt, for most of us, that's as it should be.

Chapter 3

THREE MONTHS LATER

I hadn't seen much of Natalie after that night in September. Just a couple of hurried "Hi, how are yous?" in the cafeteria. She'd called a few days after our shower "date," said she was leaving UCI for a while, something about a two-month infertility fellowship up at Cedars in Beverly Hills. I tried to engage her in conversation, see where we were going, but I had the distinct impression that she didn't want to talk about it. Maybe she was embarrassed, I thought. Probably having second thoughts in the raw light of day. She'd seemed distracted on the phone, so I let her go. For now.

In the mean time, I had a few meaningless dates with Elaine, the X-Ray tech. She was a very nice woman, certainly my type physically, she just wasn't Natalie. Our dates were okay and the sex was decent, just not earth-shaking. I guess we both knew it. We'd reached a stage of entropy in our little relationship and it was clear what lay ahead for us.

I called Elaine before leaving my place to work the night shift. We had a strained ten-minute conversation, circling the obvious for a few minutes, landing on the unspoken emotions and under-currents from our last date at long last. She'd gotten drunk and said some things she'd regretted, was embarrassed about being so badly out of control, didn't remember a whole lot about any-thing that happened after the ride home. My side of the conversa-tion was kind of stilted as well, as I was unsure about where we'd go with our friendship. We ended on a good note, though, decided to give it another try, as there was still some attraction there and Natalie was still clearly out of the picture.

New Year's Eve. Nineteen eighty-six an hour away, six months from graduation and I was stuck working graveyard at UCI. Pass out the party favors and let's get busy! Elaine was under-standably none too happy, but I had been putting my job first a lot lately. For two reasons: I loved it, and, wily bastard that I am, I'd used my work commitments as a convenient excuse to dodge further entanglements. I volunteered for this shift, so I wasn't feeling sorry for myself.

As chief resident, I had the responsibility of scheduling the house officers. Most of them were single, like me, and I usually gave them a break around the holidays, especially this one. I always tried to bend over backward, didn't want to be accused of favoring myself. This was my third consecutive New Year's Eve and so far, so good. The first two New Years were slow until about two-thirty, then all hell broke loose as the bars closed and the parties broke up. Tonight was no exception. A few beer-bottle scalp lacerations, a biker PCP overdose in Med 2 and a roomful of squalling kids with some sort of baffling rash. I turfed that mess to Peds after about ten minutes. As the big cheese, I was able to farm out the simple stuff; fourth-year medical students got the easy lacerations under a surgery intern's supervision. The OD was being handled by third-year Internal Medicine resi-dent, the delicious Jane Quan, and the kids were also out of my hair. I patted myself on the back; three and a half years and I still hadn't had to deal much with kids. I felt very comfortable handling critical Peds, I could always focus and use my skills, even on the tiniest babies; I had run a dozen or more codes and hadn't lost one yet. It was just the fevers and the earaches that got to me; too much screaming, too much wiggling. Besides, I didn't like to deal with the parents. Sad to say, I couldn't relate to the legitimate concerns that they had. Being so much younger than my brother Jake, I was practically an "only." I guess the real reason I had so much trouble with kids was that I had no real role model growing up; felt more than once that I had raised myself because Dad was always working and Mom was in the bag most of the time.

I checked the board and found it nearly empty. With nothing much to do and a few hours to kill before the mad midnight rush, I made a leisurely tour of my kingdom. I checked my look in the mirror outside of our dressing room: Not bad, I thought, spotless white coat, black Nikes. I took stock of my life as I toured the ward, decided that I was happiest in The Department, even on New Year's Eve; wasn't a drinker or a party animal and seriously couldn't see myself anywhere else but here.

UCI, like most large teaching hospitals, was designed with the ER on the first floor, a large receiving bay out back, set up like a warehouse loading dock, with eight marked lanes reserved for paramedic units. The walk-ins accessed my department through a maze of cubicles located off the lobby up front.

Irvine was built in the fifties as an osteopathic hospital, later purchased by the University of California when it began the medical school in 1967. The old place had been expanded several times over the years and now resembled a metastasizing tumor; the original dirt-brown, six-story tower surrounded by satellite offshoots and a whole row of "temporary" office buildings first set in place during the Johnson Administration. The ER was an

29

original fixture and showed its age; cracked tiles in the trauma rooms, worn linoleum and water stains soaking nearly every other ceiling tile. We were located ten feet below street level and surrounded by ramps; from where I stood at the nurse's station, one to my left led up to the cafeteria, the one to my right led up to the elevators and the nursing units.

The pressure was intense most of the time, but we had developed, over the years, unique ways to relax. Slow times at night with no ER attendings in sight usually called for a UCI tradition; Gurney Bumper Cars. We'd strap a willing or, even better, an unwilling med student onto a litter, put one on the ramp to the right, one on the opposite grade, give them a shove and let Newton's laws of physics decide the winner. A modification that I introduced, wheelchair jousting, was even better received by my people. Picture this: Two students strapped into four-point velcro restraints, hurtling down the ramps with only a cardboard tube from housekeeping wedged under their arms as a weapon. Spectacular spinouts earned extra credit, redeemable for free Cokes and microwave popcorn.

I wandered over to the Drunk and Disorderly room, located a few feet down the cafeteria ramp from Security. I loved this little corner of my Department. Found it very peaceful, strangely comforting. During the slow times I often slept on a gurney in this room, especially Tuesday nights, traditionally the quietest evening of all.

Every county or teaching hospital has its own version of the padded room. Ours was a spacious twenty-by-twenty, lined floor-to-ceiling with wrestling mats and stocked with ten or so of the special restraint wheelchairs that I had appropriated for the jousting matches. The patients were lashed to the arms and leg rests of the wheelchair with velcro straps and the rowdiest ones had their heads immobilized to padded headrests with yet another strap. Sounds medieval, but it was really the most humane way to deal with violent, large men crashing from a night of PCP or Methamphetamine abuse. Trust me, you've never seen humanity at its worst unless you've seen this spectacle: ten bellowing, bearded ex-felons, half-inch, red rubber naso-gastric tubes stuck in their noses, hopping in their wheelchairs from one side of the room to the other. Never could figure out how they got them to hop, but on a Friday or Saturday night it was like Chucky Cheese's in there: three hundred-pound men bouncing off the walls, yelling for the nurses to *"get me the fuck outa here."*

Which brings me to the next stop on our tour, Security. We lived and died, sometimes literally, according to the skill and courage of our underpaid officers. I taught all of my residents the first week in my department to make friends with the guards. I had learned this lesson first hand my third month on duty. Late on a Monday night, not much going on. Barbara Manning, who'd been charge nurse down here for ten years before I arrived, was helping me in Trauma Two. We were situated in the smaller of the two operating rooms with a gangbanger who'd been wounded in a knife fight in Santa Ana. He had a deep cut across his left forearm; Ortho had already cleared him, said he hadn't injured any nerves, so it was my job to sew him up.

Barbara had become my friend, colleague, and confidante, over many long nights and days in our home away from home. We knew each other's triumphs and tragedies and consoled each other over our minor failures in a seamless, comfortable relationship. I trusted her with my life, considered her my "office wife."

I looked into Barbara's expressive green eyes, motioned to a lock of ash-blonde hair escaping her bonnet, and gave her a smile under my mask. She adjusted her hair with her sleeve, touched my gloved hand in thanks, and flashed a smile.

I felt the patient move under my hand, returned my attention to the laceration. I was concentrating on lining up the fascia over his rotator muscles, placing chromic sutures just so, when the guy abruptly reached across me and grabbed a number ten blade from the Mayo stand. He sat up suddenly, brandished the scalpel inches from Barbara's neck, said he was *"gonna cut this fuckin' bitch."* I grabbed his wrist and tried to shove him back onto the gurney, but he broke through his leg restraints and kicked me away with a right foot to my ribs. Barbara ran for the door and stopped short at the threshold, nearly colliding with the chief of security, George "The Mangler" Gomez.

Nobody messed with George. I'd watched him in the Drunk and Disorderly room and you could tell he was perfecting new wrestling moves on the druggies. The overfed bikers were like ninety-five-pound nerds to him.

George came into the room at a full run, dived onto the gurney, landing full force, face to face, on top of the gangbanger. The litter rocketed across the room as the scalpel and my Mayo stand hit the floor with a crash. A split-second later, the head of the gurney crashed into the wall and George was instantly back on his feet, bearded face inches from the patient; he had a growl that could ignite a fire. "Hurt anyone in here, *cabron,* and I'll take that knife, cut your fucking dick off." He wrenched the kid's arm back. I could have sworn I'd heard it pop. The kid screamed; George pulled him closer, an expression mean enough to make you wet your pants. *"Comprende?"* The stunned 'banger could only nod, his eyes glued to George's twenty-eight-inch guns. Mr. Tough Guy Gang Banger had been officially scared straight, introduced to The Mangler. My new best friend.

My trip down memory lane was interrupted an instant later by a call from the desk. "Doctor Adler. Full arrest. Trauma One."

I sprinted the ten feet from the drunk tank in four steps and called on my way to the night nurse, Angela Piccioli, walking with her back to me, headed for Trauma. "What have we got, Angie? Gunshot? MVA?" This time of night, on this particular day, I expected a bad penetrating trauma or car crunch.

Still on the run, I shucked off my coat, separated the students from the gurney, and ran to the head of the bed, ready to intubate.

A few seconds later they wheeled him in. The patient looked about twenty-five, not a mark on him, clothes immaculate, no visible blood. Nothing. I noticed he was dressed ten years behind the times, in Seventies disco style; iridescent blue polyester shirt, tight brown bell-bottoms, shiny black ankle boots. He smelled as if he'd taken a bath in Stetson cologne.

As soon as we had him situated on our table, I shoved the gurney away from the wall and quickly detached the headboard. The respiratory tech, a freakishly tall and skinny guy I'd never met, helped me pull the patient all the way to the to top of the bed with a quick tug on the top sheet. I turned slightly to the tech, my eyes still on the patient's ashen face, asked for an endotracheal tube. "Give me a seven and a half." I reached out my hand as he started bagging the patient; tried to read the tech's nametag pinned to his left chest, said, "Sorry, I haven't met you."

The tech bagged the patient quickly five times while Jane Quon, the Medicine resident, did chest compressions. Satisfied with the oxygen level, the tech stopped his bagging, opened an endotracheal tube and slapped it into my hand. "Name's Bradley, Dr. Adler. Bradley Morris."

Angela supervised the lead placements and readied the defibrillator, a machine that delivered a low-voltage external shock to the heart, essential in a patient with certain irregular heart rhythms or no heartbeat at all. I nodded and turned back to watch the monitors, spoke to him over my shoulder. "Bag him a few more times while I get the scope, Bradley." He repositioned the clear plastic facemask and ventilated the patient, as I searched for the intubation instrument.

Another look at the monitors confirmed my worst fears: my crew and I were getting nowhere with this guy. No blood pressure, no spontaneous respirations, all without any outward signs of trauma. I reached behind the gurney, broke open a steri-pack tray and flicked open the laryngoscope.

The respiratory tech took the facemask away and a half-second later the patient vomited. About two hundred ccs of milky yellow liquid and a few chunks of hot dog. I immediately turned his head to the side and swept an index finger into his mouth, caught the respiratory tech's eye, motioned toward the Mayo stand at my elbow. "Grab a Yankaur, Bradley." The tech drew the clear plastic suction from under the pillow and slapped it into my hand. I inserted the laryngoscope and suctioned a pool of clear liquid from the throat. Dropped the suction on his chest, shoved the tongue down, and guided the plastic endotracheal tube through the vocal cords, into the trachea.

Bradley disconnected his facemask and switched the ventilator tubing to the ET tube. I listened for breath sounds and confirmed the proper placement while Jane Quon continued compressions.

Took a minute to scan the bank of monitors and saw what I'd known I would from listening to the incessant alarms. Blood pressure: thirty. Oxygen saturation: sixty. EKG tracing: agonal rhythm, which meant the patient's heart, long starved for oxygen, was dying. He had no coordinated pumping action in his heart at all; the resident's chest compressions and the respiratory tech's bagging were all that kept him alive.

Angela read my mind, as experienced ER nurses often did. She took a squeeze bottle of Betadine antiseptic liquid and splashed it all over his chest. Handed me a syringe filled with Epinephrine, a potent stimulator of the vascular system, the last-ditch medication we used on patients sliding into cardiac standstill.

I felt along the space between his ribs on the left side of his chest, counted down to the fourth one toward his abdomen and plunged the six-inch needle straight into his heart. Drew back a few ccs of dark red, oxygen-starved blood, and shoved the plunger home. Watched the monitor start to blip into a junctional rhythm, a weak attempt by the patient's heart to restore a normal flow of blood.

Jane Quon was clearly on the same page, voicing my plan a second after the thought had entered my head. "How about a pacer, Steven?"

Angela had the pack open in a few seconds, the Mayo moved to my right elbow. I was down to my last option. A trans-thoracic pacemaker: electrical stimulation delivered to the heart through a pair of wires from an external pacemaker through the chest wall into the heart muscle. It was threaded through the chest-wall muscles using the same sort of needle we used to inject Epinephrine, albeit by a slightly different technique.

I had done more than a dozen and felt pretty confident. A rushed moment after I'd unpacked the kit, I used the same approach I'd practiced for years, got the leads into position, secured the wires and shot another look at the monitors: heart rate of thirty and blood pressure, zero. The compressions weren't working; even worse for the patient, the pacer was barely keeping his heart from another bout of standstill. My mind was racing through the possible causes of this healthy looking man's lethal problem: Pulmonary embolus where a blood clot shuts off the lungs, cerebral incidents including ruptured aneurysms, or, considering the times we lived in, cocaine-induced heart attack.

I took another quick look at his vitals, still critically bad, and went back to the head of the bed as my team continued CPR. Grabbed a flashlight, leaned in over his head, gently retracted his upper eyelids. One look at his pupillary reflexes and I knew he was finished. His right pupil was ten times the size of his left and neither pupil got smaller, as it should have, when I shone the light at it. Brain death, probably from a ruptured blood vessel in his head, surprisingly common in otherwise healthy young patients. I set down the flashlight, heaved a sigh, and looked at Angela, who sensed the truth instantly. I tried to talk, took three attempts to get the words out through the tightness in my throat. I was completely humbled; this was the first time I'd failed this miserably. My first death. "Call it, Angie. He's fixed and dilated. Probably blew a berry aneurysm."

Even though I'd not lost one yet, I took every bad case like this one personally; hell, I thought, this patient was younger than I, twenty-one, according to the medics. They had picked him up across the street at Vertigo, a live-band dance club that I'd been to with Elaine not two weeks ago. I went into ER medicine to

35

save people, wanted to save everyone, and even though I had recovered everyone until that night, I wasn't naïve; realized after just a few months here that it was impossible to save them all. Still, a guy this young, it hurt worse than I'd imagined to lose him.

Completely despondent, I thanked everyone and officially called the code. Angela removed the EKG leads, the respiratory tech unhooked the Ambu bag, leaving the endotracheal tube for the coroner, and I was left alone with my misery.

I knew the drill as well as anyone, had conducted dozens of codes like this one and had passed all of the monthly M and M, our peer-review Morbidity and Mortality conferences, without a nick on my record. The ER attendings ran these meetings like the quintessential assholes they were. Took great pleasure in finding fault, but in the real world, who could blame them, patient care was at stake and we *needed* to be hard on ourselves.

Most nights, we had supervising attendings. Tonight was an exception. I was practically an attending, they trusted me, and the assigned supervisor, Dr. Payton, wasn't due here until crunch time, after two.

I ran through my treatment sequence, as critically as I could, and honestly concluded that the attendings would have done the same. With the same sad result.

Alone in the suddenly quiet trauma room, I covered the patient with a sheet, shucked off my gloves, and noted the time on the clock over the head of the gurney. Twelve-oh-one. Welcome to 1986, I thought, with an overwhelming wave of sadness.

A minute or two later, I walked to the nurse's station, scratched out a quick note, and went in search of the family. I'd never had to say the words, was dreading it more than anything I'd done the last three years. I had no choice; hard as it was, I owed them an explanation. The worst part: now this poor guy's parents would always associate this night with their precious son's death, a lifetime of empty holidays and pain ahead of them. I shook my head. A young guy like that. Perfect health;

dancing, having fun without a care in the world. Maybe he'd had a little headache, sudden shortness of breath, nothing serious; a few notes of music later, he collapses and it's over. Made me more convinced than ever that there *was* no God.

The next eight hours went by in a blur. After the disco patient died, everything else that night seemed trivial by comparison. Death hovered over us constantly in the ER, even on that night of renewal and frenetic celebration. We're never far away from it, of course, hence our well-intentioned defenses: the black humor, the stupid little games, even the hurried sex we indulged in from time to time in the call rooms.

Throughout the night, a steady procession of the usual crazies and abuse victims came traipsing through. We handled it all with professionalism and compassion, I must say. As always, I was proud of my team. The rest of my shift went so quickly, I had to double-check the clock when my relief came in.

Seven-o'clock sharp, I finished my notes on the last patient and made lightning rounds with my replacement, a second-year named Adam Wachtel, from NYU.

Chapter 4

I grabbed a quick shower in the locker room, changed into a fresh set of clothes, and trudged up the ramp toward the cafeteria, my legs feeling like they were encased in cement. I was too tired to make breakfast at home, most of the restaurants near the hospital were closed for New Year's, and the really good ones in Newport were too far away, leaving me with microwaved slop in the doctor's dining room.

The line was short today, I noticed, because of the holiday and the skeleton crew of residents. I shuffled over to the line, picked up some elderly fruit, dry scrambled eggs, passed over a slab of mystery meat that had a green, deadly looking sheen to it, grabbed a blueberry muffin. The menu called it "Heart-Healthy Alternative." I called it a la carte Russian roulette.

The cafeteria was mostly empty; a few half-occupied tables near the exits. I was walking toward a four-top near the door when I heard Rick Lamb yell out, "Adler, you shithead, come eat with me." I smiled at his enthusiasm this early in the morning, still didn't know where he got his energy, as hard as he worked.

I'd known Rick since UCLA. Loved him like a brother, even if he was the crudest, rudest, most sarcastic man I'd ever known.

He'd been an All-American defensive tackle for the Bruins before going on to medical school and, in line with his athletic choice, was nobody's idea of a shrinking violet. He looked exactly like his college yearbook photo, dark brown hair, brown eyes, and a slightly wild expression. He stood six-seven, two-ninety, without a bit of fat around his gut. He had the heavy brow and deep-set eyes of a classic bully and the voice of a stevedore. Needless to say, he hadn't gone into Pediatrics. He was a fourth-year General Surgery resident, headed for Plastics. Rick was a legend at UCI. He had done solo belly cases his first month as a second year, was assisting hearts as a third year, and had the best hands in the hospital. Even his attendings admitted that.

I waved at him as I walked to his table; laid my tray on the tabletop. "Hey, Rick. You coming or going?" He looked pretty good so I couldn't tell. Sparse growth of beard, eyes slightly puffy and red. Pretty much what we all looked like, all the time: The walking dead, roaming the hospital waiting to care for your sick and dying loved ones.

He took a triple-thick bite of waffle and kicked a chair into the walkway, motioned for me to sit, mumbled around the soggy mess, "Going off." I sat across from him and he swilled a half-glass of orange juice. "Been on since Thursday." Today was Sunday, which meant seventy-two hours straight. More of the same bullshit, I thought. Slavery with a Knife is what they should call General Surgery.

I popped a shriveled grape in my mouth and shook my head. "No way you've been on for three days." The grape tasted like dirt. I tried the eggs. Powdery texture with a rancid aftertaste. Tasted like it was coated with that shit the astronauts used to drink, Tang or some such crap. I spat the eggs into a napkin. "They can't work you that hard."

Rick finished his juice and slumped lower in his chair, head hanging just above his chest. "Can and do, Adler." He looked as tired as I'd ever seen him, three-quarters dead and probably wishing he were. I swear, this place, Surgery training especially, could steal your soul if you let it, erode your will to live. Medical training is filled with irony; the powers-that-be train the next generation of healers by breaking us down, bit-by-bit; destroying our health, even as we learn to restore yours.

He seemed to brighten an instant later, as if refuting my thoughts. "So, how's your hot, juicy new slit? Saw her the other day in the OR" He gave the ancient sign; two hands squeezing an imaginary pair of breasts. "Great little titties." Cleaned his fork of the remaining soggy half-waffle with a loud smack of his lips. "Give me the word when you're done with her." His tongue took a lap around his lips, eyes searching my face. "Sure love to tap her round little Asian ass."

He was a good friend, I'd known him for eight years, but I hated that term, slit. Despised it. How would he like it if I called his mother or little sister a ravenous cunt? I thought with disgust. Didn't care for his attitude today at all as a matter of fact. "You mean Elaine?" He raised an eyebrow, clearly ready for some dirt. I gave him nothing but cool. "Okay. We don't see as much of each other . . ."

"So, you fucking somebody else, then?" I couldn't believe this guy. Up seventy-two hours and all he could talk about . . . My second thought was that he'd somehow heard about Natalie. My mind shifted into overdrive at that last question. I could see it now, Lamb running his mouth about us. That's all I'd need. The dumbass would be all over the hospital, and hospitals were the worst rumor mills in the world. He'd ruin any chance I'd have with her in a couple of hours. His insinuating tone brought me up short. I hoped I could hide my embarrassment under his hot glare. "Who?"

I had to hand it to him; the guy was relentless, I wondered if he thought about anything else besides sex and surgery. I gave a weary sigh, mustered up all of my tattered self-control, even as my imagination ran wild. "No, Rick. Still seeing Elaine. When I can." I gave up on the space-age synthetic eggs, tried the muffin. Not bad. Would have been better last week, though. I started to get into it with him about calling Elaine a slit, when he tapped me on the shoulder. Nodded toward the line.

Rick brightened suddenly, a hound on the scent; pointed an index finger at the line, indicating the third person in. "Speaking of hot and juicy slits, isn't that Natalie what's-her-name?" He squinted toward the darkened foyer as I tried to look where he was pointing. "You know, Adler, that stuck-up cunt we knew from UCLA?"

I turned in my chair to look, hoped the woman he was talking about was somebody else. "Please, God," I muttered, let it be anyone else. I didn't think I had it in me to carry on like there was nothing going on between Natalie and me. Not as tired as I was.

Despite his utter lack of class, and my incipient terror, I was impressed. Even at thirty yards, in a dark cafeteria, Lamb knew his prey, could practically pick out a pretty woman blindfolded. I gave him a reluctant smile; afraid I'd give myself away if I my face revealed what I was really thinking. I kept my tone nonchalant with an effort I was proud of. "Yeah, Rick, looks like Natalie Bogner."

Lamb reached over to my plate, grabbed the rest of my rancid muffin and shook his head. "Bogner? No, that's not her name, Adler. Something else." A comically intense look of concentration passed over his broad features. Rick was a smart guy, a great technician, but at that moment his struggle reminded me of a chimp worrying over a shrink-wrapped bag of banana chips. He chewed absently on the muffin, brow furrowed. "Nah, she's married now." I could tell he almost had it. Lips pursed, palm to his forehead. "Guy that owns the Porsche dealership in Newport." He closed his eyes. "Help me out here, Adler. Husband's a lot older, used to race. Name like a dead Commie." Rick was really struggling now; I half expected to see smoke trail from his ears. I could have rescued him, of course, but I was having too much fun watching him struggle. "Natalie, Natalie . . ."

"Marx. It's Natalie Bogner-Marx, Rick." She gave Lamb a quick, disdainful look, had a warm smile and wave for me. Her voice was low and sexy; I felt my little friend straining against my scrubs. "I still use Bogner professionally, so I can understand your confusion." She set her tray on the table and I caught a trace of perfume, something Italian or French, probably cost more than my TV, I thought, as I inhaled another whiff of high-octane scent. "That and the fact that you're a surgeon."

Rick stood as if hit with a cattle prod, shot her the finger, and muttered something about "*stuck-up Amazon cunt,*" as he gathered his stuff. Grabbed his tray, nodded curtly to me, neck red to his chest, glowered at Natalie, and stalked off.

I spun to face Natalie as she settled into her chair, as relieved to be free of Lamb as I was excited to be alone with her. She was dressed in black, head-to-toe. A wool suit with a subtle gray chalk-stripe; silk blouse the color of freshly polished silver, and a thin gold necklace weighted in the middle by a round-cut diamond the size of a pencil eraser. She laid a hand on my cheek and we exchanged kisses. "Steven, I've missed you." She took a quick look around the deserted cafeteria while I drank in her essence. That voice. I was ready to sell my car, take all my money out of the bank, and move to Nice with her. She noted my obvious excitement with an amused expression on her face, the kind of look you'd get from a clerk at Tiffany's who'd pegged you as flat broke the minute you walked in the door. Took a second to look me up and down, fixed her glance at my tent-pole. "You look great." I felt like yesterday's trash after my awful night, but I'd take her compliment any day. My friend was ready to break his leash. She sipped her juice, lips wrapped tightly around her blood-red straw, gave me a pensive look. "What's it been, six weeks?"

I took a long look at her face and felt myself falling. I don't consider myself a romantic, not at all. Hell, I hardly believe in romantic love at all. Still, here she was, back in my life if just for a little while and I was struck stupid, practically begging at her feet. And it wasn't just her looks that had me twisted into knots. She was the smartest person I'd ever known. Natalie never studied; at least not like the rest of us nerds, yet she had graduated with the highest National Board scores in our class. I never once beat her on a test, and I studied harder than a dyslexic astronaut. She was always the topic of speculation among those of us in her outer orbit: rumor had it she was dating some TV actor until she dumped him for an attending in Plastics during our fourth year. She always denied it when I asked her, but I *did* see the guy hanging around a lot, sad puppy-dog look on his handsome face; said he was researching a TV role the time I talked to him after I caught him lurking in the hall outside our Physiology lab.

Given her many suitors, and her wanderlust, Natalie's marriage to the Porsche guy a week after graduation was a surprise to everybody, as well. She had a reputation as a world-class heartbreaker, went through men like Pavarotti ate canolli. Told me all the time that she'd never settle down. At least not until she finished her residency. I hadn't wanted to be cruel, wouldn't think about ruining her big day while we danced at her wedding, but guessed at the time of the nuptials at the Four Seasons that her marriage proved the aphorism: *money talks and bullshit walks.* I checked out her husband at the wedding; shorter than her by half a foot, pudgy, and at least fifteen years older.

She must have read my thoughts, as she sat across from me; her crystalline blue eyes searching my face. "We're separated, Steven." She took a delicate bite of dry toast; her eyes never left mine. "Henry and I split up, so you needn't worry about what happened the other night."

I tried hard to mask my joy. Kept my lack of surprise locked down tight inside. I fumbled out a bogus condolence. I'm a little old fashioned, my dad taught me well, and I'd never want to be a contributing factor to a marriage breaking up, but still, this was Natalie Bogner sitting across from me. I could still taste her; still feel her against my skin. I wanted to dance on the tabletop. My insecurities overwhelmed my euphoria, though. I took another look at her and thought, dream on, stupid. She looks like every man's wet dream and here you are, looking like leftover dogshit.

She gave me a look, was clearly expecting an answer so I mumbled, "I'm sorry, Natalie. Really."

I covered her hand with mine, hoping against hope for another session with her, a little rebound action, horndog that I am. "When did this happen?" Was it wrong to be happy about someone's marriage collapsing? Most certainly it was, but this was Natalie. Social niceties were for eunuchs. "The last time we talked . . ."

She took another sip of orange juice. Stole a worried glance at her watch. "It happened three months ago." Set down her bottle of juice. "Before I left for Cedars." She gave me a lascivious smile that I'll take to my grave. "Besides, Steven, the last time we saw each other, we didn't do much talking."

I squeezed her hand. My friend felt ready to explode. My voice sounded like I was forcing it through a drinking straw. "I'll remember that as long as I live, Natalie." Sounded lame, even to me, but she let me off the hook with a warm smile. I decided then and there to see where we were going, see if I had any shot at all with her. I took a quavering sip of juice, steadied my voice, even as my heart pummeled my ribs. "So, what happened?" She sat back in her chair, took a quick, halting breath. Shit, I thought, now I'd blown it. Scared her off. A random thought entered my head as she sat across from me, the silence between us awkward as a machine-gun fart on a first date: *That's why you've never had a chance with her, Adler. Because you're a fucking putz.* She looked ready to leave, I desperately wanted her to stay, didn't know when I might have this chance again, our transcendent shower sex notwithstanding. I gave it one more try: my tone just this side of frantic. "Sorry, Natalie, that was out of line."

She placed her bottle carefully on the tray, took her time, a tapered fingertip to her lower lip. "Actually, that's a good question, Steven." She slung her purse over her shoulder, grabbed her tray and stood to leave. "I've thought long and hard, believe me. Unfortunately, I don't have a good answer for you." I stood and we hugged. "Nor for myself, for that matter." She felt like a lifetime of good luck in my arms. I wanted our embrace to last forever. "Not yet, anyway." She held the hug, turned her face and gave me a quick kiss. She startled me again with that voice that could make you swindle your mother. "I'm sorry, but I'm late for rounds, Steven."

She grabbed her tray, turned and walked away, toward the tray return. A few feet down the aisle, she turned her head, caught me gaping at her ass; I didn't care. She had me hooked and she knew it. I had to give it to her; like most gorgeous women, she had what it took and she'd learned how to use it. A few steps later and I heard that voice again, carrying across the empty cafeteria, sizzling straight into my lizard-brain. "Call me, Steven. I need you."

I gave her a wave; my face ready to burst into flames. "I'll do that. Call you." Forced the words through the knot in my throat. Did I hear her right? I thought. She needs me? I *never* have this kind of luck. I wanted to hit my knees, right there in the deserted cafeteria, even though I didn't believe in God, not to mention how unbelievably tacky it would have been to thank Him for a great piece of ass falling into my lap.

Still, this was Natalie. She stood at the threshold as I struggled to find the words. "Sounds good, Natalie." I stood there blushing like a dumbass kid caught with his first hard-on. Call you? I'll do that? Sounds good? I thought, what a jackass, Adler. No wonder you can count your sex partners on one hand.

Chapter 5

I went straight home and crashed. Mornings like this, I was glad that my apartment was only a mile from campus; I was so fatigued that I almost fell asleep waiting for the light at City Drive and Chapman. The emotional hangover from the disco patient still plagued me; my first death in four years.

I woke up tight and stiff after an eight-hour nap, hit the gym across the street for the last kickboxing class, and returned to my place at about ten, physically exhausted but mentally renewed. Checked my mail and plopped on the sofa for some mindless TV. There was nothing on, so I took a chance and called Elaine. The main reason I wanted to call her, sadly, was to lay the foundation for our breakup.

"So, you finally decided to call." Her voice had an edge I hadn't noticed before, nothing at all like the sweet woman I'd dated, seduced, and bedded. "Know what I did at midnight?" I tried to break in with an explanation about the full arrest, my horrible night, but she cut me off before I could form the words. "Nothing, Steven." She choked off a sob. "The first time in my adult life. A New Year's by myself." Now *I* was getting defensive. I'd told her before Christmas that I wouldn't be available, that she should make other plans. I even took a shift off to spend some extra time with her on Christmas Eve. I knew from her tone the handwriting was on the wall and I was ready to pull the ripcord if things didn't improve in the next few seconds. Life's too short, I reminded myself. I was convinced that I wasn't bailing out because of Natalie's sudden availability. The sex was awesome and she did seem to want to see me again. Still there was no way I would put myself on the line for somebody who had so thoroughly shut me down, as Natalie had done at UCLA. On the other hand, Elaine and I didn't really have a firm commitment and we clearly weren't on the same page anymore . . . Her whining voice cut through my thoughts like a steak-knife through silk. ". . . to Mexico." Dead silence as I thought about Natalie: Her ass in my hands, her lips on mine, our legs entwined . . ."Steven, are you even listening to me? I swear."

I took a deep breath, shook Natalie from my thoughts; this kind of confrontation was never easy for me. I decided to go for the diplomatic approach. "Maybe we should get together when you've calmed down. Talk about a few things." I could hear her breathing on the line, short, staccato exhalations, followed by a couple of muffled sobs. Despite the temptation I felt to end it here and now, get on with my life, I had a firm personal rule; never break up with anyone on the phone. Too cold. Not my style at all. Nothing from Elaine's end but quiet sobs, so I decided it was time to break the silence. "Elaine? Are you still there, honey?"

"Honey? You're *dumping* me and still calling me honey?" Her voice had more than an edge now. It was eight inches of flame-hardened, tempered steel aimed straight for my brain. "You leave me without a call on the most important night of the year . . ."

I broke in, felt the urgent need to defend myself. "Elaine, I'm not dumping you. Besides, we had a terrible night. This young patient came in . . ."

"And you didn't even call me." Wracking sobs. "Not once, Steven."

It was clear where this was going. I just didn't have the emotional energy to continue, had to break this off before I started to yell at her. "Elaine, I have to go. I'm off work for a couple of days and I'll look you up on Wednesday. We can . . ."

She cut me off, her voice clipped, tightly controlled. "There *is* no we. Not anymore." Sharp intake of breath as she reloaded. "Go to hell, Steven. We're through."

Just a little overreaction, I thought, as her hang-up reverberated down the line.

I went to bed thinking about my upcoming two days off. I was aimless. No girlfriend, just the half-assed promise of one in the wings, no plans, bank account almost empty. What to do? Tossed and turned some more. What to do, Adler? I fought sleep for a couple of hours and decided around two to visit my folks in Riverside later in the morning. It had been a few months and I'd missed the family Christmas Eve get-together to be with Elaine, so I was feeling more than a little guilty. I'd called them from the ER, Christmas morning; Dad was his usual cheerful self, only wanted to know about my "exciting, glamorous life," wanted to be sure I was taking care of myself. Mom was in bed with a "headache." Mom and Dad. Mrs. Drunk and Mr. Enabler. People age, relationships evolve, but deep down, their roles never seem to change.

I finally fell asleep around four, thoughts of meeting the parents filling my head.

I awoke at seven, hopped out of bed, and took a quick inventory. Discovered that I felt pretty good. Better than that, I felt great. Even after the nastiness with Elaine. Even anticipating/dreading the trip to Riverside. I showered, shaved, dressed in my best khakis and a blue sweater, and headed out the door. Ten steps later, I slapped myself in the forehead for forgetting the presents I'd so carefully picked out; turned around and let myself back in the apartment. How could I be so stupid? I thought, with a surge of frustration. I had just emptied my savings account two weeks ago to splurge on gifts for the folks: complete sets of golf clubs. The gifts had set me back six hundred dollars. What the hell, I reasoned at the time, they *are* my parents and it's only money.

Mom and Dad had only recently taken up the sport. Dad had talked about it since I was a kid, but there had never been enough money growing up in Riverside. Their place was about two miles from a new public course on the west side of town. They seemed crazy about it, especially Dad. Mom was reluctant at first, but she seemed to be taking to it quickly, according to my father on Christmas. I smiled as I locked my apartment, had no doubt that they were going to flat-out love my gift.

Ten minutes later I was on the Five headed south to the Fifty-Five and Riverside, a song in my heart, packages safely stowed and AC/DC on the stereo, as luck would have it, playing one of my favorite tracks: *Money Talks.* "Come on, Come on, lovin' for the money, Come on, come on, listen to the money talk."

The traffic wasn't too bad. The Monday morning commute was headed in the opposite direction, toward L.A., so I made it to my exit in less than an hour. Driving through Riverside brought back a flood of memories. High School at good old Ramona High. Friday night football games. Cheer leaders, pompons, making out in the bleachers, thrilling overtime wins. I missed it all, was working nights at the Straw Hat Pizza. Got to see all my pals after the game when I served their pies.

Winter-quarter break at UCR; all my friends off campus for five days of drunken skiing at Mammoth. I was back in Riverside, working at the Sizzler across from Sears. Was I bitter? Felt deprived, left out? No, not at all. My dad had instilled a solid work ethic in me from day one. I saw how much he'd sacrificed everyday, so it was only right that I should work part time to help pay for my own expenses. I silently thanked him for showing me the way, every day; humble beginnings, hard work, and perseverance led to success in this country. Every time. I was determined to be living proof of that truism.

I drove up our street at around eleven. Not much had changed in the six months I'd been away. Same slightly run-down houses, basketball backboards on nearly every garage, endless rows of stucco one-story ranch homes in homogenized shades of tan. Looking at our neighbor's places, I was especially proud of my dad. Our house was the best kept on the block. A neat row of rose bushes leading to a freshly painted red door. Precisely laid ring of red bricks surrounding the oak tree we used to build forts in.

I let myself in and called for Mom. The curtains were drawn, muted stereo playing an old Tom Jones album, Mom nowhere in sight. It was end-of-the-world dark at eleven in the morning, every shade pulled against the weak winter sun.

I set the clubs quietly on the foyer tiles and went in search of my mother. Walked into the kitchen, found it immaculate but deserted. Took a look outside. She liked to read the *L.A. Times* out by the fire pit every morning while she fed the birds. Nobody there. Came back through the den and there she was, lying on the sofa with a wash cloth over her eyes. Oh, man, I thought. Please don't be drunk at eleven-o'clock. She looked even thinner than last summer, I noticed with alarm, like she'd dropped thirty pounds in six months. I was instantly worried about liver failure, made a mental note to get her over to her internist.

Dad told me on the phone Christmas that she was a little better. Didn't seem to be drinking so much. Seemed like the golf was helping with her "moods," which I had diagnosed as clinical depression. I hoped he was right, but we'd all been through it before. A little progress, twelve-step programs through our temple; followed by a relapse. I'd tried checking her into a formal detox program, even found a good one in Corona, less than five miles away, but she'd refused, said they couldn't afford it. I offered to pay for it; she turned me down again, said she could, "Take care of herself." Sometimes I wondered how Dad took it. Married forty years to her and he still obviously loved her. Still took good care of her. I silently wondered if, given the same circumstances, I'd be so faithful to a wife with that degree of denial, that much pigheadedness.

She must have sensed me standing over her, worse, read my unkind thoughts. She sat up suddenly, washcloth sliding down her face. "Steeeven. You're hommmme."

My worst fears realized with the first rush of her breath on my face. The smell of Seven Crown whiskey hit me with a jolt of long-forgotten pain; a jump-cut flashback of missed meals playing across my mind, broken plates, loud fights in my folks' bedroom, my brother and I fending for ourselves until Dad came out and put together grilled cheese sandwiches, an embarrassed look on his face. "She's just tired, kids," He'd say. "A bad headache today." Seven years old and I had no idea what the term "enabler" meant, but I sure got an up close and personal education on that particular interpersonal dynamic. She was never violent with us; I know my dad would have divorced her over that—she just hid in the bottle, safe from her life, completely isolated from her kids. Kids that needed her guidance, her love. For all my years in Riverside, this was my entire world: my long-suffering Dad, Jacob Steven Adler, and his alcoholic wife, Catherine Mills Adler. My parents, Jake and Katy Adler of the Riverside Adlers. Her message was as clear as if she'd hung a sign on the garage: *Welcome home, son. Where time stands still and nothing ever changes.*

I leaned over to kiss her cheek, found it cold and stiff from the washcloth. Her eyelids fluttered as she strained to focus on my face. Looked like she'd had more than one highball. I tried with all my strength to keep my voice compassionate, didn't succeed as much as I'd hoped, if her startled look was any indication. "Let me get you some coffee, Mom."

She grabbed my wrist with surprising strength. "No. Sit here, Steven." She had the veteran drinker's ability to appear more sober than she actually was. It was a talent that continually amazed me, but made a sort of sense when viewed as a defense mechanism, mobilized at a moment's notice to protect her against insult and injury.

I took a quick look at the whites of her eyes as I sat next to her on the sofa. The same couch my older brother Jake and I'd spent countless hours laughing with Dad about Archie Bunker, Gomer Pyle, and Johnny Carson, I thought, with a wave of sadness. The light wasn't good in the darkened den, but her sclera didn't seem to be yellow. What I could see under her loose blouse told me that her belly wasn't distended, so she probably wasn't in liver failure. Still, I thought, she needs to get to her doctor. Maybe this time he could talk some sense into her. The way she looked, as much as she was drinking, she was running out of chances. Once again I was surprised by her feminine intuition as she read my dark, worried thoughts. "I'm feeling fine, Steven." She couldn't keep the quaver from her voice; the slack, doughy flesh on her face belied her words. "Never better, in fact."

I settled a few feet away from her on the faded blue-and-white checked sofa, now covered with a hideous orange afghan, decided to confront the obvious, hopefully get her to commit to treatment. "Okay, Mom, but you're still drinking."

She sat bolt upright, moved a few inches away. "No, I'm . . ."

I stopped her with a look. "Mom, I can tell." She lowered her eyes, a gesture I remembered from so many shattered days and chaotic nights growing up. "But you don't have to listen to me, Dr. Standish has been telling you for years. You need . . ."

She pulled farther away, arms crossed tightly across her chest, intoxication seemingly cured by the sobering force of her indignation. "Standish is a quack. All those meetings, the pills he gave me, my God, Steven, I was sick for a month on those damned things." She took a wrinkled tissue from her housecoat, wiped a tear and sniffled; fell back on manipulation, a well-used defense she kept close as a knight and his shield. "I'd rather be dead than live a few more years like that."

That did it, I thought, with a surprising surge of anger. She was going to Standish this week or I'd make Dad commit her. I'd opened my mouth to respond when the door flew open, a rush of sunlight and welcome breeze spilling in from the front yard. "Stevie, boy. Come give your Pops a hug."

My dad came running into the den, lunch pail in his right hand, arms outstretched; childlike joy on his worn and tired face. I took him in my arms and held him tight, inhaled the familiar smells of Old Spice and sweat. My Dad. Five inches shorter than

I, bald as Daddy Warbucks, still thin and fit as a welterweight fighter.

I held our embrace and was instantly alarmed. He felt even smaller than a few months ago, his face carried more lines, must have lost at least ten pounds. A few moments later, he broke our embrace, looked me over, and shook my hand; a hot insurance prospect close to sealing the deal. "You look terrific, son. How's the hospital treating you? Are you getting enough sleep?"

I had to laugh as I held his gaze, same old Pops. Full of energy, full of love. Tireless worker with an iron grip on what it took to survive our horrible times as a family; never missed a day of work, even now in his late sixties. My dad, My hero. "Thanks, Dad. You look good, too. The hospital's great." He nodded at me, filled with pride, as if I'd told him I'd won the Nobel Prize in Medicine. "I graduate from residency end of June, and I'm sleeping as much as I need."

"Graduate?" He looked down at Mom, beaming like a brand new papa. "You hear that, Katy? Stevie here is gonna graduate again." He slapped me on the back and led me back to the sofa. "Man, oh man. How the time flies." He took a wistful look around the den and it hit me. He was lonely here. All this time had passed without his boys around to buffer his sadness. Only Mom and his memories to keep him company, and she was in her own world most to the time.

I met his look. He took half a second to recover; his dazzling smile back almost before I noticed the deep sadness in his eyes. I looked at my Pops, worn down by a hard life and a problematic marriage, and had to suddenly gulp back the tears, tried to remember why I was here. I managed to keep my voice level, even though my throat ached with sorrow and longing for Pops. "Mom, Dad, stay here. I'll be right back."

I wiped my eyes with a sleeve, went into the kitchen and retrieved the golf clubs. Dug in the zippered pocket of Dad's bag for their cards and returned to the den, burdened like a Sherpa, smile restored, determined to make it a good day for my dad.

Dad was off the couch in an instant, across the den in three steps. "You didn't! Ah, Stevie." He gave me a kiss on the cheek and I had to hide the sudden rush of tears with a fake sneeze. He swept the bag from my hands, eyes glittering like a five-year-old. "You shouldn't spend your money like this." Pops shook his finger at me, flashed me the same proud grin he gave me the first time I'd ridden a bike down our block all by myself. "I taught you better than that."

He set the bag up on its retractable legs and started rummaging through the set. "Katy, look at these." He pulled out a driver, shook it in the air. "They're those new metal woods. We saw them at the SportMart last month. Remember, I showed them to you, Katy." He turned to me, holding his brand new driver with the purest look of gratitude I'd ever seen. A look I'll carry to my grave. "Oh, Stevie, these are the best. The absolute best." He took a practice swing in the hall, missing the overhead light fixture by a couple of millimeters. "I'm gonna drive like fucking Jack Nicklaus with these babies."

"Jacob! Language!" Mom's voice broke the mood. She stood on unsteady legs to hug me for her gift. I noticed that she'd hardly looked at hers, but it didn't matter, Dad's reaction would last a lifetime. His excitement wiped out New Year's Eve in the ER, the stuff with Elaine, even Mom's relapse. Nothing pleased me more than seeing him like this, happy and carefree. Nothing.

Dad ignored Mom's jab, still over-the-moon with his new toys. He threw an arm around my shoulders, cradling his new driver like a newborn. "Stevie. You got to get a set. We can go over to Jurupa Hills, that new public course. You, me, and Mom." He set down his driver, grabbed the putter, and tested its balance-point on an outstretched palm. Looked up at me with real yearning. I knew in that instant just how lonely he was; he couldn't mask his near-desperation. "How about that? I mean later on when you're not so busy, son."

I was struck by such a strange mixture of emotions: sadness for his plight, lonely as he seemed; pride and joy for the small presents I'd given him. Here was this hard working man, the center of my life, my whole life, acting like a boy again. No way was I going to disappoint him, didn't matter how busy I got. "Sure, Pops. Any time you want." He ran over to examine my mom's clubs, showed her all the pockets and compartments on her bag.

I followed him to the den; laid a hand on his back. "I'll start looking for a set next month." He clearly liked that, gave me the radiant smile I'd seen years ago in their old wedding photos, a grin I hadn't seen on his face for years. I realized in that instant that I'd been away too much lately. I missed my time with him, more than I was willing to admit. "Maybe you could help me pick them out, Dad." His excited smile as he turned to face me was answer enough.

We spent the next hour or two in the kitchen, catching up on the past few months. Jacob, my older brother, still worked in Kansas City, at the country and western station. "WHRS," Dad told me with a wry grin. Stood for "horse," of course. His professional name was now Jake the Snake. My dad raised his eyebrows a little when he told me that news, but was obviously proud of his oldest, regardless of Jake's choices in life. Still, I knew Dad, could almost read his thoughts, *Imagine that, Stevie, a non-practicing Jew from California playing redneck, shit-kicker music in the heartland.* He would typically follow up a comment like that with a shake of his head and, "Only in America!"

I filled them in on the highlights of my past few months. Glossed over my time with Elaine, wanted no part of that emotional minefield. Mom was constantly on me to get married, give her some grandkids. She'd given up on Jake years ago; his two childless divorces and his growing emotional distance making that milestone highly unlikely, in her mind at least.

I decided to give them a little of what I loved, the ER. I regaled them with stories of exploits with my friends, Barbara Manning, Jane Quon, Rick Lamb and Dad's favorite, George "The Mangler" Gomez. He insisted that I get tickets to see him wrestle. I promised him; done deal. Overall, a good holiday, all things considered.

An hour later; the patio now fully obscured by shadows, Dad took our lunch dishes to the kitchen sink, glanced at the clock over the window and made a dash for the door, his voice trailing down the hall, "Holy shit. Look at the time."

I left Mom at the table, followed him to the foyer, and helped him into his jacket. I always hated saying goodbye to Pops. Never got used to it, even though he was constantly coming and going when we were little. I adjusted his collar and gave him a kiss. His voice was choked. All these years, all these sorrows and I'd never seen Pops cry. He tried hard this time, ultimately failed to stem the tears, looked down quickly a minute later, clearly embarrassed. "Sorry, Stevie. Can't stay. I'm late for work."

He struggled a few moments, finally regaining control; blew Mom a kiss through the archway and led me out the door. "Thank you so much, son. Those clubs? Perfect is what they are." He gave me another hug, kissed my cheek. "You shouldn't have."

I walked him to his car, the same meticulously maintained Chevy Nova he drove when I was still at UCR. He turned to face me, back resting on his door. "Stay a little while, Stevie." His eyes said it all; fear overlain with chronic worry. A look I'd seen constantly growing up. "Your mom needs you." Staying at home with Mom was the last thing I wanted to do, truthfully, but Dad seemed desperate.

I knew he was right, even as I was planning my exit. Another look into his eyes and I knew I couldn't refuse. "Okay, Pops. I can stay for a while." He gave me a clap on the shoulder and climbed into the Nova, his smile instantly restored. "Call me, son. I know you're busy, but I love hearing from you." He started the engine; I noticed the twenty-year-old car still hummed like a fine watch. "And take care of yourself. I worry."

I waved good-bye as Dad turned right at the corner, toward his crappy janitor's job at the high school, a proud man who should have risen higher in life, a man who couldn't have stood any taller in my eyes. He gave a cheery wave a moment later, as he sped up Brockton Avenue. I didn't care that my answering voice was lost in the rush of traffic noise. "Take care. I worry about you, too, Pops."

I mustered my strength, thoughts on how tired Dad looked, and went back inside. Mom was lying in state on the couch, Tom Jones crooning softly in the background. The clubs were stowed in the back hall, curtains once again drawn against the outside world. I leaned into the den; she was snoring lightly, face flushed, a half-empty bottle of Seven Crown on the coffee table. I took a minute, deciding whether to stay or go; scanned the familiar den, nothing much had changed in all the years since I'd left home: Mom's scuffed oak coffee table, the inevitable whiskey bottle an easy reach away, surrounded by a neat pile of romance novels and the beanbag ashtray Dad had bought for her in Vegas five years ago on their anniversary. The one that promised "Everyone's a Winner," in day-glow pink paint.

Nearly overcome with depression, I walked over to the couch, leaned down and kissed her cheek, warm now with the jolt of eighty-proof whiskey in her bloodstream. I felt a little better; she looked at peace. Comfortable, even if it *was* because of her self-medicated stupor.

I walked into the kitchen, rinsed the dishes, and stacked them in the dishwasher; looked around at the worn yellow daisy wallpaper, speckled white Formica countertop and red vinyl chairs, and felt oddly out of place, a stranger in my home for the first time ever. I suppose I could have sat outside on the patio, waiting quietly in the gloom for Mom to awaken. Could have stayed to make sure she was all right. See how she was really doing.

In the end I took the coward's way out and decided to leave. Couldn't seem to face her demons yet again. Too frustrating, too enervating. I told myself that I was leaving because I couldn't mess up the good memories of today. Not after having such a great time with Dad. My rationalizations did me no good. Trying to be honest with myself, I reached the inevitable conclusion: Mom wasn't the only Adler skilled in the use of denial.

I took a last look around the kitchen, grabbed an apple for the drive home and my eyes lit on a business card stuck under a ladybug magnet on the fridge door. "Douglas Standish, M.D. Board Certified, Internal Medicine." I closed the refrigerator, pocketed the business card and promised myself I'd call for an appointment for Mom. This week for sure.

A few minutes later, halfway home on the Ninety-One, I started to cry. For my mom and her frantic need to escape. For my dad who seemed to be shrinking before my eyes, worn out by hard work and worry.

I didn't believe in God, but prayed anyway. To fate, to the gods of cause and effect, to whatever cosmic force controlled the universe. I prayed for Mom to stop drinking. I prayed for Dad to have the strength to survive. Hang on just a few more precious years, Pops, I prayed. I need you.

And I prayed for myself. For the strength to make the hard choices in life. Every time. And for the courage to stare down Death at work. Every day.

Part II

"*It is love, not reason, that is stronger than death.*"
— THOMAS MANN

Chapter 6

SIX MONTHS LATER

Early October in Orange County. My favorite time of the year. The tourists had returned to Cornsilk, Iowa and Lake Wannamucka, Minnesota, the traffic had thinned out with all the kiddies back in school, and the sun was still warm enough for me to bodysurf without a wetsuit. Late afternoon, Laguna Beach, steps from our oceanfront bungalow, sun on my back, covered with wet sand, hair plastered to my head, stinking like a bilge rat. I was in heaven.

I shook the sand from my feet, toweled off and plopped into the chair next to Natalie. She was tucked deep into the shadow of our blue-and-white Cinzano umbrella, engrossed in an OB journal, an article about post-menopausal coitus, she told me with a wink. In the hour or so I'd spent surfing, she had finished half the pitcher of room service margaritas we'd started at lunch; chicken quesadillas and shrimp tacos from Las Brisas; the Mexican joint a half block up the bluff above our hotel.

I watched Natalie as she scanned the article; dark-glasses halfway down her nose, mouth slightly open in concentration, shiny black hair cascading down her back. Did I love her? Too early to say. We had an understanding. We were living that famous mantra: One Day At A Time. She certainly hadn't brought it up, but I had to admit, I was getting a little closer to speaking the "L Word." The best part for me? For the first time in my life I didn't give a thought about whether or not a woman I was involved with shared my feelings. Natalie made it clear enough how she felt about me; at least how she felt about having sex with me. That was enough for me then, as shallow as it sounds in retrospect.

Given my natural reticence with women, distrust of them even, it was a new experience for me to give myself to a woman. In every way. I'd been burned a few times in the past, so it was slow going at first. I didn't totally trust Natalie yet, didn't feel that I knew her well enough to take that leap of faith toward complete confidence in her motivation and agenda, our great sex notwithstanding. Hard as it was for me at times, I felt myself loosening up a little more every day, giving her a little more of me without expecting much in return.

We'd spent lots of time lately just getting to know each other. She knew all about my brother, Mom and her affliction, Dad, everything. I hadn't left anything out, wanted to see what happened when I opened all of those closets, let the cleansing light of day illuminate all of my skeletons. I guess I was ready for my first "grown up" relationship. At twenty-nine. She knew everything there was to know about me, of that I was confident.

Natalie had reciprocated; telling me that her folks were still married although separated for more than twelve years, since Natalie was fourteen. She wouldn't tell me the reason her parents had split, no matter how I approached that subject, wouldn't even come close. I decided in the end to let it go, as it clearly still caused her pain. She only let on that she and her dad were very close before he left and that this seemed to cause her mom quite a bit of anxiety. Said her mom used to act as if Natalie were a rival for her father's attention and affection somehow. I had to wonder, at the time, how much Natalie's mom's misgivings contributed to the separation and how that set of circumstances affected Natalie. I knew that kind of thing was fairly common in families, had read all the statistics about abuse and divorce. Still, I didn't want to pry; Natalie had very firm boundaries around that watershed event in her life and I wasn't ready to push, didn't have a clue how to break them down yet.

Natalie did tell me she was an only; born when her mom and dad were in their late thirties, grew up in San Francisco where her dad was an engineer with Hewlett-Packard for fifteen years before transferring down to Cupertino to work for Apple. She let it slip that he'd helped Steve Jobs and Steve Wosniak develop the Apple operating system. I was impressed. She had gone to private schools in the Bay area, attended Stanford for her under-graduate work, graduating second in her class with a chemistry major. I was even more impressed when she'd told me she grad-uated Stanford at twenty. I'd pegged her IQ at one-fifty. She cor-rected me one day: One-seventy-eight, don't you know!

We discovered that we had a lot of likes and dislikes in com-mon: loved rock and roll, chocolate, Mexican food, Robin Williams, stupid comedies, especially *Saturday Night Live*, slap-stick, and travel. Hated snobs, country music, Indian food, bigots, liars, and injustice. She had been to Europe every summer since she was seven. I'd never been outside the states, but had been planning a trip to Paris since I'd turned twelve, the summer I fell in love with Catherine Deneuve. Fell in love with her *Playboy* pic-torial, that is. Childish, yes, but I was *only* twelve at the time.

We discussed our philosophies of life and love; this was the area of our greatest divide. Natalie simply didn't believe in uncon-ditional love, whereas I thought it was all-important in any serious relationship. On the other hand, I was a firm believer in personal responsibility, didn't believe love forgave all sins, but Natalie went even farther, said she believed that love "had to be earned and renewed every day." I thought it was harsh at the time, wondered how anyone could possibly live up to that standard, as fallible as we humans are. Which brings up our other major disagreement in this realm: She thought, even said, she was perfect. Had never made a mistake. Said she had "very high standards" for herself, as well as those around her. Two thoughts occurred to me upon hearing this for the first time. First, how about the divorce from the Porsche Guy? Doesn't that constitute a mistake on her part? Come on, give me a break, I thought at the time, no one is completely blameless when a marriage falls apart. Secondly, I wondered how high her standards were and if I could possibly measure up to them, bumbling fool that I am. Given her inflexibility and great opinion of herself, I gave myself a few sleepless nights wondering if we were actually compatible. Wondering if what I was feeling for her was love or just stupendous, mind-expanding sex masquerading as love. As I look back on the months we spent getting to know each other, I had to conclude that I was so impressed by Natalie's intelligence, sense of humor, and sexuality, that I was able to overlook our obvious differences, her little and not so little personality quirks. After all, I rationalized, we all have eccentricities. It's just a matter of degree. The bottom line was this—I hadn't had much experience or success with women up to that point and here was Natalie, my idealized woman, suddenly and happily a huge part of my life. I took her for what she was, who she was. Took her to my heart and gave her everything I had in return. After all, isn't the selfless giving of one's faith and trust the true definition of love? I thought so at the time.

We talked about sex, of course, steeped in it as we were. Natalie lost her virginity when she was thirteen. Said her first partner was an older man. Needless to say, I wondered at the time, how much older and under what circumstances? Another area of her past that Natalie guarded zealously. She wouldn't divulge the particulars and I never asked about the identity of her first. Although I wondered about the statute of limitations on statutory rape and what precipitated her early entry into adult womanhood. Thirteen seemed awfully young to me; at that age I was very much into noticing boobs and asses, knew all about "beaver cheaters," but didn't have any first-hand information on the actual act. So, once again, I was left to my imagination on that score. Another topic to keep me up at night. She admitted to a series of men in her life, all through private school and Stanford. I'd asked her for a number, just an approximation; she was typically coy, citing a woman's right to privacy. She'd said she loved sex, needed to express herself that way. I said, "You think?" She slugged me on the arm. Hard.

All kidding aside, Natalie came to me largely as advertised: a highly sexualized, free-thinking, independent, and accomplished woman. A woman with an extremely active intellect who seemed as if she would be easily bored. Easily distracted. Once again, I glossed over these traits, assigning them a small portion of the totality of her personality; the "good" clearly outweighing the "bad." Overall, I was convinced; I was absolutely sold on "the package" that was Natalie. In short, she was my woman. My ideal.

We had been together since late April. Her divorce was still pending after more than a year of haggling; something about a snag in their prenuptial agreement. Lots of back-and-forth between the lawyers and worst of all, her husband, the Porsche Guy, Mr. Henry Marx, was being a bastard about it. He had acted like Natalie was trying to wrest Newport Motors right out from under his nose. I wouldn't mind if she stuck it to him, took his business. I loved Porsches; maybe she'd give me one for my next birthday. Besides, the guy had a net worth of fifty million. So, what was he worried about? He could still keep half of it; twenty-five million was nothing to sneeze at, although I'm sure he didn't see it that way.

The divorce hassle didn't concern me too much except that it bothered Natalie. I felt myself getting closer to her, was almost ready to start making long-term plans, despite my ingrained fear of commitment and marriage and my misgivings about our philosophical differences. Natalie couldn't make a move until her divorce was settled, of course, but she'd talked many times about a future together. As much as she complained about Henry Marx, Natalie kept a lot in as far as the runup to her divorce was concerned. She still hadn't given me the whole story of the breakup, and I decided to let her tell me when she was ready. One thing I knew without question was that she hated the legal haggling. Despised the endless conferences and phone calls, said it detracted from her practice, her life in general. She would get quiet and preoccupied after a visit with her attorney. Said they were making progress, but it could take another six months to straighten out.

I didn't care, I was living the life. I had my beautiful girlfriend, was able to afford some time off, was sending a few thousand home every month to help out Pops. He had quit the janitorial job, was down to just the insurance gig, and was playing a lot more golf. Even my mom had stabilized somewhat. Standish had put her in rehab for a month, and she had been sober for three months running. A new record for her.

We were both attendings by now. Nat practiced at Hoag Memorial Hospital in Newport, while I was still at UCI. As disparate as these hospitals were, it seemed as if we had both found our niche. She preferred a more upscale clientele; I was happiest slogging it out in the trenches; still hadn't lost my taste for the horrific case.

Natalie finished her article and gave me a glowing smile. She was tan and relaxed from our week at Laguna, a blissful time of sleeping in, room service, long runs on the beach, and sex. Bed-shaking, contortionist, sweaty sex. Our personal best was five times during an eight-hour marathon yesterday. Three times in the hotel room, once in the surf while the lifeguard was on his lunch break, and the best time, by far, a rowdy session in the men's room at Las Brisas; mariachi band playing their hearts out next door, oblivious to our lovemaking just a few feet away.

I had never experienced anything like sex with Natalie. She seemed insatiable, had taught me things I'd only read about. We tried everything. Did everything. From the first time we'd had sex in the shower until now, I'd lived in a continual state of amazement; didn't believe it could get any better, yet the next time it did. We did. I didn't want to jinx it; gift horse and all, but my suspicious nature led me to ask myself two questions: Why me? And, what's this going to cost? I had always tried to be honest with myself. That attribute had carried me through some tough times, so I stuck with it. Always. More to the point, I had no illusions about my sexuality; I wasn't the best-looking man in the world, had never been told I was that great in bed. So why the sudden good fortune? Why was this gorgeous creature turning me inside out? I decided right there and then to go to the source. To ask Natalie.

Right after we had sex, again.

She lay beside me on two hundred-fifty-a-night sheets in our rumpled bed at The Inn at Laguna. A four-star resort steps from the beach, a short walk from the vibrant nightlife of Laguna Beach. The home of artists, the world-famous Pageant of the Masters and Yearly Sawdust Festival. So said the brochure I'd read while I ran a palm down her beautifully tanned backside. She barely opened her eyes as I read the flowery copy, clearly ready for a post-coital nap.

I ran my fingers through her tangled hair and asked the question that had plagued me for weeks. "Natalie?" She opened her eyes, stretched, and snuggled closer. "I was wondering?"

"Mmm?" She reached down to cover herself with the top-sheet, breasts grazing my chest.

"Why did you come on so strong with me? You know, in the shower." She peered at me with one eye closed, the hint of a smile on her face, no doubt thinking about fools and gift-horses. "Not that I'm complaining, mind you." She moved closer, insinuated her warm, smooth thigh between mine. Man, how I loved it when she did that. "It just shocked me, is all. Out of the blue like that. Know what I mean?"

"I told you, Steven." Her voice could make a man commit a Class A felony; gladly take a five-year jolt in San Quentin for her. "I wanted you. Right there, right then." She ran her tongue around my ear. "Simple as that."

I stated the obvious while she explored my ear with her tongue, "I'm flattered, believe me. I was just wondering, why me?" She sat up, withdrew her thigh. I could feel the sudden chill, see it in her eyes, but it was time for us to have this conversation. Our relationship at this point was about sex and little else. Believe me, I was fully aware that I was living the ultimate male fantasy, the-guilt-free, no-strings, All-American-fuck-fest. Men's magazines were sold by the thousands hawking this sybaritic lifestyle. Needless to say, I would *never* dare mention these concerns to any of my male friends. I could hear them laughing now; Rick Lamb's booming voice, *"What, are you nuts, Adler?* Move over, let me take her for a ride." Despite that attitude and my own superstitions, I still wanted to know. It was more than simple curiosity that drove me. I was getting close to Natalie, needed to know why she started up with me, where she thought we were headed.

I understood that she was still technically attached to her husband; even so, she seemed to be all right with our relationship, not the least bit conflicted morally. I must admit, I was at first, but she convinced me that her marriage was broken beyond repair. We had been together exclusively for more than four months, but I still felt as if there was a lot I needed to know about her, despite how much we'd talked philosophy. Hell, I thought, there must have been any number of things she needed to ask me, too. We hadn't been intimate in medical school, that's for sure, and now here we were four years later, in bed. All the time.

She rearranged the pillows, scooted up to the headboard, and sat with her arms crossed, wide awake now. "Okay. You want to know why I had you in the shower?"

Too late to back down now. I wasn't sure where this was going, or if I'd like what she told me, but I still wanted to know. Had to know. "Yes, I do."

She took her time. There was something in her eyes. It crossed my mind at the time that she was getting ready to make something up, perhaps attempting to spare my feelings or worse; trying to cover her tracks. "I was keyed up from the case, Steven. Stress makes me horny. Every time." She ran her fingers through her hair; erect nipples straining against the champagne-colored, satin sheet. "Always has. I don't know, the excitement, the adrenaline rush. It really gets to me." I had to admit the same thing had happened to me several times. As much as I'd thought about it, I guess I'd just never had the opportunity or the balls to act on it.

She gave immediate voice to my musings, displayed her daring, her outrageous sensuality without a second thought. "I saw an opportunity and took it." Natalie had a reputation at UCLA, and I could certainly vouch for her open sexuality, so I had to wonder if I was the first "opportunity" she had seized. How many of us there were over the years? She'd always dodged answering that one. She anticipated that unspoken question in a heartbeat as well. Must have seen the suspicion in my eyes, sensed the storm clouds gathering in the cramped hotel room. "I didn't mean for it to come out so cold. Like I was on the prowl, desperate to get laid." She kept her eyes on mine, her voice steady. "Besides, It's not like I did that kind of thing every day."

"So it was just an urge. An itch you had to scratch." I had no illusions about being used by Natalie. She hadn't tied me down. Hadn't spiked my Coke with Rufies. I was *more* than a willing participant; could have stopped her in the shower anytime I'd wanted. Not that I'd wanted to, of course. I'm no fool. I'll take that memory to my grave.

She nibbled my ear lobe, hard enough to hurt, just short of drawing blood. "No, stupid. I had the hots for *you*. You in particular." She tweaked my balls, gave them a real jolt, nearly sent me rocketing up to the cheap plastic light fixture above our bed. "Women have urges too, you know."

I rubbed the circulation back into my boys, brought my head up, and met her gaze. "And I'm thankful for that." Checked my scrotum; no bruising, yet. "Every day."

She pushed my head away. Serious now, her mood shifting steadily toward darkness; a heavy sea before a storm. "What brought all this on, anyway, Steven? Aren't you happy being with me? Because if you're not . . ."

"No, Natalie, of course I'm happy. Never happier." She didn't seem to be buying it, seemed on the verge of serious anger; eyes nearly pinched shut, brow furrowed. "I just needed to know." She gave me a doubtful look, arms crossed tightly across her chest. "That kind of thing never happens to guys like me, so I had to understand it. From your point of view."

She relaxed a little; her voice once again calm, if no longer seductive. "What do you mean, guys like you? You're good-looking. A doctor." She gave me an up-and-down appraisal. "Don't tell me you've had problems bedding women?" I thought I saw a flicker of calculation pass over her eyes as she talked, a smug smile play across her lips, as if she'd had this conversation before. "You had that little Asian woman share your bed, Steven." She jabbed my chest with an index finger. "Emily something or other. . . "

"That's not it at all. This is different. Nobody's ever come on to me like that." Her smug smile had brought me up short; I wondered suddenly how she knew about Elaine. More importantly, if Natalie knew I was in a relationship, did she know Elaine and I had broken up when she fucked me in the shower? Did she even care? On a second's reflection, I decided there was no way Natalie would know about our breakup. Call me old-fashioned, but to me that fact put an entirely different spin on her actions. One I had to sort out, for my own peace of mind. So, once again, I went to the source. "Besides, how did you know about Elaine?"

She jumped up, stood by the side of the bed, reached down, and covered herself with the top sheet. "Look, Steven. It is what it is, okay?" Pulled the sheet tighter around her torso. "I wanted to get laid that night. I liked you from back in med school and we had just gone through that horrible case together." She gave me a look with the slightest trace of condescension; her voice taking on a note of sarcasm I'd only heard while she'd been talking about her ex. "Why is that so hard for you to understand?" She gave me a disgusted shake of her head, headed for the bathroom. "As for your little girlfriend, the X-Ray tech, it was common knowledge all over the hospital."

I couldn't let this go. Had to find out if she knew about the breakup before getting with me in the shower. As petty as my concern may have been to some people, I knew her answer would be an important clue to her character, her ethics.

I waited until she came back, watched her sit a discreet distance away on the bed. "Did you think that Elaine and I were still together when we made love that night at UCI?"

Even in the face of Natalie's aggressive body language, her undisguised contempt, I felt I had a valid reason to ask that question. After all, if we were to stay together long term, I wanted to know if I had to worry about her doing it again. With someone else. I knew her sexually, very well, but needed to have some sense of her values, her morals. If for no other reason than to be ready for any eventuality. More importantly for me in the short-term, to avoid the problem in the first place by just walking away. *Adios, Amiga. No harm, no foul.* Her answer, delivered in a low monotone a few seconds later, surprised me, even as it revealed a little more of her character. "Does it matter, Steven?"

I knew this much about Natalie. She was a free spirit. Even back in medical school, she *lived* to party. Didn't care one whit about the rumors circulating about her love life. I knew all this and still took a chance with my answer, risked her scorn by answering truthfully. Knew she'd probably think me weak because it *did* matter to me. "Yes it does, Natalie." She had her head down, expression masked by her hair. I tried to turn her gently toward me, she stayed where she was. "I'd like to know, baby."

She moved farther down the bed, her back to me. I saw her shoulders shake, from laughing or crying, I couldn't tell. "Well, since it means so much to you." She kept her face hidden. I was frustrated; with her back to me, I had lost any chance to read her expression, judge her veracity. She kept her voice low, again in that uncharacteristic monotone. "I did know. About your breakup."

I didn't know what to think. I was pretty sure I'd kept it to myself. Didn't remember telling anyone. A moment later, as I watched Natalie, back straight, absolutely still, I recalled my conversation with Rick Lamb on New Year's Day. Knew we'd talked about Elaine. And about Natalie. Couldn't remember for the life of me whether or not I'd told Lamb that Elaine and I were finished. I tried to reason this through; finally concluded that it could only be one of two possibilities: Lamb had told her or Natalie was lying. I simply couldn't think of anyone else who may have told Natalie.

After a few tortured seconds of self-doubt, I decided to trust my instincts and believe Natalie; Lamb must have told her, and I'd forgotten I'd told him in the first place. More than that, I decided to go beyond giving her the simple benefit of the doubt. All the way to trust. Trust in her ability to be truthful with me. I even took it a giant step further that afternoon and decided I could begin to trust her in the most important realm to me: trust that Natalie could remain faithful. After all, I thought, what is love without trust?

I even talked myself into believing that it didn't *really* matter after all. Elaine and I weren't married, not even close to being engaged for that matter. So Natalie wasn't even breaking up a couple. Not really.

Years later, I looked back on that conversation in Laguna and understood, too late, the root of my troubles with Natalie. Saw the first subtle shading of the truth, the willing misappropriation of trust. The emotional sleight of hand that, even more than her cunning sexuality, was Natalie's greatest gift.

Chapter 7

Six A.M., October twenty-fifth; back to work Monday. For some poor slobs. As for me, I was off to play golf with Pops, my work week started later that night, at the stroke of midnight. I'd bought a set of used clubs last summer, only a hundred bucks in *The Green Sheet*. They weren't fancy: old-school genuine wooden woods, steel-shaft irons, and a putter straight out of a Fifties newsreel; greenish fiberglass shaft and a head the size of a grapefruit. Hope my dad wouldn't laugh too hard.

Dad had worked hard at his game, practiced twice a week, took lessons once a month. As in all of his endeavors, my dad threw himself into golf with a vengeance; resulting in a well earned seven handicap. He played in tournaments nearly every weekend. Usually by himself or with a buddy from the insurance agency. Mom went with him about once a month. Said her back was bothering her too much to play every week.

I couldn't wait to see Pops play; he sounded more excited than I'd heard him in years. This was the first time for us to play together. I was at least as jazzed as he was. No matter what, I knew we'd have fun. Pops and I always did.

I pulled onto Greenbrier Drive, our old street, at six-thirty. Pops was in the garage polishing his clubs with an old tee-shirt, bent over his work bench in total concentration. I pulled on the emergency brake; he heard my car in the driveway and turned around, a huge smile creasing his face. "Stevie. Come here and give me a hug."

I fell into his arms, kissed his light, two-day stubble. "You look great, son." He held me at arm's length, gave me the quick once-over. "Really good. You getting more sleep? Working less, now that you're a big shot down at the hospital?"

Same old Pops. Forever proud, perpetually worried. "Yeah, Dad. Everything's good. Just got back from vacation. Had a great . . ."

Dad slapped a palm to his forehead. "Stupid me. I forgot. You went to the beach with your lady friend, Maria."

"Natalie, Dad. Natalie Bogner. My old friend from work." I had to smile. Dad had a very good mind, could quote you prices for annuities going out five years, never used a grocery list, and always came home without forgetting a single item. But names, holy shit, he was bad with names. Used to call our neighbor Morty Klein "Charlie," called Mom's friend Ruth Morris "Chrissy," and would occasionally yell down the block, "Jake, Ralphie, you boys come on home, supper's ready." Always broke my brother up. Jake and our pet boxer, Ralphie, would always sprint ahead of me, Jake giving me endless shit, all the way home.

I helped load Dad's clubs into the Porsche. Had to use a lot of imagination to make everything fit this time, what with my huge old clubs and a passenger on board. Dad was absolutely no help; he stood with his hands on his hips, a bemused smile on his face while I struggled. I gave him a look, which he studiously ignored, finally voiced my thoughts. "You coulda' helped, Pops."

"Oh, Stevie." He was having way too much fun this early in the morning, a smile creasing his face, eyes crinkled. "Where's the fun in that. Car's so small, I was waiting for you to break a couple clubs." He pantomimed a driver crashing over his knee, made a big show of pretending to stuff them in the back seat. "Get 'em in that way." He walked over to the passenger's door, threw an arm over my shoulder and gave it a squeeze. "Let's go say good-bye to your mom."

I looked over at my dad as we walked through the garage. He didn't seem to be carrying as much worry; had a bounce in his step, less concern showing around his eyes. I was glad he'd decided to take my checks. Stubborn and proud as Dad was, he'd fought me like a hellcat. Had to talk to him about it every night for a week before he decided to let me help out. A proud and self-sufficient man, my father; none better. He called me a few weeks after cashing the first check back in July; let it slip that he'd quit his janitorial job at the school and the gig as a security officer at the Price Club. Said he was going to devote more time to his golf game. Told me . . ."If that old geezer Arnold Palmer can play at sixty, why can't I?" Went on to say he was thinking about joining the P.G.A. Senior Tour. His way of thanking his son for what any man in my position would have done in a New York minute.

I took him aside before we went through the laundry room door, kept my voice low. "How is she, Pops?"

I was prepared for the worst. Her detox had gone well, according to Dr. Standish, whom I called weekly all summer long for follow-ups. But I didn't dare get my hopes up, had been disappointed too many times for that. Dad turned to face me and his broad smile put my fears partially to rest. "Good, Stevie." He opened the door, motioned for me to go first. "She's put her weight back on. Doesn't have nearly as many headaches."

This was Dad's code for hangovers; a definite good sign. Encouraged by this bit of good news, I decided to cut to the chase. "So she's not drinking, then."

We passed through the cramped laundry room; a spotless pair of harvest gold Kenmore's on the left, Dad's hand-built wall of cabinets on the right. The room was filled with one of my favorite childhood smells: fresh, clean clothes and laundry detergent. "No, son. Not that I've seen."

I wasn't totally reassured by that answer; when it came to booze, Mom was highly skilled at deception, as are most heavy drinkers. I decided to let it rest for now, see if I could pick anything up when I saw her. "How's her health otherwise?"

We went to the kitchen for some fresh fruit. Dad had made a few sandwiches; paper bags stood on the kitchen counter, neatly folded, clearly marked "Jacob," and "Steven." I was touched beyond words at Dad's thoughtfulness. Old habits do indeed die hard. As much as Dad worked while we were growing up, Jake and I always had lunches prepared, waiting for us in exactly the same spot. Mom helped out, about ten percent of the time; the rest was up to Dad.

I'd planned to take him to lunch at the course, but quickly shelved that idea. Couldn't disappoint him, as he clearly had gotten up very early to prepare. Besides, he made killer PB & J sandwiches. Just the right amount of Skippy extra crunchy and Smuckers strawberry jam. We rummaged in the fridge for apples, put the lunch sacks and fruit in a larger bag, and went in search of Mom. Halfway down the hall, he gave me a nod, his voice a notch above a whisper. "She seems all right, Stevie."

There was something in his tone. I believed Dad about her drinking, Standish had told me he was fairly certain she'd cut way back if not quit altogether. Still, I could tell something was nagging at Dad. "You're sure? You're telling me everything, right, Pops?"

He pulled me into the den. We could hear Mom stirring in their bedroom, Dad clearly didn't want her to know we were discussing her. "It's just some back pain, Stevie. Nothing serious."

My antennae went up immediately as I mentally scrolled through the possible diagnoses: renal failure, carcinoma, abdominal aortic aneurysm, all the way down to simple musculo-skeletal pain. "How long, and how bad, Pops?"

He leaned against the back of the couch. We could hear Mom coughing in her bathroom; a loose, phlegmy hack. He took his time, counting back through the weeks, searching his memory to give me a sense of her discomfort. "I'd say a month or two. She told me it just aches sometimes. Nothing serious, though." He caught my worried look, laid a hand on my shoulder. "Really, son. She said it's nothing."

"She ever wake up in the middle of the night with it? Have trouble moving?"

Dad smiled, clapped me on the back. "Stevie. It's nothing. Really." Lowered his voice and flashed a smile as Mom came into the room.

"What's nothing, Jacob?" Mom looked pretty good, a bit tired, a little grayer at her temples, but not bad, considering the way she'd abused her health for so long. Her weight was back, as Dad had said. Her color was healthier as well, no longer ash gray. Her voice was even better, I noticed as she came closer; no quaver or slurred words.

I decided to answer for Dad, afraid he'd change the subject to avoid upsetting Mom. Besides, I needed to get a sense of what was wrong with her. "We were discussing your back pain, Mom."

Dad shot me a look. Mom got on her tiptoes and kissed my cheek. "You know your dad, Steven. He worries too much." I had to admit she was moving fairly well, especially this soon after getting up. Hell, there were days when I'd need a half-hour to get going in the morning, and she had more than thirty years on me. "I think I strained it working in the garden. It's just a little twinge now and then."

I didn't want to ignore anything serious, but I didn't want to pester her, either. She seemed comfortable, so I let it go. "If you're sure, Mom." She gave me a reassuring smile. "You'd tell me if it got worse? Go see Standish, wouldn't you?"

She nodded vigorously; clearly tired of my questions, ready to move on, ever the pragmatist when it came to her health. A minute later, she zipped up Dad's sweater and shooed us out the door with instructions to have fun and stay bundled up. Handed us our sack lunches, told us we were going to miss our seven-thirty tee time if we hung around bugging her much longer. We kissed her, waved good-bye, and got in the Porsche, each of us looking forward to a full day of golf, good-natured bullshit, and P B & Js. Life just didn't get much better than that.

Chapter 8

Jurupa Hills Golf course was my first full-scale golfing experience, having honed my skills, such as they were, at the Pitch and Putt in Twin Lakes Park, beside the Twenty-Two Freeway. The Pitch and Putt, my home course, was actually just a cut above the miniature golf setup at Knott's Berry Farm. Every hole was a par three, flat as the Mojave and noisy as an airplane factory from the truck traffic whizzing by a few yards away on the Twenty-Two. The only hazards were the jackasses on the freeway yelling every imaginable expletive as they roared down the road toward L.A. One asshole even threw a golf ball at me going seventy miles an hour. Let's see Mr. Arnold-freakin'-Palmer try to sink a thirty-footer at the Masters with a Titleist flying past his ear! Needless to say, Jurupa Hills looked like a monster to me: three hundred fifty yards? That's just one damn hole? Par five? Water and sand? What, are you kidding me? Where's the fake blue grass, the windmills and dumbass clowns? I took a look at the map, brow soaked with flop sweat. I was afraid it would take us twelve hours to play. Dad said not to worry, he'd show me how.

The First Hole.

Dad showed me how. His drive carried two hundred forty yards, down the middle of the fairway. He was an eight-iron from the pin in perfect position to birdie. Blew me away. Watching his outrageous drive, I half expected his tee to spin into the air, fly up over his head and land in his shirt pocket. I shook my head, thinking: where did my old man learn to drive like Jack Nicklaus?

He walked back to the cart, not even trying to hide his shit-eating grin. The bastard. Spun his driver in his right hand about a hundred RPM, like a drum major; trying to rub it in. He gave me a smirk, his voice dripping fake conceit. "I believe you're up, son."

I trudged to the tee, dragging my second-hand driver behind me. My heart was pounding. I just couldn't be shown up by a sixty-something old man. I felt as if my reputation was at stake. Wait a minute, I thought, what reputation? Top gun at Knott's Berry Farm; ass-kicking pro at the Pitch and Putt? I was as dead as deep-fried shrimp. And Dad wasn't much help. He was too busy enjoying himself at my expense. He stowed his driver, climbed into the cart, and yelled, "Use the yellow tees, Son." I was crushed. Dad was pointing to the women's tees, down a gentle grade, fifty yards closer to the pin than the blue men's tee. Not on your life, Pops, I said to myself. I'm an Adler, and Adler men don't hit from the ladies' tee.

I teed it up, took a few mighty practice swings, and got into position. Feet firmly set just so, back straight, confident smile. Took a gigantic backswing, drove it forward, head down, left arm straight, wrists locked. Perfect. Made contact with the ball, and a little clump of grass. Dad was practically falling out of the cart, yelling something that sounded like, "Told you, Stevie." I couldn't make it out exactly, because he was laughing too hard. "Should have used the yellow tees." I turned to glare at him; he was nearly prostrate with laughter, right hand pointing at my ball, which was resting ten yards away, five yards short of the women's tee.

We spent the next three hours finishing the front nine. Looked like my time estimate of twelve hours was accurate after all. I was getting a little nervous. Had to be on duty at midnight. Nine holes left to play, and work was only eleven hours away.

We were having a blast, of course. Dad gave me a few tips; I hit a couple of decent drives and even sank a fourteen-footer. We stopped for lunch at the clubhouse, spread out our sandwiches and popped our Cokes. Dad was fussing over his scorecard. I sneaked a peek; thirty-eight, two over par, I needed a calculator to figure mine. Holy shit, I thought with a surge of pride, he *had* been practicing. Who knew my dad was such a good athlete? Pity he had to work so hard all those years.

He caught me staring, gave me a dazzling smile; wiped away the regret I was feeling about missed opportunities in the time it took him to show me his score card, pleased as an eighth-grader with straight A's. "See what practice and hard work will do for ya, Stevie?"

I shoved my card in a back pocket, still smoldering over my sixty-five-for-the-damned-front-nine score. "Yeah, Pops. Hard work and talent, you mean."

He took a huge bite of peanut butter and jelly on wheat. "Nah! You didn't do so bad, son." He swallowed a mouthful of Coke, wiped his lips with a paper napkin. "Hell, this is only your first time out. You'll get better." Chewed a little more sandwich. "Just need to keep playing."

I unwrapped my sandwich, licked the extra jam from the crust, and smiled. If his game was any indication, Pops was right, although my practice sessions at the Pitch and Putt were about as useful as a trailer hitch on a Corvette. "Hope you're right, Dad. I really stunk it up out there."

He started another laughing jag. Here it comes, I thought, a rehash of the first hole. No, this anecdote was even worse. "I couldn't believe that tee shot you hit on five." He was laughing so hard I expected Coke to fly out of his nose. "Went about fifteen, twenty yards." He slapped his hand on the table. Other golfers were starting to look. "Straight up." I had to laugh. Pops was killing me: red eyes, tears down his cheeks, he looked like the front row at a Robin Williams concert. "Almost landed on your head." He completely lost it, head on the table, shoulders shaking. What the hell, I couldn't help myself, I was right there with him, laughing hysterically. My Pops, a gentle man with a vicious sense of humor. God, did I love him.

We finished our lunch. A half-hour of laughs, insults, and great sandwiches. One of my best days ever. We talked about everything riding along the cart paths, late-October chill in the air. Jurupa Hills was a pretty course; lots of water, gently rolling fairways and plenty of shade.

We asked about each other's jobs; he was learning to be a certified underwriter, taking courses at the home office in San Francisco, seemed happy and justifiably proud to be in middle management.

I told him about the endless stream of blood and guts we saw in the Department. The gang truce had been shattered on a hot Saturday night in September: Labor Day weekend in Anaheim. Three dead, fifteen seriously wounded in a twelve-hour period. Rick Lamb and his team operated nineteen hours straight that night. The Knife and Gun Club was officially back in business, so our census was booming.

He started the cart and asked me the question I'd been waiting for all day; his eyes shaded by sunglasses, fixed on the path straight ahead. "So, son? You serious with this girl, Natalie?" I hadn't brought her home to meet the folks yet; they only knew what I'd told them. They knew that Natalie's divorce was almost finalized, knew it would be a done deal by December at the latest. The problem for me was; as far as Pops was concerned, she was still technically married. Given that little detail, it was a bit of a touchy subject between us.

I had to be careful with my answer, considering my dad's way of thinking, so I kept my tone of voice casual, hoping he'd get on to something else. "I like her, Pops. Like her a lot."

We stopped at my ball with a spray of gravel as Dad yanked on the emergency brake. "I know that, son." He wasn't going to let me off the hook that easily, that much was clear by his intent stare. "Do you love her, Steven?"

Ah, the sixty-four-thousand-dollar question. Leave it to Jacob Adler to come right to the point. I wasn't even sure how to answer that one in my mind, much less aloud, so I decided to play it safe. "I wouldn't go that far, Pops. We have a lot in common. Get along pretty well." I looked over at Dad to see how my answer was playing. He kept his gaze trained on me, his impassive face giving nothing away. "She's great. Can't wait for you to meet her."

I lined up my shot, hit a decent hack about a hundred yards, climbed back into the cart. He released the brake and shot me a look full of meaning. "I'm looking forward to it, son." He gunned the little electric cart down a long grade. "Your mom and I want you to be happy, Steven." He kept his eyes on the path. Left me wondering if this was just another father-son chat or if my dad had something else on his mind. He addressed that thought before we'd gone another yard. "She treat you well?"

Now I had an idea where he was going. I decided to tell the unvarnished truth; hopeful that, in the process, I'd draw him out a bit, learn a little something about women. No doubt I could use his help on that score. "Sure, Pops. We get along just fine."

He stopped the cart alongside his ball, stepped around the back to select a nine iron. "Not what I meant, Steven." He had a look on his face I hadn't seen since Jake left home for the last time: concern admixed with a deep longing. "Does she love you back?" He took a quick practice swing, turned to face me through the windscreen. "I guess I wanted to ask if she gives as much to you as you give her."

He slapped a perfect wedge shot five feet from the pin, replaced his club, and started the cart. "I know you pretty well, son." His look was as tender as the one he gave me when I broke my right arm in a seventh-grade football game. "You're just like your old man when it comes to love. It's easy for you to give it, you're so grateful to have it." He drove down a shallow gully, stopping a few yards from my ball. "Problem is, you don't pay enough attention to how much of it's coming back to you."

There it was; a partial answer to thirty years of questions about my parents' life together. Even an answer for my troubles with women. The dynamics of their relationship, the basis of their love for one another, revealed in his innocent concern for my welfare. In that instant I had an inkling of what Dad had gone through the last forty-some years with Mom. About why Dad stood by her, even during the impossible years when she was drunk for weeks at a time. I even learned something about myself from Pops' perspective. Why it was hard for me to trust women, why I got hurt a little more than I thought I should.

He looked over at me expectantly as I struggled to formulate my answer to the toughest question I'd ever faced. "I know what you're saying, Dad. I guess I've been burned a few times by women. I kind of know you're right about my problems." I paused, searching for the truth, needing to let it out. "Giving too much in a relationship, but I feel like this time we have a decent balance, Natalie and I."

We drove in silence to the next tee and *I* wondered if he bought it, wondered if I believed my words. Dad parked the cart and turned to face me, as serious as I'd ever seen him. "You know I love your mom, right, son?" I couldn't help jumping to conclusions. My suspicious mind again. What's he leading up to, had he been hiding problems with his health, her health, a divorce, what? My heart was pounding. Even at this age, long gone from home, I was afraid of my folks getting divorced. Even worse, I was terrified of losing one of my parents. Every child fears that loss. One step closer to being an orphan. One giant, metaphorical stride closer to our own grave.

I forced my voice through a growing lump in my throat. "Sure, Pops. Of course."

We hit our drives on the sixteenth hole. I out-drove Dad for the first time, by about twenty yards. He smiled wistfully as we climbed back into the cart. "I don't know what's come over me, Stevie." He reached over and squeezed my hand. "I didn't want this to turn into a philosophy session." We flew over a rise in the fairway; I had to brace my hand against the roof, Pops was driving so fast.

He slowed slightly, turned again to face me. "I'm not as good with words as you, but just hear me out, son." I nodded silently, expecting the worst. "It hasn't been easy for your mom and me. We've had some trouble over the years." I was really nervous now, waiting for the other shoe to drop. "But that's the way it is in life. In marriage." He kept his gaze trained on me as we hit a broad, straight section of fairway grass. "The tough times come, but they don't ever last, thank God. You gotta wait 'em out. Just keep livin' your life." He gave me an embarrassed smile. "Am I making any sense, Stevie?"

More than you could ever imagine, I thought. "Sure, Pops. You always do."

He shook a finger at me, his smile replaced by a look of pure parental concern. "This Natalie woman? If you do decide to get serious. Even come *close* to marrying her, just make sure she loves you as much as you love her."

I knew he was telling the truth, but that still begged the larger question; how does one know? How can we ever know for sure what's hidden in our lover's heart? I decided to ask the man whom I trusted more than anyone in the world: "How can I know that, Dad? How can anyone?"

He gave me a shrug. "How should I know, son? I can only go by my own experience. You just know it when you feel it." He peered into my eyes, trying to gauge how well I was following him, clearly intent on delivering his critical advice. "If you have to ask yourself that question when you're with someone? Then you probably have something to worry about on that score. But, if all you feel is love all around you, at least most of the time, you're okay." I nodded, hadn't thought about it in those terms, but he made sense. "If all you want to do is make the other person happy and she's doing the same thing for you. Bingo. You're home free."

He'd nailed it. As usual. Life according to Pops. The Golden Rule of Love and Marriage: treat your partner with all the love and respect you expect back from him or her. Simple enough concept. Hard as hell to accomplish in real life. I was the prime example of that, I thought with an inward sigh.

We reached the eighteenth tee. Pops hit another monster drive; two hundred forty yards down the left side, away from the water hazard. I hit mine a lot better, as well. Two hundred fifty yards. Straight down the fairway. Into the middle of the pond.

Pops had a good laugh at that one. Guess we'd come full circle just as the sun began to set. We pulled up to the edge of the green. Dad leaned over his bag, met my eyes, and said, "The best advice I can give you, Stevie, is this." I grabbed my goofy-looking putter and waited for Pops to sink his eight-footer. Job done, he pocketed his ball and walked over to me. "Don't ever confuse sex with love."

I lined up my putt, my mind on Natalie: the shower, Las Brisas, The Inn at Laguna Beach. Took a smooth, slow back swing, stroked it perfectly, missed it by an inch and a half. Pops picked up my ball. A gimme: "Trust me on this one, Steven. Great sex is easy to fake. Lasts about a month after the wedding." He threw an arm over my shoulder as his words hit their intended target. "Love is a different animal, altogether." We set off for the clubhouse, shadows chasing us home. He glanced over at me, the contentment I'd been searching for all these years evident in his face, in his confident tone. "You have a marriage filled with love, you're the richest man in town, son. Always remember that."

Chapter 9

I dropped Pops off at home. They wanted me to stay for dinner, Mom's meatloaf, but I had to beg off. It was closing in on six-thirty, so I knew I would have less than fifteen minutes to shower and throw on some scrubs by the time I made it back to Orange. I stayed for about five minutes, thanked Dad for a wonderful day, made a date for a few weeks later, and kissed them good-bye.

I got home at seven-forty-five, just as I'd predicted. Had less than ten minutes to get ready for my first day back at work. I congratulated myself again for staying in my old apartment. Even though I was making a lot more money, I loved the conven-ience. Besides, I'd rather have the extra cash for fun stuff. Wasn't quite ready for a big mortgage payment, yet.

I was looking forward to work. Had a great time with Natalie, but missed the gang and the cases even more. I jumped out of the shower, threw on some scrubs, and made a dash for the door. A few moments later, I had my hand on the doorknob when I noticed the blinking light on my answering machine. Hit the button, rewound the tape and listened to: Natalie. She'd heard from her lawyer. Her husband was ready to settle. She sounded excited, said it looked good for her. Said she was glad she'd hired an asshole for a lawyer.

I locked the door and ran to my car, thinking; are there any *other* kinds of lawyers?

What a homecoming. You'd have thought I had been gone for a year. Sterile gloves, blown up like balloons, with crude caricatures of my ugly mug under the distended fingers. I shook my head; the way they did it I looked like a demented rubber rooster. They'd put a placemat fashioned from an exam table paper cover on my desk; a can of Coke chilling in an emesis basin filled with ice, next to my own personal tub of buttered popcorn. Pop Secret, my favorite.

As it turned out, I didn't get to eat a single kernel.

"Medics two minutes out." Cathy Jenkins was working the radio tonight. One of the kindest, gentlest women I'd ever met and an extremely competent nurse. She had one quirk, though; tension made her swear like a longshoreman. She ran out of her cubicle, down the hall, trailing her headset cable behind her. Stopped a foot from the ward clerk's desk. "Get the goddamned pediatricians down here. We have a motherfucker of a case coming in." I'd never heard her so frantic. This could not be good, I thought, as I grabbed my coat. A minute later, I was already on my way to Trauma One, my mind racing through the possibilities. I paused for a second at the doorway, grabbed the intubation tray on my way in, slapped it on the Mayo stand and flicked the switch that powered up the monitors.

As I was setting up, Cathy Jenkins grabbed Barbara Manning at the nurse's station, nearly spun her around, and pushed her toward Trauma One. "Hurry up. Get in there and help Dr. Adler. This one's gonna be a fucking son of a bitch, Barb."

Barbara, bless her heart, was calm as usual, the ultimate professional. She took Cathy gently by the elbow, guided her toward the radio cubicle, and used her quiet voice, the one she used with the ambulatory psychotics. "Cath, we need you on the radio." She gave her the slightest push down the hallway. "So we'll know what to set up for."

Cathy seemed to awaken from a trance. She blinked twice, peeked around Barbara into Trauma One, and said, "A kid. Five year old fell in his pool. They said he's clinically dead. ETA one . . ."

The medics burst into Trauma One, radio chatter screaming from their Handi-Talkers. I took a quick look at the little boy, his skin blue as faded denim, wrinkled and pale head to toe. Almost before the medic's stretcher had lined up with our bed, we shoveled him onto the backboard, adjusting his position as we heaved him over. As soon as the patient was positioned, the crew chief hopped onto the gurney along with him, knees tucked beside the boy's chest. Never missed a beat of his chest compression.

I grabbed a number-five endotracheal tube, the small McIvor intubating blade, and shoved it in. The medic was doing perfect, rhythmic compressions, the hard-plastic backboard undulating slightly with each of his thrusts as I depressed the boy's tongue with the McIvor.

The kid vomited milky water the second I exposed his vocal cords with the blade. Barb hustled to my side, handed me a Yankaur, and I cleared his airway with the suction. Slipped the ET tube past his cords and a second or two later, Respiratory hooked him up.

Looked at the monitors. Flat line. His color still a frightening, dusky blue. Tried three ccs of intra-cardiac Epinephrine; his rate only blipped up to twenty. Fell back to ten within seconds. I looked the crew chief in the eyes, looked away quickly as he began to cry. Kept my voice confident, wasn't even close to panic. "Keep up the compressions. We're not giving up yet."

Ran to the head of the bed, checked for breath sounds. Nothing on the left, fair on the right side of his chest. The ET tube was down too far, into the right main-stem bronchus, delivering oxygen only to the right lung. Swore at myself for the botched placement; this kid needed all the oxygen he could get. Right now!

I reached down, pulled the tube back three centimeters, about an inch, listened again. Distant breath sounds but equal side-to-side.

Checked the oxygen saturation: fifty percent. Pulse was now in the thirties. Asked the crew chief how long the kid had been down. He never missed a beat, perfect CPR all the way. "Thirty minutes."

I tried and failed to keep the note of alarm from my voice; this was my worst drowning case yet. "In the water that fucking long?" I felt his carotid pulse. Fair perfusion. His color a little better. Cerulean blue lips; faintly pink trunk.

The medic kept up his perfect CPR. "Mother said she found him at the bottom." The nurses cut off his clothes, wrapped him in Mylar blankets to prevent hypothermia. "Says he was under about fifteen minutes."

Shit. Shit. Shit! Brain death usually occurred in around five minutes. Still, he's young, I thought, seems to be responding a little. No way was I going to call this code. Not for a hell of a long time. Checked his pupils. Swung the flashlight slowly past each in turn: sluggish reaction but both worked. Score another one for the good guys. Not brain dead, yet.

Checked the EKG: sinus rhythm, rate up to fifty. Oxygen saturation: sixty-five. Gave a nod to the crew chief; his cheeks were wet with tears. Had to look away from him, couldn't afford to lose it. This kid needed me.

Had Barbara take a manual blood pressure. Sometimes the electronic ones were inaccurate in kids, especially when they were in shock. She blew up the cuff. The kid moved his arm. Then his legs.

I checked his pupillary reflexes again. Briskly reactive, no doubt about it. Best of all, the kid seemed to engage when I looked in his eyes. A tear rolled down his cheek. A heartbeat later, my cheek was wet as well. A second later, I felt tears running down my neck in a sudden rush.

Loud sobbing from Barbara, the nursing students, all of the medics as they realized what we'd done.

I wanted to kiss him. He was one lucky kid. Fifteen minutes in the water, clinically dead in the field. Forty-five minutes of hard work by the best team in the county, the only thing standing between him and death.

I checked him again, my heart swelling with joy. He was pinking up nicely, making purposeful movements, trying to talk around his endotracheal tube.

I leaned over the head of the bed, toward his right ear. The room was instantly quiet; the only sound the muted blip of his EKG tracing. The crew chief watched from the corner, picked up my intentions immediately. His soft voice barely carried across the room. "His name's Jason, Doc."

He was straining against the tube, fighting with every breath. I leaned in closer to his right ear, kept my voice calm. "Easy, Jason." I wiped a tear from his cheek; his eyes met mine, a look of stark, animal terror suffusing his face. "We're going to get you fixed up now. A little later on we'll take that tube out of your throat." I ran a hand through his thick black hair. "Then you can see Mommy and Daddy. Okay?" He nodded and closed his eyes, completely spent from his ordeal.

I took a last scan of his vitals as the crew chief, a burly six-footer, jumped down from the gurney. An instant later he stood near the doorway, unashamedly crying on a female medical student's shoulder.

Jason's rate was now in the nineties, oxygen sat at ninety-two, blood pressure a little low but acceptable, all things considered, at seventy over fifty.

The Peds residents showed up, finally. Mumbled a lame-assed excuse about a bad spinal tap in the Neonatal ICU. As the Peds team fussed over "our" save, I finalized Jason's treatment, got him ready for a quick trip upstairs to Peds ICU. Dead-tired from the adrenalized ordeal, I took a deep breath and slumped into my chair.

The Peds' chief resident directed the transfer upstairs, jotted a quick note, and came over to my desk; looked down at me, and said, "Nice save, Dr. Adler." He reached over and shook my hand. I was embarrassed by all the attention. Just wanted to be alone to decompress.

I nodded an acknowledgment. "We have the best crew in the country down here. You should be congratulating them." I reached for my Coke, was surprised by the violent tremor in my hand. Hid it from the resident by folding my hands on the desktop. "Lucky for us he was in cold water."

The resident, a gangly kid named Rod Farmer, looked about sixteen to me, a spray of acne over ruddy cheeks, bright red hair and absolutely no visible beard. He nodded. "The diving reflex." He was referring to a physiological response that was especially prominent in children. Immerse them in cold water and the blood circulation to the limbs, abdominal muscles, and peripheral nervous system virtually shuts down. The brain, heart, and lungs are perfused instead as a survival mechanism. Kids have been known to survive up to twenty minutes of these conditions. That's why we try so hard for as long as it takes to save them. I'd been on hour-long codes lots of times.

A minute or two later, the Peds resident realized that I was in a world of my own, silent and outwardly calm as a monk. He caught my hint: *Discussion over, I want to be alone.*

I was left to my thoughts. The board was empty. All I had to do was go talk to Jason's parents. I was dreading that, even as I was overjoyed to deliver qualified good news.

On an impulse, I picked up the phone, dialed Natalie's number. Looking back, I was sure it was the aftermath of my extreme distress that prompted the call. Christ in Heaven, I'd thought at the time, that little boy was dead. Floppy, blue, cold. Clinically dead.

I felt a profound surge of emotions, sitting alone in my office: joy, awe, pride, mostly fear for what might have been. And the sharpest feeling of all, certainly the strangest for a confirmed cynic like me, a tiny glimmer of faith. I didn't believe in God but still, I had to wonder, something strange happened in that room. Something beyond simple science and skill. But I'm not particularly introspective; I'm more into action and reaction, so I shook it off as the dial tone droned in my ear. Besides, I reminded myself as I waited impatiently for Natalie to answer, miracles just don't happen anymore. At least not in Southern California, the home of shattered dreams and drive-by shootings.

Natalie answered on the third ring. I was vaguely aware of her voice on the other end, a muted "Hello, Hello . . ." Seemed to be coming through a tunnel. I broke off my musings with a start, nearly at a loss for words. I heard her voice once again and blurted, "I love you, Nat. I really do." There was a stunned silence, broken in a second by Natalie's quick intake of breath, an instant in which I was sure I'd made a mistake, revealed too much of myself, too soon.

Natalie's voice was nearly the sweetest sound I'd ever heard. Her words heart-felt, tone of voice far from her usual seductive whisper. "I love you too, Steven. More than you can know."

I took a few minutes after hanging up with Natalie to compose myself. Walked into the restroom, splashed cold water on my face, and checked for blood spots on my coat. I was fastidious most of the time, most especially at work: I know how I'd feel if my loved one's doctor came to talk to me in blood-splattered scrubs. I'd freak out.

Jason's parents were huddled on a pair of orange plastic chairs in the far corner of the waiting room. As miserable and vulnerable as two people could be, locked down in their horrific prison of fear. I walked over to them; they immediately turned away. Afraid to hear the truth. Afraid to hear that the world as they knew it was gone forever. Their faces, tortured with panic as they were, revealed the true meaning of love to me in that instant: we humans can survive *anything* except a parent's worst

nightmare come horribly alive. *Nothing* in this world is as important as our unconditional love for our children. Nothing.

I bent at the waist so that I could meet them face to face. They
trembled as if they were being slowly electrocuted. I put my
arms around them and hugged them tight. Whispered to the
mom, "Mrs. Stanton?" Jason's mom began to scream. I held her
tighter, tried to soothe her tremor. "Jason's upstairs in the ICU."
They searched my face, desperate for a shred of good news. I
didn't have to force a smile; I wanted them to see how overjoyed
I was. For the first time in my career, I'd thrown away my professional reserve the minute Jason left for the ICU. "He's doing
remarkably well, considering what . . ."

"He's not dead?" They were out of their chairs, tears of joy
mingled with screams and sobs. "He's going to be okay?" They
were hugging me, Jason's mom clinging to my chest. "Our little
boy's all right?"

I had never experienced such happiness. Such a profound
sense of relief. I had literally saved their boy's life, and we were
now connected forever: three ordinary humans bound by a heart-
stopping close shave. A startling turn of events none of us would
ever be able to fully explain. I melted into their arms, professional
reserve dissolved by the palpable love I felt in their embrace. I
found my voice after a few moments of tears and kisses from his
mom. "He's going to have it a little rough for the next few days. A
lot of tests, some medication." His parents looked reborn. The
only way to describe them. "There's a lot of work . . ."

They'd heard enough of my medical mumbo-jumbo; that was
clear from looking into their faces. They were only interested in
one thing. "When can we see our Jason?"

We stood apart; Jason's mom took a hankie from her purse
and lovingly wiped the tears and smeared residue of her lipstick
from my cheek. "The ICU will call you." I motioned to the receptionist's desk and instructed them to check in with the clerk.

Jason's mother reached up to lay a hand on my right cheek;
kissed me lightly on my left. "Thank you, Doctor. For everything."

She seemed to be lost in tears, her terrible fears replaced by over-whelming happiness. I could hardly contain my joy.

I shook hands with his father, nodded my head and said, "You're welcome. Glad the medics brought Jason here. Where he could get the help he needed."

Jason's parents waved me good-bye with a, "God bless you."

A phrase I'd heard thousands of times, at temple, of course, at birthday and graduation parties, holidays, even after something as trivial as a sneeze. Always thought, cynically, *Right. God! There's a concept.* Decided to ditch my skepticism in the face of these overwhelmed parents. I turned to face them halfway up the tunnel and whispered, "And God bless you, too."

The rest of the shift passed uneventfully. Nothing compared to that first forty-five minutes, needless to say. I even got some rack time. Amazing, given we were without residents to cover the ER. The whole county seemed to take a night off. Okay by me. I was spent, needed the rest.

The phone rang at four-thirty. I fumbled in the dark, knocked the handset from the cradle, heard a distant, "Dr. Adler? Dr.Adler, are you there?"

I felt along the floor for the phone, snagged the cord with my hand and traced it back to the handset. "Yeah, Adler here."

The switchboard operator apologized profusely for waking me. Told me in the tone of voice we all dread, the one that seems to portend doom, "You have a personal call, Sir. Should I patch it through?"

I sat up in bed. Confirmed the time, even as my heart beat practically through my chest. "Sure, go ahead."

Dad's voice was near panic. "Stevie. Come home quick, it's Katy. I can't wake your mom."

Chapter 10

I jumped out of bed, felt for my scrubs, and hit the light. Began to make plans to bolt. Tried to think about the most immediate concerns, like a replacement on such short notice, my thoughts consumed by Mom. What could have happened? She seemed okay yesterday, I remembered her words clearly. Just some back pain that she'd said was a minor annoyance. Hard as it was, I forced those fears temporarily to the background. I would need relief. The residents were all down in San Diego, so I'd have to get a colleague in to cover.

Walked over to the bulletin board hanging over the desk to see who my replacement would be at eight. Ran my finger down the schedule grid to Tuesday. Wouldn't you know it, I thought, it *would* be Tompkins. Our fearless leader, Robert Tompkins, M.D., seventy-year-old, semi-retired chairman of the Emergency Medicine Department. A Harvard graduate, snooty as the Queen's butler. I'd always gotten the impression from him that you had to be Ivy League or you were strictly bush league. A condescending old bastard in a starched lab coat. Full white beard, granny prince nez glasses; every time I saw him walking around the Department, I expected to see leather patches sewn into the elbows of his lab coat, a smoldering pipe nesting in the pocket. He pulled shifts in the Department maybe twice a year. Said he "Liked to keep his hands in." Typical old-school academic; couldn't intubate a patient to save his life, but he could kiss a Dean's ass from across the room. Well, it's now or never, better call him, I told myself. Dad said to hurry.

I grabbed the phone, told the operator to reach Dr. Tompkins. Told her it was an urgent personal matter. He answered on the third ring, sounded alert, focused, at five-something in the morning. What do you know? I thought, with a real sense of surprise and relief. I had him pegged as a tired old coot, nothing left in the tank. He surprised me again, didn't ask any questions, said he was on his way. Told me there was nothing more important than family and he'd be there in fifteen minutes. I gave him my thanks and he said not to mention it. Told me he'd lost his wife of forty years only last April. Said he understood what I was going through. I was instantly ashamed to have characterized him so harshly. I reminded myself, not for the first time, that it's true about walking a mile in someone else's shoes.

He came in promptly at ten after five, clean white shirt, freshly laundered lab coat, his thick white hair perfectly groomed. Took my hurried report, hustled me out the door and said, "Go be with your father and mother. Help them get a handle on this, Steven. They're going to need you."

I was on the Five headed south less than ten minutes later. Tried to take it easy, but was frantic to find out what was going on with Mom. I was expecting the worst; Dad had said that he couldn't wake her up. I was thinking she was in a deep coma or suffering from much worse.

I reached over to the car phone and punched in my dad's number. It rang twenty times. Must be at the hospital, I concluded. Either that or the medics were working on her and everyone was too busy to answer. The closest hospital to the house was Magnolia

Presbyterian, a pretty good community hospital with a decent staff about ten blocks away, in downtown Riverside.

I ran the Porsche up to ninety in the sparse traffic, kept half-an-eye out for the CHP, but wasn't that worried. After all, I had a ready excuse: a doctor, still in his scrubs, racing to a family emergency. Figured the worst that could happen would be a police escort to Magnolia Pres.

A half-mile from Corona, fifteen minutes from home, I decided to call Natalie. Rang her number, let it ring four, five times. A gruff male voice answered, sounded like he was seriously pissed, like I'd interrupted something. I glanced at the green, backlit keypad, double-checked the number display. I knew it was right, Natalie had given the number to me only two weeks ago. Besides, I'd just dialed it less than twelve hours earlier. It was the number for her condo in Irvine. Just last week, Natalie had told me it was okay to call anytime since she'd moved away from the Porsche Guy's house. Had to be some kind of mistake, I thought, as I passed into southern Riverside. So I tried again; nice as could be, I said, "hello" again.

The same gruff voice, if anything even angrier, sounded like a jealous husband. "Who's this calling so goddamned early?"

I slowed the car a little, hated to talk while driving; certainly didn't want to risk it at ninety-five miles an hour. Kept my voice polite, even though I wanted to reach through the phone, teach the jackass some manners. "I'm sorry, I'm looking for Dr. Bogner. Dr. Natalie Bogner."

Guess he didn't appreciate my civility; sounded like he was ready to permanently rearrange my anatomy. "Who the *hell's* calling at five in the morning?"

Now *I* was getting pissed. Almost said her fiancé, decided against it for a lot of reasons, not knowing what I'd stumbled into being first and foremost on my list. "This is Dr. Adler calling for her." I could have sworn I'd heard a female voice in the background right after I'd identified myself, although it was hard to tell going seventy-five in my noisy Porsche. More than a little confused, I willed myself to stay calm, as I needed to focus on my mom, regardless of this strange conversation. "I need to speak to her about a personal matter."

The connection wasn't very good and Porsches are about as loud as a single-engine Cessna, so I wasn't a hundred-percent sure, but thought I heard the rustling of sheets, the squeak of bedsprings, and again a muffled female voice. Gruff Man came back in a few seconds, shot me down like a wounded duck. "She's not here."

I was really confused now. I *knew* I hadn't mis-dialed; Natalie's number was simple as all get out: 555 8822. No way I'd forget that one. I decided to give it one more shot. Maybe I'd gotten a house-guest by mistake, I thought, as I passed Magnolia, five minutes from home. "I'm sorry to bother you, sir. Is this 555 8822?"

He was really mad now, Jack Nicholson-with-a-pitching-wedge mad. "What part of no don't you understand, asshole? Don't you fucking *get* it? She doesn't want to talk to you." Click!

I stared at the dead handset for a half-mile or so. First she isn't there? Then she doesn't want to talk to me? I didn't know what to think. As confused as I was, I knew I didn't have time to worry about it now. I'd have to call her tomorrow or the next day, get the real story. I had much more urgent things to deal with.

I pulled into the driveway just before six. Nobody around. No fire rigs, no ambulance, garage closed tight, lights out in the front room. I reversed the Porsche, heading for the hospital, when I had a sudden premonition of dread. Decided to see if Dad was still home. Maybe he'd panicked, couldn't think coherently enough to call 911. Maybe he'd fallen down running for the phone.

I killed the engine, ran up the walk, shoved my key in the lock, hand shaking like I had Parkinson's. Opened the door. Dark as a tomb in the hall and den. Muted light to my left, faint sounds of sobbing from the master bedroom. I took off at a run, made it to their bedroom in three strides.

Dad was on his knees, his face buried in Mom's disheveled hair, rocking back and forth, mumbling, "Katy. Oh, Dear God, Katy." He shook her shoulders, cried again, "Wake up, Katy. Please, baby."

I placed my left hand on his shoulder. "Got here as fast as I could, Pops." Joined him on my knees. I could see at a glance that she was gone. Her face a dusky blue I'd seen only a few hours ago on the kid from the pool. Unlike my little patient, I knew there was no hope for Mom. I reached around Dad to feel her carotid pulse. Nothing. She'd been dead for a while: her skin was nearly room temperature. The bedroom closing in on me, I closed her sightless eyes and threw an arm around Pops, joined in his raw misery.

A few minutes, maybe a few hours later, I went to the kitchen, called Johnson Brothers funeral home. An old friend from high school, Johnny Johnson, answered the phone. Hadn't talked to him since our ten-year reunion, didn't realize he was now in charge of the family business. He was the complete professional, sincere, dignified, said he'd come over personally in the next fifteen minutes to pick up Mom. I hung up the phone thinking what a surreal experience that had been. Johnny and I used to hang out, drink beer after work at Straw Hat Pizza, seemed like three weeks ago. Now he was on his way here, dressed in a black suit, driving a windowless van. He'd bring a stretcher down our hallway, say a few comforting words to us, and take my mom away forever . . .

I snapped out of my reverie a few seconds later; knew I had a lot to do, hard as it was. Dad was in no condition. I thumbed through Mom's well-used pink phone book for Jake's number; searched through more than two dozen listings, each address and phone number printed in Mom's careful, cramped hand. Called the Kansas City number. Got a recording that the line was no longer in service. Called it again. Same result. Hmm, I thought, as I hung up, Dad would have to help me with this one. Was Jake gone again? Another city, another radio gig? Still in KC but hadn't paid his bill? I'd been a little worried about Jake for months, and now this. I was seriously concerned.

Johnny Johnson showed up as promised, did his job quietly and efficiently, hugged and kissed Pops on the cheek, came up to me and gave me a bear hug, told me how sorry he was. Said he'd give my mom the best. He told me not to worry about anything; wanted me to call him later that day or the next. He used his professional griever's voice. "When you feel up to it." I nodded my thanks, walked him to the door and watched his assistant load her in the van. Walked to the cargo door, laid a hand on her shoulder and said a silent good-bye to Mom.

I walked the five-foot distance from the front door to the den, each step an effort in concentration, dreading seeing my dad. Pops was slumped on the sofa, head in his hands. I sat next to him, an arm around his shoulder. He looked over at me a minute or two later with red, dry eyes, his voice a hoarse whisper. "She died way before I woke up, Stevie. I tried so hard to help her. Nothing worked, Son." He sobbed quietly against my chest. "She was so cold, Stevie. Nothing I could do."

I hugged him closer. "I know, Pops. Nothing anybody could do." I held him on the sofa the better part of a half-hour, my thoughts occupied with isolated, random memories: My first day of school, walking hand-in-hand with Mom. A block or two from Sonnenberg Elementary School. She stopped, leaned down to me, moistened a hankie she always carried with her, and wiped a spot of jelly from my cheek. Said she loved me. I searched my memory as long as we sat on the sofa. Went backward through all of my thirty years, every one of the holidays, birthdays, graduations, everything. Try as I might, I couldn't remember another time she ever said that to me. Realized with a rush of shame that a few years ago, I'd stopped saying it to her, too.

I had no trouble at all with the bad memories. They came back as a harried, flash-cut clip reel of childhood terror: burned dinners, shouted threats, screaming fights with Dad, a lot of them so bad I thought my helpless kid's world was going to come crashing down; leave me in some stranger's house, stuck forever in foster care. I had no trouble at all remembering the gut-wrenching fear that Jake and I shared. Whispered conversations in our room late at night about Mom and Dad getting divorced, the terror we both felt about having to live alone with our mom.

A large part of me knew I should be focusing on the happy times, especially sitting on the sofa; Dad crying softly on my chest. Still, I knew that I had to come to grips with this sudden shock in my own way. With total honesty. I wanted more than anything to say I loved my mom. More than that, I wanted to know that she loved me back. Try as I might, I just couldn't. I respected her, of course. She demanded it. I protected her. Any son would. But, to this day, I don't believe she loved me, or Jake. She only loved her bottle and the predictable, soothing manner in which it anesthetized her pain.

Mom's service was two days later at the same funeral home Johnny Johnson and I used to take all of our friends to when we were eight. We used to organize scary tours on Halloween night; midnight rides through the receiving bays, three or four little boys pedaling their bikes like the hounds of Hell were on their heels, zombies closing in as they screamed their way home

I was a little surprised by the sparse turnout. Mostly friends of Dad's from work. I was disappointed that nobody from his insurance job bothered to show; thankfully nine or ten from his janitorial days, dressed in inexpensive, ill-fitting suits, were by his side. I could see from across the room that they loved Dad, seemed genuinely grief-stricken by his loss. True friends.

Johnny Johnson had, indeed, done his best. Mom looked like a waxy replica of a younger Catherine Mills Adler. I found some measure of comfort looking at her in the casket because it seemed to me as if she'd found the peace of mind she'd been searching for all these years. Pops refused an autopsy, and I supported his decision. Dad said, "I don't want to think about somebody cutting up my Katy." I had to do some tap dancing with the local coroner on that one. Told him that she *had* been attended to by a physician, namely me, in the weeks before she died. Otherwise, state law would have mandated a post mortem.

I was left to speculate on her cause of death, thought that a pulmonary embolus or dissecting abdominal aortic aneurysm were the most likely candidates. With a deep pang of guilt, I recalled her complaints of back pain the day Pops and I played golf. I excoriated myself the entire two days leading to her funeral for not insisting on an examination, right there in our house. Knew I could have picked up the aneurysm with a cursory exam, had that been the case. My dad, as usual, was philosophical about it. "It was just her time, Stevie. Nothing either of us could do."

I looked around for relatives while I prepared my eulogy, shook my head sadly. It was just Dad, Uncle Mike, and I. My grandparents had died five years previously in a car wreck back in New York. Dad only had his brother Mike, and Mom was an only child with a ninety-two-year-old mother of her own in a nursing home in Philadelphia, too ill to attend. We'd tried for two days to reach Jake: three telegrams, endless calls to his job, FedEx letters. Nothing. Earlier that morning I had finally reached his boss at the radio station. He told me what the secretaries couldn't. "Jake was on suspension for comments he'd made on air." They hadn't seen him for a week. I was worried, of course, but Jake was known for this. Trying to prove to everyone who cared about him that a man *was* indeed an island. I missed him more than I'd thought possible that morning. Promised myself I'd hunt him down, no matter what.

An hour after we'd started, everyone had paid his or her respects, walked up to see Mom in her coffin, and it was now up to me.

I trudged up to the mahogany podium, still unsure about what I'd say. I passed the pitifully sparse two rows of mourners, felt everybody's eyes on me as I took my place to the right of her simple, white casket.

"I deal with life and death everyday at my job. I've helped bring people into the world, eased their pain on the way out. I thought I'd be prepared to lose a loved one, with all the practice I've had at work. I see people in distress every day, unimaginable pain and suffering that never seems to end." My Uncle Mike met my eyes, wiped away a tear. "My mom, Catherine Adler, suffered. As we all do. She suffered in silence most of the time, lived through her pain the best way she knew how." Pops nodded slightly at that, dry, swollen eyes trained on mine. I broke off my gaze, afraid I'd choke up; such was the depth of Pops' pain.

"She raised two sons, took great care of my father . . ." I looked back at my dad; his eyes glittered in the soft light of the parlor. ". . . And we all know how hard that must have been for her." I got a ripple of polite laughter from the mourners, a heart-rending smile from Dad.

I tried everything I could think of, standing in front of the mourners, tried to conjure up pleasant anecdotes, reasons why I loved Mom, why I'd miss her. In the end I failed miserably. Couldn't think of a thing to say on her behalf, almost died of shame and guilt standing there in stumped silence, right next to her coffin. I opened my mouth and said, in a voice I hardly recognized, "Dad, Uncle Mike, Jake, and I want to thank you for coming here this morning, and for honoring Mom." I looked over my left shoulder at the mounds of red roses and irises, seemingly bursting with vibrant life, even as they continued to wither and die. Looking over the group of friends and family, I was finally able to let go. I thought about the good times we had as a family, put aside the bad ones. I knew it was only a start; that it would take weeks, possibly years to come to terms with our relationship. A moment before I left the podium, I tried to remember if I'd told Mom I loved her the day we went golfing. Finally realized I hadn't, that I'd missed countless opportunities to make things right with my mother. My heart aching for all that could have been, I decided to tell her once more, hoping against hope that she'd somehow hear me. More than that, hoping that after all these years, she'd believe me.

I walked the five feet over to her casket, the eyes of the congregation on my every step, the years of regrets, fears, loneliness, and despair weighing heavily on my shoulders. I paused at the casket, lay my hand on my mom's cheek and said, "Rest now, Mom. I love you." I fought tears and lost. "I know you tried to love me, too."

Mom was laid to rest under leaden skies a mile from her home, overlooking the rolling fairways of Jurupa Hills and the dry Santa Ana riverbed a mile beyond. Dad held up pretty well, until we started tossing handfuls of dirt onto her casket. I held him as he slumped in my arms, sobbing his final good-bye to his wife of thirty-nine years.

I saw Pops in a new light as we stood by her grave. I had always admired his devotion to Mom, his incredible patience. As Jake and I grew older and the fear of our parents' divorce receded, we used to talk about what we'd do if we were married to someone like Mom, drunk a lot of the time, belligerent when she was, inattentive when she wasn't. We had decided as adolescents, then and there, to never make a "mistake" like Pops'.

Looking at Pops that day at the cemetery, I realized Jake and I had overlooked one crucial factor in evaluating our parents' lives together. Dad really *did* love Mom. Thoroughly and unconditionally. He tolerated her faults, accommodated to her behavior the best way he knew how. Her passing had simply crushed him.

I tightened my grip on his shoulder as they lowered Mom into the ground; made a silent vow to give myself to the woman I married, to give her my unconditional love, no matter the cost.

We drove back in silence, each of us lost in our own memories. Uncle Mike declined our invitation to stay for dinner, said he had to get back to Bakersfield for a meeting. Dad never asked, as I knew he wouldn't, so I volunteered to stay the rest of the week with him. He put up a fight, said I'd miss too much work, lose income, had a handful of other reasons, but his heart clearly wasn't in it. Besides, I couldn't think of any place in the world where I was needed more.

Chapter 11

THREE WEEKS LATER

Dad and I had a good week together, all things considered. Played some golf, reminisced about Mom, Jake, and the good times. Even touched on some of the not-so-pleasant times. I had learned more about my dad in the last few months than I had the previous thirty years. We had some long talks about love and marriage, during which he told me that in his opinion the secret to a long marriage was patience and forgiveness. He told me that a woman without forgiveness would be miserable forever. And, of course, by extension, her husband would suffer greatly, as well. He admitted that he had been an enabler with Mom, surprised me by knowing the technical definition with all of its psychological nuances. He had no regrets, no apologies, said, "It was what your mom needed. I tried everything I could think of to make her stop drinking. Nothing worked. She had to have *somebody* in her corner." He had stopped a minute to compose himself. "She didn't have very many friends, so I was it. The drinking was always there. Sometimes more than others." He gave a resigned shrug, his tone wistful. "I guess it was just in her makeup."

We cried a lot, of course, as much from nostalgia as from acute grief. Dad realized that she was miserable in her life, trapped in a situation she couldn't escape. As the week passed, I could see acceptance begin to appear in his eyes, hear it in his words. He said over and over, "My Katy can rest now." He apologized to me for "putting you boys through so much." I reminded him that we went through it as a family and besides, he was a rock to Jake and me. I told him flat out that I wouldn't be the man I was, had it not been for his guidance.

By the end of the week, I think we were both ready to move on. Dad wanted to start "organizing the house." Said he wanted to finish some projects he had put off. I really think he needed to be alone with his thoughts; say a final good-bye to Mom without having to hide his emotions. I could certainly understand that; I did as well.

Sunday afternoon I waved good-bye to Pops from the street, noticed how small he looked standing at the door, diminished by his grief. He had refused my offer to stay down in Orange with me, and deep down, I knew it was best for both of us to be alone for a little while. I made plans to see him the next week and headed for home.

The first thing I did when I got back to Orange was check my messages. I hadn't heard from Jake or Natalie the whole week, and I was a little worried about my brother and more than a little peeved at my girlfriend. My machine had fifteen messages waiting. Two from Jake, ten from her, the rest from well-wishing colleagues. My brother said he had been backpacking in Yellowstone when we'd called. Said he'd get back to me later that week. Hoped the funeral wasn't too hard on me or Dad. He promised to call Dad, come over to see us as soon as he could get away. Overall, Jake had sounded more relieved than saddened by Mom's death. I could definitely understand that after what we'd experienced as kids.

Natalie's messages were interesting, more for what she didn't say than what she did. She made no mention of my call early Tuesday morning; seemed surprised that I hadn't called, even though I'd left a half dozen messages for her about Mom. Her subsequent messages seemed increasingly irritated, then somewhat frantic, as she was having trouble locating me. Come to find out, she was in Lake Tahoe, had left at ten the morning Mom died, said she had called all over trying to find me. She said she finally reached the department chairman, who told her about Mom. Her last message told me how sorry she was. For Dad and me, and because she couldn't get away from her meeting in time to attend the funeral.

I went into my room, unpacked, flipped through my mail; crap, bills, and even more crap, and lay down on my bed to collect my thoughts. I had been anxious to talk to Natalie, needed to clear up the "mystery" surrounding my call to her condo. I wasn't an especially jealous man, but I needed to know who belonged to the gruff voice. I remembered clearly telling Natalie I loved her after taking care of the drowned little boy, was positive that she didn't hesitate an instant to say she loved me, too. Even though I knew that declarations of love, no matter how heartfelt, were subject to change at a moment's notice and didn't imply a firm commitment, I was still bothered by the situation, had to get her side of the story. The whole state of affairs had made me confused and anxious, a circumstance I didn't need from my girlfriend.

I took a quick shower, dressed in a pair of stolen UCI scrubs, and gave her a call. Dialed carefully, digit-by-digit; the same number I'd punched in early Tuesday morning appearing on my handset's display. She answered on the first ring.

"Hello."

"Hey, Natalie, it's me."

Her voice was relieved, then excited. "Steven, are you all right? I've been so worried. You must be exhausted, sweetheart."

My place seemed suddenly cold, as if exposed to the elements; must be the temperature difference between the shower and my bedroom, I thought. I carried the portable phone with me into the hall, adjusted the thermostat a few ticks upward. "It's been a little rough, but I'm feeling better every day. You know, trying to process it."

She sighed on the other end of the line. I could almost see her sitting cross-legged on the sofa, a lock of hair curled around her index finger. "You sound kind of tense, Steven. I know you've been going through hell with your mom." I could hear muted music in the background, sounded like Bach. "More than that even. I don't know, you sound kind of angry. Anything else going on?"

There it was, my opportunity. I knew without thinking that I had to risk it. Had to take the chance that we'd be finished if the answer wasn't what I wanted to hear. I walked back to the sofa, plopped down with my legs stretched out in front of me. "Yeah, there is one thing, Natalie."

A long pause; during which I could hear her shallow breathing, soulful piano in the background. "Go ahead."

"Tuesday morning? I called your place on the way to my Mom's?"

"Okay."

I'd expected more. I guess I'm naïve, but I had half-expected her to come forth with a logical explanation, get us back on track with an innocent, truthful rendering of the call. Especially if she were feeling guilty about it. Was she stalling or just didn't want to talk about it? I thought, as the silent seconds piled up. "Seemed like you didn't want to talk to me." Nothing at all on the other line but a faint rustling of fabric and funereal music. I decided to get to the heart of the matter, hoping to provoke a response, any response. "At least according to the guy who answered."

"Steven." I sat there staring at my wall clock, the seconds dragging by, utter stillness on her end a physical weight on my shoulders, as I waited for her explanation. "It's not what you think."

112

"What is it, then?" I leaned closer to the coffee table, took a sip of Perrier, tried to settle my nerves. "I'm not trying to make demands on you, Natalie. I just need to know, is all." Nothing in the speaker but the finale of Bach's Concerto No. 5. Restless and anxious from Natalie's evasiveness, I felt a need to fill the void, start her talking. I stood and paced my tiny den. "I know we're not engaged, but I thought we had an understanding. Thought we were going to be exclusive with each other." I could hear her steady breathing, almost read her thoughts through the line. "Remember, we talked about it in Laguna?"

"Nothing happened, Steven." She seemed a little defensive, her tone a lot sharper than I'd expected, as if I were the one at fault. "You have no reason to be worried. None at all."

I tried to picture her new condo as I walked to the kitchen, had only been there for a few minutes a week after she'd moved in, five days before we left for our vacation. It was in a brand new building, her unit overlooked a park fronting Jamboree Road, the main thoroughfare bisecting Irvine. Small den; hallway to the left, a bedroom on the left, a bathroom on the right, her suite at the end of the corridor. I remembered the boxes in the hall, the spare bedroom a mess; computer half set up on a glass and chrome desk, file cabinets against the left wall, floor-to-ceiling bookcase on the right side. Boxes of books and files scattered across the white Berber carpet. No room for a bed in that tiny space, I was sure of that. Leaving only the master suite: Natalie's four-poster king-size, antiqued white bedside tables and an entertainment center/armoire that housed her thirty-six-inch Sony. My heart sank. No other explanation. Had to be another guy in her bed. What else could it be? I kept my voice on a tight leash; afraid I'd give her hell and provoke an all-out screaming match. I walked back to the den, restless as a two-year-old, thought, what am I worried about? If it came to that, so be it. Still, I wanted to hear her side first. I guess I owe her that much, I thought diffidently. "I'm listening, Natalie."

"You're right about us having no commitment, Steven." Her voice had a pedantic edge; sounded like she did when she lectured her oblivious teenaged mothers about birth control. I heard a quick intake of breath, followed immediately by a slow exhale. Almost like a smoker would do, shortly after lighting up, I thought. I'd never seen Natalie smoke, but she had let it slip a few weeks ago that she smoked when she was really nervous. She blew out another breath, her voice more subdued. I had to strain to hear. "I meant what I said. I am falling in love with you, Steven. I just don't know where we're going yet." Another jittery breath. "I don't want to be pinned down."

Natalie was clearly reluctant to answer my question. More than that, she seemed obstinate, evasive even. I'd seen it more than a few times in the past few months: She was reverting to form, on the defensive at first, followed by a quick shift to attack mode. As much as Natalie had come to mean to me, I decided to press her, make her tell the truth. Otherwise, I'd have just folded up my tent and moved on. That was what I always did when the going got rough with my previous girlfriends. I settled again on the couch, gaze fixed on the clock. "I understand that, Natalie. Believe me. But we'd talked about this in Laguna." I heard a sudden burst of background noise, sounded like she'd turned on the local news. "We had decided, you and I, to only date each other." Another slow exhale of breath on her end, followed by a deep, irritated sigh. "We seemed in agreement." I gripped the portable phone harder, felt the tension rush from my hand all the way to my shoulder. "I know that's how I remember it, Natalie."

"I know that, Steven." Her voice could chip ice. "But I already told you that you shouldn't worry about this."

Shouldn't worry about it? I thought about that for a second. Tried to put her words into perspective. Here I was almost thirty, in my first long-term relationship, and I was convinced that I loved her. Felt as if she loved me in return. And she's telling me not to worry because she was in her bed with another man? I'm just not that trusting. Who the fuck *would* be? I thought. Couldn't accept it. Just couldn't. "No, Natalie, that's not how I see it." I tried to stay calm, even with a fresh surge of anger mixing with the emotional hangover of Mom's death. "The way I see it is that you slept with somebody else." I couldn't hold back any longer,

114

let my voice carry the full measure of my resentment. "I called your place unexpectedly, talked to a guy I've never met and now I'd like an explanation."

"I didn't do anything wrong." She sounded defiant, her breath coming in short spurts now. "I have nothing to apologize for, Steven."

"I don't want an apology, Natalie. Just an explanation." I had a hard time tamping down my anger. I could almost see us going up in smoke, tried for one last stab at a conciliatory tone. "I mean, nobody's perfect. If you made a mistake this one time. Let's just talk about it. See if we can go on from here."

Her tone again defiant; an undercurrent of brazen arrogance. "I don't make mistakes, Steven."

I almost choked on my Perrier. Here she goes again with the perfection, I thought with a derisive snort. She didn't *sound* like she was joking. But I couldn't believe she was serious; who *doesn't* make mistakes? God knows I've made my share. I stood and walked to my bedroom, running a jittery hand through my hair. "Come on, Natalie. Be serious. I'm not asking for blood here. Not even an apology, really. I don't care if you consider it to be a mistake or not. Just tell me what went on." Dead silence again, the idiotic TV news muted for now. "I deserve to know."

"First of all, I *was* serious, Steven. I don't make mistakes. Ever." I let that one sink in; she rushed to fill the silence while I shook my head, blown away by her conceit. "It was nothing, Steven. I already told you that."

"But you *were* sleeping with someone, weren't you? I heard what I heard, Natalie."

There was a minute or two lull, I was starting to wonder if she'd put down the phone, left the room in a huff. "Goddamnit, Steven, if you must know." I heard a furious intake of breath, followed by a slight dry cough. A moment later, another cough and quiet sobbing. "It was Henry."

The Porsche Guy. Her nearly-ex. Jesus, here we go, I thought. Sex with the ex. I tried to process this bombshell while the seconds ticked by like hours. "Why, Natalie? Why would you do that?" I stared out at Chapman Avenue through my bedroom window: a steady stream of traffic, people rushing away from their jobs, home to their loved ones. "I thought that was over."

Her voice was choked, nearly inaudible. Either I'd stripped away her defenses, her arrogance, with my attack, or she was the greatest actress in California. "It is, Steven. I told you I loved you. I meant it. We just . . ."

"You just what, tore off a quick one for old times' sake?"

Her voice a lethal weapon. Back on offense, I thought, she never gives up, shifts moods quick as a chameleon, should have been a prosecutor. "No need to be crude, Steven."

"Well, pardon me, Natalie." I was seething. All she'd done for the past three months was complain about this guy. *He was stealing her future. He was an unreasonable pig. He wouldn't listen to anything.* All that vitriol and now this, she was sharing her bed with him. I threw the phone on the bed, frustration squeezing my heart. A moment later, I picked it back up, listened to dead silence for a few seconds, convinced she'd hung up on me. I realized with a fresh spurt of anger that I hadn't even slept with her in the new place yet. Gave it to her again. "We're not all perfect, like you."

"You don't need to be sarcastic, either. It doesn't become you." My hand was tight on the handset, knuckles a bloodless white. "And I won't apologize for something that I did for reasons that have nothing to do with you and me, Steven."

I was having a little trouble breathing. "You're kidding, Natalie. Tell me you're fucking kidding."

"No, I'm trying to be very honest with you, Steven. I did this for Henry. This one last time. Why can't you believe that it has nothing to do with you?" She blew out a breath while I held mine, ready to explode. "Nothing to do with us."

I couldn't believe this shit from her, the woman I thought I loved, the woman who claimed to love me back. "So, it was just your way of saying good-bye."

"You make it sound so cheap, Steven. Like a consolation prize or something."

"Sounds like it to me." I knew it was childish of me, but I let my sarcasm come out again, tit for tat against her acerbic bullshit. "Sorry about the divorce, Henry, but thanks a bunch for the nifty settlement, I'm off to be with someone else." I was surprised by my tone of voice; I'd never allowed myself to get so out of control. "Here's a last roll in the hay to remind you of what you'll be missing."

"I'm not that cruel, Steven." She was openly hostile now; I could picture her clearly: clenched teeth, circular, bright red spots of color high on each cheek. "I wouldn't manipulate someone like that. Especially when they're as vulnerable as Henry is right now."

Charity, thy name is Natalie, I thought with a vicious surge of anger. "So you threw him a mercy fuck. Is that what you're telling me, Nat?"

She seemed to let that one go, the only evidence of her exasperation I could detect being a prolonged sigh. "Okay, Steven. You win, it was a mercy fuck."

"A fuck is still a fuck, no matter the motivation. At least where I come from, Natalie."

"I'm going to pretend I didn't hear that, Steven." She lighted another cigarette: I could hear the familiar quick inhalation, followed by a dry hack. "I want you to think about what I've told you. Remember what I said about this not affecting us. Unless you let it." She sounded as if the words were sticking in her throat. "At least as far as I'm concerned. If you see it differently, let me know." She paused a few moments; I could hear her muffled sobs as I let her words sink in, incredible as they seemed at the time. "And when you've calmed down, come over here and we'll talk about it. About us."

At that moment in time, I wasn't sure I'd take that step. I knew I'd have to think long and hard about it first. Decide if she was worth it, if we were worth all this crap I'd been getting from her. I decided, after a few seconds' reflection, to do just that. Exhausted by our fight and all the rest of my horrible week, I let it go, walked back to the den, stretched my back, phone balanced on my shoulder. "I'll sleep on it, Natalie. Good night."

"All right, Steven. Do that." She sounded worn-out, defeated. "Call me."

"I will, Natalie." Maybe so, probably not, I thought with real sadness.

I had the phone nearly back into the charger when her voice, soft and helpless as a child's, came through the speaker. "I love you, Steven. You know I do."

She showed up at my door three hours later, knocked softly until I came out from my room and let her in. She came into my arms a moment later, led us to my bedroom and lay down beside me, her legs entwined with mine on top of the comforter. She was shaking; her words seemed to stop halfway up her throat. "Hold me, Steven. I need to know we're all right." She kissed me lightly on the lips, held it for a few moments, and looked up into my eyes. "You mean everything to me, Steven. Please don't hate me."

I pulled away, looked into her eyes, searching for the truth, for a clue to her illogical behavior. "Why would I hate you, Natalie? We just had an argument, that's all."

She sounded like a little girl, terrified anew that she was about to lose a big part of her life, her security threatened. "Then, you're not going to leave me?"

I tried to hide my shock. Just a few hours ago, she was telling me she never made mistakes, didn't need to apologize, and now she was worried we were splitting up. I wondered about the depth of her guilt concerning this situation. Wanted to know why she thought this way. Decided that I had to know. "Why would you think that?"

She didn't hesitate for a second. "You were so mad. I thought you weren't going to call, so I came over." She settled deeper into my arms, reached down and drew the covers over us. "I don't want to lose you, Steven. Can't you see that?"

"Of course I can. I just wanted an explanation, Natalie. Nothing more."

Her gaze was steady, eyes locked on mine. The little-girl voice was gone, replaced by a slightly older, worldly-wise, womanly tone. I could see something pass over her face, a sense of clinical calculation: as if she were considering a slightly risky investment. "I'll explain everything, Steven." She held my gaze; I realized, again what a talented actress she would have been. "Then we'll be okay?"

I'd never seen her like this. Her expression changing in a matter of seconds: earnest calculation gone in a heartbeat, replaced by childlike hope, with an undercurrent of seduction. Even her challenging, confident tone of voice took on a note of pleading. I shook my head slightly, tried to get a handle on this "performance" of hers. "I guess that depends on what you tell me." More importantly, if you're telling the truth, I promised myself.

She seemed to sink into the covers, head resting on my chest, heart beating like a trapped bird against mine. "Henry was so bad, Steven. I'd never seen him like that." A start, but not nearly enough, I thought. She didn't seem to be the type to fuck somebody just because he was depressed. She was too savvy for that; always needed something in return, even with me, at first. Natalie watched my face closely; I gave her nothing, just lay there listening. A moment later, she laid a thigh over mine, moved closer under the sheets. "He was hysterical. Said he couldn't face life without me. Said he was thinking of hurting himself."

I gave immediate voice to my first thought, not at all ready to buy her story. "You should have just calmed him down. Told him to see a counselor. You didn't have to fuck him." I moved an inch or two farther away. "Christ, Natalie."

She rested a hand on my thigh. "I tried that, Honey. He wouldn't listen. Said he just needed *me*. Didn't need to see a psychiatrist."

119

She was into it now, voice high-pitched, staccato delivery, her face alive. "He told me he was afraid, that the divorce was moving too fast."

"You still didn't need to sleep with him, Natalie. We had an agreement."

She moved her hand to my penis. "I tried to stop him, Steven. I did."

I leaned on an elbow, tried to get a look at her face, pulled a few inches away from her again. "You're not saying he raped you, are you? I mean, come on, he *did* spend the night. At least he was there at five in the morning."

She began stroking me. For the first time ever with Natalie, I didn't respond. Her voice was husky, lids lowered. "I didn't mean it to come out that way, Steven. I meant to say that he just wouldn't stop. He was kissing me, holding me down. We were in the bedroom and . . ."

"You let him. Why didn't you just tell him he had to leave? Didn't you think about us? About what it would do to us?" Of, course she didn't, I realized with a start. She never thought I'd find out. I knew her next answer would be the key to any future we might have together. I needed to know, right now, how much of this explanation was actually Natalie just covering her goddamned tracks.

She kissed my neck, stroked with a little more urgency. "I told him about us. Told him we were serious." She nibbled my ear. "I told him we were thinking about getting married." There it was. I certainly hadn't brought up *that* subject. We'd danced around it, no doubt about that, but her statement, in this context, had really taken me by surprise.

I wasn't about to let this go, not by a long shot. "And you still fucked him, Natalie. Even after that admission about us, you still made love to him?"

"We didn't do anything like that, I swear. I talked to him for over an hour, finally got him to calm down." Her words came out in a rush, voice rumbling through my chest. "We ended up talking for several hours. Just talking. I swear." She lifted her head, met my gaze. "He said he was too tired to drive, so I let him sleep in my bed."

She rubbed her thigh against mine. I could feel her excitement, even as I kept mine firmly in check. I held her chin in my palm, stared directly into those depthless blue eyes. "You're telling me, with *total* honesty, that you didn't make love to him?" She never wavered, looked directly back into my eyes. "I need to know the truth, Natalie."

She gave me a quick kiss on the lips, settled back into my arms. I considered myself to be fairly skilled at ferreting out lies, did it every day at work. Patients lied all the time, abusive parents lied reflexively, even my staff and residents lied to me. Looking back on that moment, I remember a woman who was resolute in her belief that nothing happened. Natalie was absolutely convincing; her account told with just the right amount of detail, admixed with plausible human frailty and contrition. A sense of weakness that was that much *more* compelling coming from a woman who'd claimed to be infallible. She was credible in every detail, every nuance. More impressively, she was facing a man intent on finding the lies in her story. A man who wanted to know exactly what position he occupied in her universe. She knew intuitively that there was simply too much at stake for me to buy into her story willingly. She knew me well enough to be able to gauge my skepticism. So, she moved in to seal the deal, persuasive enough to have sold snowmobiles to Saudis. "I've told you the truth, Steven." She rubbed against me, breath hot on my neck. "Nothing happened." She kissed me hard on the lips, broke it off. Held my face in her hands. "Nothing at all."

I had to hand it to her, no pun intended. She did her job. I was convinced. Better said, I was hooked.

Chapter 12

ONE MONTH LATER

Needless to say, we made up that night in November. Natalie was loving, plausible, and remorseful. I guess one could say that at that point in my life, Natalie was everything I'd ever wanted in a woman. I'd held out as long as I could, as much as she was driving me crazy. I was proud of myself at the time, knew I needed to keep a clear head while I listened carefully to Natalie's explanation, measured the depth of her veracity. To put it bluntly, I had to keep my "little head" under control, so my "big head" could do the heavy lifting. After the storm had passed, and I was reconciled to the facts presented to me, nature took its course. It's true what they say about make-up sex. I was nearly late for my shift that morning.

Time will tell, of course, if "little" or "big" head gave me the best counsel that night.

I had signed up for a medical conference in San Francisco several months previously, nearly forgotten about it until the department secretary reminded me the week before I was to leave. I wondered later what possessed me to schedule an out-of-town seminar this close to Christmas; finally decided to make the best of it and ask Natalie to come along.

Much to my surprise, she was delighted. She told me her practice was a little slow at the moment; no elective surgeries this close to the holidays, and all her prospective mommies were due long after the first. She immediately took over planning our trip, okay by me as I was swamped at work. Natalie made all of the flight arrangements, chided me for waiting so long, gloated over finding us a "bargain" fare of five hundred bucks round trip. Each! That's what I get for being such a lunk-head and forgetting about the conference, I thought at the time.

She came to my office all excited the next day, fistful of brochures in hand, said she'd been to the travel agent, going over a few hotels.

She closed my door, ran around my desk and jumped in my lap. "We could stay near the wharf." She waved a flyer for the Holiday Inn on the Embarcadero in my face.

I grabbed it out of her hands, scanned the photos and ad copy, pointed to the picture of the plain, no-nonsense lobby with a smile. "This looks nice, honey." I watched her out of the corner of my eye, caught the skeptical look in her eyes; decided to have some fun with her. "Luxurious, spacious, close to everything." She looked crestfallen, hard as she was trying to hide it; a slight downturn of her mouth, a tightening of her eyes. "What's it cost, a hundred a night?"

She took the brochure from my hand. "Sixty, Steven." She shuffled the flyers, deftly as a Vegas croupier, came up with one far glossier, obviously costlier. "Look at this one, Steven." She was practically giggling. "The Saint Francis."

My heart sank faster than the Dow on Black Monday. The Saint Francis. Union Square. A few miles from the budget-minded Holiday Inn might as well be in another galaxy. I wasn't a cheap person. Not at all. Hell, I thought with immediate dread, the freakin' Saint Frances must cost . . .

"It's only two-fifty, Steven. For the Saint Francis. Can you *believe* it?"

No, I couldn't. I looked around my office for the defibrillator. "A week?"

She punched my shoulder. "A *night*, silly. We're not talking about the YMCA." She opened the brochure, eyes sparkling like a kid on her birthday. "It's close to everything. The galleries. The cable car's right out front." I had to smile through my pain, I hadn't seen her this happy. Ever. Pleased as I was outwardly, I was still dying inside. Two-fifty a freakin' *night* for four nights and five days? Add in fancy dinners, dancing, this could easily run into a couple of thousand bucks, I thought with a sinking heart. Wait a minute, I realized with a start, I hadn't even included . . .

"Shopping! Oh, Steven, did I mention the shopping? Saks, Nordstrom, Fendi, Neiman Marcus. All within walking distance." She took a short breath while I recalculated the damage. "All the Christmas decorations will be up." She gave me a big kiss on the cheek. "San Francisco. Our first Christmas together."

I was starting to get choked up. Eight thousand at least! Holy shit, I'd have to work double shifts until Labor Day to pay for it. I felt her eyes on me, tried to hide my discomfort with a weak smile. I looked deeply into her eyes and saw unadulterated bliss. Unmistakable love. In spite of our troubles a few weeks ago, no way I would ever disappoint that face. Despite my best intentions to seem happy, my voice sounded forced, even to me. "Sounds good, honey. Why don't you book it."

She smiled sweetly, a little too sweetly; I thought at the time, which is why I wasn't surprised when she swatted me with the Saint Francis brochure, kissed my cheek and said, "No worries, sweetheart. I already did."

I smiled back, shook my head and shooed her out of the room. "You're too much, Natalie." She waved from the doorway, as excited as I'd ever seen her. "Let me get back to work." She blew me a kiss. I scooted her out the door. "Gotta pay for this trip."

She lingered a moment in the doorway, her smile radiant, our fight now completely forgotten. "Thank you so much, Steven. We need to take this trip." I couldn't argue with that logic, we had been struggling a little lately. Besides, I loved her. I knew it with sudden clarity that day. I returned her smile, happy as she was. "We'll have a great time, Steven. I promise."

I waved as she closed the door, my thoughts on December fifteenth. Beautiful San Francisco, my favorite city. Christmas. Natalie. A romantic hotel. I was as excited as she, deep inside. I rearranged my paperwork, sighed, and said, to the closed door, "I have no doubt about that. None at all."

I glanced at the clock: ten minutes to go before my shift. Grabbed a pen and made a to do list. Confirm the course schedule. Make sure I was covered here for the week we'd be gone. Notify Dad. And, most importantly, go to the bank and withdraw some cash. Lots of cash. Lord have mercy, I thought, please let this be a memorable trip.

And it was.

Chapter 13

Friday night and Saturday morning were a blur of drunken dancing in the penthouse bar of the Saint Francis, followed by the sleep of the dead until one in the afternoon. We were both exhausted from our residencies, our tumultuous lives, and the recent trouble we'd had as a couple. In the end, Natalie was right. We *did* need this trip. I loved her more than ever in San Francisco. We felt totally compatible, completely comfortable as a couple, all of our spats forgotten in the most beautiful city in the world. A city that looked like a Dickens landscape come to life. Who could ask for anything more?

We spent a couple of hours laughing through breakfast at the Buena Vista Cafe down at the wharf. A few Irish coffees later, we were ready for some exercise. Fifteen minutes after we'd finished our meal, we jumped off the cable car in front of our hotel, ran up to our room, dumped the bags on the bed and freshened up. I loved Natalie's energy level, among a whole list of other attributes. More importantly, our lifestyles meshed perfectly. She loved active sports as much as I. We had similar sleep patterns; both early risers, loved to work hard, but enjoyed our downtime even more.

She came out of the bathroom a few minutes later with a serious look on her face. I wondered for a second if she were feeling ill. She walked a step closer, stopped beside our bed, leveled her gaze and said, "I love you, Adler." She stepped into my arms; rested her head on my chest. "With all my heart." I held her close, thought I'd never been happier, never more fulfilled. To love as deeply as I did at that moment and feel so loved in return was the true essence of happiness. Pops was right; I felt like the richest man in the world.

We decided to spend the rest of Saturday shopping. Natalie was right, again. The best of the best were just a stone's throw from our lobby. Dressed, refreshed, and fed, we made a last check of our wallets: credit cards, cash, I.D. and we were out the door, ready to tear it up.

Natalie could indeed tear it up: Attila the Hun with a platinum Amex. We were up and down Geary, hitting Saks, Neiman Marcus, and Nordstrom, one after the other. I looked like a pack mule after an hour at Saks. Had to call a taxi to take the stuff back to our room after Needless Markups. Was dead on my feet in Nordstrom, sat in one of their comfy chairs with a glazed expression while Natalie laid waste to the shoe department. She came over to me, shoebox in hand, mumbling to me about Manolo somebody or other. All these names: Jimmy Choo, Fendi, my head was spinning, felt like I'd gone ten rounds with Mike Tyson.

I tried to find my happy place cuddled into the leather chair Nordstrom generously provided for people like me: husbands and boyfriends on their last legs. A place for the weak to watch the strong do their thing. A place for men to take stock of their wallets and hope like hell that they could check out of their hotels without having more money wired from home. I had no such worries. Natalie was shopping for herself. I just had to buy some presents for Dad and Jake and, of course, something for Natalie. Besides, my girlfriend was now officially loaded. Her divorce from the Porsche Guy had been finalized three weeks before. She was sitting on five million and a brand new four-bedroom house in Newport. She'd let it slip that morning in the shower. Asked me if that was why I loved her so much. I couldn't answer her at that precise moment. Had her left nipple in my mouth. What a life I'd fallen into. From a dateless, lonely guy in Riverside to the boyfriend of a gorgeous Newport sophisticate in eight short years.

A moment or two into my reverie, she came and sat beside me, a tired smile on her face, brand new, expensive-looking Jimmy Choos on her feet. She walked back and forth in front of my chair, gave me the full catwalk attitude. "You like?"

I had her come closer, bent and examined the beautiful stitching, the supple leather, wafer-thin sole, and gave her a thumbs up. "Very nice." I hated to ask, didn't really need to know, but couldn't help myself, nosy bastard that I am. "How much? Ninety?"

She put her foot back on the carpet, laughed discreetly. I caught the sales girl laughing at me as well. This could not be good. Natalie leaned over and whispered, a hand to her mouth. "Three-fifty, sweetheart." She modeled them for me again. "These are Jimmy Choos after all."

Three-fifty for a pair of shoes? They better propel me down the street for that price, I thought. I forced myself to speak. "They're nice. Really nice, Nat." The salesgirl approved. I was rewarded with a bright and shiny Nordstrom smile. Good boy!

Natalie paid for her nine pairs of shoes and we headed for the escalator. My woman looked rejuvenated, fresh as a newborn. I was ready for a nap, or a run. I decided on a run.

Natalie said she wanted to do some shopping on her own, so I told her that would be fine with me. I knew instantly what she was up to. Some serious shopping for her man. Couldn't put one over on Steven Adler. I am nobody's fool.

I graciously offered to shlep the packages upstairs, agreed to meet her in the lobby bar at five thirty. She kissed me good-bye with a knowing wink, and I flew up the elevator, carried along by dreams of Natalie's Christmas gift to me. Armani suit? Burberry briefcase? Rolex? New Porsche? Not likely unless she shopped somewhere besides Newport Motors. No problem, a sparkling blood red Ferrari Spyder, then? I was clearly losing my mind, must have been delirious from the long day of shopping. A man of simple tastes, I would have been happy with a new tie. To add to my collection of four.

I finished my five-mile run around the City in forty-five minutes. Slow for me, but I had a few handy excuses to fall back on: a lot more traffic to deal with in comparison to Orange, the hills, of course, and lastly the coronary-on-a-platter I'd had for lunch at the Buena Vista Cafe. I was happy enough, though. I had my thoughts of the wonderful weekend with Natalie to keep my spirits up. Add that to the endorphins released into my tired brain while running and I was on a true runner's high.

Natalie met me at precisely five-thirty. I was a little late, had to get my hair just right. This was going to be a special night. I was going to make sure of that.

She met me with a big smile and a warm kiss on the lips. "Hey, don't you look nice?" I gave her my old killer-jock high school grin. She was right, of course. I had it nailed. I had pulled out the Suit. My one and only Armani Black Label that I'd splurged on with my last check as a resident. Cost fifteen hundred bucks, took nearly my entire check, but I was determined to have one really good suit. This suit did, indeed, make the man. Wool as soft as chamois, black, of course, a perfect fit; as if Giorgio had tailored it himself. I chose a dark burgundy Hugo Boss tie with a subtle embossed pattern, over a plain white shirt. I knew Natalie would love it, and she did. She took another look and frowned at her own outfit. She looked gorgeous of course, chic

130

as a Vogue cover in her black wool suit, but try telling your woman that. I finally convinced her that she could change after we had a drink or two. She happily agreed as I signaled for a waitress.

The lobby bar at the Saint Francis fit the hotel's ambience to perfection. Picture an English library of a certain age: floor-to-ceiling bookcases filled with books that people actually read. Muted floor lamps giving off a suffused glow and rich butter-soft burgundy leather chairs. A movie set that you could actually sit in, have a conversation while you sipped your Cosmopolitan. Very nice.

Natalie ordered a Martini. I stuck to a Coke. She raised an eyebrow at that and I mouthed, "Later," as the waitress walked back to the well to place our orders.

She cupped her chin with a palm and studied me closely. "So, handsome, what's with the fancy duds? I mean, it's only six and you look like you're going to the opera."

I smiled at the compliment, didn't think of myself as handsome, certainly not a sharp dresser, but knew, in all modesty, that I looked pretty good. "I just wanted to rise to your level, couldn't look like a bum in scuffed Nikes when you're sporting brand new Jacky Chans."

She set her Martini back on its fancy sterling silver holder, gave me a shake of her head. "You're crazy, Dr. Adler." She reached for my hand. "Guess that's why I love you so much."

I had a bit of my Coke; felt slightly ridiculous sipping a kid's drink in such a fancy place, still couldn't keep the grin off my face. She reached over for my hand. "I'm glad you're having so much fun, Steven." She ran a thumb along the back of my hand. "I'm having an incredible time." She looked happier than I'd thought was possible, truly carefree for the first time since we'd gotten together eight months ago. "Could you believe the selection in those stores? Much better than we get in Newport."

Frankly, I couldn't remember what was in those stores. It was a three-hour blur to me. One rack after another of well-constructed, expensive garments. I wondered to myself, who *bought* all that stuff? I looked over at Natalie and had to laugh.

Her wonderment and enthusiasm spoke volumes. She was really into that kind of stuff. Here she was, a very intelligent physician, virtually at the top of our class at one of the best medical schools in the country. She had graduated from a prestigious program, ran a successful practice, and she was raving about the selection in a department store. Another lesson I had better learn about women. You can never generalize about what's important to them. She cleared her throat discreetly, waved her hand in front of my face, *Earth to Steven.* I blinked a couple of times, smiled sheepishly. "I'm sorry, honey. I was daydreaming."

"About?"

"You, actually."

She signaled for another Martini. I waved the waitress off. Shot a look at my watch, which Natalie caught immediately. "Got another date, Giorgio?"

"No, smartass. I'm tied up. Won't be available for a long time. Hopefully for the rest of my life."

She gave me the strangest look. Her eyes said it all: *Where are you going with this? Let me know while I try to settle down over here.* She kept her voice calm, even as I was able to read the wealth of emotions in her eyes, puzzlement, hope, a little fear. Her voice was as enticing as sex-on-satin. "Why thank you, Dr. Adler. You make a lady blush."

I kissed her palm. "I see the room is getting to you, too. Pretty soon we'll be asking for scones and tea." I gave my watch another anxious glance. Rose from my chair before Natalie could ask. "Let's go for a walk, Natalie."

She had taken her shoes off, looked completely exhausted, comfortable in her deep leather chair. I hated to break her mood, but really wanted her to take this walk with me. She must have read my thoughts, my insistence, as she smiled, reached down for her shoes and said, "I'm all yours."

She rose gracefully from her chair, extended a hand and we left the bar. I signaled our room number to the waitress, who scribbled it into her notebook with a cheery wave.

We stood in the cold breeze whipping down Post Street, Natalie sheltering in my suit coat, the wind whipping her skirt around her knees. I looked down, could hear and feel her teeth chattering over the hum of the traffic. She met my gaze, lips nearly blue. "I'm freezing, Steven." She shivered against me. "Are we going far? Shouldn't we get a cab?"

I turned my eyes to the store directly across the street. Natalie followed my gaze and gave me a quizzical look. "We've been all over town, Steven." Shuddering against my chest. "Aren't you tired of shopping?"

As a matter of fact I was, but I had just one more stop. The light changed and we ran across the street hand-in-hand. Her cheeks were flushed a deep red: she was easily the most beautiful woman in San Francisco. A few steps later, the blue-suited doorman smiled and opened the heavy vaultlike copper door, trimmed in antique silver. Tipped his hat to Natalie and said, "Welcome to Tiffany and Company, ma'am."

Natalie was really puzzled now. Confused and excited. She knew my economic circumstances, was sure that I wouldn't, couldn't get her a Christmas present from Tiffany's. She said as much as we strolled along the central aisle, surrounded on either side by the world's prettiest jewelry. "Steven." She was a good whisperer. Just the right inflection, not too loud while still carrying lots of feeling. "Do you have any idea how expensive their pieces are?"

I considered pulling out my "slack-jawed yokel" voice, but had second thoughts when we reached the last counter on our left, staffed by a woman who made the Queen of England seem like Roseanne Barr. She gave me a quick, appraising once-over, forced her reedy voice through a deep layer of condescension. "May I help you, sir?"

She even had the accent for Tiffany's; that lockjaw honk peculiar to Connecticut prep schools. Didn't matter to me. I would *not* be intimidated. Natalie gave me the strangest look: *What the hell are you doing, Steven?* I returned the clerk's imperious glare; gave as good as I got, but kept my voice friendly, even as I detested her attitude. "Yes, ma'am." I held up a hand. "If you'll excuse me for just a moment."

I turned to Natalie and knelt on the thick pale blue carpet, Natalie's right hand in mine. I looked up into her eyes and spoke the words that would change my life forever. "Would you do me the great honor of being my wife, Natalie?"

She lost it completely; her reserve gone in a rush of happy tears. A hand in my hair, pulling my head up to plant a luscious kiss on my lips. A hug so hard, I could barely breathe, followed by a whisper so soft I had to strain to hear it. "Yes, Steven. Of course I will." She pulled me up off the carpet, we kissed again and she said, "I love you Steven. More than my life."

I held her tight, my heart nearly bursting with happiness and pride. "I love you too, sweetheart. More than you could know." I have to say Tiffany's went nuts. In an ever-so-dignified Tiffany and Company way. The Queen behind our counter was beside herself with joy. She gave Natalie a stiff nod and muttered, "Best wishes, Ma'am." Her face cracked a half-millimeter smile as she turned to me. "Congratulations, sir." She had the expectant look I'd come to recognize from my day of high-end shopping in Union Square. Oh, that, I thought. First the cash. Then the ring.

Natalie was way ahead of me, a-bride-in-a-diamond store. Eyes alive with excitement; darting from tray to tray, drinking it all in. Was I worried? Not on your life. I'd done my homework in their store at South Coast Plaza down south. Knew the price range and had withdrawn what I'd *hoped* would be enough to cover the freight. The old bag behind the counter was actually quite helpful. I had to give it to her, she clearly knew her stuff, gave us a lecture on color, clarity, and carat weight. The Three C's of diamonds, don't you know.

In the end, we settled on a ring we both loved. Two carats of flawless diamond, marquis cut in a platinum setting. I was proud of myself, as well as a little scared; thirty minutes with the Queen of England and I'm a diamond expert.

Natalie tried it on for size, and I was rendered breathless for a few seconds. Not only because of her beauty; richly enhanced by the glow of love. More for the enormity of this transition in my life. Two or three semi-serious relationships in thirty years and now this. The woman I'd loved from afar comes breezing into my life. Eight months later, we're engaged. Trust me, I wasn't having buyer's remorse, not even when Her Majesty presented my bill. Ten thousand dollars. Delivered to me on a Tiffany and Company blue velvet tray: Shocking prices cosseted in the prettiest presentation imaginable. The Tiffany's Way. Not at all. I just couldn't believe the drastic changes I'd gone through. Graduation, Mom's death, now this. I was overwhelmed.

Natalie was radiant. The ring was too large, naturally. The Queen promised she'd have it sized and delivered to the hotel on Monday, and we were done. Officially engaged.

I was overjoyed, both by Natalie's answer and of course, by the circumstances. But I must admit, I *did* sweat a rejection right there in the middle of Tiffany's. My heart had been pounding into my throat. No way I could have gotten out of that situation with my dignity intact, had she turned me down. Not to worry, she didn't, and so we began our official life together.

We walked across the street hand-in-hand, back to our hotel, carried along as if in a dream: San Francisco, Tiffany's, Union Square decorated like Disneyland, tinkling bells, excited couples all around us. I took a look at my fiancée, realized for the first time that I was engaged to the beautiful and talented Dr. Natalie Bogner. My life was now complete. Perfect. Standing on the corner of Stockton and Post, I thought, what more could anyone ask for?

Chapter 14

FIVE MONTHS LATER

"Dr. Adler, we have a head injury three minutes out." Cecilia Perez, our new Communication nurse, poked her head in my cubbyhole and delivered the news with quiet professionalism. A big improvement over Cathy Jenkins' histrionics and foul mouth. Poor Cathy. She was fired the day I left for Mom's funeral. Seems she was on with the Department Chairman. Got really excited about a car crunch being helicoptered from the Ortega Highway. The way I heard it, she got flustered, called Dr. Tompkins "shithead." Needless to say, he was not amused and she didn't get to finish her shift.

"What have we got, Barbara?" I walked to the intubation cart, checked the scope. Barbara Manning was bustling around Trauma One, an armful of IV bags against her chest.

"Cecilia said we're getting an S.U.V. rollover from the Five. ETA two minutes."

"Any particulars?" I opened the handle of the scope, checked the light, then walked over to the foot of the bed and helped Barbara set out the monitor cables.

"It's a young boy, think she said sixteen. I don't know anything else." Finished with the monitors, she stored the IV fluid on the top shelf, turned to help me set up the trach tray. "Said it was a scoop and run."

I snapped off my sterile gloves, took a last look around to be sure we were ready. "Look like an organ donor?" UCI was the only active trauma center in Orange County, so we saw all of the worst accidents. About thirty percent of our head trauma victims came in so mangled by high-speed accidents that they were brain dead on arrival, especially the motorcycle riders stupid enough to race around without helmets. We had an excellent transplant team on standby around the clock. Anytime we got a really bad trauma in a young patient, we'd try to give them a heads up.

Barbara had no time to answer; the medics rolled in a second or two later, with a "red blanket," an injured patient covered with a ruby red Mylar sheet, the universal sign of critical trauma. The patient, an adolescent male, was lashed to a back-board, hard plastic cervical restraint device on his neck. I bent over to help transport him to the bed, then ran around to the head of the gurney to examine him.

"MVA rollover at oh-eight-hundred, thirty minutes ago." The medic, a short, red-faced man in his late forties, jotted a note on his clipboard, checked the transport, and came closer to continue his report. "Name's Roger Hardaway, fifteen. Alert, oriented times three in the field, drowsy with two episodes of emesis en route."

I checked his airway: breath sounds, and did a quick skeletal survey, palpating his long bones and ribs for any obvious tenderness and deformity. The survey was negative, so I went to a quick neuro check.

Leaned closer to his right ear and asked the boy what happened. His voice was garbled, his breath carrying the coppery scent of fresh blood. "Don't remember." He coughed, spat a wad of filmy pink liquid, which I quickly suctioned, and then closed his eyes. I had to shake him awake. "Dad was driving. Car hit us. Hard." He tried to sit up; straining against his restraints, shouted, "Where's my dad?" The nurses had to lean on his chest, the kid was shouting, crying hysterically. "Dad? Daddy?"

I shot a look at the crew chief, who gave me a thumbs down, which meant the worst possible news: dead on scene. I shook my head, asked the chief, "Anyone else in the vehicle?"

I'd known Ricky Sutcliffe, the crew chief of Engine Company Nine out of Anaheim, for five years. He was a gangly six-ten, stubbly red beard; intelligent green eyes under a heavy brow. Never saw him show any emotion at all. And we'd been through some horrible times together. He tried to hide it, but I could see him nearly disintegrate before my eyes as he scanned his report. He came a little closer to whisper the news, trying to avoid agitating our patient further. "Five dead on scene, doc." He took a moment to compose himself, blew his nose in a tissue Barbara handed him discreetly. "Family in a minivan. Hit by a drunk in a pickup."

I pulled him away from the boy, didn't want him to hear this horrible news. "Jesus, Ricky. It's barely nine o'clock."

He gave me a world-weary look. I'd been here long enough to know what he was going to say. "Fucking drunks don't care, doc. Asshole's probably been blitzed all damn night long."

I was afraid to ask, didn't actually give a shit; he could be dead in a ditch for all I cared, but did anyway. "Where's the drunk?"

Barbara answered for Sutcliffe, a disgusted look on her face. "He's in three."

"Minor lacerations and contusions, right?" Her nod and saddened expression was all the confirmation I needed. God does indeed protect drunks and fools. I used to believe He protected kids as well, but looking at this poor broken boy on my gurney, I had serious doubts.

I walked back to the head of the table, tried to rouse our patient, ran a fist-full of knuckles down his sternum, shouted next to his ear, "Roger. Roger!" Nothing. Yelled his name again, he gave me a lethargic grin. "Am I in Heaven?" Looked around Trauma One, glassy eyes on Barbara's white scrubs. "What's on TV tonight?"

I motioned to Barbara, who was busy at the patient's arm, starting another IV. "Barb, call a stat Neurosurg consult." The kid was slipping rapidly down the coma scale, a numerical system we used to determine the patient's neurological status, which gave us a fairly accurate way of predicting hir or her outcome. More importantly, we used it to direct our treatment. Roger was sliding from a Stage I, the least serious injury to a II or III. Stage IV was consistent with brain death. I did a quick pupillary check while Roger had his eyes open. The left was reactive; the right was dilated and sluggishly reactive to my flashlight.

I ran to the side of the bed to assess his motor function, joined Barbara, who had just run back in from the hallway, gave her an urgent whisper. "Barb, is Neuro coming? This kid's a two-three now. We need them ASAP." I had Roger try to squeeze my hand with his left. Nothing. Had him try to move his left leg. Nothing.

Ran to his right side, did the same maneuver. Found a strength rating of four out of five for his upper and lower extremities, normal for a trauma victim in mild shock.

Went back to the head of the bed, he was under deeply again. No response this time to shouts, mild pain from my knuckles rubbing along his breastbone, nothing. Checked his pupils again. The right one was nearly completely dilated, his left mid-point in size and sluggish.

Grabbed my intubation scope, Barbara at my side. Turned my attention to his throat, held my hand out for the tube. "Barb, give me a six and a half." Roger was now solidly in Stage III. I needed to intubate him immediately and start positive airway pressure in order to lessen the swelling in his brain. She handed me the tube, I slipped it past his vocal cords and Respiratory hooked him to the ventilator.

I checked the placement and turned to the Respiratory tech. "Give him five of PEEP." I had given an order to give the patient a small amount of positive airway pressure, so his brain swelling would be partially improved until Neurosurgery could see him.

I walked over to the monitors, squinted at the flashing numbers: pressure a little high, pulse low, a very bad sign; his cerebral edema was getting worse. I went over to the door, yelled to our secretary, "Where's Neuro? We won't have time for a CT. This kid's going down too fast."

The nursing students at the side of the bed started to cry while my back was turned toward the gurney, my attention on the secretary. I spun around a minute later and Roger was posturing. His arms and legs were flailing uncontrollably as the swelling in his brain worsened to the point that he was in danger of brain stem herniation. Herniation was usually the prelude to irreversible brain death, followed quickly by death of the patient as the respiratory and cardiac centers in the brain failed. It was a simple matter of physics. The brain was contained by the rigid bony confines of the skull and serious swelling would literally choke the life out of the central nervous system.

I ran to the head of his bed, scanned the numbers. "Give him two grams of Mannitol, Barbara." She had already hung the powerful diuretic agent, was adjusting the drip before I'd finished my order. Our first line of defense in cases of brain herniation was to give a powerful diuretic drug like Mannitol to unload the body's fluids in an effort to combat swelling. Agitated as hell, worried about this poor kid, I yelled through the doorway, "Where the fuck's Neuro?"

"Right here, Steven. What have you got?" I heaved a sigh of relief. Don DeMaio, the chief of service at UCI, walked over to my side. He had come down personally. Unlike his colleagues in other departments, he often saw the cases in the ER first, leaving the junior attendings and house staff up in surgery. Said he missed the blood and guts in the Department. I didn't care what his motives were at that point, I was just glad to see him. Nothing much got to me anymore, but bad Neuro crunches could go south in a big hurry, and it had been five years since I'd done any burr holes.

DeMaio walked to the other side of the bed and did a quick neuro check, while I gave him a report. "MVA about an hour ago now, Don. Came in as a One, slipped to a Two about five minutes ago, now a Three. I intubated him about two minutes ago."

DeMaio checked his pupils, nodded slightly, and went down to his extremities as I continued my findings. "Flaccid on the left, four out of five on the right."

The Neuro surgeon used a wheeled device studded with pins to assess Roger's sensation for pain. Nothing. Looked up at Barbara, then me. "Give him Mannitol?"

I nodded as I checked his pressure. "Two grams about two minutes ago. Right after I tubed him. He was decerebrate just before you got here." DeMaio raised an eyebrow at that; about as much emotion as I'd seen from him in the last five years.

His tone was matter-of-fact; as if he were ordering a hamburger. "Then we have a problem, Steven."

I rechecked the boy's blood pressure. Ninety over forty. Ordered Respiratory to increase the positive airway pressure to ten. My voice was tight; I didn't like where this was going, not at all. "How so, Don?"

"I have two teams working upstairs; we're going to have to do burr holes down here."

Bad as it was, and this case was the worst I'd seen in months, my team rose to the occasion. We did this procedure in Trauma One less than once a year, but Barbara was ready for anything. We were going to open this boy's scalp and drill a large hole in his skull to let the brain decompress in order to relieve the pressure. He was so close to brain death that there was no time to confirm the diagnosis with a CT scan, no time to properly transport him to the OR. So we went for it.

DeMaio turned to my charge nurse and calmly gave his orders. "I'll need a Stryker drill with a three-and-a-half bit, the saw, two-millimeter vascular clips, and Cushing retractors, dear." He signaled for the other nurse to start shaving Roger's scalp, turned again toward Barbara. "Could you get that for me as soon as possible, please?"

Barbara walked three steps to the cabinet, chose a large metal tray wrapped in sterile paper, and began laying it out on the large

Mayo stand. "We have everything here for you, Dr. DeMaio. Do you need anything else? Anything from Central Supply?"

DeMaio snapped on a pair of size eight surgeon's gloves, bent over the table, took a moment to examine the tray, and nodded his approval. "This will do nicely." Looked over at me, gave me a microscopic grin. "You have an excellent staff down here, Steven." He directed the staff nurse to quickly shave Roger's head from his forehead to beyond his ears. Told the medical student lurking near the intubation tray how to prep the scalp. "Just once over with Betadine, would you, dear?" Chose his drill bit and tested the drill, as the room filled with the high-pitched scream of compressed air. "We're in rather a hurry."

I moved to the left side of the patient's head, ready to assist DeMaio, fastened my surgical mask as Barbara helped me into my gown; responded to his compliment of a few moments ago. "We have the best crew in the county. No doubt about that, Don."

"Hmm." He had already begun his incision, a twelve-inch slice all the way through the scalp to a shiny layer of tissue called the Gallea, immediately on top of the skull bone. Looked up briefly from his work, pointed to a bleeder halfway along his incision. "Watch the bleeding, will you, Steven?" Barbara handed me a plastic applicator that looked like a staple gun, five inches long, made of clear plastic, containing a series of spring-loaded plastic clips. I quickly applied them to the bleeding vessels along the scalp, finishing with a row of about ten on either side of the scalp. DeMaio looked up from his incision into the Gallea, satisfied that the bleeding was controlled. "Excellent, Steven." He pulled the scalp away from the operative site with his hands, created a pocket of exposed skull bone the size of a standard envelope. "Slide the Cushings in there, would you please?" Barbara handed me a pair of curved retraction blades, specially designed for this purpose.

DeMaio attached the cranial burr to what looked like a standard electric hand drill. He gave it a test, adjusted the burr, and started to drill in earnest. The noise was deafening; sounded only slightly quieter than a jet engine, because this type of drill was powered by pressurized nitrogen gas, fed through a hose snaking from the wall, along the floor and into the handset. DeMaio entered the skull with a stainless steel, three-inch burr, gently cut through the thick tissue of the dura and got an immediate return of fresh and clotted blood. He sounded as calm and collected as a TV golf commentator. "Just as I'd suspected, Steven. A temporal-parietal subdural. Bad one by the looks of it." He was describing a very serious blood clot under the dural lining that surrounded the brain by the temple, just above the ear. The mortality rate in a bad injury like this one could be up to seventy percent. He smiled under his mask, master of the understatement. "Lucky for our young man here that you and your crew were on today, Steven."

I took a look at the patient, his face swollen and purple from his forehead to his nose. "We're lucky to have more than a few good crews down here, Don."

DeMaio looked up as his senior resident came into Trauma One. "Ah, the estimable Dr. Landon has arrived." DeMaio motioned for him to gown and glove, returned to the incision, and carefully teased the brain tissue aside as he applied an electric cautery device to several small bleeding vessels. Looked up briefly at his gowned-and-gloved resident. "Why don't you come and relieve Dr. Adler, Landon. I'll let you tidy up in here, help you put in the bolt."

I snapped off my gloves and helped Barbara set up the intracranial pressure monitoring device. A few more minutes of hemorrhage control and DeMaio was almost ready to thread a thin plastic catheter into the space between the two sides of the patient's brain, so that we could monitor the brain swelling after they'd closed the incisions. Typically, after the catheter was in place, the monitor's plastic hub was then screwed into the bone of the skull, hence the name, bolt.

Less than thirty minutes after DeMaio and I had started, the patient was on his way to the ICU, monitor in place, head swathed in gauze bandages. He walked over to the sink, snapped off his gloves, and shook my hand. "Nice job, Steven. Really." DeMaio washed his hands in the sink, turned to place a hand on my shoulder. I'd known him since my aborted Surgery residency; he was my first attending as an intern. "You should have stayed in Surgery. You have good hands. Excellent judgment." He dried his hands on a paper towel. "Who knows, you might have made it all the way to Neuro."

I shook my head. "Thanks, but no thanks, Don. I'm happy down here. I like the action."

He turned to murmur orders to his chief resident, finished a few moments later, and gave me a grave look. "This poor kid's in for a rough go of it. I'm afraid he's going to be gorked." Bad news, almost the worst for a young, healthy boy. He was likely going to be paralyzed, possibly permanently, that is, *if* he woke up. Worse for him, he could even face the grim prospect of spending the rest of his life in a nursing home, "locked-in," unable to communicate verbally with the outside world. What an unspeakably terrible break. Fifteen, his whole family wiped out by a goddamned drunk, and now this. I suddenly wanted to hit something. A malevolent thought passed quickly: I would love to hit a *drunk* something if only I could get away with it.

I shook off my vicious thoughts, nodded to DeMaio. "Jesus, Don. What a world." He nodded sadly, turned away from the sink, and directed the residents and nurses up to the floor, said he'd be right along after he went to talk to the parents. I wanted to spare him the trouble, had to clue him in. "They're gone, Don. Medics said the rest of the family was dead on the scene."

He shook his head, tension and anger clear in the set of his mouth, his tone of voice. "Goddamned drunk drivers ought to be shot. On the spot. Every last fucking one of them."

No truer words, put it on the ballot next November, I thought, as I walked him to the nurse's station. "I couldn't agree more, Don."

DeMaio, lost in thought, walked across the room to Barbara, leaned close and whispered something in her ear. She smiled weakly in return, whispered something back to him. A moment later, he gave me a nod and rushed up the ramp to the Neuro ICU.

I got home late that night, around midnight. Let myself into the apartment; the place smelled like it had been abandoned. Which, in a sense it had been. I was there to pick up a few of my things; bedding, toaster, some odds and ends in my closet. I had moved out of the old place a few days ago; it was getting to be a hassle driving back and forth to Newport all the time with the endless errands I had to run. Wedding stuff, moving stuff, honey-do stuff, closing one home and opening another stuff. I missed my old apartment on Chapman. The convenience, the low rent, even the noise. Funny how we get used to a place, simple comforts, familiarity, even the annoyances. Natalie's house, on the other hand, was huge, four thousand square feet; state of the art everything, an ocean view, three-car garage. Great crib, awesome neighborhood, just not my home. Yet.

A half hour later, I pulled into her driveway, locked the Porsche, and let myself in through the front door, punched in the alarm code. Only took me three tries this time. The last time WesTec Security had come bursting in, guns drawn. Boy, was that embarrassing.

I set my stuff on the floor and went looking for my lady. "Hey, Nat. I'm home."

The foyer light was the only one on. The living room to the right, step-down den to the left were both deserted, nothing but the floor-level night-lights on in the gloom. I flipped on the kitchen light, checked the mail stacked on the center island: bills, bills, and more bills, all for Natalie. My junk would likely come in a week or two. No matter, I thought, the bills could wait.

I opened the fridge, looked for an apple, found a good-looking ripe Gala, closed the door and a piece of notepaper fluttered to my feet. I bent to pick it up, scanned it quickly in the dim overhead lights of the kitchen: "*Dear Steven. Got called in for a delivery.*

The casserole's on the second shelf. Maria made taco salad, your favorite, sweetie. Put it in the micro, nuke it for about two minutes. Be home soonest. Love, Me." There was a tiny postscript, drawn in the bottom corner in Natalie's forward-slanting, perfect hand. *"Did you get another band??? Please say yes!!!"*

I took a huge bite of the apple, mumbled between chews, my voice bouncing off the freshly stained rosewood cabinets. "Sorry, Honey. No-can-do with the band. Saving lives all day." I walked through Nat's eat-in kitchen to the adjacent den, turned on a table lamp, and sat on her eight-foot, butter yellow leather sofa. Five thousand bucks at Z Gallerie, she had told me last week. More than twice what I was able to send to Pops every month, I realized with a start. The girl had expensive taste. Glad one of us is rich, I thought, as I flipped on the TV. I realized, as I took a look around the redecorated space, that I kept thinking of all of this stuff as Natalie's. Oh, well, maybe I'd get used to saying "ours," but I knew it would take me a while. This married stuff was going to take some getting used to. Of that, I had no doubt.

I took another huge bite of my apple, flipped through the channels. Seventy-some stations of round-the-clock cable TV and the only thing I could find was Jay Leno. His guests were David Copperfield and Cher. Boring! I punched the power button just as Jay was yucking it up with his bandleader, stood up, chewed up the last of my apple and went down the hall to "our" bedroom. Still sounded strange to my inner ear, though. I stowed my bedding in the linen closet, stripped off my jeans and sweater, walked into the bathroom, threw them in the hamper and started the shower.

I took a look at my face in the mirror as the shower warmed up, was shocked to see how tired I looked. Nothing at all like the horny young buck rutting his way through San Francisco. Looked more like my dad everyday. With a quick stab of panic, I checked my hairline, spun around and checked for a bald spot in back. Heaved a sigh of relief as I gazed at my perfect sandy blond hair. Vanity, thy name *is* Steven.

I grabbed a towel from the pile and checked the water temp. Just right, a few degrees over room temperature. Opened the door and stood for a long few minutes under the pulsating spray. Heard a voice. "Steven?" Natalie. It sounded like she was calling from the hallway; muffled by thick walls and carpeting, her voice seemed a half-mile away.

I turned off the water and yelled to her. "In here, baby. Taking a shower."

I caught her reflection in the mirror as I restarted the water. "I'm right here, Steven." She seemed tired, tense. "No need to shout." She stretched against the countertop, back impossibly arched, softened her voice. "Just get home?"

I lathered my chest, poured some water over my hair. "About ten minutes ago. How'd it go?"

I could hear her slamming a bureau drawer, her shoes hitting the hardwood floor. "Routine prime-ip. They take for-fucking-ever." More slams, sounded like the closet door this time. "The stupid nurses in OB stopped the pit drip, so I was stuck waiting for three hours." Her voice rose above the noise of the shower, she seemed really pissed. "Like an idiot. Decided to stay at Hoag. Didn't want to drive all the way home, just to go right back." Natalie often complained about the nursing staff, at least once a week since I'd known her. She was famously impatient, I'd even heard from some of the nurses at Irvine that she could be very difficult. Had heard her called a bitch by more than one member of the nursing staff. One of them went so far as to call her "an impossible cunt." Yikes, that one would have left a mark! I knew better; we were all that way, had to be Type A personalities just to get through our training. They could talk all they wanted, call her anything they could think of, I just chalked it up to hospital politics, jealousy, and overall chronically disgruntled employees. It was that way everywhere.

It sounded to me as if she'd had a rough night. Her patient was a prime-ip, a first time mother; they always took much longer to deliver. She sounded mad that the nurses had screwed up the IV medicine she gave the patients to assist in cervical dilation. Overall, not a good night for my Natalie. Made me glad that I'd stayed at UCI. Barbara and her crew were golden. Prime example: the kid we did this morning was stable; even DeMaio was optimistic.

Happy to be home, I soaped my back and called to her in the bedroom. "Why don't you come in." I put a little extra lechery in my voice. "I can soap you up *real* good. Wash all those hard-to-reach parts."

At first I thought she hadn't heard me. I listened more closely and heard Natalie murmuring, sounded like she was on the phone. I gave up temporarily, washed my hair, deciding to let her finish her conversation, probably giving orders to post partum, I thought.

A few minutes later, I finished up, still heard her talking on the phone, so I reluctantly turned off the water. Shit, I thought, after a day like mine I could have used a little slip-and-slide.

I toweled off and walked into the bedroom. She had her back turned away from me; stretched out under the covers, phone cradled to her chin. I slipped into a pair of scrubs, tried to be inconspicuous, in case she was giving orders, didn't want to break her concentration. Her voice was low, almost intimate. "Yeah, I did too." A second later, lost in her conversation, Natalie jumped when I dropped my hairbrush on the floor, nearly dropped the phone, turned toward me an instant later and murmured into the hand-set, "Gotta go. Yeah, tomorrow's good."

I went to the bureau and pulled out a fresh pair of scrubs, gave her a bright smile over my shoulder. "The hospital?"

Natalie gave me a puzzled look, as if she hadn't heard my question. "The hospital what, Steven?"

I pulled on my scrub-top and padded over to her side of the bed, leaned down and kissed her lips. "On the phone just now. You giving orders to the floor?"

She turned her back and fluffed the pillows, turned back toward me a few moments later, reached down and pulled the duvet up to her chin. "Oh, that." A faraway look on her face, she smoothed the sheets, made room for me by scooting closer to the edge. "Yeah, they called me about the, ah, the IV orders. For my post partum patient. The one I went in for." She reached for the remote, flipped on Jay Leno. Cher was singing "I Got You Babe." She looked pathetic up on stage without Sonny. A tight faced, artificially bolstered shadow of her former self. Natalie smiled up at me as I took a good look at my beautiful fiancée, snuggled into her fancy "hotel style" sheets. "Come to bed, Steven. You look tired." She pulled back the covers; I noticed she was wearing the teeny-tiny, oh-so-sheer panties she'd worn for me in San Francisco, the night we got engaged. The ones I pulled off with my teeth the minute we got back to our room. I hadn't seen her wear them in months; she usually stuck to basic white cotton bikinis for everyday. Maybe, it's going to be my lucky night after all, I thought, as I climbed into bed.

I slid over her to my side, the right side, away from the telephone. Natalie got a lot more calls at night than I did, actually all the calls, so it made sense to let her have the phone side. I'd always slept on her side, and was having a little trouble getting used to my new position. I leaned over to kiss her. Cher was laughing with Leno about her latest boyfriend, Macaulay Culkin. Started to rub her back, whispered in her ear, "Hard night, honey?"

She returned my hopeful kiss with a peck on the cheek. "They've all been hard lately, Steven." Her voice was tense, her mouth a thin, tight line. "The wedding, my practice. I hardly have any time for anything anymore." I reached up and started to massage her shoulders. Her tone of voice now sounded a little more promising, the irritated professional gone for now. "Mmm, that feels good, Steven." She arched her neck, settled deeper into the pillows. I was on my game. A little massage, a little kissing; bada bing, bada boom, a little nookie. A winning parlay. Worked everytime. Learned it at UCR: Horn-dog 101. Except tonight. A few rubs later, the prosecutor's voice was back; I felt my erection melt like snow on Memorial Day. "That's fine. I feel much better, Steven." She removed my hands, gently, gave me a weary smile. "I'm a little tired, sweetie. Rough day."

I crept back to my side of the bed, crestfallen, heartbroken, and horny as a gorilla. Like to compare days, honey? Bet mine was way worse than yours, I thought, with a flash of irritation. Tired as she looked, I decided to let it go, give her the benefit of the doubt. Laid a hand on her shoulder. "See you in the morning, then."

She leaned over to kiss me on the cheek. I noticed she was wearing her favorite perfume, *Iviore*; it had cost me two-fifty an ounce at Saks. Strange, I thought at the time; she'd told me long ago that she didn't like to wear any scent at work; too many of her patients were sensitive to it, especially the pregnant ones. Her voice was low; she seemed already on the verge of sleep. "We'll catch up tomorrow, promise."

Natalie flipped off the TV, thank God. Cher was starting to blather about a "wonderful new weight loss product" that she and Macaulay Culkin were hawking. A half-hour later, I lay there trying to decompress from my awful day, wide awake at one-thirty; my mind occupied by thoughts of crushed skulls, brain death, and our wedding day, which was rushing toward us like an out-of-control Metro Link train.

As I remember that night now, I was happy, I know I was. But I was worried too. And I didn't know exactly why. Couldn't put my finger on it. Must have been too tired to think it through with any degree of insight.

An hour or a couple of days later, I was asleep, strapped to the cab of a runaway train, a bloody zombie dressed in tattered scrubs at the controls, when Natalie shook me awake, her voice way too loud for my dream. "Steven. *Steven.*" She shook me again; I jumped a foot. "Did you get a chance to call for a new band?"

Fuck me! I thought with a surge of annoyance. The Band. I'd forgotten all about it. Must have been occupied with real life in the ER. I tried to keep the irritation I felt out of my voice. "Sorry, hon. I was super busy today. I'll call . . ." Big yawn, couldn't stay awake another second. Bloody zombies on a runaway train calling my name. ". . . tomorrow."

I felt her move away, toward her nightstand, thought I heard her say something that sounded a lot like "Typical."

151

Chapter 15

We were married the following Saturday in Laguna Beach, on a perfect day, twenty or so of us gathered on a windswept bluff overlooking the Pacific. Just a small group of our nearest and dearest, Pops, her mom, Laura, and my brother, who showed up at the last minute with a big surprise, a new wife named Olivia and three step-kids, the cutest set of twin eight-year-old boys imaginable named Harry and Kenny, and a six-year-old girl named Stephanie, beautiful curly blond hair to her shoulders, deep brown eyes, glorious smile. We were instantly in love with our new family; Pops was in heaven, already spoiling his grand-kids, took them to Disneyland by himself the minute they unpacked at our house. Kept them out all night for ice cream after. The guy was like a kid himself.

The ceremony was a blur of emotions and bittersweet joy. I guess most weddings are. Pops was my best man; Jake gave Natalie away as her dad was "too busy to come down from Seattle." I knew Natalie was secretly crushed, even though she tried to hide it by saying, "He'll never get over Mom. That's why he won't come down." I knew it went deeper than that, knew she was covering up; I caught her crying in the bathroom after she'd called him. She wouldn't even talk about it for a week, kept her feelings on that score buried deep down inside.

Despite the sticky family dynamics, the ceremony was beautiful. She was beautiful, the perfect blend of restrained sexuality and wholesomeness, Natalie was every inch the radiant bride in an off-white gown molded perfectly to her figure, flowing like liquid silk over her hips, stopping just an inch or two below her knees.

We had reserved the restaurant next to the gazebo at Las Brisas and spent the next few hours laughing till we cried, reminiscing and planning our future. Pops caught my garter; Laura caught Nat's bouquet while the kids tore up the place. The best party ever.

As the reception wound down, I sat with Natalie at a table overlooking the ocean, the only sounds the crashing surf ten yards down the bluff. I looked at my new wife and thought, after all this: here we are, joined forever by a bond of love. She gave me a weary smile. I kissed her cheek. It felt good to be married to her, really good. After all of our trials and tribulations, I was excited to begin our life together.

Las Vegas, my beautiful new wife, and a five-day honeymoon sounded like paradise at the time. To be accurate, in retrospect, I'll call it faux paradise, a Vegas specialty. It's not that we had a bad time, it was just sort of a let-down after our red-hot courtship. We stayed at Caesars Palace, a truly unique hotel, right in the middle of the strip. Our room was on the fifteenth floor; if not quite the bridal suite, at four hundred a night; it was pretty nice. We had a sitting area with a sofa, wet bar, and tiny desk; the bedroom had the requisite king-size bed, marble bath, and inch-thick towels. Natalie was impressed; she told me it was only her second time to Vegas; the first one several years ago, when she was sixteen, with her mom.

Why was I disappointed? I look back and can point to one or two things. Natalie seemed a little distracted, kept telling me nothing was wrong, but she just didn't seem herself. Didn't want to do much, wanted to sleep most of the time. She told me she wasn't ill, "just wanted to relax." That was okay with me, up to a point. This was my first, hopefully my last, honeymoon, and I wanted to tear it up. Make some memories we could look back on and laugh about, recollections that we could sanitize heavily and tell our kids about.

The second thing was the sex. I hate to complain, we still made love every night, but it just wasn't the same. The passion wasn't there. I was thrilled beyond belief to have Natalie as my wife; who wouldn't be, but she just seemed *different*. Not disinterested, exactly, it's as if she wasn't into it as much as before, almost like she wasn't in to *me*, either. Whereas before we got married, she would come once or twice almost every time we made love, and seemed to want it four or more times a day, after the ceremony she seemed to be satisfied with a ten-minute session. She would come very quietly, if at all, and then would immediately roll over and go sleep.

I was happy enough just being married. Natalie? I didn't know whether or not the fire had gone out already or it was just the accumulated stress that was bugging her. Try as I might to cut her some slack, the fact remained: here we were on our honeymoon and she had turned into a librarian. Strange, to say the least. A day or two into our honeymoon, I chalked up her lethargy to post-wedding fatigue and possibly some mild depression. I started to ask her about it a couple of times, but she didn't want to talk about it at all, she just kept sleeping. Feeling adrift and confused, I was left to explore Vegas.

The city that never sleeps. How true was that slogan? Let me tell you how I saw it. Monday morning, our third day there, five-o'clock, I couldn't sleep, Natalie was conked out and I decided to roam the hotel. Before we'd left I'd budgeted a thousand for gambling over the five days we planned to be at Caesars. I'm anything but a big gambler; work too hard for my money and never got much of a thrill throwing it away. Over the weekend

Natalie had lost two hundred, I'd won three hundred, so we were a hundred bucks up. I never played anything more complicated than the slots; Natalie lost her wad at the blackjack table. She was a big hit with the other gamblers though, wore her tiny black San Francisco dress and really drew a crowd. Disquieted as I was by her attitude in Vegas, I must admit it was nice basking in her reflected glory, even if the surroundings were a bit of a downer to me.

I walked through the casino level, looking for a café. What a depressing sight; stick-thin matrons bent over nickel slot handles, cigarettes hanging from their mouths, a fixed expression of frayed expectation on their faces. The constant sound of rattling coins and hacking coughs competing with the housekeeper's vacuums. I got so dejected walking through the casino, I decided on the spot to ask Natalie if she wanted to go home early.

Only one problem. I got back to the room and she was gone.
   I changed back into my scrubs, got back into bed and tossed and turned, wondering where she was. Ten minutes later, the rising desert sun started to blast through a crack in our blackout curtains and I finally gave it up, turned on the early news, wondering where my wife had gone. It was already eighty degrees outside: perpetual summer had started in April and I was stuck here in Sin City, bored to tears. Too early to go to the pool, couldn't play golf because I hadn't brought my golf clubs, since I figured we'd be making love night and day. Yeah, right. I thought, with a little selfish sigh. Eight o'clock and nothing to do, nobody to do it with. The time had started to hang heavy on my hands.

She came back to our room around nine, dressed in her tight black bike shorts and a white sweatshirt, flushed from a workout in the second-floor gym. I gave her a cheery wave from under the covers, my voice happier than I felt. "Hey, you're up early." She nodded without a word and went straight into the bathroom; a few seconds later I could hear water running, followed by the sounds of her brushing her teeth. Not much of a greeting, I thought, more than a little pissed. I hopped out of bed and joined her in the bath, kept my voice light. "Have a good workout?"

"Uh huh." She had a mouth full of toothpaste, back to me as she rinsed her mouth. She picked up a towel, wiped her mouth; turned to give me a pale smile. "Sure. What have you been up to?"

I stretched and yawned. "Nothing much, went downstairs, wandered around, got a cup of coffee in a dump called Gladiator's."

She stood facing me, arms folded over her chest. "Ugh. I saw that place on my way to the gym." She shook her head, ran a hand through her hair. "Pretty tacky, huh?"

I leaned in to kiss her, she turned her face and I caught her cheek, something she'd done more and more often lately. "Like most of Vegas. They go overboard with all the themed crap here."

She left the bath; turning slightly as she passed by me, walked to the bureau for some fresh clothes, selected a pair of jeans and a white sweater, brushed by me again on the way back into the bathroom. Turned to face me, her expression grim. "Gonna take a shower." She made a move to close the door. I started to take off my shirt, sensed a good moment to reconnect with her. She quickly closed that opening with a look of unmistakable dismissal; her voice cool as the bathroom marble. "I'll just be a few minutes, Steven."

I felt like I needed to force the issue; this was getting sort of ridiculous. "Want some company?" She was already closing the door, clearly wanted me to wait outside. I was more than a little put out, given all the fun we'd had with showers in our time together, but decided in the end to let it go. We had three more days in Sin City, plenty of time to straighten this out. As much as I'd tried to be fair, I failed to keep the disappointment from my voice. "I guess not, then."

She leaned into the black-marble shower, which could easily accommodate two couples, and adjusted the flow and temperature, gave me a shadow of a smile. "Next time, Steven. Promise."

She turned her back, stripped off her top and saw me staring in the mirror. I caught her look, noticed how she unconsciously covered her breasts with her hands and decided to take her obvious hint. I closed the door with a disgusted shake of my head and climbed under the covers. What the hell brought that on? I wondered.

She came back in a half-hour later, flushed head to toe from the hot water. At least what I could see was flushed; she had one of Caesars complimentary white terry robes tied tightly around her waist; just her neck and legs peeking out from the oversized wrap. I patted the bed and opened the covers. "Come on in, Natalie. I've warmed it up for you."

She sat on the edge of the bed, slipped into her jeans, dropped the robe on the floor in a heap, shrugged into her sweater. Kept her back to me. "I'm not tired, Steven. You go ahead though, take another nap."

I threw the covers aside and walked to the foot of the bed. This was getting a little nuts. She sat with her arms crossed tightly across her chest; her eyes were red, from crying or the steamy shower, I couldn't tell. I caressed her cheek with my right hand, tried to meet her gaze, which she kept trained on the carpet. Cupped her chin with my palm, raised her face to meet my gaze. "Natalie, are you going to tell me what's wrong?"

She returned her stare to a point on the floor; her face expressionless, tone flat. "Nothing, Steven. Just feeling a little down." A moment later, she looked up into my eyes, then quickly recast her eyes downward. "It's not you." She seemed on the verge or tears, her voice a hoarse whisper. "Please don't think it's you."

I sat beside her on the bed, put my arm around her shoulders. She sat stiffly; I could feel her move a fraction of an inch farther away. "We need to talk about this, Natalie. I know there's something bothering you." I tried to draw her closer, she increased the distance by scooting her butt closer to the window. "Are you happy being married, honey? Is there something I've done?" I tried to kiss her hair; she started sobbing lightly. Shit, what was going on with her? I thought with a rush of panic. She had never been this depressed while we were going together. She had her moods, just like I did, but I could usually bring her out of it quickly. Moods notwithstanding, I understood this about her; Natalie saw the glass as half empty; I was the genuinely optimistic one in our relationship. We both had our ups and downs; every couple does, just never like this. She was starting to worry me.

She turned slightly to face me, eyes brimming with tears. I held her closer, a few seconds and a couple of muffled sobs later she relaxed slightly, settled into my arms. She blinked away her tears; I ran a thumb along her cheek to dry her face. She struggled with her composure, met my eyes. "I have something to tell you, Steven." She shook in my arms, nearly inconsolable. What could have upset her so badly? I immediately thought about her mom; she'd called from New York, safe and sound, so what else could it be? Her dad had called from Seattle, offered his belated congratulations. Natalie was upset after *that* call. She'd had a chronic problem with her dad; that was clear to me from the second time we went out on a date, and the bastard had made it much worse by his cowardly behavior when he skipped our wedding. This time she was *really* angry with him, understandable in that he failed to show for his only child's wedding, but still, we'd talked that through, she seemed to be okay with it for now, promised me she'd have it out with him in person. So why this? Why now? I was completely puzzled, more than a little alarmed.

I whispered in her ear, "You can tell me, Natalie." I held her chin in my palm, she closed her eyes against the tears. "You can tell me anything. You know that."

She kept her eyes tightly shut. "It's just . . ." She shook against my chest; I tried to console her by holding her tighter, she only cried harder. "I've never done something so stupid, Steven." She sobbed on my shoulder, felt like she was coming apart at the seams. "I've ruined everything." She met my eyes; I saw fear for the first time in nine years of knowing her. Naked vulnerability. I didn't know what to think; she had always been in rigid control of her life, never made a mistake, according to her, and now this. I needed to hear her tell the truth; couldn't wait for another moment, my mind running through the possibilities, Natalie having an affair being first on the list. I truly didn't believe that she could contain herself much longer. Even more worrisome than having an affair: I expected her to say she'd made a huge mistake marrying me, wanted a quickie divorce. At least we're in the right place, I thought with a degree of resentment that brought me up short.

I tried to keep my voice calm, even as I started to come apart, myself. "Tell me, Natalie. Just tell me."

She buried her face deeper onto my chest. "I'm pregnant, Steven." She was sobbing uncontrollably now, her cries reverberating off my ribs. I was shocked speechless, completely terrified by the sudden prospect of parenthood, then, after a few moments of reflection, overjoyed. Thrilled beyond belief. A baby! We were pregnant! Married less than seventy-two hours and we were pregnant. Boy, was I stunned. Stunned didn't even begin to cover it. Natalie had always been obsessive about her birth control regimen. Being an OB doc, she had an endless supply of samples, and her colleagues rendered her excellent care; saw to it that all of her needs were met on a moment's notice.

I can't fully describe the maelstrom of emotions I felt that morning: elation, followed by intense worry for Natalie's welfare, fear of the unknown, unbelievable pride, and finally, ultimately, love. Love for my wife, and an almost unbearable, all-encompassing love for the little one growing beside me. Lost as I was in the happiest moment of my life, I *had* to know how this miracle could have happened. I held her at arm's length, my heart filled with contentment. "But, I thought you . . ." It was impossible to control my voice with the feelings swirling around inside, I'd hoped Natalie would hear only joy, not the tight clench of fear that I felt in my chest.

She shook harder, refused to meet my gaze. "I *did*, Steven." She sounded defensive, ashamed, I needed to nip that in the bud. I was elated. Her shoulders shook. "Sandra gave me a sample." She blew her nose on a tissue. "A new low-dose estrogen pill." She sniffled, her voice choked and barely audible. "I'm so sorry, Steven. I don't understand . . ." I held her closer; she trembled as if she had just been pulled from a frozen pond. "All our plans. My practice. Both just starting out." I couldn't believe what I was hearing; she was concerned about her *job?* Sure, we both loved our careers, but all I could think about was our son or daughter, how I wanted to be sure Nat's pregnancy was going to go smoothly, that our baby would be healthy. I was still ecstatic about the wonderful news. I was shocked by Natalie's words, again, for the second time in less than a minute. "Oh, God, I'm so sorry, Steven." She looked at me with an expression that I'll never forget; as if she were mortified by her stupidity, in a hurry to rectify her mistake as soon as possible. "I just found out before the wedding, honey." She finally met my eyes, her expression earnest and back in control. "I can have an . . ."

I put a finger to her lips, didn't want to hear her speak that word about my child, about *our* child. I wasn't opposed to abortion, had no religious or moral problem with it, truly believed that it was up to the woman and her partner, if he was still in the picture. But I was *adamantly* opposed in this situation. Never in a billion years would I even consider it. "How could you even think that about our baby, Natalie? I thought you loved me. Thought you wanted to have children with me."

She pulled away from me, tears dried in the time it took to speak my peace, her voice once again in control. "Later, Steven. After."

I let my arm drift downward from her shoulder, sensed the direction of this discussion by the firm set of her lips, the intense tone of her voice. "After what? After we have a million in the bank? You already have that. After you're department chairperson? After we have a bigger house? We have more that we need already." I didn't believe she was serious, couldn't accept it for a second. True, she hadn't mentioned wanting a family while we were dating, not specifically, but I'd seen her with kids at ER Christmas parties; she seemed totally at ease with them, eager to interact on their level. I realized, of course, that having children so early could put an enormous strain on a relationship, that even after five years of marriage a new kid was a huge adjustment; still, we loved each other, were financially secure beyond our wildest imaginations, and had a lovely home near the best schools in Orange County. I simply didn't see the problem. Not at all.

She stood and faced me, arms crossed, expression set. "This isn't only about you, Steven. It's my life, too. My body."

I stood toe-to-toe with her, didn't want an all-out battle this early in our marriage, but felt strongly that I had to do what I could to get her off this dangerous course. "I know it is, Natalie, but it's my child, *our baby* you're talking about flushing away." I laid a hand on her shoulder. "Think about what you're saying to me, Natalie. Take a minute to consider how I feel."

She shook free of my grasp. "I *have* thought about it, Steven. I've known for over a week. And I've decided it's too soon for us." She saw the stark flicker of outrage in my eyes, regrouped quickly; rested a gentle palm on my cheek. "We have to get to know each other first, see if we even *want* children." She could see in my set expression that I would not be easily dissuaded, not about this and not at this time of my life. If I wasn't ready to have babies at this precise moment, and the reality was still just sinking in, I was more than ready for the next stage of my life. Mom's death had exposed the tenuous nature of life in the most direct way imaginable. I found myself thinking of the future more and more these days. Natalie instantly misread my open expression for acquiescence, pressed her perceived advantage. "I know deep down you agree, honey. It's just not the right time."

I took a few measured breaths, composed my thoughts to avoid overreacting. "It's never the right time, Natalie. Ask any married couple." I anticipated her objection before she could voice it; we'd been over this ground many times in our dating relationship. "Except the infertility couples, of course, they're an obvious exception. The rest of the married people I know? They weren't ready at all, not financially, not emotionally, most of them, but you know what, Natalie?" She raised a finger to object, I hurried on, anxious to make my point. "They all say that it changes their lives. Completely. Gives their relationship new strength, a new purpose."

She backed away, set her feet a few inches farther away from mine. "Exactly, Steven. *Everything* changes. Nothing is ever the same." Her tone was challenging, louder than she needed it to be in the quiet of our room. "Ever again." She seemed more than ready to fight, tears and fears forgotten now. "I'm afraid, Steven. Afraid that it will be the end of us."

I knew her misgivings, could understand her hesitancy; still, there was no way I'd yield on this point. "It won't unless you let it, Natalie. Unless we let it change the way we feel about each other." I wondered at the time how much this was about us and how much it was about Natalie. Wondered if she was really as selfish as she sounded that morning. I took hold of her shoulders. "Look me right in the eye and tell me this is not about you. Not about your job, your precious body image, Natalie."

I was instantly worried that I'd gone too far; she let her gaze fall, seemed ready to break down again. Her voice came from a place I'd only heard from a time or two before; she was almost childlike, withdrawn, not at all the confident, occasionally over-bearing woman I'd come to know. "I'm just so worried, Steven." She looked up again, her eyes glistening with tears. "No one's just loved me for who I am, who I want to be." She swiped an arm across her eyes. "My whole life I've had to be perfect, to be everybody's dream-date. The perfect daughter." Took a hitching breath. "The perfect doctor, the perfect lover, perfect wife." She laughed derisively, her gaze raking my face. "Look how that worked out, Steven. Daddy won't even come to my wedding. Henry kicked me out in less time than it takes to finish medical school." She blew her nose on a wadded-up hankie, crossed her arms and took a step closer. "I try so hard to make people happy,

I try to be the best, try to be perfect and it's never good enough." She shook her head bitterly. "Everybody leaves me, Steven." She took my face in her hands; I was as chilled by her words as by her icy grip. "Don't you see, Steven, I'm terrified that you'll leave me. Find someone younger, without all my baggage. Afraid you'll just leave."

She wasn't making any sense. She had to know how much I valued her, how much I needed her. I'd never seen her act this way, never imagined such deep-seated insecurity was in her makeup at all. I had to put a stop to this fight; too much was at stake, not the least of which was Natalie's well being, our marriage. Our baby. I stepped forward and held her in my arms. "I married you because of who you are, Natalie. I've loved you since medical school, you know that." I held her chin, kissed her cheek. "I didn't marry you for your looks, your job, your money, *or* your house. I wanted *you* and I want you to live with me until I die." I held her gaze, kissed her lips. "Maybe it is too early for us to have kids. That's what everybody tells young couples." I stroked her hair. "But who cares what everybody else says." I held her tighter. "I want you to want our baby too. I want you to be a hundred percent behind me in this, otherwise, I don't know if we can be together, Natalie." She looked into my eyes; searching for a way out of this dilemma, saw only my absolute resolve. I watched for a few moments, saw her fear dissolve slowly into acceptance. "You have to know this is right for us, honey."

She laid her head back on my chest, gave a deep sigh. "I just need to know that you won't leave, Steven. I couldn't take that."

I leaned down and put my face against her belly, imagined that I felt the first stirring of our new life together. I gently kissed her there, said, "We're in this together, Natalie. Forever. All three of us."

Chapter 16

SIX MONTHS LATER

I got home late after a truly boring shift in the ER, the first time I can remember that I'd wanted to be home, rather than at work. The entire day had felt slow and disjointed; the whole Department seemed to have come down with a case of terminal ennui. It had gotten so bad that around five-thirty I'd gone out to the nurse's station, taken the first case off the top. Which led directly to my cut fingers.

Natalie, of course, noticed them as soon as I came in the door, her voice filled with concern. "Steven, what happened to your hand? Come here. Let me look at it." Natalie met me in the foyer, took me by the elbow, a worried look on her face as we made our way to the kitchen. Barbara Manning had bandaged my thumb and forefinger with a huge stockinet dressing and about five yards of gauze; I looked like I'd had an amputated thumb reattached.

It was throbbing like a son of a bitch, felt like it had been run over. "It's nothing, honey. Really." I opened the fridge and took out a bottle of juice. "I cut it at work. Nothing to worry about."

She started laughing and I knew without asking that Barbara had finked me out. She had spilled the whole stupid story: a fifty-something CPA had been my one and only case, the first one on the pile. Serves me right for getting so restless, I thought, as my thumb pulsated in rhythm with my heart. What a case it was. Seems as if the CPA had a hot date with a twenty-two-year-old waitress from the Five Crowns in Corona Del Mar. Things progressed as they will on a date, and our patient had a big problem. His little friend stayed little. Despite what he described as "furious attention" from his lady friend. So, how did this genius solve his problem? By jamming two *huge* solid gold wedding bands over his penis. Seems the guy knew just enough about hydraulics to save his date. Too bad he didn't know as much about anatomy. This Low Rent Lord of The Rings got the blood pumping in the right direction, nature took its course, and a few minutes later, he had a nice erection. Everybody was happy in Corona Del Mar. Problem was, his wedding bands were too tight, so the blood had nowhere to go and he was left with a painful, dark-purple Louisville Slugger throbbing away in his pants.

Which is where I came in. Two hours and about a thousand turns of our ring cutter later, he was free. So how did I cut my fingers? They weren't actually cut, just macerated, bruised, and skinned. From turning that freakin' little wheel so many damned times. Think of a scaled-down can opener, with a diamond-studded wheel in place of the blade, a winged handle that cranks the wheel, and you have the picture. Now imagine yours truly turning and turning that little handle for two hours straight, until that jackass patient of mine was relieved of his obnoxious, massive, stupid boner.

And Natalie was absolutely no help at all. The bitch. "Barbara told me he's going to be good as new." She put an arm around me and nuzzled my cheek, her hand around my bicep, laughing like an idiot. "Thanks to you. My big, strong, cock-saving hero."

I took a gulp of my juice, eyed her suspiciously. "You're in a good mood."

"What's that supposed to mean? I'm always in a good mood." She slapped me on the chest, a smile spreading across her face. "Well, almost all the time." She placed my right palm on her stomach, beaming with pride. "That is if Tyler will stop jumping around in there."

Oh, my God, not with the Tyler nonsense again, I thought. "Tyler? You're not serious, are you Nat?"

She took a minute to think it over, eyes scrunched in concentration. "Actually, I've thought of some more names since the amniocentesis." She pinched my lips together, stifled my outburst with a laugh. "Don't give me any crap, Steven. I've been looking through baby books waiting for you to come home."

She led me to the den, sat beside me on the sofa. "How about Reggie?"

I took another sip of juice. "Fine if he's going to be six ten and a power forward at Duke." She reached over and pinched my ass. "Next."

She gave me an evil look, stole some of my juice. "What about Zander?"

I almost choked on my drink. Took a quick look at her and she couldn't contain her laugh; her head on her knees, shaking the couch. "You idiot. Take all day to think up that clunker, did you?"

She took my glass and walked toward the kitchen, motioned for me to follow. "Come on Steven, we're late."

Damn, I'd forgotten. Tonight was Tuesday. Lamaze Night. I was exhausted from saving The Penis That Ate Orange County; the last thing I wanted was to drive back to Irvine for a class. But, I reminded myself, I was the one who practically talked Natalie into having our child, so it was the least I could do. I heaved a tiny sigh as my thumb throbbed like a locomotive. "Of course, our Lamaze class."

She shrugged into a sweater, pulled it taut over her sleek, swollen belly. She looked prettier than ever, womanly, complete.

Gave me a shake of her head. "You forgot, didn't you, honey?" She grabbed her purse from the center island, walked with me to the foyer. "If you're tired, I can just go by myself."

I held the door as we walked into the garage. "What, and let one of those horny husbands pick you up? Not on your life. I've seen the way they look at you." I opened the door to her Mercedes, helped her with the lap belt. "While we're doing the *hee, hee, hee*, those horn-dogs are checking you out, doing the *uhm, uhm, uhm.*

I climbed into my seat and started the car. Adjusted the mirrors and dialed in some Brahms. Natalie reached over and stroked my cheek. "That's very sweet of you, Steven. Thank you."

I backed into our cul de sac and headed toward MacArthur and the Five. "Thank me for what. I'm just trying to be a good daddy is all."

She laid her head on my shoulder. "And you will be. I can tell. But I'm talking about the way you said I'm still attractive." She kissed my cheek. "You're always so sweet. So patient."

We passed the Newport Center, looming off to our left; it was starting to spit a little rain; the TV guy had predicted a whole half-inch overnight, what passed for a vicious winter storm in Southern California. I flipped on the wipers and kissed her hair. "You know I love you. Besides, you *are* sexy, Nat. Sexy as hell."

She turned on the heater, all the way to eighty. I started to roast, but said nothing, as she was frequently cold, even as I was sweltering. She gave me a frown. "Even with this huge belly?"

I put my right hand over our son. "What belly? What could he weigh, four, five pounds, max?" I turned right onto the southbound Five; the traffic was miserable, much worse than usual even with only a drop or two of rain on the road. California drivers were the worst when it came to weather. They still drove seventy, eighty miles an hour with no space between their cars. God, I'd seen some horrific wrecks on nights like this. I took my eyes off the road as we came to a complete stop, taillights stretching south to infinity. Looked at Natalie's silhouette in the darkened car. "And look at you, Nat. You've gained what, about twelve pounds?"

I knew she was inordinately proud of her figure. You simply couldn't tell she was pregnant from the back. She exercised constantly; this was going to be one lean and mean baby boy, I thought. She reclined her chair, touched her belly again and smiled broadly, the expression of the truly content. "I guess it doesn't matter, does it, Steven?" She shifted her weight slightly and looked me full in the face as I merged into the fast lane. "As long as Zachary is healthy."

"You're shitting me, right?" I was overjoyed. I slammed on the brakes as the moron in front of us braked suddenly for no reason, reflexively protecting Natalie from sliding forward with an arm around her belly. "You like Zachary, too? No Tyler or what was that other one you sprung on me at home? Zaster?"

She pulled my hand to her lips, kissed my palm. "Silly, I never liked those names. I was just having fun with you." I swerved around the idiot in front of me, merged over two lanes as I saw our exit, Bake Parkway, coming up on the right. "You tried to hide it, but I could tell. It's like I wanted to name him Percy or something." I eased down to fifty and hit the exit. She turned up the music, a wonderful piano solo filling the car. I felt as if God Himself were playing for us. "I liked the sound of Zachary Adler from the moment you said it." She shifted my hand farther to the right, just as Zachary let loose a huge kick. "Feel that, honey? Zachary's happy too. I think he likes his name as much as we do."

Natalie was right. That night in Lake Forest was one of the happiest in my life. Natalie seemed completely at peace, content as I'd ever seen her. Our baby was vigorous and active; we were healthy and very comfortable financially. I couldn't count all of my blessings, they were so numerous, so meaningful. My wife looked over at me in the reflected light of the streetlights, and I understood what it meant to be fulfilled: our little son happily kicking, anxious to start his life with us, a family who was ready to shower him with love. And two parents more in love than ever, ready to sacrifice anything to make sure he was safe.

We parked at the community center, behind a huge Chevrolet dealer hard beside the Five freeway. I came around the front and helped Natalie from her seat. She rushed into my arms and gave me a long, deep kiss. A minute or two later, I broke away with a look of genuine surprise on my face, leaned over to steady her footing on the rainy sidewalk. "Thanks, honey. What'd I do to deserve that?"

She linked her arm in mine and led me down the path to the open glass door. We could hear the "heeing and hooing" from ten feet away. "You talked me into the best decision I've ever made." She gave me a look filled with the gratitude of the truly blessed. I fell in love with her all over again. She lowered her voice as we walked hand in hand up the slick sidewalk. "Forgive me?"

I gave her a light kiss on the lips. "Forgive you for what? I knew all along you'd do the right thing. I knew what kind of woman I married."

Chapter 17

FOUR MONTHS LATER

Zachary was born early on a Tuesday, December fifteenth. Four-fourteen in the morning early. Stands to reason, his mom and dad were both morning people, too. Natalie woke me at two o'clock, said, "Either I have to pee really, really bad, or it's time." I raced around our room, throwing clothes onto the bed, searching in vain for my shoes, looking for my camera in the bathroom. Natalie was calm and still as a yogi. She slipped into a pair of sandals, changed from her nightgown into a pair of scrubs that she had laid out the previous night, grabbed her overnighter, and was waiting in the foyer, anxious smile in place, a couple of minutes later.

I, on the other hand, was still a mess. Shirttail flapping, mismatched socks and hair that looked as if I'd been electrocuted.

We arrived less than ten minutes later at Hoag. Sandra Wilson was there; Alan Nachman was as well. I was surprised to see him, as he'd just left Irvine a month earlier for private practice. I greeted him warmly, and he responded with characteristic modesty; "Sandra asked me to come in. I wasn't on call, but thought, what the hell?"

I shook his hand, felt real gratitude for his sacrifice. I knew his wife was pregnant too; he looked like he'd not slept in a month. "Thank you, Alan. This means everything to Natalie and me. You're a true friend."

He took over Natalie's wheelchair from the orderly and hustled her into the elevator, bound for the third-floor delivery suite. Shook his head dismissively. "You can thank me later." An impatient Sandra gave him the twirling-finger, hustle-up sign, and they disappeared silently behind the closing doors.

I stepped off the elevator a few minutes later into chaos: the delivery room was blaring Guns and Roses, Nachman's favorite. I wasn't sure I wanted Zachary to be born into a world that loud, didn't want him to be hyper from the get go, didn't want him to turn out to be another Axel Rose or Slash, that was for sure. I prevailed upon Nachman to use another tape; he picked a musty oldie from the sixties, Herb Alpert and the Tijuana Brass. Nachman rolled his eyes as they transferred Natalie to the bed, gave me a good-natured dose of sarcasm. "Slow enough for you, Gramps?" He hooked her up to the EKG monitor. "Sorry I don't have any Lawrence Welk tapes. They were all buried with my great-grandfather."

I was glad for the insult, it took my mind off what was happening. "Yeah, yeah, yeah. Just do your damn job, Alan. That's all I ask."

The next forty-five minutes passed in a blur of screams, agonizing pushes, sweat, and tears, culminating in the appearance of our pink-faced, dark-haired, bawling, baby boy. Sandra let me cut the cord. I was so nervous that I almost cut above the top clamp instead of *between* the two Kellys. A rookie mistake I would have berated an intern for all the way until the end of his shift. Sandra was cool about it, though; she just guided my hand to the proper position, made it look like she wasn't even helping me. Natalie caught it, though; she gave me a secret smile and a look of complete happiness I hadn't seen since we'd gotten engaged in Tiffany's.

A minute or two later, I went to Natalie while the nurses cleaned and checked Zachary. He had an APGAR score of nine/ten, a sign that his oxygenation and neurological parameters were perfect. I said a silent prayer of thanks as Natalie lifted her head to check on the pediatrician's progress across the room. I leaned down and whispered, "Are you all right, honey?" She looked exhausted; I took a sterile towel from Alan's stand and mopped her brow. Nachman hadn't had time to insert an epidural catheter for pain control since Natalie was already dilated to nine centimeters when we hit the delivery suite, a fact that amazed Sandra Wilson, who kept going on about prime IP's never coming in at more than five centimeters dilation, taking forever to deliver. A familiar refrain at the Adler household; Natalie often played the same tune. Said, "*They always come in at two in the frigging morning, too.*" I guess we proved that adage as well, I thought with a smile.

She turned her pale, drawn face to mine, answered my question through pursed lips. "Not too bad."

She was still breathing like a fighter finishing the twelfth round, face white as the ceiling tiles. I glanced down at Sandra, who was bent to her work, repairing what she'd mumbled was a "*Grade I episiotomy.*" I didn't even want to think about how much those sutures would hurt Natalie. With or without anesthesia. At that moment, I had a brand new appreciation for motherhood and all of its painful sacrifices.

She laid her head on the pillow, too worn out to move, her voice a hoarse whisper. "Is he okay, Steven?" More accelerated breathing from Natalie. I timed her respiratory rate at thirty-two, a little alarming in a healthy young woman. I shot a look at Nachman, who was clearly unconcerned, whistling along with *Tijuana Taxi* as he was administering a dose of IV Morphine.

While Nachman was pushing the Morphine., the circulating nurse took Zachary from the pediatrician, an elderly woman with kind eyes and a slight intention tremor, named Mary Fox, walked over to the head of the bed and handed me our son. He was swaddled in a blue sheet, weighed as much as a loaf of bread, and was barely big enough to span the length of my forearm. He had a swirling cap of black hair plastered to his skull, blue eyes like most newborns, and the pinkest cheeks I'd seen this side of a Disney cartoon. I cradled him carefully as Natalie raised her head for a closer look, her eyes bearing a mother's unique combination of concern, refuge, and love. I leaned closer so she wouldn't have to strain, Zachary's head nesting perfectly in my palm.

I looked down at that beautiful face, felt his breath on my hand, and I was instantly, completely in love. Natalie looked at me with tears streaming down her face, her pain a thing of the past. "He's really ours, isn't he, Steven? Look at him. Our perfect Zachary." I leaned closer and she gave Zachary his first kiss, her breath light as a promise on our boy. She met my gaze, smiled. "Our son."

I kissed my wife's pale blue, trembling lips and handed her our precious son. I stood with tears in my eyes and watched with amazement the bonding of mother and child as her eyes met Zachary's for the first time. All of my anxiety and earth-bound limitations were gone in that instant, as I knew with certainty that I had just glimpsed the true meaning of life.

The first month of Zachary's life was a whirlwind of feedings, diaper changes, naps, cries, laughs, and awe. I never knew how much I'd needed this. Never knew how much it would change me. Parenthood had been a nearly unfathomable concept to me, like being an astronaut or a big- league baseball player, something we all wanted to do but knew nothing about. I had an idea of what it entailed; I saw parents and kids at work every day, of course. Still, until Natalie told me the news on our honeymoon, it hadn't become real to me. Now that we'd been home as a family, being Zachary's dad was everything to me.

Natalie breast-fed, so during the first month feedings were her special time with our son. I got up every four hours, just wanted to help out: fetch and change his diapers, get water or juice for Nat; best of all, play with Zachary until he fell asleep. A week after we brought Zachary home, I was gorked out of my mind with sleep deprivation, but as with most parents of newborns, I fought my way through it. Did whatever needed doing. Even kept working, albeit on a reduced two-shift-a-week schedule.

Three or four weeks after we'd brought Zach home, Wednesday, three o'clock in the morning, he was especially fussy and Natalie was on the verge of collapse. I couldn't calm him with my usual routine of coos, stories and gentle rocking, so I decided to take him on a tour of the house while he fussed and fretted on my shoulder. He cried all the way to the kitchen, screamed while I took him down the hallway and seemed on the verge of apoplexy in his nursery. I was out of ideas, ready to join Zachary in his abject misery. Wanted nothing more at that moment than to cry hysterically, suck my thumb until I slept, such was the depth of my fatigue. I'd checked his diaper, dry as a bone. He had let out a burp that would have blown out a grass fire just a few minutes before, so I was stumped. Mystified and exhausted. Completely out of tricks, I decided to rock him in his favorite chair. One more time. He was still screaming at the top of his lungs, his little face red as my car. More to calm myself than to soothe Zachary, I started singing one of my favorite songs, John Lennon's *Imagine*. God how I miss that man, I thought, as I rocked my son and sang his haunting, beautiful lyrics: *"Imagine all the people living for today . . . Imagine all the people . . . Sharing all the world . . . You may say I'm a dreamer, but I'm not the only one, I hope some day you'll join us, And the world will live as one."*

I looked down at my son: his eyes were wide open; he lay in my arms, still as fog on a lake. I knew at his age that he couldn't focus completely on my face, but even in the shadowed nursery, I saw something in Zachary's eyes. Absolute trust, serenity, and love. We fell asleep together in that rocking chair, the house quiet and warm. Natalie told me later that she came looking for me around five, said her breasts were engorged and she'd wondered why Zach wasn't crying. Told me she watched us for a long moment, overcome with emotion. Said she crept back to our room quietly as she could, got into her robe and came back to the nursery with the video and still cameras.

I still have that precious memory, kept in a safe place, away from all the cares and worries I've had all of these many long years.

The photo, framed in silver, rests in a place of honor on my desk. I look at it often, especially in the dark times, and think of Zachary and me, safe and sound in his room, bonded from the very beginning, destined to be together forever.

Part III

"Where there is great love there are always miracles."
—Willa Cather

Chapter 18

FIVE YEARS LATER

September 13th, the first day of school. Zachary had dragged Natalie and me all over Newport trying to find just the right backpack, school supplies, and, of course, Nikes. Running shoes like his daddy's. I couldn't believe how much kids carried to school these days; fill his backpack with oxygen canisters and Zach could lead me all the way up Everest.

The past five years had been ones of discovery for Natalie and me. We learned more every day from our son than we'd ever learned in all the years of college or medical school. He had taught us patience, fair play, and, most importantly, loyalty. There were several kids in our neighborhood, at least two dozen, and we'd met them all at one time or another. Zach was far more gregarious than I; he put his mom to shame as well, coming home from preschool with another pal almost every week. The Adler home on Bayside Place was *the* happening spot for sleepovers.

As every parent does, I took this occasion of his leaving the nest to reflect on Zachary's milestones. First word: hamburger, believe it or not. Natalie was crushed. I was elated; knew we had a polysyllabic genius on our hand, was ready to sign him up for early enrollment at Stanford. We were prejudiced, of course, but Zachary always seemed a little ahead of the curve. Walked and talked at nine months, he started to memorize his favorite book, *The Cat in the Hat* at eighteen months.

I buckled him into the car seat, gave him a thumbs-up and we were off to the Country Day School just off Pacific Coast Highway, overlooking Newport Harbor. The school had a great reputation: ninety-percent of its graduates finished college. Who kept track of all these kids? I asked myself when we signed him up. The place had been in business since the early Fifties; it must have had several thousand pupils in that time. The Day School needed four recommendations from "prominent members of the community." We chose Natalie's colleague Sandra Wilson, my friend Rick Lamb, who was now the busiest plastic surgeon in Orange County, Alan Nachman and, surprisingly, to me at least, Natalie's ex, the Porsche Guy, who was gracious enough to lend his influence. I made a note to myself after hearing that to go around to his dealership after dropping Zach off. It was time for me to meet the famous Mr. Henry Marx to offer my thanks. And to check him out.

We arrived at the circular drive entrance to Zach's school at five till eight. Zachary was squirming in his seat, ready to climb out of the car. He caught my eye in the rear view mirror. "Dad?"

I found a spot near the far edge of the parking lot and killed the engine. "Yes, son."

I caught another glimpse of him in my rear view mirror. Now that we'd stopped at his school, the bravado I'd seen in his eyes had started to slip. His voice cracked, I could see the glint of tears in his eyes. "Do I have to go? I don't want to." He couldn't hide his terror any longer. Try as he might to put up a brave front, he was crumbling. "Can't I just stay home with you? Until

Mommy finishes delivering babies?" He was breaking my heart. A large part of me wanted to give in, even as I knew that would be the worst thing for him in the long run. He was into some serious pleading now, brow furrowed, lips tight. "Please, Dad?"

I closed my door and walked around to the back to unhook his seat belt. Leaned in to pick him up, my voice filled with forced reassurance, even as the lump grew in my throat. "You can do it, champ." I slipped the buckle off and reached my arms out to help him out of his car seat. "Remember, we talked about it?" He stayed put, arms crossed over his chest. "Jamie McDonald is going to be in your class. You like Jamie, don't you?" Jamie lived two doors down, and the two were inseparable. Jamie, a really cute redheaded boy, was like a second son to us. I put my arms out again; Zachary reluctantly squirmed down from his seat. After a moment or two of stubbornness on his part, frustration on mine, he looked over my shoulder and saw Jamie in the Mercedes next to us and decided all at once to be brave. I nodded vigorously, relieved, even if it *was* peer pressure making him feel more confident. Gave him a reassuring nod. "That's it, buddy." I took his hand and closed the door. His face looked a little brighter; he'd stemmed the flow of tears with a backhand swipe of his long-sleeved tee. "See, I told you Jamie'd be here."

Zachary took his time getting out of the car, clearly reluctant to make this crucial first step. He watched Jamie and his mom climb the ramp toward the classrooms and gave me a hurt look, sad to be left behind by his friend. "You sure I have to do this, Dad? Why can't I just stay home? Learn stuff there?"

I had to admit to some serious second thoughts of my own that morning. Here was my son, barely five, already leaving home to spend five hours a day with a bunch of strangers. How could this be? He was sleeping on my chest; so tiny he barely reached my waist as he snoozed just a week or two ago. We were running with the ducks at the Back Bay only yesterday, Zach in his yellow coveralls, Natalie and I chasing him all over the dunes, exhausted and happier than we had a right to be, while his little boy's giggle scared all the birds away.

He had just gone to a sleepover at Pops', whom he absolutely adored, spent the whole weekend with my dad, came back home grubby and outrageously spoiled. Zachary called him Papa, came back all excited with tales of Papa's tools and his new electric golf cart. Told Natalie and me that Pops had driven him "All the way to downtown" in the cart and that they had gone "A hundred miles a hour." My son was too young to go to school. I wasn't ready for this to happen. I came so close to taking him home that Monday morning. Consequences be damned, I thought. He's too young, and I'm not ready for this either.

I was jolted out of my reminiscence by the clanging of the loudest school bell I'd ever heard. It sounded like an air-raid siren in the quiet of a September morning.

Afraid we'd be late on his first day, I took him firmly by the hand and went in search of Room Twelve, his home for the next year. Kept my voice light. "Come on, buddy. It'll be fun. You'll see."

He wasn't going to be convinced by that; one look at his stubborn five-year-old face told me that. He went into the stall routine. One I'd used on more than one occasion with my own dad; literally dug his heels into the gravel walk. "Did you like school, Dad? Did Mommy like school?"

I had to practically pull him, but a minute or two later, we'd reached the top of the ramp. Maybe if I could just keep him talking, I thought, we'd be home free. I looked along the corridor of classrooms, we'd entered the hallway at Room Ten, so Zach's had to be two doors down, toward the gym. I smiled down at my son, who was clearly expecting an answer to this most important question. I sensed that it was all or nothing time. If I said no, we'd be in a foot race for the car; if I said yes, it would open up yet another avenue of questions. I loved my son, he was my whole world, but he absolutely had Natalie's argumentative personality. I woke up in a cold sweat at night: visions of my son as a lawyer. Natalie caught me screaming last week after that dream, called me an idiot for worrying so much, reminded me that the law was an honorable profession, too. Still, my son an attorney? I couldn't see it. Politician, used car salesman, grifter, maybe.

We stopped at the entrance of "Kindergarten Room Number Twelve. Miss Hoover's Room," proudly signified on carefully hand-lettered blue card-stock paper taped to the door. I looked down at my son, gave him a confidence-building smile, even as I felt my heart sinking like a stone. "Look, buddy, we're here."

He tugged on my sleeve. "But, Dad. You didn't answer."

I could see the other kids circling the room, trying to find their assigned desks, didn't want Zach to feel conspicuous if he were to come in too late. I knelt on the concrete and stared directly into his eyes. "Yes, Zach. I loved school and your mom?" He nodded solemnly; even at his age, he knew who had the brains in our family, Mom. "She was the best. In every grade."

That seemed to satisfy him. He took my hand, marched me into the classroom, directly to Miss Hoover, a kind-looking sandy blonde in her early twenties. We stopped at her desk. Zachary extended his hand and said, "Hi, Miss Hoover. I'm Zachary and this is my dad, Dr. Adler." He shook her hand gravely, like an ambassador from another world, one where civility and manners still counted for something. I was so proud of my son at that moment; I couldn't concentrate enough to respond. Zachary bailed me out, pointed a tiny index finger at me. "He's a emergency doctor."

Miss Hoover bent slightly at the waist and smiled at Zach. "Nice to meet you, Zachary Adler." She straightened and gave me a wink, held out her hand. "And you, too, Dr. Adler." She surveyed her class of fifteen wiggling five-year-olds, still circling their desks, making a game of it now, screaming every time one of them made a mistake and took the wrong desk. I could see an idea forming in her eyes."So, do you work at Hoag?"

I watched my son calmly walk the rows of desks until he came to his, marked in big block letters on a white piece of paper. He stowed his backpack under the desk and sat down, ready for business. Gave a high-five to his buddy Jamie McDonald, sitting directly across the aisle. I said a silent thanks to the administrator for working that one out. Jamie was scheduled to be in Room Eight. I had to also thank my Type Triple-A, compulsive wife for ferreting out the information and making the arrangements. I returned my attention to Miss Hoover, who stood next to me with an expectant look. "No, I work at UCI."

She gave me a radiant smile. "Even better." She motioned for her class to sit down and turned to me. "How about a field trip later this year? I'm sure the children would be fascinated."

I would have thought it would be better to wait until they were older, but she looked so enthusiastic and I knew that Zachary would love to show off his dad's "office," so I nodded. "Call me and I'll make it happen."

She clapped me on the shoulder and ushered me toward the door. Guess it's time for me to go, I thought, with a jolt of panic. I took my time getting to the door, sneaked a quick peek at Zachary, who was deep in conversation with Jamie, oblivious to my leave-taking. Kids, I thought, they always take it better than their folks.

I had four and a half hours to kill, and Natalie wasn't due home until six at the earliest. I didn't feel like going to the beach, so I decided to pay a visit to Newport Motors. It was time to meet the Porsche guy, AKA Gruff Voice, in person. If I took it easy on him, maybe he'd give me a good deal on a new 911.

Ten minutes later I pulled Natalie's Mercedes onto the lot, just off busy PCH, near the Back Bay, about five miles from our house. I parked in the visitors lot and walked along the rows of shiny new 1992 Porsche Carreras. I got to the second one in line, a gorgeous gunmetal gray coupe, when a salesman caught my eye. He approached, intent as a cruise missile, closing in on me before I could duck back to the Mercedes. Held out a hand. "Morning. In the market for a new 911? Gonna trade the Benz?" He shook my hand. "Tom Wilkes." Pointed to the gleaming car. "Give you a good deal on this one."

I was waiting for him to say, "What's it gonna take to get you home in this little baby?" next. I shook my head, admiring his obvious sales talent, intrigued by this hot car, despite my very different mission. Shook his hand. "Steven Adler. Nice to meet you, Tom." It was hard for me to say no; I was practically drooling over the beautiful sports car. "No, thanks. Just looking."

He was undaunted, must have seen the lust in my eyes. "This one here's Anthracite Gray. Saddle full-leather interior. Two hundred thirty horse." He ran a hand down the car's flared rear fender: ardent lover stroking his hot girlfriend's ass. "Zero to sixty in five point two. A hundred and fifty top speed. Drives like sex-on-wheels, I promise you that."

Despite my best intentions, he had me thinking. Mine *was* nineteen years old; not bad for a Porsche, as their engines were bulletproof if properly maintained; besides it *had* been years since I'd splurged on anything, and we weren't exactly hurting for money. I knew with certainty that five more minutes with this guy and I'd be running to the car for my checkbook. With a last, longing look at the coupe I summoned the last of my sales resistance and shook my head. "Actually, I came here to meet Mr. Marx."

The poor guy was crushed. He withdrew his hand, wiped his fingerprints from the polished gray fender and took a deep breath. "You a friend of his, Steven?"

Not exactly, I thought with a wicked inner laugh. "He's a friend of my wife. Dr. Bogner."

That got his attention. He'd clearly been with the dealership long enough to know a little about their divorce. Who knew what this guy'd heard? I thought. He gave me a new, frankly calculating look; intrigued by this new bit of potential gossip, his easy sale forgotten for now. "No problem, Steve, let me go get him." I hated being called Steve. Especially by a stranger. He gave me a quick look, one that practically shouted, *"So you're the other guy. You don't look that great to me."* I'll be right back."

I was left to admire the Porsche. I circled around, checked out the tires, outrageously wide and extremely low profile. Checked out the interior: six speed, high-end stereo, built-in cell phone. Outrageous. Checked out the price. *Sixty-two-thousand?* Christ-on a crutch, I thought. Mine had only cost thirty-five hundred!

Of course it was a pale copy of this beast, still a twenty-fold run-up in price in the last ten years? Yikes!

"Beautiful, isn't she?"

I was so engrossed in the window sticker that I didn't hear him come up. Must be a tag team, I thought. Send in the closer if the first guy strikes out. I turned toward the second stringer and stuck out my hand, "Steven Adler. And you are?"

"Henry Marx." I was nearly speechless. He had a voice like Colonel Klink, straight out of Düsseldorf, not at all like the gruff-voiced "Charles Bronson" I'd talked to when my mom died. Shit, this can't be, I thought, as I gaped open-mouthed. His voice wasn't even in the same ballpark. I took a closer look at him, thought maybe he had a cold, a sinus infection; hell, maybe he'd gotten smacked in the throat, I thought, as my mind started to whirl. This just couldn't be happening. Natalie was very clear that time a week or so after that call, when we had our argument in my apartment. She told me straight up that Henry had broken down and stayed at her place. Told me nothing had happened, that she took pity on him because he was so upset. Marx was staring at me, his smile wearing a little thin. "So, you're Dr. Adler. It's so nice to meet you."

I took his hand, nearly swallowed his fingers with mine. He couldn't have been more than five-six, weighed at most a hundred and thirty. I looked at him closely, barely remembered him from Natalie's first wedding, hadn't even had a chance to talk to him, depressed as I was that she was marrying someone else. Selfish shit that I am, I'd totally ignored him. I had the same impression standing in his lot that I did at the wedding: he looked nothing at all like I'd expected in her ex. Even worse, listening to his voice, there was no doubt about it now, he was *not* Gruff Voice. I had to put these fresh doubts about Natalie aside. Here was this apparently nice gentleman, wasting his time so he could meet me and I was gawking at him as if he were a carnival freak. I forced out a reply, sounded ridiculous even as I voiced it. "I wanted to meet you." I swallowed the bile in my throat. This changed everything. She's lied about it from the start. Without hesitation. Without remorse. "To thank you." I was finding it hard to breathe. "For your recommendation to the Day School." I wondered now about the phone call I'd overheard two nights before the wedding. The one she claimed was to the hospital. I started to wonder about a lot of things. I felt his eyes on me, the weight of his unspoken questions. "You were most kind." She'd been distant, seemed disinterested in sex since the honeymoon. I believed, wanted to buy her explanation that the wedding and reception; then the pregnancy and Zachary exhausted her. I wanted so desperately to believe Natalie, even while my gut was churning. Marx gave a tiny cough; I looked down into his friendly, open face, felt my whole life spinning out of control like the tilt-a-whirl on the Balboa Pier. "Natalie and I are very grateful, sir. I just wanted to let you know."

He took me by the elbow, started to lead me toward his office. "Come, sit down with me. We can have a cup of coffee." He had the kind face of a guidance counselor, the smooth charm of a born salesman. I was ready to throw up my breakfast. He mistook my nausea for sales resistance, pulled a little harder.

I shot my cuff and glanced at my watch. "I'd love to, Mr. Marx." I had to talk to her about this. She has to come clean. Has to tell me the truth, I thought, with real malice. I could hardly focus on his face; my vision seemed to be narrowing as the pressure in my head increased. "But I have an appointment with our accountant at ten." He gave me a genuine-appearing frown. I could see why Natalie still had warm feelings for him; he was nice, unaffected by his vast wealth, a total gentleman.

Funny how life works, I thought, standing there in his lot. I went there hoping to ridicule him, hoping to put the seeds of jealousy I'd felt about him and his fucking gruff voice away for good. Now this. I was facing an open chasm. I'd uncovered a pack of lies. She'd obviously been with someone else. Damn her, she'd probably slept with another guy just before the wedding, too. That's what that call was all about; I knew it deep in my gut.

The one she claimed was to post partum. My mind reeling, I wondered how much more I'd discover. How much more thoroughly she'd destroy my trust.

Marx released my arm, gave me a quizzical look. "Nothing serious, I hope." I hadn't noticed the thin line of sweat on my upper lip, he clearly had. "Nothing like an audit or anything, is it, Steven?" He watched me wipe the sweat from my lip and brow with a hankie, gave me a conspiratorial wink. "Those fucking Nazis from the IRS can be a major pain in the ass, no?"

I could hardly stand still another second. Had a sudden urge to run over to Hoag and have a talk with Natalie. I forced a quick breath, took a second more to look at Marx's concerned face, and willed myself to calm down. I'd have to pick the right time. After I'd had a few hours to go over the sequence again. Make sure I wasn't jumping to conclusions. There was way too much at stake to make a mistake now. I was suddenly aware of his stare as the sun shimmered on the bay to our right, glared off the long, neat row of Carerras. I tried my damndest to focus on his words, even as my mind ripped through Natalie's pack of lies. "No, Mr. Marx, this is just routine tax stuff. Nothing bad."

He gave me a business card from his suit pocket, clapped me on the shoulder. "I hope so, Steven." Gave me a wave as he walked between the last pair of cars, peeled off toward his office. "Say hello to Natalie for me. Give her my best."

I waved in return, walked to my car and sat inside, willing my fingers to work the ignition. I tried my best to salvage a shred of hope regarding this revelation, tried to see the good things about Natalie. Prayed that she would have an honest explanation. Deep down, though, I knew the real truth. I knew she'd lied, what else could it be? Knew in my heart it hadn't been the first time. I wanted to trust her, needed to trust her, but I'd come to know Natalie, really know her, and I had to admit that it probably wouldn't be the last of her lies.

Chapter 19

I drove aimlessly through Newport, trying to formulate a plan, perfectly groomed palm trees marching silently past my windows as I tried to work through my options. I couldn't go home; Maria would be busy supervising the cleaning crew and planning tonight's menu. Besides, I always did my best thinking while driving. Only wished that I'd kept the Porsche; I suddenly felt uncomfortable in Natalie's S Class. I had to keep an eye on the clock; as much as I needed to drive, there was Zachary to think about. He needed me to be there on time to pick him up, and there was no way that I'd disappoint him. Thinking about my son brought the whole situation with Natalie into sharp focus. I'd read all the studies about the effect that divorce had on kids, and although I had no intention of going that route, it still scared the shit out of me. The statistics didn't lie. More than sixty percent of children of divorce were divorced themselves at least once later in life. About fifty percent never finished college and, according to several studies; about seventy five-percent did not achieve the same life and career goals as their peers from intact families. A truly sobering thought. I pictured my small little guy, embarking on his education, advanced for his age, with the world opening in front of him, and it brought me up short. I decided there and then to discuss it with Natalie that night. I knew that I'd always fight for our marriage, try counseling, whatever it took to keep us going. I didn't want Zachary to become a statistic. Ever. So I resolved to keep calm, but get to the bottom of Natalie's behavior tonight. And that's what I intended to do.

I headed back to Newport from the Balboa Peninsula at around twelve-thirty; still thirty minutes to go until I picked up Zach. I had done some serious soul searching in the last two hours and made a promise to myself that I'd keep my problems with Natalie from my son at all costs. Not an easy task to be sure, since Zachary was sensitive like me.

He'd demonstrated an extremely sensitive "kid's radar" on many occasions. Like most children, Zach could tell in an instant if all was well in our home.

I pulled into the parking lot at the Country Day School at ten till one, typically compulsive, predictably early. I wasn't the only one; the car park looked like the used car lot at Fletcher Jones Mercedes. I was parked half a mile from Zach's row of classrooms and decided to take a walk around campus to kill some time.

The school sat on a bluff over the Back Bay, an estuary of Newport Bay that overlooked the Peninsula and Catalina Island off to the northwest. The ten-acre site was one of the most coveted parcels in Orange County and was landscaped like an arboretum; each tree tagged with species identification, common name, and flowering schedule. We were overjoyed when Zachary got his acceptance letter. I kid you not, he ran up the driveway bursting with pride, carrying his first "thick envelope." We were as proud as if he'd been accepted to Stanford Med.

I sat in the shade of a jacaranda and watched the other parents attempt nonchalance; a glance at a watch, a nervous smile, a "Hi, how are you." We were all boiling inside. Couldn't wait to see our kindergartners run out of their rooms.

The bell rang at one and we sprang into action, it looked like a half-off sale at Barneys, a pack of parents rushing toward the door, anxious to catch a glimpse of their five-year-old superstars. Zachary was the last one out. I watched him shake Miss Hoover's hand and give her a little wave as he made his way toward the door. I liked that he was polite, but being the overanxious dad that I was, didn't want him to be a teacher's pet, didn't want the other boys calling him Poindexter or anything.

He saw me sitting under the jacaranda, ran full-speed, and jumped into my arms. "Dad. It was so cool. Miss Hoover? She's so smart. And Jamie? He sits right next to me. And, Dad? You know what?"

I held him tight, feeding off his incredible happiness, the horrible shock of meeting the Porsche Guy evaporating in the warm glow of his excitement. "What's that, son?"

I took his hand and we followed a group of parents and kids down the ramp toward our car. He looked up at me with a look that melted my heart, filled with the wonder of discovery and the confidence born of conquered fear. "We're going on a field trip." He shook free, ran ahead, and beat me to the car by five lengths. "To the beach. Tomorrow. To catch some crabs." He was practically vibrating with enthusiasm. "Isn't that neat, Dad?"

I opened his door and buckled his safety belt. "Cool as can be, Zach. A field trip on your second day, huh?" Adjusted his belt tension. "Things sure have changed since I was in school."

I walked around the back of the car, buckled in and started the car. He met my eyes in the mirror. "Oh, Dad. Not more junk about when you were little. Yuck."

I pulled into line behind about ten other cars and waited my turn to exit onto Newport Boulevard, kept my eyes on his. "What's wrong with that? I thought you liked hearing about the old days."

Zach was waving out his window at Jamie McDonald, two lanes over in the block-long line of cars. "That was millions of years ago, Dad. Who cares about that?"

I caught a glance of his profile in the rearview mirror and shook my head, filled with wonder; he looked like he owned the world, a five-year-old with his whole life in front of him, two parents who adored him, and the prospect of the best education in southern California. All Zachary had to do was try. There are defining moments in life. Incidents that show us that all of our hard work and worry were worth it. The sacrifices were given for a good cause; the risks taken for the right reasons. One look at his face and I knew that I'd tackle my upcoming difficult times with Natalie with a renewed conviction: to protect my son's welfare at all costs.

I had planned to take Zach for a treat after school, thought about a trip to the Balboa Fun Zone, a ride on the ferry, Chucky Cheese's, one of the usual suspects. I had settled on a destination, was about to suggest the Fun Zone when I looked back into the back seat at the intersection of PCH and MacArthur Boulevard, a couple of miles from school. Zachary was sound asleep in his car seat. Tuckered out from his big adventure at the Day School.

Five minutes later, I parked in the garage and managed to hustle him into his room without waking him. Maria almost woke him; she was so excited to ask about his day, I barely stopped her in time with a finger to my lips. She *"oohed and aahed"* over his new clothes, smothered him with silent kisses and helped me put him to bed.

He slept until three, a few minutes after Natalie swept through the door, fresh from surgery.

She gave me a quick kiss on the cheek, waved to Maria, and spun around the kitchen. "Where is he? Is he okay? He didn't have any trouble, did he?"

Maria took over; carried Natalie's handbag to the foyer, took her jacket and sat her down next to me, smiled at Natalie. "Señor Steven. He brought little Zachary home one thirty." She raised a finger to her lips, theatrically imitating my gesture. "He sleeping so long. I check him a few minutes ago." She rested her head on her hands. "Mister Zachary very tired."

Natalie gave me a look; brow furrowed, lips pursed. "He's all right, isn't he, Steven? Should I go wake him?" She bolted out of her chair, took a tentative step toward the hall. "He didn't get hurt on the playground, did he?"

I went to the sink to get a glass of water, turned my back, and stared out at the Pacific, placid and welcoming as a Monet landscape. This was going to be harder than I'd thought. I needed to keep it light until I had a chance to talk to her alone. I took a swallow and turned to face her, forced a smile, kept my voice reassuring. "Of course he's all right, Natalie." I took another sip of water, had to force it down, my thoughts on the encounter with Henry Marx. "He's just tired. Big day and all."

She came over to the window, laid her head on my shoulder. "Our little boy is growing up." She took a sip of my water. "Pretty soon he'll be asking to borrow your car."

I turned away and rinsed the glass, not in the mood for small talk. "Guess so."

She leaned over the sink, craned her neck; caught my eye. "What's wrong with you?"

Not now, I thought. Zach will be up any second. Kept my tone light, tried to concentrate on something pleasant. "Nothing. Why do you ask?"

She hopped up on the counter, trained her gaze on my face. "Like hell. You've been distant since I came home. Hardly looked at me, can't even make eye contact." She crossed her arms over her breasts, ready to attack. "Are you pissed at me, Steven?" I averted my eyes to the backyard. Maria, sensing trouble, had left a few minutes earlier; made herself scarce by pretending to sweep up in the cabana. "Look at me, Steven." Natalie reached for my chin, pulled me to face her. "I come home after a full day in surgery and it's like I'm not even here. Like I'm intruding in my own home."

I kept my voice under tight control, even as I wanted to scream at her. "I said there's nothing wrong, Natalie." I leaned over to kiss her; she immediately backed away, clearly angry now.

"Don't bullshit me, Steven. I can tell when you're mad." She moved a foot away, her butt sliding across the black granite. "God knows I've had enough practice."

There it was, her opening salvo. As much as I wanted to keep this civil, I still needed to have my say with her and if that was the way she wanted to play it. . . .

"Mommy, you're home." Zachary came running into the kitchen, stocking feet skidding to a stop in front of Natalie, arms outstretched, smothering her with kisses as she leaned down to pick him up. He fell into her arms, planted a huge kiss on her lips. "Guess what, Mommy?" He kissed her again. "We learned about the alabet today. I already knowed it, though." He scrunched up his face in a fit of concentration. "ABCDEFG. We learned one plus one." He held up two tiny fingers. Showed us both. "That makes two. We learned how to spell cat. C A T." He took a quick breath; I laughed until I nearly cried. "And we're going to the beach tomorrow. To learn about crabs. They pinch real hard." He pinched Natalie's forearm and giggled. "Like that. And, guess what, Mommy?" His eyes were wide, face aglow. "Miss Hoover is nice." He shot a glance at me. I nodded. "And she's pretty."

Natalie hopped off the counter, set him on his feet and raced Zachary to his room, leaving me in the kitchen with my thoughts, the bitter residue of our spat lingering like smoke from a tire fire. I followed after, watched as she paced him down the hallway, their voices echoing off the tiles. "Last one to Zach's room is a rotten egg."

"Nuh uh! You're rotten." Zachary squealed with delight, a three-year-old in a grown up kindergartner's body.

I could hear Natalie's voice from his room a long hallway away, filled with laughter. "No, Mister Adler. *You* are."

Dinner was a happy hour or two of school anecdotes, Maria's homemade Sonora enchiladas, and laughter. Zachary told us about the pet gerbil in Miss Hoover's room; he giggled his name trough a spray of milk: "Stinky." He informed us that the girl who sat in front of him, Olivia, was "Yucky, but sorta cute." I raised an eyebrow at that one, decided to keep an eye on my son, didn't want him entangled with some kindergarten hussy.

A few minutes after dinner, Zachary announced that he was "Going to my room now." Seems he had some homework. The first day of kindergarten and the kid had homework. We followed him to his room where he sat at his miniature desk, ready for some serious studying.

We sat on his bed, watched him work. I wanted to be helpful, but felt like an intruder, didn't want to interfere with the learning process, knew right then that I had a lot to learn about parenting. I hated to interrupt, but couldn't help myself. "Anything we can do to help, son?"

He stopped his rummaging through the utensil compartment over his desk long enough to turn our way, his voice and manner all business. "I kinda need to be alone."

We looked at each other, nodded, and made a hasty retreat. Natalie took a last look at Zachary, hunched over his desk. "I can take a hint; how about you, Daddy?"

"I'm gone." Put an index finger to my lips. "Must be some sort of secret project."

Zachary heard that one. He looked up from his paper and gave us a grin. "Nope. Miss Hoover just wants us to draw a picture." He turned back to his work, orange crayon in hand, tongue out in concentration. "Of our moms and dads." He picked up a blue one and set to work, waved us out of his room. "So, I need to do this for awhile. Then I'll show it to you."

An hour later, Zach came into the den, carrying two sheets of typing paper in his outstretched hands as if he were carrying the original Magna Carta. I patted the sofa and made room between Natalie and me. He sat solemnly with his back against the cushions and presented each of us with our portraits. I had blue-gray hair, fluorescent green clothes, and a huge, loopy grin. Natalie had green clothes as well, flowing black hair nearly to the floor, and a very serious look on her face. In her arms was a pink stick-figure baby. Zach pointed to my picture and said, "Your clothes are green because you always wear them." He waited a beat as I murmured my approval. "When you work as a emergency doctor."

I nodded, very impressed by his subtle shading and attention to detail. "I'm glad I'm smiling, Zach. It's important to be happy at work, right buddy?"

"Uh huh." He nodded vigorously and turned his attention to Natalie. "And Mommy is dressed in green cuz that's what *she* wears. When she makes new babies." He pointed a green-stained index finger at the stick figure in her arms. "Like that one there."

Natalie smiled and kissed his forehead. "I like the picture very much, Zachy." She looked closer and a frown depressed her lips. "But Mommy's not smiling in hers. Not like Daddy. How come?"

Zachary met her eyes and explained his reasoning to us, voice steady, hand resting on his mother's. "Because you cry a lot. At night." He stroked her face, compassion far beyond his years evident in the tender touch of his hand. "I can hear you. In the hall. Lots of nights."

I looked at Natalie, who quickly averted her eyes. A minute or so later, Zachary sensed our discomfort and broke the awkward silence by carefully gathering his portraits. He hopped off the sofa, tucked the papers under his arm, and walked down the hall toward his bedroom. Natalie shot me a look. "Go get him, Steven." She was pale, whether from shock or shame, I couldn't tell. "Make sure he's all right."

I stood and leaned closer, whispered so he couldn't hear from the hallway. "We need to talk. Tonight." She nodded silently, motioned me impatiently toward Zach's room.

By the time I'd gotten to his room, he already had his jeans and tee shirt off, ready for his bath and bed. I helped him strip off his underwear, ran a bath, and set him in the tub. Washed his hair with a soapy washcloth. "You know Mommy and I love you very much, right, Zach?"

He was preoccupied with a new boat I'd bought him at Target the previous weekend, a going-away-to-school present. He pushed the red-and-white sailboat the full length of his bathtub, burbling like an inboard-outboard engine. Finished his lap, looked into my eyes, a guileless expression on his face, utterly serious. "I know, Dad."

I soaped and rinsed his back, raised his feet and scrubbed between his toes. "And you know that Mommy is very happy to have you, right buddy?"

He pushed his boat to the bottom of the tub, giggled as it righted itself, surrounded by a halo of bubbles, missing his arm by mere inches. "I know that too."

I washed his face, scrubbed behind his ears, and kissed his cheek. "Mommy just cries when she's sad. About work. Mommy and Daddy love each other very much too." I felt terrible saying that, filled with doubt as I was, still, he needed to hear it. "You understand that, don't you, Zach?"

He twirled around and around in his tub, trailing the sailboat behind a mini tidal wave, water sloshing onto the floor tiles. "Uh, huh." He paused in the middle of his turn and gave me a look that nearly stopped my heart: the naked fear of a child mixed with the piercing insight of an adult. "Then why does Mommy say she hates you?"

I looked up as Natalie came into the room. We exchanged shocked looks, tried to cover our acute anxiety with forced laughter. She sounded as if she were choking on her words. "Mommy doesn't hate Daddy, honey. Not at all. Mommy must have been . . ."

Zachary stood suddenly in his tub, put his arms out toward Natalie and said, "I'm tired, Mommy. Could you tuck me in and read me a story?"

She turned to the towel rack and pulled out his favorite "Elmo" towel, wrapped him in a bear hug, and said, "I love this little guy so much." She nuzzled him close to her breast, murmuring soothing words as she motioned me out of the room.

An hour later, she came into the den, her face drawn, lips tight, as she plopped down next to me. "What brought that on, Steven?"

I slid a little farther down the sofa. "You tell me."

She bit at a cuticle, eyes locked on mine. "So, we're back to this, are we?" Her voice was steel, the same tone she used late at night when a nurse refused to get her telephone order straight. "You've been pissed all night, Steven. I'm tired and would like to go to bed early for the first time in a week." She gave a theatrical sigh. "But you clearly have something on your mind, so why don't you just come out and say it." She turned slightly away from me. "Get it over with."

I moved into her line of sight, met her glare. She refused to look away, clearly ready for whatever I had to say. "I met your husband today, Natalie." She blinked but said nothing. Her eyes narrowed slightly, but her face remained impassive. "At his store."

Her voice was sharp enough to cut granite. "My *ex*-husband? Why would you want to meet Henry?"

I took a few calming breaths. I didn't typically shrink from confrontation, just didn't enjoy it. "I went to thank him for helping Zachary get into the Country Day School."

"Really? Any other reason you were so anxious to meet my ex-husband?" She drew her legs under her butt, inched farther away from me. Condescending note in her voice. "Collecting dirt on your wife, maybe?"

"I didn't know you had anything to hide, Natalie."

Unmistakably nasty tone. "If you have something to say, Steven, just come out and say it." She looked at her watch, skewered me with a look of pure malice. "I would like to get to bed sometime tonight. I have a seven-o'clock C-section."

"All right. I'll get right to the point." Here it was, the worst moment of our life together. My head was splitting, gut roiling.

"Why did you lie, Natalie? About that call the morning my mom died."

She whirled around to face me, face red down to her neck, eyes narrowed. "What the hell are you talking about, Steven?"

"I called you on my way to Riverside." I had a tendency to jumble my thoughts when I was excited or mad. I willed myself to stay focused, didn't want to miss-state anything, needed to get to the truth. "You said the man who answered was your ex."

She practically spit her words across the sofa. "And it *was*. I *told* you that the time you confronted me on the phone." She shook her head, lips twisted into a sneer. "Honestly, Steven. Get over it. That was *five years* ago."

"That's not the point, Natalie." She turned away, arms held tightly against her chest. "The man I talked to wasn't Henry Marx." There, I'd said it. She didn't move a muscle, I'd have given anything to watch her face; she kept her back firmly toward me. "I want to know who it was."

She turned back to me, her face a mask of barely contained fury. "You're out of your fucking mind." She was spitting now, her words hitting with a physical impact. "You're accusing me of lying based on a voice on the phone from *five goddamned years ago?*" She stood suddenly, nearly knocked her water bottle from the coffee table. "You're pathetic, Steven. So fucking paranoid." She paced a few feet from me, face set, lips white. "I told you the truth. I *always* tell the truth." She stopped pacing a foot from me, leaned forward, practically screaming in my face now. "I was with my *husband*, Steven. No one else." She tapped my forehead with her index finger. *"Understand?"*

I felt like slapping her hand away, stood up instead, inches from her face, barely able to control my voice. "The man on the phone that morning? *Whoever* he was. Didn't have a fucking German accent. Like the one your ex has." She took a sideways step, moved toward the hallway. I spun her around. "Tell me who it was, Natalie. Tell me why you lied to me."

She wrenched her arm free. "Let go of me, goddamnit." She shook a finger in my face. "I told you the truth, Steven. Believe anything you want." She tapped my forehead again. I slapped her hand away this time. "Get it through that paranoid brain of yours. Nothing happened." She was shouting so loud, I was afraid she'd wake Zachary. *"Nothing."*

I moved to block her path. "I know what I heard, Natalie. The voice on the phone that day was *not* your husband." I gripped her wrist again. Harder. "Not even close."

She jerked her arm free, sidestepped me quickly, before I could reach her arm, turned toward the hall. "I will *not* stand here and let you accuse me of lying about something you *think* you heard five years ago." An instant later, she turned and slapped my face, hard enough to blur my vision. I looked into the face I'd loved for fourteen years and saw only naked aggression and loathing. "You ought to go to a fucking psychiatrist, Steven. Get your head straight before you destroy this family."

I tried to catch her as she ran toward our bedroom. She was too quick, and we were too close to Zachary's room; he'd hear us for sure. I stood shaking silently in the hall, returned a few minutes later to the sofa, smoldering mad, absolutely convinced I was right. I'd seen beyond Natalie's façade, glimpsed her true nature tonight, for the first time since I'd known her.

I went to work two hours later, afraid this was the beginning of the end.

Chapter 20

I'd asked around work, as discreetly as possible, for the names of a few good marriage counselors. The only problem was that everyone who gave me names based on their personal experience was currently divorced. Not exactly a ringing endorsement of counseling. Barbara Manning had the best advice; she was still seeing her therapist, a Ph.D. psychologist in Irvine even four years after her divorce. She admitted that the man hadn't been able to save her marriage, but still trusted him enough to use his counsel as she went on with her life. She cautioned me that it wouldn't be easy, but more importantly, she said we'd need to "dig deep" to get to the root cause of our problems. Anything less would likely lead to separation or divorce. I hated more than anything to hear that, but secretly knew it anyway. Divorce was so pervasive in our society; how could it be otherwise?

The rest of the shift was a battle of concentration over emotion. The residents were rounding into shape for the upcoming graduation, so they needed little or no supervision and the Department was slow, so I spent a lot of time in my office, planning my moves and considering what we'd just been through. Zachary clearly knew a little about what was going on with us. He had been way ahead of me; Natalie crying at night was a surprise to me. She had her moods, just like I did, but seemed to come out of them quickly, actually faster than I did. Still, she tended toward depression, particularly during her pregnancy. She'd gone for days, especially on the weekends, without getting out of bed, often stayed in her scrubs, hunkered down in bed, with a stack of journals on her covers, TV at a low level. I didn't think much of it at the time for two reasons: I knew she was tired physically, and I'd had no experience with pregnancy at all. As always, when a person is confronted by crisis, the mind searches the past for clues. I recalled the time I came home one day near the end of Natalie's term to find her wedged in the corner of the closet, rocking back and forth, just staring off into space. She explained her actions at the time by saying she was "Just straightening up some things and had gotten nostalgic about her childhood." Said she'd just had a flood of bad memories from the time her mom and dad split up. I chalked it up at that time to emotional overload and hormones. Still, I had to wonder, as I sat in my office, if this weren't one of the signs of severe depression I should have been more aware of.

Natalie didn't talk much about her parents. She'd told me they were "fairly happy" for the most part, didn't seem anxious to have any other kids, although Natalie was a little lonely being an only child. She said that her dad was "very affectionate" with her. Would dote over her constantly, read her bedtime stories until she was eleven or twelve. She said she always had a lot of trouble sleeping even into her early adolescence. Told me her dad would lie down next to her on her double bed, hold her in his arms until she drifted off. She wasn't very open about her mom. Natalie did tell me that she thought her mother was "a little jealous" of the close relationship she shared with her dad. Talked about how she used to hear them fighting late at night. As I looked back on those conversations with Natalie, a strange, random thought occurred to me. Natalie didn't seem bothered by the fact that her mom was upset by her father's seemingly overboard affection and caring. She didn't seem concerned that it caused friction in her parent's marriage. The way I saw it, from listening to her, she actually seemed proud of it. Seemed to almost be in competition for her father's affection. Natalie even confided in me one night, with unmistakable pride, that her dad told her that she "understood him better" than her mother.

I asked Natalie several times what she thought happened to her parents' marriage. I was particularly interested because I was keenly aware of the statistics: children of divorce are more likely to have serious relationship troubles. This was certainly true in her case, as she'd only lasted three years with Henry Marx. She was very close-mouthed about her parent's break-up. She *did* say that it happened a little while after her mom had found her dad still in her room at four in the morning. Her father had apparently fallen asleep on her bed, above the covers, she hastened to add. Natalie said her mom was furious, said she'd "seen enough" and "couldn't take the humiliation anymore." I wondered at the time if Natalie was telling the complete truth, wondered if there was more going on with her father than she was willing to admit. I knew how commonly that sort of overboard affection and excessive cuddling could lead to sexual activity and was aware that it could have a lasting, devastating effect on women for decades. We'd had rotations in Psychiatry in medical school, of course, and we'd learned that eating disorders, depression, borderline personality disorder, even multiple personalities, were more common among female victims of adolescent sexual abuse. I wouldn't put Natalie in any of those severe categories, except for the depression, and I had no direct evidence that her father had touched her inappropriately or, even worse, had sex with her. Still, I had to wonder if her behavior: her lying, the intense possessiveness, the multiple partners at an early age, and her extreme sexuality, at least in the beginning of a relationship, weren't themselves symptoms of a deeper need, a more powerful force. I wondered, not for the first time, if Natalie could only relate to a man sexually. She told me on many occasions that her relationships "started out really hot, only to cool a few months later." She even admitted she was afraid it was because of her. Something "lacking" in her makeup. She seemed to think that every man got tired of her pretty quickly and eventually left her. I was incredulous at first, because my experience from the outside looking in during medical school was entirely opposite: Natalie was *the* object of desire; all the males in our class somehow caught in her sexual gravitational field.

Natalie contradicted this opinion without hesitation; said that abandonment was *the* pattern, the constant, in her life, starting with her father. She clearly had never gotten over his leaving the family when she was fourteen. She seemed nearly overcome with grief the few times she talked about those days when her family split up.

I thought about all the times Natalie warned me when we were starting to get serious that she tended "to be easily bored" with men. That she liked to "play the field." I found that highly contradictory at first, had a hard time reconciling that with her obvious fear of abandonment until I gave it some more thought. It became clear to me, after careful reflection, that she would push men away, go on to another, before they "got rid" of her. She even said she was always the first one to break off the relationship, said she wanted to be the one in control "at all times."I knew, now, that this was a defense mechanism on her part to preempt the possibility of abandonment and maintain the control she so desperately needed. As I dug deeper into her past, pored through the discussions we'd had, I came to the conclusion that Natalie *did* use her sexuality to get her way. She used her skills to capture a man, to keep him, and ultimately, by withdrawing her sexual favors, to control him. I realized, with a growing sense of depression, that I was just one in a long series of Natalie's conquests. Another target of her emotionally warped modus operandi.

I wasn't at the state of epiphany yet, hadn't even approached a level of complete insight into the multiple facets of her personality, but most of what had happened to us, from our courtship through last night's argument, became a lot clearer. Natalie was feeling rejected or at least at loose ends as her marriage to Marx was nearing an end. She saw me as a friend, even another target, as someone whom she could "win over" with her sexuality. She was probably aware that I was at least somewhat committed at that time to Elaine, and she moved in anyway. She got me.

I had to admit, looking back, that the early months of our relationship were mostly about sex. Sure, we had a lot in common as far as career goals, dreams, and aspirations were concerned, but our time together was mostly about fucking. Night and day. I wasn't complaining, not at all, had no regrets about that facet of our relationship, as we clearly had and *still have* some chemistry together. Having thought that, I was aware, even as my lizard-brain was overjoyed with the constant love-making, that there should have been more to our relationship. We should have been talking about deeper things.

Even the times in San Francisco make sense in that light. Natalie seemed ambivalent, to say the least, about getting engaged, almost frightened, despite her excitement in Tiffany's. In retrospect, she may have been right. We probably should have gotten to know each other better, on other than a sexual level. She was probably feeling a little overwhelmed, maybe even trapped, but I was so insistent, so "romantic" that she got caught up in the moment, probably felt she had little choice.

The more I thought about it sitting in my office in the middle of the night, even her opinions about love made a lot more sense. She had told me on many occasions that she didn't believe in unconditional love. Not at all. That amazed me, as I felt very strongly that forgiveness and unconditional love were two of the constants, along with total honesty, of a lasting relationship. She just didn't buy it. Said she "couldn't tolerate mistakes." Natalie had told me, since the first days of our relationship, that she had never made any herself and that she "held herself and the people in her life to very high standards." I knew, for the first time, why she was so sensitive to perceived betrayals, why she was so unforgiving and rigid. If indeed her dad had abused her, she would never be able to give enough of herself to trust another man, never be able to admit to being wrong in any substantial way. She couldn't afford to lose that sense of control. She needed it to keep the man-of-the-moment in her life. Needed it to survive. Literally.

Even the worst time we'd had as a couple, until last night, made some sense to me. I had never been unable to explain, to my own satisfaction, why Natalie was so opposed to having a baby, even to the point of wanting an abortion. I believe now that she felt trapped, wasn't ready to commit to me, even after we'd married. She seemed to always need an escape hatch, an exit strategy from the men in her life, for use at the time and place of her choosing. After all this crap in our life, I think I understood why. She felt that a child would change everything. She couldn't cut and run if she sensed her man growing tired of her, if she felt the urge to find another partner, to validate her sexuality all over again. That's why she fought so hard to have our son aborted. Under close scrutiny, that's the only explanation that made sense to me.

Startled out of my musings, I looked up at the clock on the wall when my replacement, Paul Krivitsky, opened the door. He came over to my desk, shook my hand. "Steven, you look like you've seen a ghost." He hung his jacket on the back of the door, turned and sat in my guest chair. "Checked the chart rack. Slow night, huh?" He stretched and yawned. "Barbara said you've been in here for two hours. Wondered if you were all right, so I came to see for myself." He gave me a concerned look; we'd been friends since internship, and Paul was very adept at reading my moods. "So, I'm asking you, Steven, *are* you okay?"

I gathered my stuff from the desk and stuffed it quickly into my duffel bag, anxious to avoid spilling my troubles on such a good friend. I needed to tell my concerns to my wife, hopefully to a counselor. So, I took the usual man's route out. Denial. "Nah. I'm okay." I clapped Paul on the shoulder, looked him right in the eye and lied. "Everything's great." I opened the door and smiled with one foot in the hallway. "Hope it's as quiet for you." I moved closer to the hallway, anxious to escape his concerned stare. "Take it easy, Paul."

He gave me a half-hearted wave as I closed the door. His expression said it all: he didn't believe my bullshit. Not for a second.

Ten minutes later, I was on the Fifty-Five, halfway home, the Porsche on autopilot as I navigated the sparse morning traffic. My two hours of solitary rumination had cleared my mind, as always, and I felt more than ready for the next few hours. I made a pledge to myself to make a date with Natalie for counseling, tonight if possible, by the next day at the latest. I now felt that I was armed with at least some understanding of her personality, of the rationale behind her actions recently. I felt a renewed confidence that we could work it out, could go on from here and rebuild our relationship. We just had to, for Zachary's sake. I knew she loved him as much as I, realized deep down, that she probably loved him more than she did me. I didn't care about that at all. I only wanted to stay together. To be a family again. I wasn't ready to forgive her for that night a few months before we got married. I knew without a doubt that she'd lied to me about her husband being in her bed. She still had to apologize for that. It wasn't enough for me to understand her actions, I needed to be able to forgive her. I needed her to be honest enough to admit her mistake. For the first time in her life. I wasn't a saint, far from it. I wasn't holding her to impossibly high standards, not at all. The fact remained: she owed me her truth. Her fidelity. I gave mine to her without reservation. As I turned the corner onto Bayside Place, I realized that I could probably find it in my heart to forgive Natalie. I just wasn't sure she'd let me in far enough to admit she'd been wrong. Realized with a fresh wave of depression that I wasn't even sure she wouldn't do the same thing again.

I parked the Porsche in the garage. The space to my left was empty; Natalie's Mercedes was gone. She'd probably left for work early, anxious to avoid a confrontation, I thought, as I opened the back door.

I knew without a doubt that I faced an uphill battle with my wife. Knew it would be nearly impossible to break through her barriers, the armor she'd built up over a lifetime to protect herself from pain. We all carried our own personal, customized shields into battle every day; otherwise we couldn't face the harsh realities of slights, real and imagined insults, and genuine physical pain that was waiting for us right outside our doors.

I sorted through the mail with half my attention, the other half on the daunting task of breaking through *both* of our defenses, finding the common ground that every couple needed to claim in order to survive as a unit. I said a silent prayer that God would help me pick the right therapist, that he or she would find a way to reach both of us in this, our hour of greatest need.

Chapter 21

TWO WEEKS LATER

Natalie and I had reached an uneasy détente in our relationship over the past ten days. I'd slept in the guestroom for a couple of nights, slowly worked my way back to our room. Natalie admitted nothing, explained nothing about the guest in her bed. I had the definite feeling that she didn't think being with another man at that time in our relationship was anything to be ashamed about, hence the lack of remorse. I didn't agree, of course. I don't think I was being old-fashioned or prudish about it, just held out for my principles: it was simply dead wrong for her to violate our relationship that way. We clearly had an understanding that we'd be exclusive, we seemed to be working toward a more permanent relationship and it was wrong for her to sleep with someone else. End of discussion.

Our rapprochement did not include sex, not yet. I think she was still punishing me for calling her out for lying, and there was simply nothing I could do about it. I called three of the marriage and family counselors I had been referred to, and we finally decided to see one that Natalie had met during her volunteer work through Hoag. She said the therapist was a specialist in saving marriages; she was supposedly batting about fifty percent. I thought they *all* should be specialists in such a critical endeavor and fifty percent was scarily low, but kept my comments to myself and decided to keep an open mind.

The therapist had her office in Corona Del Mar, on Marguerite, a block south of PCH, two blocks from the ocean, and about ten minutes from home. Her name was Olivia Tanner, and Natalie informed me that she was a Harvard graduate. I didn't care if she was a night-school grad from Tijuana Tech, as long as she would be fair and effective.

We pulled into her parking lot ten minutes early. I turned to Natalie and asked, "Are you up for this?"

She checked her look in the vanity mirror, made a few minor adjustments to her hair, and closed the visor. "Remember, this was your idea, Steven." She reached for the door latch and opened the passenger door. "I'm just doing as you asked."

Not such a great attitude considering the stakes, I thought, with a sinking feeling in my gut. She had fought my efforts to go to counseling almost from the start, saying, in effect, that we could work things out. Besides, she'd said, "we're professionals, smart adults, we should be able to figure this out for ourselves, especially if we're committed to staying together." Even as I'd agreed with her in principle, I had to admit to some serious reservations about unburdening myself in front of a stranger. Still, given those anxieties, I wanted to try everything possible to avoid a catastrophe.

I opened my door, came to her on the sidewalk and linked arms. "This is for all of us, Natalie. I thought you understood that." She pulled her arm away and started up the flower-lined sidewalk, walking double-time toward the two-story brick building. The ocean breeze was up, the strong smell of kelp in the air. I hustled to catch her, hoping that the therapist wasn't spying on our little scene from her office. Caught her by the elbow, spun her gently around. "We need to do this for us. For Zachary."

She broke away, walked faster, increasing the distance between us with each step. A few feet from the door, she turned to face me, her face a complete blank, cheeks slightly flushed, eyes narrowed. She brushed a strand of hair from her eyes. "I just want to be on record with this, Steven." She turned to open the door, leaving me in her wake. "Nothing she will say, nothing you say will change my mind." She lowered her voice as we entered the foyer, deserted except for the receptionist sitting behind the frosted glass panel. "I didn't do anything wrong." She stole a look at the secretary, who was preoccupied with the phone. Turned back to me on the threshold, her voice an urgent whisper. "*You're* the one with the problem, Steven. You and your paranoia." The receptionist hung up the phone, turned to talk to a tall, dark haired woman in a navy blue suit. Natalie's voice was flat, eyes boring into mine. "Get this straight. Whatever you think happened that night didn't affect us at all." She smiled quickly as the receptionist opened the window, turned again and whispered in my ear. She repeated her mantra of the past few months, delivered in a vicious, low monotone. "Just get over it."

I was suddenly filled with resentment. She had effectively boxed me out, made it impossible to respond, much less have the last word. She had also pushed my buttons, something she was increasingly adept at. Not a good frame of mind to begin counseling. Probably what she had in mind, I thought acidly, as I found a seat in the cramped waiting room.

The woman in the dark blue suit came through the receptionist's door and gave Natalie a hug. She was at least five-ten, spare, aerobics instructor's frame, suffused with the obvious glow of excellent health. She had even, fairly attractive features, no great beauty by any stretch of the imagination, but very pleasant and presentable, with a professional woman's brisk manner. She smiled my way, extended her hand, and said, "Dr. Adler, I'm so happy to meet you. I'm Olivia Tanner. Come in, please." She led us down a short corridor to a dimly lit consultation room at the end of the hall. She made a sweeping motion with her arm as she walked toward an armchair dead center in the smallish room. "Please, make yourselves comfortable." She then indicated a five-foot, dark brown upholstered sofa and a matching armchair positioned a foot or so closer to the door. "Wherever you feel like sitting."

Natalie chose the sofa, walked the full length of the couch, to sit at the far side, away from the door. I considered taking a place next to her, finally decided to sit in the armchair, liked the sightlines better in that I could see Natalie's face and the therapist's reaction without being obvious about maneuvering for a better look. If Tanner thought anything about our seating arrangements, she gave no hint of it. Clearly, this was not the first time a troubled couple had game-played the seating arrangements.

Settled in our positions, she smiled at me and said, "I'm fairly casual in my therapy style. Democratic, I guess you could say." She looked from me to Natalie, warm smile in place, eyes making direct, lasting contact with each of us in turn. "I'll ask you each to tell me why you're here and what you hope to accomplish. You may talk as long as you like, but I ask that you not interrupt the other person." She had the barest hint of a Boston accent, sounded a little like Jacqueline Onassis after she'd spent a few years in Manhattan. "Okay with both?" She smiled as we nodded in unison. "Fine. Why don't we start with you, Steven?" She flipped open a small leather-bound pad and turned on a mini recorder poised on the arm of her chair. "I'm sorry, Doctor. Is it all right if I call you Steven?" She gave me a hopeful smile. "I feel as if I already know Natalie, but maybe you'd feel more comfortable with Doctor."

I shook my head, tried to calm my nerves by thinking of something pleasant, settling at length on Zachary and our recent trip to Knott's Berry Farm. "Steven's fine, Ms. Tanner."

She smiled again, a professional attempt at true intimacy. "Olivia, please, Steven." She smoothed the crease on her trousers with the flat of her palm. "Now, if you would, tell me why you think you need marriage counseling."

I cleared my throat, took a reflexive last look at Natalie, who was busy studying her manicure. "I want to save our marriage, I guess. I mean, I'm sure that I want that. That *we* want that." I willed myself to slow down, acutely aware that I was rambling. "I'm sorry, Olivia." I stole another look at Natalie, she had a slight, smug smile on her face. "I'm a little nervous."

"Of course." She motioned for me to continue with a subtle nod of her head.

"I feel as if Natalie and I have some problems. Some serious problems." I caught Natalie staring at me in my periphery; she looked away suddenly, seemed to be studying the Dali print on the opposite side of the room as I struggled to order my thoughts. "There have been a couple of incidents where I've felt she wasn't telling the truth."

"That's not true and you know it, Steven." She whirled on me, fire in her eyes. "My God, just get over it!"

Olivia raised an index finger, her tone low, nonjudgmental. "Natalie, please."

She turned slightly in her chair, nodded to me again. I regrouped, willed myself to stay calm. "Trust is very important to me. I guess it is to everyone, but especially to me." I wondered how deeply I should get into my background. I'd always had trouble trusting women; guess it had to do with Mom's neglect and her undependable nature. I just wasn't sure how germane it would be. Olivia seemed to anticipate my reservations; no doubt she had seen it many times in the past.

She leaned forward in her chair, eyes fixed on mine. "Why do you feel it's particularly important to you, Steven?"

I decided at that point to ignore Natalie. I needed to get this off my chest, if only to give Olivia enough background to help us. I was embarrassed to unburden myself like this, but the stakes were so high, I knew I had no choice. "My mom. She was sort of neglectful. Sort of distant. I don't know, I just didn't feel as if she loved me very much. I hadn't given it any deep thought until recently, but it's pretty obvious that I have trouble trusting women because Mom let me down so badly." I took a deep breath, looked into Olivia's open expression. "I mean, I didn't exactly have a great role model to grow up with. It's caused me a lot of problems. And it still does." I took a sip of water, waited for Olivia to scribble her note.

She looked up from her tablet, gave me a tiny smile of encouragement. "Yes. Go on."

"Actually, it was worse than being neglectful, she was an alcoholic. Never gave my brother or me much affection." That sounded too harsh, even to my ears, so I softened it a little, gave Mom a little benefit of the doubt. "I guess she was hurting too much to be able to give us anything extra."

Olivia looked up from her notepad, nodded stolidly. "And this has caused you problems?"

"I'm sure it has. Actually, I hadn't given it much thought. Until Natalie." I glanced at her on the sofa; she was staring at a point over Olivia's left shoulder. "I mean until I became serious with Natalie. I had a few relationships with women before her, not a lot, but they always seemed to disintegrate after a few weeks, at the most a few months. I would find some excuse to leave, something I didn't like about them and we'd be over."

She bowed her head, jotted a quick note. Looked up again, flashed her professional smile. "Were they faithful to you?"

"I suppose so. But, I never had a relationship that lasted enough to be truly committed, so it wasn't as important as it is now."

She kept her placid gaze on me, her voice low. "So you want to be able to trust Natalie, is that right, Steven?"

I glanced again at Natalie; she sat forward in her seat, seemed ready to pounce; Olivia cut her off with an index finger to her lips, turned back to me, motioned for me to answer. "I guess that's why we're here. Why I'm here. Yes."

"What is it that has caused you to distrust your wife?"

I tried to meet Natalie's eyes; she was looking down at the carpet, as if she were looking for verbal ammunition in the cream-colored, patterned Berber. "I think she was unfaithful to me. Before we were married."

Tanner kept her eyes on mine. "Why would you think that?"

I explained my reasoning about the voice on the phone, the obvious discrepancy with Marx's Germanic tone and Natalie's refusal to admit what she had done. Olivia listened without interruption, making sparse notes, stopping me only for a few seconds as she reached for another pen. I went on to explain that her behavior didn't fit within my standards. Told Tanner that as far as I was concerned we'd had a commitment. One that I honored and one that I trusted her to honor as well.

She adjusted the gain control on her mini recorder, turned her attention back to me. "And you feel she's jeopardized your marriage by lying about this?"

I could see Natalie off to my left; watched as she crossed her arms tightly across her chest and turned to face the wall. "Yes, I do. Without doubt. I trusted Natalie. Like no other woman I'd ever been with. I trusted my life to her, my heart and soul. I wanted nothing else except her love. I wanted us to be together forever." I turned slightly in my chair, tried to meet Natalie's gaze, she continued to give me her back. "Now, I don't know. She's not going to tell the truth. Doesn't seem to want to get past this."

"Could you trust her again if she admitted to you what you think she did?" She looked up from her notepad, her tone earnest. "What you believe she did that night?"

I didn't hesitate for an instant. That was exactly what I wanted. I wasn't sure I could trust her, but it was an important first step. One I felt we had to take. "I'd give it a try. That's the best I could do at this point."

Natalie spun to face me, her face flushed, turned then to Tanner, voice clipped. "See, Olivia? That's exactly what I was talking about. Steven can't get past his damned paranoia."

Olivia took it in stride. She simply shifted her focus to Natalie, gave no hint that she was out of line or too aggressive. "Okay. Let's hear your side now, Natalie."

Natalie took a sip of water, focused her gaze on Olivia. "He's making so much out of this phone call. All of his stupid accusations are making me sick." She took another sip of water, glanced briefly in my direction before returning her focus to the therapist. "All this shit from him about a phone call and we weren't even married yet."

Olivia held up a hand to stop for a second as she replaced the tape. "Sorry, Natalie. Now, you believe that the incident, if it happened, was not significant because you had no commitment to one another? Is that correct?"

Natalie nodded vigorously, clearly in her element, relieved to be on the attack once again. "There are two issues here. First, I was not married at the time, so my actions were my responsibility alone." Her voice was strong, confident. "Secondly, I stand by my statement to him that my ex-husband spent the night with me." She crossed her arms again while I tried, yet again, to reconcile her version of the truth with what I heard. Deemed it patently ridiculous. Impossible.

Olivia seemed to read my thoughts; looked first at me, then at Natalie. "Do you really believe that you had no commitment at that time? When the two of you had an agreement to be exclusive? When you were clearly headed for a more permanent arrangement?"

"I don't see it that way. Not at all." She turned to look me full in the face, head held high, voice secure, challenging. "Steven doesn't understand. I need a certain degree of freedom." Once again using the tone and cadence of the undefeated prosecutor. "I tend to chafe under a lot of restrictions."

I raised a hand to interrupt; Olivia stepped in with a discreet shake of her head. "Do you mean an open marriage? Is that what you want, Natalie?"

She gave a slight, shy smile, which told me all I needed to know. This new information fit perfectly with what I believed about her psychological makeup, about the need to feel in control, the urge to stray from one new man to another. She gave the bombshell question short shrift; I wondered at the time if her demur was for my benefit or for her friend, the therapist's. "I wouldn't go that far." She studied my face, tried to get a read; I shifted my gaze to the carpet, reeling from the possibility, hell, the near certainty that she did, indeed, want an open marriage. "I still want to stay married to Steven. We have a son to think about and I don't want him to grow up in a broken home. I've been there and it's Hell on earth for a kid." She tried again to meet my eyes; I suppressed a wave of nausea by concentrating on the geometrically patterned carpet, my thoughts on this new, harrowing reality. Her voice sounded a half-mile away. "It's just that he wants to crucify me for something I may or may not have done. It's just ridiculous."

Olivia took her time; seemed to be mulling her next question, as she looked first at me, then back at Natalie. "Forgive me for asking, Natalie, but I need to know, *Steven* probably needs to know. Why did you marry him, so soon after your previous failed marriage, especially given your need for freedom?"

Natalie looked down at the carpet, seconds passed and I thought, not for the first time, that she was about to say it was all a mistake, that I had somehow rushed her into it. She looked at Olivia, nodded slightly and then looked at me, her eyes intently on mine. "I've given that a lot of thought lately." She held my gaze. "I needed him. Needed the emotional stability Steven gave me, from the time we got together." She took another sip of water, turned to face Olivia, her voice barely audible in the hushed room. "I'd been through a lot in my life, too. I'd never felt so safe with a man, so much at peace. I just responded to him that way, and then he wanted to marry me and I was overwhelmed." She stole a glance at me. "He gave me all the stability and comfort I'd never had with a man. What I'd needed all along without even acknowledging it to myself." She gave me a wan smile. "I knew I could depend on him, knew I'd grow to love him."

"Steven?"

I looked up from my reverie, not sure how to proceed, reeling from her words, especially the intimation that she didn't love me when we married. Even with that shock, I was still anxious to salvage this mess, to move on. Despite her seemingly heartfelt emotion, I wouldn't give in on this issue, trust was way too important to me, her absurd notion of an open marriage notwithstanding.

I decided that I'd just have to say what was on my mind, come what may. "I don't give a damn what she says about an open marriage." I shot her a glance; she refused to meet my eyes, back in defensive mode. "As far as I'm concerned, you either want to be married or you don't. An open marriage is sanctioned cheating. Nothing more." I tried once again to catch Natalie's eye; she was now fully absorbed in the Dali. I returned my attention to the therapist. "As for her lies. I only know what I heard. I'll never forget that voice on the phone. It was too unusual, too out of character for Natalie, at least I thought so at the time." I took another long drink of water, got ready to tell the rest. "I can't stay married to someone I don't trust. I have too much history with untrustworthy women to feel any different. I'm not a psychiatrist, don't read Freud, but I *do* know myself." I looked again over at Natalie to judge her reaction. She sat stoically, worrying a piece of tissue between her hands. "I get very anxious, really upset when my world is insecure, when the person I love doesn't seem to love me, too. I guess you can call that childlike, but that's the way I am." I shifted slightly in my chair, stared directly into Olivia's face, no longer afraid to unburden myself to this stranger. "I don't consider myself needy, don't have to be told all the time that someone loves me." I turned to my wife, met Natalie's eyes at long last; she seemed ready to cry. "I just need to rely on that love. So I can give it back to her. I just need her to be available to me. Without strings. I know she needs her freedom, we've known each other for fifteen years, but it's different for me. I'm a different person than she is." I looked away, acutely ashamed to have Natalie see me cry. Turned my gaze back to Tanner. "I have to know my wife is behind me, right there with me at all times." I glanced once more at Natalie, we were both crying silently now. "Otherwise, I'll just move on."

Olivia finished her notes, nodded gravely and turned to Natalie. "Anything else?"

Natalie blew her nose, turned to face me, reached for my hand. "I *do* love Steven. More than he knows. And I love my son. Our son, with all my heart." She moved to the edge of the sofa closest to me, squeezed my hand. "I want to stay married. Don't want him to leave me. To leave us." A few moments later, clearly overwhelmed, she broke down completely, the first time I'd seen Natalie sob since Las Vegas. I moved to the sofa, sat down and held her close as she shook in my arms. "I can't be left alone again. I just can't."

Olivia got up and left the room on the pretext of visiting the restroom, leaving us alone for a few minutes.

I gave Natalie time to compose herself, waiting for the words I needed to hear. She looked up after a few minutes of quiet crying, dried her eyes with a tissue and said, "You're not going to leave me, are you, Steven?"

Not what I'd hoped for, but I had to think about the future, about our son, so I swallowed a little of my pride, incorporated this new, hard-earned knowledge of my wife and said, "As long as I can trust you, Natalie. I'll stay." She blinked back tears, rested her head on my chest. I forced all the conviction I could muster into my voice, "I need you to be faithful to me. At all times."

"Then you're not going to leave?"

She raised her head, looked into my eyes; hers were red-rimmed, swollen, but dry of tears. I held her gaze, my voice low. "I need you to say it, Natalie."

"I will, Steven." She kissed my lips, clung to my shoulders. "I'll be faithful. I promise."

Olivia came back into the room as we sat on the sofa, lost in our respective thoughts. Natalie wasn't going to apologize, that was pretty clear. I had to decide, right there and then, if that was enough for me. Life is compromise, there's no doubt about that. Knowing what I did about Natalie, I could understand her need for perfection, her real trouble admitting fault. I didn't like it, but I'd married her and this was what I'd gotten. My thoughts went immediately to our son, as always. He was thriving, top of his class, and his welfare was more important than my principles, hands down. I knew Natalie was never going to change; adults rarely, if ever, did. So, in the end, I settled for her assurance with the nagging fear that I'd have to be wary, alert. I needed to protect my interests after all, and there was only so much I could take. I took her face in my hands and said, "I'm going to hold you to that, Natalie." She nodded vigorously, anxious to put this past her. "Seriously."

Across the room, Olivia glanced discreetly at her watch. "I think we've made progress today. The important thing is we know where we stand, individually. We know what each of you needs from this relationship and that's always the first step to understanding. To security." She gave us an expectant look. "Agreed?"

We nodded in unison. If only that were true, if only Natalie's telling me the truth, I thought.

She stood and gave us each a hug, ushered us toward the door into the hall, pausing at the foyer as she told her secretary to give us a follow-up appointment in a month.

We drove home in virtual silence, my thoughts consumed with what I'd given and what I'd gotten in return: no admissions and a devalued promise to be faithful from her, in exchange for baring my soul and laying myself out for more pain, should she stray. Not the bargain I'd hoped for, but a truce of sorts at the very least. I decided I could live with it for now, in the best interests of our family. I also decided that I wouldn't, couldn't accept another incident from her. I just couldn't give that much of myself away.

Enveloped in an uneasy quietude, we pulled into the garage ten minutes later. Natalie turned to face me, took my hand in hers. "I love you, Steven. You know I do."

I turned off the engine, pocketed the key, feeling uncertain, slightly lost. "I know. And I love you, too." She turned to open her door, I did the same. I came around the front of the car and caught up to her at the back door. "It's just that I need you to . . ."

The door burst open and Zachary ran into her arms. "Mommy. You're home." He kissed her full on the lips and turned to me, a complete portrait of joy. "Daddy's home too! I missed you guys so much!" He hopped down from Natalie's arms and led us by the hand into the kitchen, humming with excitement. "Come see. Maria and I made a special treat for you." He dropped our hands, ran through the door, raced to the kitchen and whispered something in Maria's ear, turned again to lead us into the kitchen. "You're gonna love it. I promise."

I looked at Natalie, shrugged, didn't have a clue what he'd done, couldn't wait to find out. He walked to the center island, a step ahead of a beaming Maria, who was carrying a stainless steel cookie tray. The wonderful aroma of fresh-baked Toll House cookies filled the kitchen. I craned my neck for a peek; Zachary shot me down. "No fair. Close your eyes, Dad."

I did as I was told, opened them a second later as Zachary announced the all clear. Maria was standing behind Zach, her face creased by a huge smile. "He make all by his self." She kissed his head. "He so cute."

I came closer, inhaled the rich scent of chocolate and butter, and took a look at Zachary's masterpiece. He'd baked a chocolate chip cookie the size of a flattened volleyball, studded with M&M's. I couldn't quite make out the designs, they looked like three stick figures, so, at the risk of hurting Zach's feelings I asked, "Is that us on the cookie, Zach?"

His smile wiped away all the pain of the afternoon in Corona Del Mar. "Yep. I call it my Adler Family Cookie." He smiled at Natalie, who could no longer hide her tears. "For the best Mommy and Daddy in the whole world."

We hugged for a minute, maybe an hour, all four of us crying and laughing. My son, my precious son, as usual, had put everything in perspective for us. Wisdom far beyond his age, compassion and love enough to embrace the world.

After a few minutes, Zachary abruptly broke away, a concerned look on his face. "Mommy? Daddy?" He was serious now, clearly upset as he met our eyes. "You don't have to cry. I'm gonna let you eat some of it, too."

Chapter 22

TWO YEARS LATER

*Z*achary's school offered golf classes, not surprisingly for upscale Newport, and he had become a pretty good grade-school golfer. Natalie and I got him a set of junior clubs for his seventh birthday and he had been bugging me for weeks to go play golf with his grandpa. Today was the day.

We were halfway to Riverside when he turned to me, his expression totally serious, little-boy-voice steady. "Dad?"

I merged into the car pool lane at Coal Canyon and settled into an eighty-mile-an-hour groove, checked the traffic in my mirrors and turned to my son. He had grown at least five inches in the last two years, lost all of the fullness in his face and acquired the wiry body of a soccer player. I was struck then by his strong resemblance to Natalie: prominent chin, piercing blue eyes, and a perfectly proportioned face, framed by glossy, straight black hair. I was going to have to watch him closely in a few short years, keep him away from all those grade school floozies. I checked the traffic, a few seconds later took my eyes from the road, turned slightly toward him, "Yes, Zach."

He cleared his throat, took a sip of his bottled water. "When I grow up." He kept his eyes on mine as we hit an open stretch of freeway. "I want to be just like you. An emergency room doctor."

I turned my attention back to the traffic, grinning like I'd won the lottery. It's every parent's dream to have their children admire them that much. I wanted him to choose his career on his own terms, would never steer him toward my path, but still, I was so proud, so happy, I could hardly keep my attention on the drive. "What brought that on?" I reached over and ruffled his hair. "I mean, the last time I asked, you said pro golfer."

He turned to face me, shook his head. "Nah. That's just kid stuff. I want to help people. Take care of them when they're hurt bad. Like you do."

He had clearly taken to my environment when I'd hosted his class. Twice. Once with Miss Hoover in kindergarten, and as recently as one month ago with his third grade. He'd asked dozens of questions the first trip, wanted to know what we did with all the blood, of all things. Guess he'd heard Natalie and me talk about our cases once too often. His class loved Trauma One, of course, couldn't get enough of the beeping, flashing monitors and gleaming equipment. They looked like curious visitors to an alien land. Barbara and I had them dress in cover gowns, paper bonnets, and shoe covers; they were too cute for school. I felt an overwhelming sense of pride for my son, joy that he'd seen the value in my profession, awe that I'd done something right in parenting him. "You sure you don't want to be an obstetrician, like Mommy? Deliver babies, bring joy and happiness to moms and dads?"

He scrunched up his face, as only a seven-year-old can do: upper lip nearly colliding with his nose. "Yuck, Dad. All those screaming babies? Besides, I hear Mom leaving all the time real late at night." He gave me a considered look; clearly he'd given this some serious thought. "I like to sleep too much."

224

From the mouths of babes. I'd reached the same conclusion after my rotation in OB. Too many wailing babies, screaming moms and the hours were horrendous. I ruffled my son's hair. I had taught him well.

An hour later, we pulled up to Dad's house; he was sitting in an old lawn chair in the garage, dressed like the serious golfer he was, clearly fidgeting to get his day started. I hardly had the car stopped in the driveway and Zachary was already out, his arms outstretched for grandpa's hug. "PaPa. I can't wait to show you." He ran into Dad's arms, was hoisted practically to the top of the garage by my dad, who smothered him with kisses. They had bonded almost from the instant of Zach's birth; every time we had trouble settling him down the first week home, Pops would rock him in the chair, humming a tune only he knew and, like magic, Zachary would fall asleep. More often than not Natalie and I would fall into bed, exhausted from round after round of feedings and changings. We'd nap for an hour or so, awaken to find Pops and Zachary playing quietly in his room, Zach's soft baby giggles and my dad's hearty laugh filling the house with the sounds of love.

Zach sat perched on Pops' lap. "Dad got me some new clubs. At Nevada Bob's." Zachary motioned impatiently for me to join them in the garage, anxious for his grandpa to admire his new rig. "They're really cool, PaPa. You gotta see 'em."

He jumped down and dragged us out to Natalie's car, took the key from my hand and popped the trunk. He turned and deftly threw me the keys, grabbed Dad's hand and pointed to his new blue bag and junior Callaway set, gleaming in the trunk.

Pops leaned down and whistled as he extracted the cut-down driver, an exact replica of his own, new model. "Man oh man, Zach. You're gonna out-drive your old grandpa with this baby." He checked the balance as Zach seemed to glow with pride. "I better take some vitamins before we go." Pops gave me a wink. "No way I can keep up with my grandson now."

Zach pulled the driver from Pops' hand, ran to the grass and proceeded to show his grandpa what he'd learned. "Watch, PaPa. My teacher told me to keep my left arm straight. So that's what I'm doing." He took a couple of practice swings, perfect arcs that barely ruffled the grass. "See. I'm gonna kill that ball. Hit it way farther than my dad." He took another vicious swing and gave Pops a broad smile. "Right, PaPa?"

Dad elbowed me in the ribs, his infectious laugh echoing off the garage door. "No doubt about that, Zach. No doubt at all."

Laughing all the way, I went into the garage and grabbed Dad's bag, went around the car, and loaded them in the trunk. Dad and Zach were already in the back seat, Pops working on the seatbelt as I started the car. I flashed Dad a look in the mirror. "Guess you guys are ready, huh?"

Zach put his hand on Pops' knee. "We've been waiting forever." He strained to grab a look at the dashboard clock. "Come on, Dad. Our tee time is only a half hour from now."

I shook my head as I backed out of the driveway. "He sounds like you, Pops. Can't wait to beat up on his poor Dad."

Pops ran a hand through Zachary's hair, gave him a warm smile. "I taught him well, Stevie. This grandson of mine is going to be the next Arnold Palmer. Just you wait and see."

Zachary gave my dad the purest look of love and devotion I could imagine as we made the turn on Brockton. My life had never been better than that morning; couldn't see how it could improve much after witnessing that look.

We arrived fifteen minutes before our tee time, much to Pops' delight. He immediately jumped out of the back seat, came around and helped Zach from his, and grabbed their clubs from the trunk. "We're gonna go warm up at the driving range, Stevie." He took Zach's hand as they pulled their carts along the path toward the fenced tee boxes, gave me a wave. "Go sign us up, we'll be down there knockin' 'em dead."

Zachary turned to face me. "You're in so much trouble, Dad. We're gonna knock 'em dead." They slapped high-fives and giggled like a couple of idiots as they raced to the tee box. My dad looked thirty years younger, happier than I'd seen him since before Mom died. God, don't let anything happen to him, I silently prayed. We love him so much. Those two are my whole world.

I unloaded my cart and bag, dragged it the length of the parking lot, which felt like half a mile, finally reaching the clubhouse out of breath, sweating in the March sun. I huffed and puffed up to the counter, where a white-haired, former touring pro named Jim Reber greeted me warmly. "Just you today, sir?"

I parked my cart near the glass counter and caught my breath. "No. There are three of us. My dad and my son." I reached for my wallet, ready to charge the carts and rounds on my Amex. "Name's Adler." I checked the right pocket. Nothing. Fished around my back to the left, empty. Shit, I'd never done this before, I thought with a start. Maybe it's in the golf bag. The pro was watching me with detached amusement, had clearly seen it a dozen times; the harried golfer, patting all of his pockets looking for his . . . "Damn, wallet's in here somewhere. Just give me a minute."

"No problem." Reber went off to help an impatient foursome at the end of the counter while I dug through all five pockets in my bag. Not there.

I swore a blue streak to myself, could now clearly see my wallet and cell phone on the kitchen island. Recalled in that instant that I'd been distracted at the time by Zachary calling from his bedroom as I got ready to leave. He needed help picking out his clothes, wanted to be sure he looked good.

I made a snap decision to leave my clubs there, go get Pops and borrow some money for the round. Didn't want to disappoint the two guys, not at all. I further decided to run back to Newport and get my wallet and phone that afternoon, since Zach and I had planned to stay overnight with Pops. Natalie had a meeting in San Diego, so it was boy's night out in the big city. I cursed myself again as I walked to the driving range. All these great plans and me with no fucking money!

Pops saved the day as he whipped out his Visa card. Not without a snide comment or two to my son, of course. They had a good laugh about "The Absent Minded Professor," asked if I'd left my game at home, wanted to know if I remembered how to swing a club. Pops even offered to buy lunch and sodas along the way. Zach chimed in as they slapped hands again, "Good thing, huh, PaPa? Otherwise we'd have to go through the garbage!" They laughed and snorted all the way to the carts. Zach rode with Dad, of course, and I was alone in the following cart. I felt like a horse's ass for forgetting my wallet, but still was looking forward to the time of my life.

Pops drove first on the first hole. Another beauty down the middle of the fairway, about two hundred and thirty yards. Zachary was next. From the man's tees, I noticed with a swell of pride. He took a couple of hearty practice swings and belted one a hundred and seventy yards down the right center, getting a generous roll over a rise in the fairway. I was shocked, proud, and a little nervous. I couldn't help but think about my first tee shot here a few years ago, the one that . . .

I could hear them laughing in their cart, heads down, snickering like a couple of teen-aged girls. "Barely made it to the woman's tee." Zach doubled over with laughter, his face as red as Pops' sweater. Dad pointed to the yellow tee box. "Your dad had to take another stroke penalty." I could have heard Dad's laugh in the next county as he filled Zach with stories of my god-awful golf game.

I carefully teed it up, took a tentative practice swing, cringing inwardly, dreading fresh humiliation. I hadn't had much time to practice, with my new schedule, Zach's school, and counseling with Natalie, in short, life had gotten in the way. I was nervous as George W. Bush at a Mensa convention as I teed it up. I looked over at their cart, which was rocking on its springs from their raucous laughter. "All right, you guys. Enough of the hilarity. I've gotten a lot better lately." *God, please don't let me shank it. Please don't let me . . .*

"Hit it even shorter." Pops was practically out of the cart, Zach draped all over him as I watched my tee shot dribble off the tee box, into the rough a total of ten yards from the blue tees. Holy Mother of God, I thought, I'll never live this down. I slunk over to my ball, gave it another whack. I hit the shot of my life, thank goodness, a screaming low liner down the middle of the fairway, landing about ten yards shy of Zach's ball. I walked silently back to my cart, feeling at least a little better about myself until I heard Pops' braying laugh as they peeled out along the cart path. "He almost caught you on that one, Zach."

Zachary joined in the hilarity as I shoved my club in the bag. "Right, PaPa. Except he's lying TWO." I started the cart as the two amigos raced off to their second shots, yours truly, the dork in the following cart, already one down after only the first shot.

We broke for lunch after the ninth hole. My game had picked up nicely; I was shooting a fifty-one, fifteen over par, while Dad sat at thirty-nine and Zach, that little monster, was at thirty-eight, two over par. He had developed a killer short game at school to compensate for his understandably short drives. And, like Pops, his putting was lights out: we'd sat in my cart at eight and watched with total amazement as Zach sank a twenty-footer around two breaks, over a two-foot rise. I looked at Pops, he was sitting open-mouthed, finally managing, "How'd he learn that shot?"

I drove the cart over to theirs and shrugged my shoulders. "Had to have gotten it from you, Dad. You've seen me putt."

Zach climbed into the cart, sat by his grandpa, soaking up the adoration like a sponge. He was truly on top of the world; his dad and PaPa all over him, alive with the first rush of success and confidence. He seemed to grow older, taller, almost before my eyes.

I sat at our lunch table, caught him looking at my dad as Pops described Zach's tee shot on five, his longest of the day, a beautiful two-hundred-yarder that led to his first birdie. Zachary was totally secure in his loving family. He looked as if he could conquer the world, as if all of his dreams would come true and that everyone he loved would live forever. I will always carry that look with me, the essence of youthful happiness: my son, Zachary.

We finished our round at three, packed up our gear and headed for Dad's house. I had explained the wallet and cell phone situation with a fresh surge of humiliation. Pops said, "No problem, Stevie. We'll take showers, go to the store for some steaks, hit the video store, and meet you home when you can."

Zach chimed in with a few suggestions about videos, calling for *Night of the Living Dead, The Exorcist,* and *Halloween.* Man, kind of gruesome for a seven year old, I thought. Boy, was I wrong. Both Dad and Zach shot down my suggestions: *Caddyshack* and *Old Yeller* as "too babyish." Outvoted two to one, *Halloween* it was.

Chapter 23

Thirty minutes later, I was headed south on the Ninety-One, laughing in the empty car about one of the best days of my life, filled with hilarity, love, and the unbeatable rush of exercise outdoors. A perfect day all around. The traffic was light, late afternoon too early for the supper and party crowd, too late for the people traveling to the beach from Riverside and Redlands.

Still smiling about the game twenty minutes later, I pulled into the driveway, hit the garage opener, and gave a momentary start. My new atlas grey Carrera, freshly detailed and covered, was parked in its usual spot on the left, but there was another car in Natalie's spot beside it. Strange, I thought. She'd told me she was going to take Sandra with her in my Porsche, wanted to show off her newly learned ability to drive a six-speed. I killed the engine, opened the door, and walked between the two cars, checked the strange one out: a brand new, black, BMW M Five that I didn't recognize. Hmm, Natalie must have gone with someone else, I thought. Must have carpooled with Sandra.

I walked through the kitchen door, scanned the spotless granite counter for my keys. Nothing. Maybe I left them in my room, I thought. I must really be losing it, I could swear I'd left them in here.

I grabbed a bottle of water from the fridge, opened it, and took a huge swallow, parched after the six-hour match. Started down the hallway toward our bedroom. Stopped a few feet away. Heard sounds from our room. A masculine voice, crude and insistent, followed quickly by a grunt, and then a loud, low moan. My wife. No doubt about it. I'd heard that sound so many times over the past nine years, been thrilled out of my mind by it, since the first time in the shower at UCI. I knew Natalie so well by now that I could even tell when she was faking and when she *really* came, a subtle but unmistakable difference in pitch and urgency that I heard once again as I slumped against the hall. Natalie moaned three times in succession as she cried out, "Rick, oh, Rick. Oh, God, Rick."

I took a few moments to decide whether or not to open that door. I had no doubt, of course, who I'd find in my bed, our bed. Rick Lamb had the most distinctive voice I'd ever heard. Piercing, authoritative, gratingly arrogant. I had to admit, deep down, I wasn't that surprised. Natalie had put on a good show for the therapist, said and done all the right things. She almost had me convinced, even as I came to know her true nature through counseling, even as she unwittingly confirmed my suppositions about her past, her problems with the use and abuse of sex. I'd deluded myself into thinking she could change, that she *wanted* to change, for Zachary at least. She'd even made a point of making love with me like she did in the old days, with a few new twists, a few extra moans, ultimately, however, without any of the passion she shared with me before we married.

I decided, after a few more seconds of gut-wrenching reflection, that it didn't matter anymore. I wasn't going to hide from her, from this. She didn't deserve any consideration on my part. Not at all. Besides, whose feelings were I trying to spare? What a joke, I thought, with a hot surge of rage and humiliation, my feelings were shattered, and my precious Natalie was happy, ecstatic even, that was clear even standing five feet away behind a closed door. As for Lamb, my supposed friend? I wanted to beat his arrogant plastic surgeon's ass to a bloody pulp.

I took a few steps forward and opened the door . . . to Natalie on her knees, suspended over Rick, ass in the air, working him into a sustained frenzy. A heartbeat later, they both looked up as I stood by the door. Natalie with a horrified look of guilt and surprise, Rick with a look of undisguised triumph.

I walked a few steps closer. Natalie jumped to her side of our bed, buried herself in the covers, Lamb stood to face me, not in the least ashamed of his nakedness, much less his predicament. I looked down at my wife, shook my head sadly, and quickly turned back to Lamb, drove my right fist through his nose, stopping only when I hit the firm bone of his upper jaw. Wiped the satisfied smirk right off his face. He bent at the waist and coughed out a spray of blood all over my pristine, white Berber carpet. One look at his purple face and the spreading stain on my carpet and I was newly enraged, as much by the mess he'd made of my rug as by his brazen acts with my wife in *my* bed. Coughing and spitting, face covered with blood, he looked up at me with a priceless look of surprise, and to my immense satisfaction, fear.

I took a handful of his carefully styled, thinning blond hair, put a hand on his back and hustled him toward the door. I hardly recognized my voice, filled with murderous rage as it was. "Get the fuck out of my house, Lamb." Halfway to the hall he grabbed a towel from the chair near the door and stole a look at my wife, who lay partially hidden under the covers.

I turned and glared at Natalie, cowering on her pillow, face blanched, save for the blotches of red, high on her cheeks; the residual heat of her sexual arousal, the tell-tale mark of her betrayal. Lamb stood there like an oversized boy, towel held to his bleeding nose. I stuck my finger in his face, tempted to hit him again. Turned his head to face my wife. "You want that worthless cunt so badly, you can have her."

I let go of his hair, pushed by him and started to leave. An instant later, Natalie jumped out of bed, ran to meet me at my bureau, trailing her sheet as she ran, voice choked with emotion. "Steven. Please." I nearly threw up my lunch. She reeked of cigarettes and sex. "Let me explain."

I kept walking, picked my wallet and phone from the top of the dresser, shook her hand from my elbow, snarled at her, "It's over, Natalie. You wanted your freedom in the worst way. That's all you've talked about for weeks." She looked ready to cry. Like I could give a shit. Couldn't care less about her precious fucked-up psyche at that moment. "And now you have it."

She grabbed my elbow again, spun me around. "What about Zachary?"

I wrenched free and spat the words in her face. "Don't talk about my son, Natalie. Not now." I waved an arm at Lamb, my voice filled with barely contained rage. "Not with his fucking handprints all over your tits."

I made my way to the kitchen, Natalie a half step behind, sheet dragging on the floor. Turned to face her, blood hot in my veins. "I'm going back to my dad's for the rest of the weekend." I looked down the hall at Lamb, struggling into his jeans, towel held to his face with his free hand. "Take the rest of the time to fuck each other senseless for all I care."

She stood there in the middle of the kitchen, her eyes dry, a sense of calm permeating her face. "Fine. If that's the way you want it, Steven. Just bring my son back here by Sunday night."

I stood three feet away, in our newly remodeled kitchen, a short distance from my wife of eight years, my friend for twenty, lover for nine, and realized with a painful certainty that I really hadn't known her at all. I knew the lover, I'd had experiences I'd never imagined were possible with her. I had come to know, in the past two years, the sexual predator Natalie. Knew her even better now. I'd been pursued by her, "captured" by her; I knew with clarity that afternoon that I was only the latest in a long, unending string of sexual roadkill.

That early Saturday night in March, after all those years together, I'd finally glimpsed the real Natalie Bogner. The egotistical, narcissistic, calculating, lying, manipulative Natalie, a hideous persona she'd taken great pains to hide from me, out in the open at last. I summoned all the calm I could muster, didn't want to make a spectacle in front of her, didn't want to show any weakness even though my world was caving in on me. "I still live here too, Natalie. I'll be back with our son long before his bedtime. In time to do his homework." I took a last look at Lamb and Natalie, standing side-by-side in my kitchen, my wife and my replacement standing in a space I'd spent thousands on just six weeks ago. I wanted to render that asshole Lamb unconscious. The two of them standing there, Lamb with his battered nose, my wonderful wife with her forced and ridiculous self-serving anger: a last visual insult to cap this horrible night. I looked from one to the other. "I'll call first, so you can clear out your lover, Natalie." I pocketed my keys, turned to leave. "Got to keep up appearances for the neighbors, right?"

I took a last look at my disheveled wife and opened the garage door. Natalie stood on the opposite side of the kitchen, arms folded, sheet tightly bunched over her breasts; her face truly ugly now, filled with naked derision. "You do that, Steven. Then you can get the hell out of *my* house." She tightened her grip on the sheet. "Just drop my son off and find another place to sleep."

Like hell I will, I thought with a surge of venomous anger. No doubt about it now, I realized. She had carved out the battle lines. Typical Natalie, ever the pragmatist. Let her do what she wants, I thought, I'll find a new place when I'm good and ready. I shook my head. "I'll be back tomorrow and then we'll talk." Lamb had slunk halfway down the hallway, his nose dripping blood onto the bath towel. "About all this." I took a last look at my former friend's ruined face and felt nothing. No sense of retribution, no sense of triumph, just a yawning emptiness, one that threatened to take me down; swallow my soul. I looked back at my wife's contemptuous expression, saw clearly what lay below the exterior beauty: the cunning focus of an animal starved for another fresh kill.

I moved into the garage, shook my head sadly. Turned again to face her. "All this goddamned shit you've brought down on us, Natalie. Just so you could fuck somebody else." I was totally disgusted; the way she'd acted, her inappropriate aggression, she just didn't seem to care. About anything. "So you could get off for the millionth time since you turned twelve." I took a stuttering breath, shot a last glance at Lamb. "Hope he was worth it."

I closed the door to the garage; made my way between the cars, heart pounding hard enough to shake my ribs. Halfway to the driveway and her Mercedes, Natalie threw open the garage door; voice sharp enough to lacerate. "He was. He's *way* better in bed, Steven." She looked ready to pounce, advancing steadily through the garage. I felt only a growing sadness as my rage receded. She was three feet behind, flushed bright red all the way to her chest. "Bigger, too." I kept walking, unable to comprehend how this woman I'd loved and had a wonderful son with could debase herself so completely. I refused to turn around, wouldn't give her that satisfaction. "They *all* were, Steven." I shut her out, numb from the sudden, final disintegration of our life together. She was shrieking now, a heartbeat away from meltdown. "Every . . . fucking . . . one . . . of . . . them."

I opened the driver's side door and settled into the seat, fumbled the key home, managed to get it started, and backed out of the driveway. Natalie ran to the edge of the garage and screamed her last. The Newport Beach Divorcee's Rallying Cry: "Get the best lawyer you can afford, Steven. You're going to need it."

I didn't lose it until I'd reached the northbound Fifty-Five freeway, a half-hour from Riverside. Then it hit me like a bad diagnosis. Zachary's life would never be the same. He would forever be labeled a child of divorce. A statistic. I had tried everything with Natalie, urged her to get a separate therapist, a psychiatrist who could help her get to the root of her behavior. She'd consistently and adamantly refused. Had a dozen excuses. Her defenses, in the end, were too entrenched, too impenetrable to save her. To save us. Her stubborn denial, her past, and, her present behavior were going to cost us unspeakable pain, endless regrets, of that I had no doubt. I realized without thinking, however, that no one gets divorced in a vacuum. I had to bear some of the blame; every cuckolded husband, every unfaithful wife does. The only blameless soul in this disaster was Zachary.

Lost in a daze of pain and regret, I merged onto the Ninety-One, slowed the car unconsciously. I was twenty minutes away from changing my son's perfect world forever and in absolutely no hurry to get to that wretched juncture in his life, in our life.

Chapter 24

I ended up stopping three times on my way through Riverside in an effort to compose myself, finally found myself at a gas station a block away from Pops' house, wet paper towel over my eyes, breathing like an asthmatic, my thoughts a swirling mess. No closer to control after an agonized fifteen minutes, I threw away the towel, looked in the stained and cracked mirror, and decided to wait. To wait until Zachary was in familiar surroundings, with the people he loved, the things that gave him comfort. I knew that Pops would have a million questions, more importantly that he would be of great help with Zach; still, I couldn't bring myself to break this horrible news so far from home. The impossible task would be acting as if nothing were wrong tonight, as if my son's world wasn't forever changed. That wasn't going to be easy. Not for someone like me, whose emotions were on display for everyone to see, and not for my precious son, who could pick up his parents' mood by listening to their greeting. Like all children, Zachary had the most sensitive radar for trouble that one could imagine. These days, it must be something children picked up in school. From the kids in their class who've been through this kind of trouble, I thought, with a crushing sense of despair. I took a deep breath, put on a weak smile and tried to force myself to feel happy for my son.

One look at Zachary and Pops in his backyard patio, and I knew I'd made the right decision. Zach was bent over the charcoals, Mom's old gingham apron wrapped three times around his waist, a look of total concentration on his face. He looked up as I closed the slider and came over to the barbecue. "PaPa let me light the fire and now he's letting me cook the steaks." He grabbed a T-bone with his tongs, carefully as if he were handling plutonium, turned it over and gave Dad a huge grin. "About ten more minutes, PaPa?"

Dad checked the steak with a fork and nodded. "Sounds about right, Zach." Pops turned his attention to me, patted Zachary on the back. "Why don't you stand watch here while your dad and I set the table."

He opened the door for me, carefully closed it, and walked me to the far edge of the kitchen. I was instantly alert, guessed in an instant what was going on. "She called, didn't she, Dad?"

He stood with his back against the sink, a look on his face I'd only seen twice, at Mom's funeral and the day Jake moved to Arizona. "About an hour ago. Said you had a terrible fight. Said you were talking about a divorce."

I felt completely adrift, like a toddler at the controls of a jumbo jet. How could I explain this to the man I loved more than my life, who loved his whole family, including Natalie, with all his heart? His expression, of near-total devastation, told me that it would be impossible. A few seconds of soul searching while starting at Pops' face was all I needed; I decided to tell him straight up about what I came home to. "Natalie was unfaithful, Dad."

His voice was shaking. "And you're absolutely sure about this?"

I watched through the window as Zachary checked the fire, oblivious to our discussion in the kitchen. "I caught her in bed, Dad." Zachary gave a cheery wave; we both faced the window and returned his greeting. "With a friend of mine from residency."

Pops could no longer hide his emotions; he looked crushed, his face ashen, eyes filling with tears. "What're you going to do?"

"I have to leave, Dad." Zachary came and knocked on the door, waved for me to come and help him. I motioned for him to wait a few seconds, turned back to my dad. "We've been through counseling for over two years. She knew what was at stake." I walked over to the door, poised to open the slider. "The worst part is it's almost like she can't help herself, Dad." I waved to my son, who was struggling to land the steaks with his fork. "I'd do anything to avoid this, Pops. Avoid hurting Zachary. She's given me no choice."

I opened the door; Dad came closer, kept his voice low. "Just be sure you protect him." We smiled at Zachary, who had the steaks safely on an aluminum platter decorated with the Oakland Raiders logo. "He's the important one."

I nodded to Pops, unsure if that were even possible, whispered, "I know, Dad. I know."

The next day passed like an hour. I was dreading Sunday night, frantic as I was to shield Zachary from the fallout that was coming, wishing with all my strength that I could just stay there at Dad's with my son. Build a new life in Riverside. But I knew that wasn't fair to Zach, wouldn't do him any good to uproot him from all of his friends, his school, especially in this period of savage life change. So we said our good-byes to Pops and piled in the car for the long ride home. Zachary was asleep before we left Corona; I was wide-awake, gut roiling from the impossible prospect of telling my son that his family was splitting. How do you tell your son that he won't have an intact home anymore? How in the world do you tell a seven-year-old that everything will be all right when they see you walk out the door, one last time, taking his security and happiness with you? The closer we got to Newport, the fog surrounding our car like a funeral shroud, the less I knew. The more scared I became. I was now

like Zach. A scared, lonely little boy, facing the biggest loss of my
life. Uncertainty my only guarantee.

We got home forty minutes later and Zachary ran to Natalie,
wrapped her in a tight embrace, and kissed her all over. "How
was San Diego, Mom? We had a fun time with PaPa. Dad sucked
at golf and I got to cook the steaks. And they were delicious." He
turned and beamed at me. "Daddy told me." She hugged him
for at least five minutes, tears streaming down her face. Zachary
pulled away and reached a tender hand to her cheek. "Why are
you crying, Mommy? Did I do anything wrong? PaPa *told* me I
could cook." I watched in agony as Zachary backed away from
her, afraid he'd done something wrong; thoroughly disgusted
with Natalie in that split-second. He seemed ready to cry; I
wanted to slap her. "It's not my fault, Mommy."

She kissed his cheek, as I died a millimeter at a time. "No,
Honey. Mommy's crying because she's so happy to see you.
That's all." She led him to the den, sat him down on the sofa
beside her. "Now, tell me all about your weekend. Sounds like
you had a wonderful time."

Zachary patted the cushion beside him, smiled as I sat next to
him. He reached out a hand and held mine, my big seven-year-
old boy, still young enough to need my touch. I wasn't going to
make it through this, wouldn't be able to make him understand
this horrible tragedy, I knew, as I watched his animated face, listened to his excited voice. How could I ever make him understand something that I couldn't make sense of myself? Something
I'd dreaded my whole life, with my parents, especially with
Natalie? Now a sudden, awful reality.

I sat on the sofa, in a spinning world of pain, hearing
Zachary's words, feeling his joy, even as I knew I'd have to go
soon. Even as I knew he'd never get over this night. Never see
his parents in the same way.

I didn't hate Natalie. Not yet. I hated what she'd done.
Despised being in a situation that I'd tried so hard to avoid, tried

242

to insulate myself from. I looked at her, a few inches away on the sofa, and thought: all the work I'd put into trusting this woman, the first woman I'd let get this close to me. All for nothing. Destroyed in an afternoon by her selfish needs. By her urge to have just one more conquest. I'd never understand it; how could I ever hope to make a seven-year-old make sense of it?

We had arranged, during a tortured hour-long telephone conversation that morning, to have me sleep in the house that night, after we told Zachary the bad news. I wanted to be there for him, wanted him to have that little last bit of security. I'd told Natalie that I would stay in a motel the following night, then try to find a rental condo close to them while we decided to either separate or divorce.

An hour after we'd gotten home, the time had come. I looked over at Natalie, who nodded solemnly, her eyes filling with tears. I swallowed my pain and began the hardest conversation I'd ever had. "Son, Mom and I have something to tell you." Zachary looked from me to Nat, his eyes keenly on our expressions, hyper alert to the tone of voice he was hearing. I knew instantly that he'd sensed there was bad news coming, could feel a cloak of depression descend on the sofa as I struggled with my composure. Natalie buried her head in her hands and sobbed, unable to hide her pain any longer. Zachary put his head on her shoulder, rubbed her face with his hands, the innocent victim of our family tragedy comforting the villain. His compassion, misdirected as it was, seemed more than I could bear. I took a deep breath and let it out. "Son, you know Mom and Dad love you more than anything, don't you?"

Zachary looked at me as the last remaining support fell away from our world. His expression held the bottomless pain of every lost child, the crushing disappointment of every betrayed loved one. I had to concentrate just to breathe, thought my heart was going to stop. He had dissolved into tears, was hardly able to mumble his reply. "Don't get a divorce, Daddy." He clung to my arm, my heart in a million pieces. "Please, Daddy." He collapsed in Natalie's lap. "Please say you're sorry, Mommy, Daddy. Please don't do this."

He was inconsolable; I was nearly incoherent with grief. In the end, it was Natalie who spoke first, her voice choked with tears. "Daddy's going to stay tonight, then he's going to have a brand new place for you to go to, Zachy." She wiped his tears with a thumb on his cheek. "Just until Mommy and Daddy work things out."

He clung to that shred of hope as a rock climber to a wobbling piton. "Then you're not getting a divorce? Huh, Mommy?" He looked then at me, this was even worse, now he had a false sense of hope. I hated Natalie for the first time, then. For the cruel hoax she was perpetrating on our son, for fucking that goddamned son of a bitch Rick Lamb in our bed, for lighting a torch to our life. Zachary's voice tore through the last shreds of my composure. "Right, Daddy?"

I couldn't lie to him, couldn't raise his hopes, only to see them crushed a few weeks later. "Mommy's right, son. I'm going to get a new place. Just for you and me. Then we'll have to see."

I'd unleashed a new torrent of tears again, hated myself anew, hated the whole fucking mess, more than I hated death. His panicked tone shattered my resolve. "But you're still going to be my Mommy and Daddy, aren't you?"

I hugged him tight as he shook with sobs, my heart simply incapable of standing any more pain. "Of course, Zachary. We'll always love you. Always be your one and only Mommy and Daddy." I took Natalie's hand and we hugged him as a family. One last time. "Right, Mommy?"

She couldn't speak. Simply held onto our past with all her strength as Zachary sobbed against my chest.

As bad as that night was, and it was my worst by far, the next day, when I left our home, was worse. As long as I live I'll never forget my little boy's look the moment I walked out the garage door for the last time. The last time I left our home, left his life as his full-time Dad. He stood there, hugging his mother's leg, face smeared with tears, unable to even raise a hand and wave. He looked like a seven-year-old who'd already been through a lifetime of heartache. I knew I had to find the courage to say the words, to look my son in the eye, even as I walked away from his perfect little world.

I went back to him on legs that refused to move of their own accord, held out my arms, and felt him run into my hug. I kissed him on the head, held him tight, and said, "I love you more than you'll ever know, Zachary." He kissed me on the lips and I dissolved in tears. "You're my big boy. I'll get you through this. I promise you, honey."

He held my hand as I walked to my car. I could feel the smothering weight of disappointment with every step we took. Felt as if we were walking along the ocean floor, the sand sucking us down with every step. I stopped at the driver's door, straightened his school shirt, and gave him a last kiss. "I'll call you right after school. Okay, Zach?"

Natalie came over to the car a moment later and held his hand, pulled him slightly toward her house. Nodded sadly to me. "Drive carefully, Steven. Call us when you're settled." Settled? I thought. That seemed as foreign a concept as quantum physics to me that Monday morning in our garage.

I gave Zach another kiss and said, "Be brave, son. We're going to get through this. All of us." He gave me a weak nod, returned my kiss, and I closed my door. Let down the window and said, "Remember, honey. Daddy will call you this afternoon. The minute you get home from school." He nodded through his tears as I backed the car into the driveway, nearly unable to breathe. Zachary waved with all the dignity and courage I'd expect from a battle-hardened Marine, and a minute later, I was gone, alone with my thoughts. Not at all ready for my new life.

Chapter 25

TWO MONTHS LATER

A lot had happened in the past eight weeks. I'd called every divorce lawyer in south Orange County, forty-eight of them, without success. Seems as if my lovely wife had visited all of the "sharks," the slobbering bulldogs of the legal profession, paid a consultation fee to them, regardless of whether or not she wanted their representation. The lawyer I finally hired, Samantha Harris, told me it was common practice among the savvy divorcees in our litigious little county. Seems that Natalie had done her homework; she had cut me out of the shark pool by seeking advice from the baddest and the meanest, leaving me with the leftovers: wet-behind-the-ears newbies, or people from outside the county. My wife was represented by Raul Gelder, recently featured in *Los Angeles Magazine* as, inevitably, "The Shark of Newport," a regular fire-breathing king of torts. Samantha heaved a nervous sigh when I'd spoken his name, told me with more than a touch of awe that Gelder had represented the former Mrs. Donald Warren, ex-wife of the housing billionaire, landlord of the Irvine ranch, the largest undeveloped parcel of land left in Orange County. She gave me a little courtroom gossip that turned my guts to liquid. Seems that the randy Mrs. Warren had been caught in bed with the ranch manager, Andy Stephens, twenty years her junior. Her husband had it on tape. They had an "iron-clad" prenuptial agreement. Problem for Mr. Gelder? Not at all, according to Samantha. He got the ex-wife a settlement worth fifty million bucks. And alimony of twenty thousand a month until she reached the age of sixty-five or got married. Married? I had to laugh. Why would anybody get married under those circumstances? Samantha brought me out of my soul-killing reverie with a jolt. "Steven? Are you listening? This is important."

Although clearly not in Raul Gelder's league, Samantha Harris was no slouch. I'd gotten recommendations from three friends, people I trusted, some of whom had been on the other side of the courtroom from her. They all praised her preparation, her toughness, and her intelligence. I did my homework as well, looked her up in Hubble, the one-stop place to do your legal shopping, an exhaustive listing of all attorneys in the state. I'd found out that she was second in her class of two hundred at UCLA, law review, clerked for the California Supreme Court. All the important stuff the best lawyers did. I put my full faith and trust in her. All right, my critically wounded faith and brain-dead trust in her. Hard as it was, I scraped together her twenty thousand-dollar retainer and hoped for the best. She had just started my verbal tour through the divorce morass when she'd been sidetracked by the Raul Gelder saga. I signaled my alert attention to her story, took a sip of water, and settled in for the bad news. And man, oh man, was it bad.

She folded her hands on a fresh legal tablet, sat forward in her chair, and began. "Now you understand, don't you Steven, that you have virtually no rights in divorce court?" I started to bring up the constitution; she preempted me with an upraised hand. "I know what you're thinking, about a fair trial, due process under the law, and all of that." She shook her head sadly. "Forget it. The judges in Orange County, especially down at your division in Newport, favor the custodial mother almost a hundred percent of the time."

I had decided, even before hiring Samantha, that I'd be totally honest about the circumstances of our breakup, wanted my lawyer to understand that the divorce was largely Natalie's fault. So I began my sad little story. "What if the woman was at fault? What if . . ."

She cut me off again with a sarcastic laugh; she'd clearly heard it all before. "Tell me, Steven. Is your wife . . ." She consulted her notes. ". . . Natalie Bogner, M.D., a drug addict?" I shook my head, a sinking feeling permeating my stomach as I sensed where she was going. "Is she a whore? Does she work Fifth Street in Santa Ana at night? Do any call-outs to the carriage trade at the Four Seasons in Newport Center?"

I wanted to answer in the affirmative in the worst way. Even though Natalie didn't take money, I'd learned so much in the past few weeks, that I'd begun to wonder. I'd heard from three colleagues in the last month, each with direct knowledge about Natalie's multiple affairs. When questioned about their silence during our marriage, they said, to a man, "You seemed happy, Steven. We didn't want to rock the boat." With their reluctant help, I pieced together the truth a little at a time. Natalie had carried on a long-term affair with Lamb. One that predated our marriage. I further found out that the "Gruff Voice" belonged to her attending at Irvine, a doctor in his late sixties, named Sol Estes. I'd stumbled into one of his lectures by mistake a few weeks ago, sat mesmerized in the back of the room as he droned along in that unmistakable voice about the incidence of fibroids in Latinas.

A few moments later, back in my "real" world, I felt Samantha's stare and nodded weakly again. "I get the picture." I took another sip of water, it only made my acid stomach worse. "So what's the worst-case scenario?"

I took a look at her across the maple conference table. Samantha Harris was reasonably attractive; stood about five-six, with the wiry build of a distance swimmer, short, businesslike brown hair, and functional makeup. She wore no wedding band, no jewelry of any kind. I'd heard from a colleague that she was divorced from a judge up in Redlands. Heard she'd cleaned him out. A definite good sign. Aware of my appraisal, she flashed a sad grin, the kind a jailer gives a condemned man he's gotten to know as they take that long, last march together. She took her time, scanned the few pages of my story spread out before her on the legal pad. I'd told her all of it. Nat's settlement from the Porsche Guy, the house in her name, my income, her income, our cars, our investments, everything. I was starting to feel the urgent need to empty my bowel as she flipped back and forth through the pages. Shit, I thought, being on death row would be more fun. She looked up after about a year and shook her head. Again. "The bottom line, Steven? This county does not treat fathers fairly. Not at all." She glanced over the financials, which she'd circled with a red pen, and a moment later looked up again, meeting my hopeful stare with a look of seen-it-all fatalism. "You make a hundred and fifty and Dr. Bogner makes three fifty, right?"

"That's about right, why?"

She turned to her computer, loaded a software program she'd told me about the first time we'd met, the same one the judges use to determine child support and alimony. Wish they could see the truth on their little program, tell who was really at fault in this "no fault state," I thought bitterly, as Samantha crunched the numbers. When the hard drive stopped whirring, she slipped a piece of paper from the printer and swung her chair back to face me. "Now, these figures are only approximate and the judge, of course, has wide latitude in granting spousal support." She adjusted her glasses, gave me a seriously depressing frown.

"They don't have any latitude with child support." I nodded impatiently, steeling myself for the jolt of electricity to light up my brain, the lethal bolus of potassium and Fentanyl to stop my heart. "Looks like she'll be awarded three thousand a month for your son and about fifteen hundred a month for herself." She looked up from her notes, met my glazed expression with an impassive one of her own. "How does that sound?"

Like a prison-yard gangbang, I thought, with a sudden surge of abdominal cramps. I had just rented a condo at two thousand a month; my take home was barely eight grand after taxes. Take away three for Zachary and fifteen hundred for her, the car payment with insurance was about a thousand, and that left me with ... five ... hundred ... dollars. A month. I couldn't talk, tried a sip of water, made my throat even tighter. I managed to squeak a question though my constricted throat. "Are you sure? I mean, don't they take into account her income, her property, anything?"

Samantha tried to be soothing. I knew she was trying, but there's only so much sympathy a lawyer's face can convey; it's like a soap opera actor trying to do Shakespeare, there's a lot of room left for interpretation. She gave me her best impression of a concerned friend as she delivered the bad news. "No, they don't. The custodial parent has all the leverage. You must never forget that, Steven." How could I forget it when I was looking at financial Armageddon? I had about fifteen thousand left in the bank; at my current budget, that would last about six months. I knew without a doubt, that I'd be saying good-bye to the car. Maybe I could get custody of Zach, I thought, with a rush of optimism. Samantha resumed her legal sermon. "The mothers all claim outrageous expenses, of course. Lessons of all sorts for the children, exorbitant child care and clothing expenses, therapists, tutors, vacations, you name it." She added the coup de gras, the last fucking thing I needed to hear that morning. "And her lawyer, Mr. Gelder? He once got his client two thousand a month for a massage therapist." She gave a small laugh, a sign of professional pride, or jealousy. I didn't care which; I wanted to puke as she prattled on. "Can you believe it?" I was so depressed that I couldn't believe I was still alive. A few mumbles later, Samantha had finished her spiel; her expectant look told me that it was my turn.

"What if I go for custody of Zach? I'm not bitching about paying child support, not at all, I just think he'd be better off with me."

She suppressed a laugh, caught my hurt look and immediately regrouped into somber, ball-busting lawyer mode. "You're serious, aren't you?" I nodded weakly. "Excuse me please, Steven. In that case, two words. Forget it." I raised a hand to interject; she continued to speak over my objections. "Not going to happen. Not in this county. Not with this judge." She was rolling; my gut was ready to explode. "They all live in the past, these stupid judges. When women all stayed home baking cookies, cleaning and nesting, waiting for the little ones to come home. I know what you're thinking. Dr. Bogner is a career woman with a busy practice, loads of assets, but trust me, Judge Barta, a mean son of a bitch by the way, he'll still see her as Mrs. Cunningham, waiting for little Richie to come home from school."

I decided it was time to grasp at straws, put a stop to this metaphorical hemorrhage. "What about shared custody?"

She searched my face, recognized, no doubt, the look of a man clinging to a life preserver, hoping those finned fish bumping against his legs were just dolphins. "Too early, Steven. Maybe after a few years."

"A few *years*? What, like two or three?"

She glanced again at her notes. "Zachary is almost eight, right?" I nodded, my head ready to explode. She lowered the boom. "Maybe when he's twelve or so."

"Twelve? Jesus, that's more than four fucking years from now." She gave me a frown. "Sorry, I didn't mean to swear. I'm just upset, is all."

A placating smile, an upraised hand. "No need to apologize. I've heard worse. I just want you to be realistic, Steven. The system is slanted sharply away from you. Away from all fathers. You will *not* get custody. Not initially." She smiled, the first genuine warmth I'd felt from her all morning. "But take heart, Steven. Zach can choose to live with you when he turns thirteen." Great, five and a half fucking years from now, I realized with a fresh round of cramps. "Besides, everybody gets through this intact. Trust me."

I wanted to trust Samantha. Had no choice but to trust her, but still, I couldn't believe for a second that everybody would get through this intact. I prayed silently for Zachary, for me, and for Samantha. I prayed for the judge to have wisdom and for Samantha to have the mental acuity to battle this guy Gelder. Most of all, I prayed for myself. To have the strength to make a new home for my son. To be there when he needed me the most. Everything else was secondary.

She came around her desk, checked her watch and walked to the coat rack. "We have thirty minutes to make it to the O.S.C. Do you need to visit the restroom before we leave?"

Like I'd eaten a box of Ex-Lax for breakfast, I thought, as I excused myself and left the room. Here we go, the first Order to Show Cause. The initial step into that frightening and dangerous void called American Divorce Justice. I wondered, not for the first time, if I should bring a bulletproof vest and a couple fresh pairs of Depends.

"Orange County Superior Court. Honorable Judge Christopher J. Barta presiding. Please take a seat and come to order." The bailiff took her seat in the far corner of the courtroom, at a tiny desk that looked like it cost fifty bucks at K-Mart. The courtroom was nothing like I'd expected. Cramped, dingy; crowned by a very low ceiling, rimmed with boxes of charts, and filled with a nearly palpable residue of fear and disappointment. It had the musty smell of a basement library. My hurried trip to the bathroom wouldn't be the last today, of that I was sure.

We took our place at the table marked "Respondent;" Natalie sat with her lawyer at the desk marked "Complainant." Natalie had filed against me, didn't wait even a week to serve me at work, in front of all my friends, so she had the first say in court, or, more precisely, her lawyer did. And what a piece of work Mr. Raul Gelder was. A preening, condescending, five-foot-three piece of shit in a three thousand-dollar suit. A booming actor's voice, smooth tanned face, and a thick pompadour of steel gray hair swept back to an impeccable collar line.

The judge swooped in, settled down on the bench and glared at Samantha. Judge Barta looked about ninety, sparse silver threads of hair like stripped electrical wire plastered to a cone-shaped skull, beady eyes hidden behind tiny rimless glasses that were tinted slightly yellow. Great, I thought, cataract glasses. Blind justice incarnate. He sat there on the bench, surveying the two tables in turn, hands working in a prayerful gesture that made me think of Mr. Burns, the evil nuclear power plant owner on Zachary's and my favorite TV show, *The Simpsons*.

He cleared his throat and his reedy voice squeaked through the P.A. system. "On the matter Bogner versus Adler. OSC re: child and spousal support? Are we ready to proceed, people?"

The lawyers rose as one. I started to stand, Samantha laid a hand on my shoulder and smiled as she shook her head. "Samantha Harris for the Respondent, Dr. Adler, your honor."

"Raul Gelder for the Complainant, Dr. Bogner, your honor." Gelder turned slightly and gave me a glare, puffed out his scrawny chest. I gave him my "mad dog" stare, the one I'd learned from the gang bangers I'd treated at UCI. He didn't seem at all intimidated; kept his flat, reptilian eyes trained on mine.

The judge caught the silent exchange, took immediate control. "Mr. Gelder, care to begin, or would you like to continue your little staring contest with Dr. Adler outside?" I was impressed. Maybe I'd misjudged Mister Burns. Maybe he was going to put Natalie's pit bull in his place. Teach him some manners.

"Of course, your honor." Gelder's voice was like an announcer's, clear, strong and authoritative, the kind of voice that could make you buy life insurance. On your dog. I was instantly worried. "Dr. Bogner asks for four thousand five hundred per month child support and two thousand per month spousal support." I almost shit my pants; he was talking about ninety percent of my take home pay. I glanced over at Natalie. She knew exactly what I made; she had paid all of our bills. All at once it hit me as she returned my glare with a frosty stare of her own. She was out to gut me. One last twist of the knife. A final screwing I'd never forget. I kept my eyes locked on hers. She had cut her hair; it barely touched her ears. She looked every inch the successful, driven career woman. I shook my head; she immediately looked away, a secret smile playing across her lips as she turned her head toward the judge. Gelder droned on, an actor born to his role. "Dr. Bogner has extraordinary expenses that make these figures reasonable and customary, your honor." A moment's pause and Gelder asked and received permission to approach the bench. He handed the judge a sheaf of copied checks and financial statements, strutted back to our table, plopped an identical bundle on our table along with a smug smile for me. "As you can see, Dr. Bogner has had to pay for Zachary's therapist, a mathematics tutor, a sports coach, and daily child care in the combined amount of two thousand per month. In addition, you will see that Dr. Bogner has had to seek counseling with her psychiatrist on a twice-weekly basis, the costs of these visits totaling eighteen hundred dollars per month."

Gelder returned to his table. I leaned closer to Samantha and whispered, "This is ridiculous, she has insurance to pay for that. And a sports coach, give me a break." Samantha warned me to be quiet. Too late. The judge gaveled me down with a fierce look that wiped away any fantasy I might have harbored regarding his benevolent nature. I was shell shocked, mumbled a weak "Sorry," as Samantha took a sip of water.

Judge Barta spoke from on high, his breathy voice cracking with emotion. "Control your client or I'll have him sit outside. Is that clear, Ms. Harris?"

She stood and I sneaked a look at Natalie, caught her evil little smile and quickly looked away. Samantha answered in a clear and confident voice, "Crystal clear, your honor."

The judge nodded his cadaverous head, cleared his throat loudly in the microphone. "Since you're standing, why don't you get on with it? Present your facts?"

"Gladly, your honor." Samantha stood ramrod straight, her manner self-assured, controlled. "Your Honor, Dr. Adler asks for full physical custody of the minor child Zachary and child support in the amount of five thousand dollars per month from Dr. Bogner. Additionally, Dr. Adler seeks four thousand per month for spousal support." I could hear whispered murmurs from the table to my left, kept my gaze on Samantha. She was amazing, I thought with a gush of optimism. We hadn't even discussed this. Maybe it would work after all. She reached down, grabbed her cup and took another sip of water. "Dr. Adler has an extremely flexible schedule as an Emergency Room physician and would easily be able to arrange his life to accommodate his son's school and after-school activities in order to give the minor child Zachary the attention he so clearly deserves in this most difficult time of his young life." Gelder rose to object; Barta waved him down with a curt gesture, a judicial "sit-the-fuck-down." Samantha acknowledged the judge with a nod. "Thank you, your honor. Dr. Adler needs this level of support in order to provide Zachary with the level of care and comfort he has become accustomed to." She took a quick glance at my financials. "Dr. Bogner lives in a house with an appraised valuation of five million dollars. Dr. Adler would have to rent an equivalent home in the same neighborhood until such time that he could afford to buy. Dr. Adler will be incurring child care, transportation, and school costs that more than justify this level of support." She smiled down at me, full of confidence, radiating professional aplomb. I was on top of the world, believed she'd done it.

Gelder could sit still no longer. He was on his feet, a nasty sneer directed at our table. "Your honor, if I may. Dr. Adler has no experience as a parent. He lives by himself in a small rental condo ten miles away from Zachary's school. Whereas Dr. Bogner has everything young Zachary needs to flourish right there in her home. His books, his furniture, his friends close by, his school a few blocks away and a full-time, live-in house-keeper that Zachary has grown up with, a loving woman he calls his "auntie." In short, your honor, Zachary is *already* home." He sat down at the table next to my loving wife, pointed at me as if I were a triple murderer. "Don't let that man tear his secure little life apart. Keep Zachary with his mother. Where he belongs."

Samantha stood to rebut. The judge glared her back into her seat. "I've heard quite enough, Ms. Harris. Give me a moment and I'll render my decision." I took a stuttering breath, felt my guts clench again, sensed Gelder and Natalie staring at my face, felt their smug, self-satisfied smiles as Mr. Burns shuffled a stack of papers on the bench. "I'm ordering that full physical custody of the minor child Zachary Adler remain with Dr. Bogner and further that Dr. Adler pay directly to Dr. Bogner the sum of three thousand dollars per month child support and fifteen hundred per month spousal support due the first and the fifteenth of each month in two equal installments. Said awards to remain in effect until trial." He grabbed a huge, month-at-a-glance type calendar and slid his chair to the edge of his desk, consulted with his court clerk, a skeletal woman in her seventies, turned back to us a few minutes later. "The trial will commence in three months' time, on Monday, August fifteenth at nine sharp. As for visitation, I am granting Dr. Adler alternate weekends to commence at six P.M. Friday and to conclude promptly at six P.M. Sunday." He banged his gavel, harder than I'd thought necessary, and stood to leave.

I turned to Samantha and couldn't contain myself another second. "That's it? Just four days a month? How can that be fair?" She leaned over to shush me. I couldn't stop, was too close to melting down. "This is total *bullshit*, Samantha."

She took my elbow and towed me to the doorway, hissing in my ear. "This judge is an asshole. Trust me. He *will* cite you for contempt if you keep this up. And he *will* throw you in jail. Zachary doesn't need that, now does he, Steven?"

We'd made it to the corridor. Gelder and Natalie brushed by, all smiles as Gelder reached over to shake Samantha's hand, putting on a big show for my benefit. He then offered to me; I felt like spitting a huge one into his palm. He didn't miss a beat. "Suit yourself, Doctor. Remember, this is strictly business." He took Natalie's arm, guided her down the packed hallway, a proprietary arm around her waist. "Right, Dr. Bogner?"

Her reply was lost in the din of litigants, bailiffs, and courtroom junkies. Typical for Natalie, she just had to have the last word: she turned to face me and mouthed her favorite retort, "*Loser.*"

A half hour later, following an excruciating post mortem, I said my good-bye to Samantha, who vowed to fight on, cautioned me to stay calm, and said finally that the initial award was always the highest, said she'd get it "knocked down to something reasonable next time."

I found my car in the parking structure. Snatched a thirty-dollar parking ticket from the windshield with a muttered curse, "What a great goddamned, fucking day!" I started the Porsche and made my way down the ramp to the street below, thinking of what I'd have to do immediately in order to meet Barta's ridiculous order. I patted the Porsche's dash and said a silent good-bye. It didn't hurt too much. I knew I'd have to sacrifice, knew it would be brutal. And, in the end, it was.

The important thing, I reminded myself as I merged onto PCH, was to keep Zach's head above water. He was first, foremost, and only, my top priority. The Porsche could go bye-bye, not a problem. As for Natalie and her reptilian lawyer? They could go suck an egg.

Chapter 26

TWO WEEKS LATER

Our first weekend together and I had been looking forward to it like a holiday in France. I'd called Zachary every night after school, just to keep in contact; we talked about school, his pals, occasionally his life, although the divorce became the proverbial eight hundred-pound gorilla you have living in your guestroom, too big to ignore, too painful and potentially dangerous to deal with, just yet. We made plans to go to dinner on Friday night at Zach's favorite, *Dive,* a place built and outfitted like a submarine. They had it all: a periscope in the middle of the place, ear-splitting claxons to announce a birthday celebration, and authentic two-inch-thick portholes to look out at the parking lot. The food? Well, lets just say it was like all the food in the military. Lukewarm, gooey, and packed full of carbs.

I picked him up at five till six, anxious as a teen on his first date. It had been more than two weeks since I'd actually seen my son, what with the courtroom wrangling, finalizing the judge's stupid order, and coordinating schedules with my lovely wife. I parked the car, threw open the door, bolted to the front door, and rang the bell. Boy, was that a strange sensation; standing like a door-to-door salesman outside my own home, waiting to see my flesh and blood. Natalie had informed me the previous week that she had changed the locks, warning me not to try and use the old one, said she "didn't want to embarrass me." I wondered about that, of course, seemed like just another game she wanted to play. Samantha confirmed this, said this was very common with custodial parents. She went on to predict that Natalie would "find my pressure point." She explained that divorce battles always came down to two basic bones of contention, money or the children. She said that women in particular tended to use one or the other as a weapon against the ex-spouse. I knew Zachary would be target number one, since money was not an issue; I'd liquidated all of my extraneous assets, including the Porsche, in order to fulfill my obligations.

I waited impatiently, like a schmuck, for Natalie to open the door and deliver my kid. I tried with all my strength to keep my mind on the weekend rather than the humiliation and boiling rage that Natalie clearly had intended me to feel.

After what felt like thirty minutes and three rings of the doorbell, the door finally opened, precisely at six P.M. Maria answered the door with the saddest smile I'd seen in years. She bid me welcome and I started to come into the foyer. Maria shook her head, her expression one of acute grief. She came a step closer and whispered, "No, Señor Adler. I go get Zachary. Missus Natalie say you wait outside." She watched as my face fell, took instant pity on me and gave me a warm hug. "I so sorry, Señor Adler. I really am." She wiped a tear with her sleeve and turned to get my son, a whispered parting shot over her shoulder, "This is not right. This trouble." You've got that right, I thought. Halfway to the hall she turned and gave me a wave. "I be right back."

There it was. I was now officially banned from my past. What a shitty thing to do, but totally in character from my viewpoint. Natalie and her three hundred-an-hour asshole had inundated Samantha with motions and frivolous paperwork: the classic pre-trial blizzard designed to make the other side spend money. A mean and nasty trick that Gelder was particularly fond of. Natalie had indeed picked a mouthpiece who reflected her core values: pettiness, vindictiveness, and insatiable greed.

All of those loathsome thoughts dissipated like fog in a Santa Ana wind as my son ran into my arms. Even though it had only been three weeks since I'd seen him, he looked taller, more mature. I hugged him close, inhaling his scent, and felt my eyes instantly water. This wasn't right. Not at all. I should be with him constantly. He needed me. I needed to be with him like I needed to breathe. I made a promise then and there, to fight to the end to make that happen. Natalie and her lawyer be damned, I was going to get either full or at least half-time custody of Zachary if I had to spend every cent I had. Zachary broke off our hug and looked in my face, eyes etched with concern as he saw my tears. He took my hand, his voice breaking. "Dad, are you all right? Aren't you happy to see me?"

I picked him up, slung him over my shoulder and ran to the car. "Don't I look happy, silly?" I raced around the front lawn like a crack-head as Zach squealed with delight. I had missed that laugh so much, I realized, while running around the yard. I wished I could bottle that sound; that feeling of unrestrained joy and make billions selling it to divorced dads all over the country.

On top of the world once again, I set him down beside my brand new, three-year-old, used Nissan Sentra, an okay, perfectly fine car, but not the fancy new Porsche Zach was expecting.

He was just a kid, couldn't hide his surprise as I opened the door for him. "Dad, what happened to your car?"

I buckled him into place and ran over to my side, slid behind the wheel. "I sold it, son." He gave me a curious look; Zach and I had talked a lot about cars; he was turning into a car nut just like his old man. We'd rhapsodized nonstop about Porsches and Ferraris until Natalie seemed ready to scream, so I knew I had to be honest with Zach, about this and about everything, he deserved nothing less than the straight truth. "I had to sell it, honey." I started the Nissan, backed out of the driveway. "Things are a little tight for Daddy right now."

We made it down the block and I was almost bowled over by my son's next statement, his heart-melting compassion. "I have some money, Dad." He reached over and laid a hand on my knee. "I don't need it."

I fought the lump in my throat as we turned the corner onto PCH. My empathetic, beautiful son. I realized, not for the first time, how very special he was, how undeserving of him I was. I looked over at his earnest face as we stopped at MacArthur and ruffled his hair. "Don't worry, buddy. We have plenty of cash. It's just that the car was eating into the money I needed to help take care of you. And you come first." We turned north, headed for the San Diego Freeway and Costa Mesa, home of *Dive*. A few minutes later we were merging onto the freeway, Zach's hand in mine. I was filled with such love and longing, I could have died happily in that instant. I gave him a broad smile. "Ready to eat, Zach?"

He settled back into his seat and gave me a thumbs up. "I could eat a rhino, Dad. Totally."

We laughed as the Friday night traffic swarmed around our little car, bouncing along in the slow lane as we headed for a new life together.

The restaurant was everything I'd expected; loud, exhilarating, tacky, and fun as a trip to an amusement park. Zach ate like a pro linebacker: a hamburger bigger than his face, fries, chocolate milkshake, and we shared a hot fudge sundae served in a goblet the size of a goldfish bowl, "Death by Chocolate," for dessert. I was feeling overstuffed, sleepy and more than a little nauseous; my son was, in a word, wired. There was a video arcade attached to the restaurant and he dragged me in, begging me for "just five minutes, Dad."

An hour and a half later, we stumbled to the car, completely overwhelmed by flashing lights, fake guns, and screaming kids. I'd only been in arcades a couple of times before with Zach, and only for a few minutes or half an hour. I'd never realized before the two basic truths about arcades; they are as loud as a jet engine factory and as addictive as cocaine. I went through forty dollars of quarters fighting aliens, driving race cars, and shooting ghouls in a haunted castle, Zach's favorite. He got nearly to the end of the last level, an accomplishment of epic proportions. I was conflicted to say the least; as I didn't want my son to waste his life on video games, yet still admired his skill with the little blue-plastic, electronic gun. The other kids treated him like a rock star. Zach was beaming.

A half hour later, we were on the San Diego freeway, headed back to my place in Irvine, when Zachary turned to me in the darkened car. "Dad, you know what?"

I changed lanes, settled into the fast lane as we passed Newport Beach and the exit to "our" old home. "Yes, son?"

He kicked off his shoes and reclined his seat. "This car is really comfy. I can stretch out way better than I could in the Porsche."

I glanced over at my son, warm and cozy in my little Nissan, a car that cost less than the engine in my other one, realized the only important thing to him, to me, was that we were together. I was once again reminded of this basic truth: kids only need love, nothing fancy, just a clean, safe place to sleep and unconditional love.

Ten minutes later we were home. A block-long row of identical brown stucco boxes. A two-bedroom condo off Van Karman in the heart of Irvine. Convenient to the freeway and work; but a world away from Zach's leafy, expensive neighborhood in Newport. We parked in the carport, grabbed Zachary's overnight bag, and climbed the back stairs to my apartment. I decided halfway up the stairs to take Zach to South Coast Plaza first thing Saturday morning and shop for the clothes he liked. I hated having him shuttle between two homes, would never get used to it, but at the very least I wanted him to have all of his favorite things, his stuff, at our home too. With all the dislocation in his life, he needed to have that security.

I opened the door and showed him around. It was pretty standard apartment fare for Southern California. They called it a condo, but it was really just a slightly upscale apartment: den/living room in the entryway, leading to a kitchen with a tiny table, and a small deck overlooking the communal pool. Zach ran out onto the deck and nearly jumped out of his shoes. "Dad. Can we use the pool?" Natalie's house, our old house, didn't have a pool; we used to take Zach to the country club across from Newport Center to swim. He liked it, but was always bugging us to put in a backyard pool. Natalie consistently refused, citing the small yard, health and safety risks, and maintenance hassles as her excuses.

I joined him on the deck. The pool was less than fifty feet away, sparkling in the gloom, surrounded by lounge chairs, a small stand of Liquid Amber, and a cabana that sold soft drinks, nachos, and candy bars. "You bet. In fact, we're going shopping in the morning. Gonna get all your stuff, so you don't need to keep bringing that bag with you."

"Swell, Dad. I'm gonna go look at my room." I followed his footsteps down the hall. His was the first room on the left; the bathroom on the right belonged to him as well. I had tried to furnish it the way he liked; small bureau, queen-sized bed, and a couple of nightstands. Try as I might, it didn't feel right. I watched from the threshold: Zachary jumping on his new bed, testing the springs and I realized something was missing. Zachary. His toys, his posters, his scent. All the little-boy stuff I'd grown to love, things I'd taken for granted at the other house. This room seemed like a replica of a boy's room, sterile and generic. Something we'd have to work on, Zachary and I. A trip to Target would do the trick, I knew, as I watched him acclimate to his new place. Zachary didn't seem to mind; he was racing around the room, checking out the closet, the drawers, the nightstands. After a few laps of his tiny room, he plopped his bag on the bed and smiled up at me. "This is a way bigger bed than the one at home, Dad." He must have seen me wince, even though I covered it with a quick smile. "I mean at Mom's home, Dad."

I sat next to him on his brand new bed, put an arm around him. "This is home too, Zach. Always." I kissed his head, inhaled the comforting smells of French fries, little boy sweat, and new clothes. "We'll make this work, son. I promise."

We sat there for a few minutes, just holding each other, getting used to our stark new reality. A moment later Zach looked up at me with childlike wisdom and said, "I know you will, Daddy. Because I know you love me."

"Whole bunches. More than anything in the whole world, Zach." I hugged him closer. "More than you'll ever know."

We watched a little TV, some mindless sitcom about kids in high school that Zach pronounced "beyond stupid." That didn't prevent us from laughing like fools, of course. At ten, I showed Zach his bathroom, laid out his toothbrush and soap, marched him into the shower, and went to the kitchen to straighten things up. He came out ten minutes later, smelling fresh and soapy, dressed in the jammies I'd bought for him just before the trouble started; a flannel set of *Star Wars* pajamas that were already getting to be too short for him. He was going through a growth spurt, no doubt about it now, I realized. Looked to be headed for my height of six three. I asked him if he needed anything more; he shook his head, clearly ready for bed.

I followed him to his new room, watched him climb into bed, and came over to tuck him in. He looked happy, content in his new space; I was nearly overwhelmed. Having him home with me, even in this new and sterile place, was what I'd wanted since I was kicked out of our house. *All* I'd wanted since the trouble started. He looked so comfortable, so safe, yet, at the same time, so vulnerable. I decided then and there to talk to him this weekend about the divorce. I needed to find out how badly he'd been hurt, how much this had affected him. More than that, I needed to start helping him adjust to his new world. A moment later, I smoothed the blankets up under his chin and kissed his head. "Good night, son."

I lingered for a few moments, finally moved to the doorway and reached for the light-switch. He leaned on an elbow and motioned me closer. "Dad?"

"Yes, Zach?"

He looked slightly embarrassed, his voice barely above a whisper. "Could you tell me a story?"

He hadn't asked for a story in more than two years. I knew that kids regressed when they were stressed, and a divorce was only slightly less frightening than the death of a parent to a small child, so I completely understood.

I lay down beside him and pulled him into my arms. He looked up at me with an expression of complete trust mixed with heartbreaking longing. A look that nearly shattered my soul. Again. A look that seemed to say, *Why do we have to live like this, Dad?* A look that made me nearly faint. Made my determination to have our discussion that much stronger. I could almost read his emotions as I looked into his eyes: The disjointed feeling of shuttling between two homes, the frightening loss of security, the divided loyalties he had to be experiencing. It must have been terrifying for him to go from a loving family to this; where every time he told me how much he loved me, he had to think about his loyalty to Natalie. As sensitive as Zach was, it must have been killing him to go back and forth emotionally. I couldn't begin to imagine his pain. The bottom line in this whole mess was: this was my son, my whole world, and he needed me like he'd never needed anyone before.

I'd rather cut off my right arm than see him suffer anymore. I knew I couldn't change this situation; Natalie had made that abundantly clear. She'd said reconciliation was out of the question, and I'd had to agree; she'd so clearly stepped over the line. So here we were, stuck in gruesome reality. Nothing to do but keep fighting the system and make the best of it.

I hadn't a clue about what kind of story to tell my son, settled eventually on the tale of a boy named Timmy and his dad, Brian. They traveled together to a new land, a place very different from the one they knew. A place with new rules, new expectations. Their journey filled with uncertainty. They didn't know how to get there, or what they'd find when they arrived. Timmy and his dad faced challenges and trials all the way to their new place, but no matter how bad it got, they stuck together. Always.

We fell asleep together on his bed. I awoke a few hours later, started to go to my room. Zach rolled over, flung an arm over my chest and said, "Stay with me, Daddy." He moved closer, murmured, "Please."

And so I did.

Chapter 27

Our first Saturday together was, in a word, bliss. I woke up at seven, a little disoriented since I'd never slept in his room. Zach was conked out, all curled up under his new blankets, deep in the sleep of the innocent.

I went outside, collected the paper, and plopped on the sofa, scanning the *Times*. This was an entirely different life, no doubt about that, yet I had Zach with me, even for a short time, and nothing could ever change that. I'd arranged my work schedule so that there were no conflicts all the way till Christmas and was going to take a week or two off for the holidays. I was planning a surprise visit to Mammoth, wanted to teach Zach snowboarding. He'd been telling me all about it since his birthday, seemed that all his little pals were already into it. I was looking forward to it; had long wanted to learn myself, and it would be a great opportunity to get some fresh air and exercise. Besides, Mammoth is one of the prettiest places in the country.

Zach stumbled into the bathroom at around nine. I could hear him opening and closing drawers, looking, no doubt, for his stuff;

as he always liked to take a shower before breakfast. I walked down the hall, knocked on the door, and said, "Morning, buddy. Sleep well?"

I could hear his muffled voice from the shower, felt glad that he was making himself at home. "Sure. How about you, Dad?"

"Never better." I heard the shower door close and opened the bathroom door. "How about French toast and bacon for breakfast?"

He opened the door slightly and peeked out; his hair soapy, a loopy grin on his face. "Do you even know how, Dad?"

I took a handful of cold water from the sink and dumped it on his head. "Watch your mouth, boy. Of course I do."

He screamed from the impact of the cold water, closed the door and laughed. "Maria taught you, huh?"

I shook my head; this kid didn't miss a thing. I had to cop to that one, I couldn't cook anything except spaghetti and grilled cheese sandwiches. With this new arrangement, I'd best hurry up and learn, I mused. Actually our housekeeper, Maria, *had* sent me a bunch of her recipes. She had gone out to lunch with me two weeks after I'd been evicted by Natalie and taken pity on Zach and me. She'd told me she was heartbroken, wanted to be sure her little Zachary was well fed. Bless her heart, I was really going to miss her. She loved Zachary like his second mother.

Zach started singing in the shower, I didn't recognize the tune, another hole in my young-boy-stuff education. I sat on the countertop. "Of course she taught me, Zach. Otherwise we'd be sentenced to a lifetime of cold cereal and toast."

He stuck his head out again, his hair standing straight up. "I knew it." He stared expectantly. "So, Dad? Are you gonna go make it or stay here while I take a bath? Sheesh!"

I backed out of the bathroom. "Man, oh, man, I can tell what my job is around here." I walked down the hallway; happy as I'd been in months. Shouted toward the bathroom, "Why don't you wear your sweats today, son? It's going to be a little windy. Okay?"

His muffled voice from the shower. "'Kay."

Breakfast was surprisingly good for my first time ever. I'd used a little too much cinnamon and too many eggs, but otherwise it was "better than Denny's," according to my son, the food critic. We decided to drive over to Disneyland. Zach's choice. I actually wanted to take him sailing, didn't want to fall immediately into the cliché of being a "Disneyland Dad," but gave in reluctantly as he was so intent on it. A half-hour after breakfast we were dressed, scrubbed, and packed; ready for our big day in the Magic Kingdom.

Nearly there, I pointed out the dirty gray form of the hospital from the Five freeway. Zach said, "I've already been there, remember, Dad?" I must be getting old, I thought, I was sure he'd be interested in seeing my workplace, forgetting that his whole class had been there less than six months ago. I tried again, pointing to my old apartment complex, a long row of depressing, dung-brown buildings looming on our left. I didn't raise my son to be a snob, but he pronounced it "yucky." Funny, it seemed all right a few years ago, but on second thought, maybe he was right and I'm just too cheap to notice.

We'd picked a good day for the park; not too crowded, not too hot for May. The best part? I'd snagged some forty-percent-off tickets from the medical school. We both got in for fifty bucks. Couldn't beat that.

We had a ball, even though it was just the two of us. I'd asked Zach in the car on the way over if he didn't want to call one of his friends, see if they wanted to come with. He shook his head, said, "Maybe next time, Dad." Being hypersensitive as I was lately, I'd wondered at the time if he were ashamed of our new budget housing. Most of his friends lived behind the gates, at the Pelican Hills Golf Course across from the Newport Center. He put that ridiculous fear to rest halfway to the park, when he leaned closer and said, "Can I have my friends over to your house sometime, Dad?"

I mussed his hair. "You mean our house? Of course. Just say the word. I can switch bedrooms with you, so you and your friends won't be so cramped."

"Really? That'll be awesome, Dad. I can have 'em over for swim parties. And barbecues. PaPa taught me all about it, you know."

"I sure do. Those steaks the other night were just right." I felt a renewed sense of confidence; Zachary seemed happy that Saturday morning. Decided to go to the source for confirmation. "This is going to be okay, isn't it Zach?"

His voice was barely above a whisper, his tone wavering. Not the ringing endorsement I'd naïvely hoped for. "Yes, Daddy." I should have known better. Zachary's reaction reinforced my resolve to talk this over with him. I'd expected sulking, depression, even regression with Zach. That's what I'd read about when I did some research before the hearing. Even though he was obviously stunned, this early after the trouble, Zachary seemed okay with the arrangement, had clearly given it some thought, said he was looking forward to the next time at my place.

The trip to Disneyland was pure enjoyment. I had to give it to Disney; you really did forget your troubles when you entered its gates. We made the whole circle: Tomorrowland with the hokey, futuristic shrinking ride, the submarines, miniature cars, in short, everything. I counted the rides; we had gone on thirty-five attractions, some more than once, by the time the parade started at nine.

We'd scoped out the perfect viewing place; the curb in front of the Main Street turn-around, close to the exits and right in front of everything. Zach was holding up better than I. We had walked at least twenty, what had felt like fifty miles, stood in line for about eight hours, yet he looked like he could do it again. Until we sat down. He started out sitting next to me, jumbo popcorn in his lap, eager expression plastered on his face. By the time the parade started a few miles away in Adventureland, he was on my lap, fast asleep. I had to will myself to stay alert now, even though I was just as tired. It felt wonderful holding him, reminded me of the picture I had on my desk when he was about a month old. He had grown so much since then, yet he was, and always would be, my little boy. As I sat there with Zachary in my lap, I realized sadly that Disneyland wasn't the same without Natalie. We were last there two years before, for Zach's fifth birthday. We'd raced around the park like fifth-graders, joking, chasing each other, and living it up. Despite all the trouble we'd had recently, a part of me still missed her, missed our togetherness as a family. I wondered at the time if one ever really gets over that feeling.

The parade rounded the bend to our left, and Zach awoke with a start. He didn't miss a beat; jumping to his feet, his hand in mine as the brightly colored floats scooted by, electronic music blaring. He looked like a TV ad for the Magic Kingdom: bright eyes, fresh-scrubbed looks and unmistakable excitement. He pointed to the sky a few minutes later. "Look, Dad. Fireworks. My favorite."

I had to crane my neck around a float carrying Snow White to see clearly. The fireworks show had just started over the Castle, a few hundred yards away in Adventureland. This version was timed to the electronic music and was thrilling, even to this exhausted forty-year-old guy.

We reluctantly left the park at eleven. Zach had begged me to go to the Matterhorn one more time. I was tempted; it had been a spectacular day, didn't want it to end, but had to admit to being tired. He took pity on me, grabbed my hand, and said, "It's okay, Dad. I know you're kinda old now. We can go home to bed."

"Old, huh?" I started running for the parking lot, anxious to show him up. He took off a split second later; was resting against the sign for the tramway before I huffed and puffed up to the line, wearing a smug expression that seemed to mock me by saying, *What took you so long?*

Back home after midnight, I showed him again where his night light and his bathroom were, and he shooed me out of his room with an impatient, "Good night, Dad. Love you."

I kissed him and said, "Love you too, buddy boy."

Sunday, Bloody Sunday. I guess reality had set in for both of us. I awoke feeling restless and undeniably depressed. The weekend had gone by like an hour; filled with renewed bonding, love, and total fun. I knew this would happen. It was inevitable, there were only so many hours in a day and when you looked at our so-called arrangement in the cold light of day, it became clear that Zachary and I would only be together for forty-eight hours every two weeks. Out of a whole month. No wonder I was depressed. I sat on the sofa, listlessly scanning the *Times*, hoping that my son would fare better than I.

Fat chance. I could hear him rustling around in his room a little after eleven. Not making a lot of noise, but not exactly bouncing out of bed, either. I walked down the hallway and listened at his door. Thought I heard muffled cries. I knocked on his door and called his name. Nothing. Opened the door and there he was. Curled up on his pillows, knees under his chin, crying openly, his face red, mouth down-turned as he watched me come into his room. I walked over to his bed, sat down, and held him tight. "What's wrong, son? Are you feeling all right?" I felt his forehead with the back of my hand: cool and dry. I asked him again; he burrowed deeper into my chest.

"I don't want to go home, Daddy." He was sobbing now, even as my heart was sinking. "I wanna stay here. With you." He threw his arms around my neck. I felt all of his anguish, mixed with my overwhelming sense of longing in the depth and strength of our love, the power of our hug, wanted more than anything to make this all go away. To take him to school in the morning and tell him that everything was fixed when I picked him up that afternoon. I wanted him to have the life he deserved, with two full-time parents who loved him dearly. I wanted what every parent wants for their children. To have it better than they did as kids.

Hard as it was, I knew this was the time for our discussion. I held him close, his sobs vibrating on my chest. "We need to talk about this, son." He burrowed deeper into my arms. "I need to know how you're handling this, Zach. So I can start to help you."

"I don't know if I can do this, Daddy." He grabbed a handful of my sweatshirt, his arms tight around my neck. "Sometimes I want to run away from Mom's." He choked back a sob. "Call you to pick me up."

I gently cupped his chin with my palm, brought his face level with mine; waited until his eyes met mine. "You can't ever do that, Zachary. Understand?" I felt my throat nearly shut completely as I held him close. "You can never leave Mommy's without telling her where you're going, Zach. Never."

He lowered his eyes. "I know, Dad. It's just so hard." He met my gaze again, tears filling his eyes. "I just want it back like it used to be."

So do I, son, I thought, as tears began to run down my cheeks. More than you know. "I don't think that's going to happen, Zach. So we have to find a way to make this work."

He hit me between the eyes with his next question. The one I'd been dreading for the past two months. "What about me, Dad. How come you can't fix it with Mom? Can't make her take you back home?"

How could I tell my innocent son the truth? How could I begin to tell him what was in my heart? There was no good answer to his critically important question. I couldn't lie to him, would never do that, yet I couldn't divulge the true story, needless to say. In the end, I relied on platitudes, even as I excoriated Natalie in my mind, berated myself for putting up with her outrageous behavior long enough for it to blossom into this mess. "I can't fix it, Zach. I can only do the best I can with you. Right here in our new home."

It was impossible to gauge Zach's reaction to my weak answer. He fixed me with a stare that chilled me to the bone. I'd expected more tears, more sobs. He simply nodded, his expression placid. He took his time, eyes on mine, and said, "I don't know where to turn. I don't know what to say to Mom sometimes." He sighed as my heart sank. Zach looked so depressed, I was instantly worried about him, decided then and there to arrange a session with Olivia Tanner. "She's mad all the time. Always yells about my homework and how lazy I am." This brought a fresh rush of tears to his eyes, a surge of anger to my heart. I held him closer. "I'm not good enough for her."

As much as I'd been dreading this talk, the reality was much worse. Zach was being systematically destroyed emotionally and psychologically, and it was more than I could bear to see him in such pain. I hated like hell to come to Natalie's defense, but knew that Zach needed us both, regardless of her attitude. "Mom's just upset, like all of us. Just remember that she loves you, honey. We both love you with all our hearts." He shook his head against my chest. "Really, Zach. She does love you. She only wants the best for you."

He looked again into my eyes, a lifetime of sadness in his watery blue eyes. "I try, Daddy. I really try to be good for her." He blinked away his tears, trying to be brave. "But nothing works."

He was telling me that he was ready to give up. That he couldn't take the strain of meeting Natalie's impossible expectations, while trying to be happy-go-lucky when he was with me. I knew without thinking that I was overmatched in this struggle. Hoped with all my heart that Olivia would be able to help pull us through. "We only ask you to do your best, son." I ran a hand through his hair. "I'll have a talk with Mom, make sure she understands this, Zachary." I gave him a kiss. "Promise." He kissed my cheek, seemed to calm a little. "Is there anything else bothering you, Zach? Anything you want to get off your chest?"

He shrugged and looked at the floor, clearly ready to talk but uncertain where to begin. I waited him out, my mind whirling with emotion: sadness, guilt, fear, finally a firm resolve to make this better, any way I could. A few moments later he looked into my eyes, his voice low. "I don't know where I belong, Daddy. Your place or Mom's." He wiped his tears with his pajama sleeve. "It's like I don't have a real home anymore. A home like all my friends have."

A spike through my heart: the stigma of divorce. The very thing I'd been hoping to avoid, for Zachary's sake; the American Curse, our society's very own Scarlet Letter "D." I searched my mind for a comforting answer, came up empty. "You have two homes, Zachary. And two parents who would do anything to make you feel secure. Anything to make sure you knew how much we loved you. Always."

"But it's not the same, Daddy." How could I refute that logic? I knew without a doubt that he'd been facing peer pressure of the worst kind, already. Just a few weeks after our separation. I understood, on a cellular level, Zach's impulse to flee; wanted in that instant to take him to Riverside, Vegas, New York, anywhere, to start a new life. Knew, of course, that it was an impossible dream.

"As hard as this is for all of us, Zach, we have to get used to it." He met my eyes; I noticed that his were red-rimmed but dry. "I know this is hard for you to believe, but give it some time and it won't feel so bad to you. Won't seem so hard to come here after being at Mom's for two weeks."

He surprised me, not for the first time, with his depth of understanding, his maturity. "I didn't mean to make you feel bad, Daddy. I love coming here. It's just . . ."

I gave him another kiss. "I understand, son. You're having a hard time adjusting. We all are, believe me." Take that to the bank, my precious son, we're *all* in Hell together.

He hugged me tighter. "Will this ever get any better, Daddy?"

I decided to tell him about Olivia Tanner, about my plans to have him work through his pain, get him started toward an accommodation. "It will, Zachary, but we're going to have to keep talking about it. As a family." He nodded, clearly anxious to hear the rest of it. "I'd like it if we could go see a counselor. A friend of Mommy's and mine. A nice lady who would love to help you out. Help us out."

His weak smile seemed to signal his ambivalence, but his words offered the first encouragement I'd had all morning. "Sure, Daddy. I'll do that."

We sat there in each other's arms for a few minutes more. He calmed at last. I managed a tenuous hold on my emotions and gently held him at arms length, stared directly into his face. "I know this is hard for you, Zach. It's killing me, too, but this is the best I can do for right now. Understand?"

He nodded and wiped his eyes with his *Star Wars* pj's. "I guess." His breath was hitching as he tried mightily to stop his sobs. "It's just." He forced his voice to stop breaking, met my eyes with astounding courage for a devastated seven-year-old. "It's just that I don't want this to end, Daddy. I want to stay here with you. And with Mommy."

There was nothing I could say to make him understand our situation, despite our plans for counseling. The facts remained: he was blameless, totally innocent, yet he was suffering much more than Natalie or I. Despite my resolve to make our situation better and notwithstanding our heartfelt talk, I knew this. His world had been shattered, his security had vanished for reasons he never even imagined existed. How do you tell a seven-year-old that his parents can't get along? That his mommy can't stop fucking other men? That his daddy can't help her? Can't show her how much it's hurting him, hurting their son? How can you make a seven-year-old understand that a senile, asshole judge in his eighties, who probably doesn't even remember what it's like having young kids, is telling his daddy how often and for how long he can see his child? Shit, I couldn't understand that the longest day I lived, how in the *hell* could I expect my son to get it. The whole world, at least our little part of it, had gone insane. My wife takes up with a friend of mine, trashes our family, and I'm here trying to explain to my son why we can't be together more than four fucking days a month. I wanted to scream, to punch somebody. Zachary looked up at me, expecting the wisdom of the ages, expecting his daddy to make it all go away. I tried my best, I really did, but all I could come up with was a promise. A promise I prayed to God was not worthless. A promise I prayed would bear fruit. I owed him that much. "Son, I promise I'll try to change this." He swallowed his tears, hugged me again and I could feel him relax, even as I excoriated myself for giving him hope. I hastened to add the lawyer's disclaimer, a new and unwelcome part of my life. "But you have to remember, son, that it's not up to me. It's up to the lawyers, Mommy, and the judge."

He seemed satisfied with this. Jumped off the bed and ran for the bathroom, even as I plunged into depression at the thought of facing Judge Barta and He Who Crawls Upon The Earth, Raul Gelder. Seemingly an instant later, Zachary's voice was almost back to normal, his tears gone. "Okay, Dad. I'll remember." I heard the door slam and the shower start, feeling like a lowdown shitheel for promising something I had no reason to believe was possible. I could hear his voice through the door. "Can we have French toast again? It was really good."

The rest of the day passed like a minute. We decided to go to the Irvine Spectrum, an open-air entertainment and retail mall that had just opened beside the Five freeway, a few minutes from my condo. They had five restaurants, seventy stores, including a two-story Barnes & Noble, a huge arcade called Gameworks, and every imaginable movie in town playing 'round the clock at a thirty-three-screen theatre, even a five-story-tall 3-D Imax. Zach was impressed; I was relieved. He seemed to be less depressed, if a little more subdued than he was at Disneyland. We were both acutely aware of our impending deadline of six P.M. It weighed on us like a twenty-ton anchor. Zach asked at least a dozen times if, "We had to go yet?" Asked me, "Is it time yet, Dad?" The poor kid was dreading every passing second, even as we tried to cram

another bit of fun into our waning time together. I felt like a condemned prisoner, waiting in vain for the Governor's call.
Zachary put on a brave face, but by five o'clock, he was clearly
depressed. Try as I might, it was no good. He knew we had less
than an hour left. Worse than that, by far, Zachary knew that he'd
have to wait almost two weeks to be with me again. A lifetime for
a seven-year-old.

He held my hand on the way to the parking lot. The clock we
passed by the Barnes & Noble rang once at five-thirty and I felt
completely down. We dragged ourselves to the car in near total
silence, drove back to my place and collected his clothes. We had
squeezed in some shopping early Saturday morning, so at least
next time he wouldn't need to drag his stuff all over town, but
there we sat, silently depressed, twenty minutes to go. I looked
at him; he nodded gravely. A few minutes later we trudged
down to the car.

We were halfway to Natalie's, lost in our shared misery, silent
as monks. "I had so much fun, son." I held his chin in my palm;
he stared at the floor. "Can't wait for next time." He lifted his
head, stared straight ahead as we got off on Jamboree and
turned left. "Maybe you can have one of your friends over for a
sleepover Friday. How would that be?"

He glanced over at me, eyes wet in the reflection of the streetlights. "Sure, Dad. I'll ask Jeremy."

We turned the corner on MacArthur, five minutes from
Natalie's. "Great. Can't wait to meet him. You guys tell me what
you want to do and I'll make it happen."

We turned the corner onto her street. Zach was deeply into
himself, shoulders slumped, head down. "Maybe I can get tickets for an Angel's game. How about that?"

My throat was so tight I could hardly make enough sound to
talk as we pulled into the driveway. Zachary's voice was that of
a four-year-old, thin, reedy, scared. "Sure, Daddy. Sounds great."

I stopped the engine, shoved open the door, and came
around the front to help him out of his belt. He got out; we

slogged up the walk hand-in-hand, Zachary's overnight bag slung over my shoulder. Zach rang the bell; a minute later the porch light came on, and Maria opened the door. She was ecstatic. I was nearly ready to pull the plug. "Zachary, my little *pipito*. Welcome. Come in. Come in."

Zachary turned and gave me a ferocious hug. I kissed his hair, kissed him on the lips, and told him how much I loved him. How much I was looking forward to next time. I held him as long as I could, not nearly long enough to last another damned fortnight. "I'll call you tomorrow night, son. Promise."

Zachary gave me another kiss and said, "I love you, Daddy. Can't wait for next time, either." Maria had him by the hand. I wanted with all my heart to be able to come in, somehow make peace with Natalie, be a family again. I would have done anything, spent anything to make that happen for my child. A heartbeat later he was saying good-bye again as the door slammed in my face, Zachary suddenly gone as if sucked into an airlock. Completely adrift, I was left alone on the porch.

The porch light went out before I got to the car. I opened the door, sat in the dark for a few minutes, reflecting on my life. On the absolute absurdity of returning my son to my home, not even knowing what his life was like behind that closed door. Not knowing what he thought, what he said or felt. I felt detached and miserable.

A few moments later, I turned the key, took a last look at the front windows and watched Zachary pull aside the curtain and give me a wave. I returned the wave with a forced smile and made a promise to myself to make two calls first thing in the morning. One to Olivia Tanner; the other to Samantha Harris. Tell them both to try and set this right.

Chapter 28

As it turned out, I got a call the next day before I'd had a chance to make mine. A call from Zachary's school came into the ER around noon. From the headmistress, Ms. Phyllis Stevenson, an old-school educator whom I'd met a few months previously at Zach's back-to-school night. I'd found her to be a pleasant, if straight-laced matron in her seventies. She certainly looked the part: blue hair in a severe bun, tailored dark suit, a severe, intimidating manner; radiated a no-nonsense attitude about running a school. Ms. Stevenson seemed to be a woman who brooked absolutely no bullshit at all. I knew as soon as I'd heard her voice that it was bad news.

And it was.

She informed me that Zachary had been involved in a fight. I immediately asked if he were okay. She assured me, in her high, patrician tone that he was. Halfway through my sigh of relief, she dropped the bomb. Zach had fought not one, but two other boys. One was fine; the larger of the two, a kid named Jimmy Wong, was in the Nurse's office with a nosebleed and a fractured nose. Oh, shit, I thought, now the fun begins. Angry calls from the parents, lawsuits, and endless hassles. My mind was whirling. Ms. Stevenson's whiny voice brought me crashing back to Earth a few seconds later. "We are thinking of expelling Zachary, effective today, Dr. Adler."

I was stunned. Zach had never had any trouble at the Country Day School. Not until the separation. I was desperate to make this go away. Knew that Zach would be crushed if he were forced to leave his school. We argued back and forth for a few minutes, during which she informed me that Zachary "had been acting out for weeks." I rose to his defense; she shot me down, told me he'd been reprimanded for swearing, roughhousing in the playground, and lying about his homework. Repeatedly. I had no choice. I had to make a deal with her. Anything to save him from another debacle.

In the end, we agreed to mandatory after-school counseling, with written reports from the therapist to the school office. Luckily for us, Olivia Tanner was well known to Ms. Stevenson; was actually a contributor as well as a consultant in the school's counseling department. I promised to make an appointment for all three of us on Friday. Jesus, how bad was this going to get? I thought, after we hung up.

We met at the familiar office on Marguerite, a few minutes before our one o'clock appointment. Natalie stood by her Mercedes, arms folded, dressed in a tight black skirt and form-fitting white sweater. I wondered at the time if she'd dressed that way purposely, a way to "show me what I was missing." I couldn't deny that she looked good. Then again, she always did. It was what she hid deep down inside that was revolting. She nodded a hello as I thought, childishly, what, no big, juicy kiss?

I ran to Zachary, lifted him into a big hug, and kissed his cheek. Set him down on the brick pathway. He was clearly nervous, obviously contrite over the fallout from his fight. We'd talked on the phone that Monday night and he'd given me his side of the story. Said he'd been teased by the Wong kid for weeks. The little bastard had called him an orphan, a loser, and a retard. Zachary told me the twerp threw the first punch and missed. So my son stepped up and cleaned his clock. I was secretly pleased that Zach had punched him out, didn't blame him at all for defending himself. Still, I knew we needed this time with Tanner. Needed to get on the right path. I had to admit to some serious reservations regarding Natalie, though. I looked at her a few feet away as she stood at the threshold, impatiently tapping her black Fendi pump while I reconnected with Zach. I said a silent prayer that she'd be cooperative and nurturing, just this once.

God must have been busy.

Olivia welcomed us back to her familiar consult room. We hadn't seen her since the separation, despite my pleadings to Natalie, and she seemed genuinely saddened by our predicament. We introduced her to Zachary and she told us, again, to choose a seat. This time I chose the sofa, Zach hustled over to sit next to me, and Natalie was left with the armchair in the corner.

Olivia sat and smiled at Zach, made small talk about his school, hobbies, and TV. I'd noticed how nervous he was; his voice was squeaky, gestures jittery, and my heart went out to him. I had to hand it to Olivia, though; she had a way with kids and after a few minutes of talk, Zach seemed to be a little more relaxed. Olivia adjusted her recorder a few moments later and got down to business.

She smiled at Natalie, turned her attention then to Zach. "Zachary, tell me about yourself."

He shot a quick look at me. I nodded my encouragement. He turned reluctantly back to face Tanner, his voice barely above a whisper. "Do you just mean school stuff, or everything?"

Olivia leaned forward in her chair, her arms open; voice calm and reassuring. "Anything you want to tell me, Zach."

"I guess everything's okay." He turned to look at Natalie, who quickly averted her eyes. I could tell he was looking for acceptance from her, for permission to speak freely to Tanner. I was disappointed, again, in her dismissive attitude. I gave his shoulder a squeeze and he turned again to Olivia. "I'm just kinda scared. About all this stuff going on."

Olivia nodded, kept her voice low. "You mean the separation?"

Zachary looked her right in the eye, his voice rising. "No, ma'am, the divorce." He gave Natalie another glance; she refused to meet his stare. "Mom says they're getting divorced. I heard her say on the phone that she couldn't stand my dad."

Natalie sat forward in her chair, black silk skirt riding high on her thighs. "That's not true, Zachary. I never . . ."

Olivia cut her off with a stern look. I was overjoyed, wanted Zachary to be able to express himself without restraint. Tanner turned her attention back to Zachary. "How do you feel about the separation?" She shook her head slightly. "Sorry, Zach, the divorce."

I looked down at his hands; Zach had his fingers interlaced in a death grip, his back rigidly upright. "I just want things to be like they were." Olivia nodded for him to continue. He kept his eyes trained on Tanner. "And I want my mom to stop hating Daddy." He took another nervous look at Natalie. "I want her to stop hating *me*."

Natalie was out of her chair, face flushed, either from embarrassment or anger at Zachary, I wasn't sure. She took a step toward the sofa; Olivia motioned for her to sit down. She sniffed back her tears and turned to face Zach. "How could you say that, Zachary?" She didn't even try to keep the note of self-pity from her voice, I noticed with an inward sigh. Her expression belied her words; she looked mightily pissed. "You know I love you."

Zachary sat beside me in stony silence as I willed him to respond. The seconds passed as Olivia and Natalie kept their silence. I leaned closer and whispered, "Go ahead, Zach. Say whatever you want."

Olivia scratched out a note and looked at each of us in turn, no doubt assessing the family dynamics. She caught Zachary's eye and said, "Would you rather just talk to me, Zach? Have your folks step outside for a few minutes?"

He nodded and I stood to leave. Shot a look at Natalie, who'd already jumped from her chair, stood near the door with her right hand on the doorknob, her back and shoulders rigid. Zach looked up from the sofa and held my hand. Looked at Olivia. "Can my dad stay?"

Tanner turned toward Natalie, a questioning look in her eyes. Natalie nodded curtly and left the room.

Olivia waited for me to settle on the sofa, changed her mini-tape, and smiled at Zachary. "Tell me, Zachary. What's really on your mind?"

I held his hand as he began his story, his tone halting at first, gaining strength and confidence as he continued. Despite the surroundings, he seemed to feel safe with Olivia and me. He told us how Natalie continually yelled at him to do better in school. How she told him that he'd never amount to anything and how he'd disappointed her lately. How tired she was by her work schedule and how much of a burden it was to "straighten things out at school for him." In a nutshell, the poor kid was feeling worthless. As if he were a burden to her. I was shocked, even knowing her as well as I did. Knew without a doubt that this was yet another manifestation of her psychological problems, transferred in a concentrated form to our son. Knew that I couldn't let this go on. Not another minute longer. Samantha was going to have to do something. Even if it meant sending a subpoena to Olivia.

Zachary went on to tell us that he felt torn. That he didn't want to lose either of us. Didn't want to disappoint us. He'd said that he felt Natalie pulling away from him, withdrawing her love because he was disappointing her. He told Olivia that he had trouble sleeping; he was so worried about saying or doing the wrong thing around Natalie or me. I was in emotional freefall; my son was in crisis. Olivia asked him straight out if he

wanted to hurt himself. He answered right away that he was trying to hang on, trying to make sense of this, and wouldn't think
of doing anything that stupid. Still, I knew that I'd have to keep
a close eye on his moods, be ever alert.

As bad as I'd imagined this would be, Zachary was peeling
away all of my veneer of denial, showing me in the most
straightforward way the true cost of divorce. He was saying that
it took an enormous amount of energy, as sensitive as he was, to
make *us* feel happy, to convince Natalie and me that he was
doing all right. While, in reality, he was reeling. He was using all
of his limited seven-year-old coping skills just to survive. Who
wouldn't act out at school under those conditions? I thought.

Olivia commented in the appropriate places, asked probing
questions, and took copious notes while I was left to make
some sort of sense out of our family drama. I knew we'd found
the right therapist. Toward the end of the session, I could see
Zach open up to her; tell her things I'd never dreamed of. Tell
her things he'd never tell me alone, much less divulge with
Natalie present.

We ended the session on a positive note as Zachary promised
to call Olivia night or day if things got any worse. He gave her a
hug as we stood to leave, promising that he'd "try to talk with
my Mom in the room, next time."

I shook Tanner's hand, gave her my heartfelt thanks, and ushered Zachary to the waiting room and Natalie. Zachary ran into
her arms, hugged her tight, and apologized for sending her out.
I turned and went back into the consult room in the midst of
their reunion and silently closed the door.

"What do you think?"

She sat at her desk, removed her mini-cassette, and gave me a
weary smile. "I think he's pretty typical. More articulate than the
average boy his age, but he's actually acting appropriately, given
the circumstances."

I stood by her desk, dying to ask my most important question as she stowed her recorder, ready for the end of the day. She looked me in the eye and I came out with it. "He's not in danger of . . ."

She didn't flinch. "Unfortunately, Steven, everybody's capable of hurting themselves under severe stress. Surely you know that." I nodded, my thoughts on the dozens of overdoses and suicide attempts I'd treated. Never thought I'd have to consider that horrible prospect hitting so close to home. "Having said that, I don't consider your son to be particularly high risk."

I breathed a sigh of relief, desperate to cling to any shred of hope. "What can we do to help him?"

She stood and walked me to the door, gave me a thoughtful smile. "Just love him, spend as much time as possible with him. We'll help him get through this."

I shook her hand again. "Thank you, Olivia. I think he really likes you." I had my hand on the doorknob, paused and looked back at her. "Do you think he should be with me full time?"

She took a second or two to answer, clearly weighing the pros and cons, answered at length in a low whisper, a wary eye on the waiting room. "That's for the courts to decide, Steven, but if you need a report from me, I'll let the judge know what I think."

I looked in the foyer: no sign of Natalie and Zach. Checked outside: her car was gone. A minute after making a return appointment with the receptionist, I left the office playing Olivia's last words in my mind. Even though she'd couched her answer in professional tones that were predictably vague, I felt they promised a faint glimmer of hope in an otherwise bleak and troubling day.

Chapter 29

SIX MONTHS LATER

The trial. I'd been waiting for this, dreading this, since we'd split up. All of my friends and colleagues had warned me that it would be down and dirty street fighting, especially since Natalie had hired Gelder. Samantha and I tried to settle it prior to trial, but there was no way to deal with Natalie and her pit bull. Samantha told me after our last court-ordered settlement conference that Gelder *never* settled; he preferred the showiness of a trial, felt he got his clients a better deal that way. Great.

Life with Zachary and without him, settled into a kind of odd rhythm. He was always hyper-excited to see me on Friday nights; we were typically deep into depression hours before six P.M. Sunday. All in all, he wasn't doing well. Not at all. Despite the counseling. I'd talked to his teachers, visited with them a few times since he went back to school two months ago, and the news was not good. His grades had slipped dramatically, from all "E's" for excellent to a mid-"P," or passing range. Not only that, but I'd been called twice in September with reports that Zach had been nearly involved in fights again, during lunch; Zachary told me later that some kids in his school were teasing him because "he came from a broken home." I can't adequately express my sadness upon hearing that news. I had a long talk with him; told him to just ignore the taunts, hang out only with those kids who are supportive, kind. He asked if that meant only other kids from divorce. That was a tough one, as I knew that's exactly what tended to happen after a breakup. I wanted him to have a wide circle of friends, just didn't want him to be taunted anymore. I ended up spouting a platitude: that he should choose his friends wisely.

Monday morning, November fifth, Division Two-A. Judge Christopher J. Barta presiding. I could recite that spiel in my sleep. We'd had a month of pretrial motions and consultations to get through. Samantha had briefed me on courtroom etiquette, the proper way to answer Gelder's questions, and most importantly to her, demeanor. She didn't want any negative emotions from me on the stand, as it would hurt our case. Didn't want my attitude toward Gelder, Natalie, or the judge to be readable by the parties involved. A tall order indeed, since I considered her lawyer to be a scum-sucking piece of shit, the judge to be a senile dilettante, and Natalie? She was just being herself. A self-absorbed, duplicitous, grasping manipulator. Keeping all that tucked inside while I testified would be a piece of cake, I thought with an inward laugh. Nothing at all.

The bailiff gave his speech and we were off and running. No fancy opening statements since there was no jury to impress, no grandstanding and no bullshit, as the judge looked like his hemorrhoids were bothering him. Looked like a duck hunter who was pissed because he'd left his favorite shotgun at home.

Raul Gelder had the floor first. He called my ex-wife. I'll summarize her testimony thusly. Small lies, bigger lies, and outrageous, goddamned enormous lies. She testified that Zachary was depressed after the visits with me, said he "didn't like to go over to my place because it was so small." She lied that she was barely scraping by on my nearly five thousand a month contributions, even though I knew for a fact that she brought in over twenty thousand a month after taxes and that she owned a five million dollar home free and clear thanks to the Porsche Guy. She told another whopper when she said that Zach's poor school performance was due to "my ex-husband's refusal to help with our son's homework on the weekends." She went on to state that Zachary told her that "Dad doesn't care what I do after I graduate. He just wants to have fun with me."

I almost came out of my chair with that one. Natalie turned and fixed me with a haughty glare that nearly sent me over the top. Demeanor be damned, I had to set this straight, I thought, with a smothering sense of frustration. Nothing like love denied to engender something close to hatred. A firm hand on my shoulder, Samantha turned her back on the judge and whispered urgently in my ear, "Do *not*, under any circumstances, respond to any of this crap when *you're* up there. Understand?"

I nodded, eyes on my ex-wife, a tight rein on my impulse to verbally abuse her. I knew with total conviction that morning that you can never fully understand another until you've seen that person under stress. I had just been introduced to The Full Natalie. A person who would tell outrageous lies, slander her own son to get what she wanted; the public humiliation and impoverishment of the person she once claimed to love. They should put her on TV. She put on quite a spectacle.

We broke for lunch and I was up next. Was I ready? I didn't feel like it at the time, was nervous as I was before my first appendectomy in Surgery all those years ago. I couldn't eat a bite of the rotten cafeteria food at lunch. But I was determined to give it my best, and my best was usually damned good.

Samantha led me through a number of softball questions that we'd rehearsed in her office. "Yes, I was going to get a raise in my salary, to one ninety the first of January." She asked me about my living arrangements and I answered that my dad was ready, willing, and able to move in with us to help care for Zach while I was at work. This had not actually been arranged yet; it all depended on the support payments. Olivia's report was on the Judge's dais and it was a good one. She'd recommended shared custody and we were hoping for full physical custody, half-time at least. That should negate any child support I might otherwise owe Natalie and the spousal support could be hammered out at a later time. I only wanted to straighten out the custody order, get Zachary with me most if not all of the time. It was what we both wanted. I had already looked at a number of rentals in Newport, just a few miles from Zach's school and had budgeted in the new, higher rent, should our plans go well.

Samantha asked about his schoolwork, trying to refute Natalie's deceptive testimony. I looked directly at the judge and testified that I had indeed helped with his homework, in fact I was the only one to show up at his teacher's conferences. I doubted that his teacher even knew what Natalie looked like, but was proud of myself as I kept this little dig to myself. Samantha did a good job turning Natalie's testimony against her by referring the judge to Natalie's financials, which clearly showed a net monthly income of twenty-two thousand, even without my forty-five hundred in support. Her expenses, including tuition and supplies for Zach's school, her personal stuff, the house, everything, totaled ten thousand. Given those irrefutable facts, I was sure we were home free. Until Gelder started in on me.

He began with a couple of friendly establishment questions, like how long I'd been a doctor, how long at UCI, prospects for advancement, trouble at work. All of which I answered with aplomb. Then he got nasty.

He circled around the witness dock; an undersized shark scenting chum. "Did you ever strike your wife, Dr. Adler?"

I was speechless. We'd had more than a few fights, especially after the incident with the gruff voice, even after we'd started counseling, but I was sure that I'd never hit her. Would never even think about it. On the other hand, would Natalie hit me? Yes, and I had the bruises to show for it a few months ago, I remembered, as I glared at my ex.

I turned, looked him in the eye and answered an emphatic, "No. Never."

He gave me a malicious grin, the kind you see on the bad guy in horror movies as he closes in on the clueless teenagers. "Are you stating, for the record, under oath, that you've never struck your wife?" He strutted back to his table, gave Natalie a confident smile, turned again to face me. "Is that your testimony, Doctor?"

He had me scared. I knew I'd never laid a hand on her, but didn't know what they had to impeach me with. A doctored photo, some old medical records? I searched my memory for any injuries that Natalie had suffered and then it struck me. We had been horsing around one or two months after we'd gotten married, typical, stupid, pre-sex stuff in our bedroom. Natalie had fallen out of bed when I went to tackle her. She fell against her bedside table, striking her abdomen on the sharp wooden edge. I'd been nearly hysterical at the time, worried that she'd lose the baby. We ended up in the ER at Hoag Hospital, had an ultrasound and everything checked out okay. That was the only incident I could remember in the eight or nine years we were together. Still, I wondered what else he might have up his sleeve. I decided to skip the explanation about her fall, worrying at the time that it may sound worse than it really was. I answered in a less than steady voice, "No. I did not."

That sent his table into a near frenzy. Natalie handed him a manila envelope; he tore into it; looked so eager I half expected him to use his teeth, took out three photos, rushed back to the dock, shoved one of them in my face. I scanned it with a dawning sense of dread: A five-by-five color shot of a woman's abdomen, slightly bruised over the splenic region in the left upper quadrant. There was a left hand over the bruise, with a distinctive engagement ring on the fourth finger. My heart sank with the sickening realization that the ring was the one I'd bought in Tiffany's that day in San Francisco, nine years ago. It had cost me ten thousand way back then. I wondered, as I watched Gelder place a copy on the judge's bench and a duplicate in front of Samantha, how much that picture of her ring was going to cost that day. Gelder walked slowly back to face me, he looked practically orgasmic, gave me a wolfish grin. "Do you recognize this picture, Dr. Adler?"

I took a few minutes to examine it, stalling for time as my pulse rate jumped over one fifty. I knew I couldn't win if I lied; they probably had other documents. I'd had an idea about Natalie's devious ways, long ago at the beginning of our relationship, just didn't think she'd stoop this low. I decided after stalling until the judge looked ready to hit me, to answer honestly. "The only thing I recognize is the ring." I looked helplessly at Samantha; she was busy jotting down notes. "It looks like Natalie's." I felt flummoxed by this horrible surprise, added an unnecessary detail in a voice I didn't recognize. "My ex-wife. Her engagement ring." I caught Natalie snickering and felt the first gout of pure, murderous hatred in my gut.

Samantha, bless her heart, came to my rescue. She jumped up as soon as I'd finished my fumbling answer. "Objection, your Honor. Lacks foundation." She moved to the side of our table, fixed Gelder with a malignant stare. "This picture could have been taken anytime. Even last week." She was really worked up now, neck veins bulging, face red as my tie. "We have no evidence at all that it's even the Complainant's abdomen." She threw a legal tablet on the table and sat heavily. "This is a travesty, your ..."

Barta held up a hand, glanced at Gelder as he would a clump of dog shit stuck to his loafers. "Sustained, counselor." He took another visual swipe at Natalie's attorney, one that almost made me feel sorry for him and shouted into his microphone. "If you try another stunt like that, Mr. Gelder, I'll have the bailiff reserve you a nice five-by-ten cell for the weekend." He gathered our file and stood, bent at the waist, glaring down at Natalie's table. "Clear, counselor?"

Gelder looked like a deflated balloon, his voice had lost its power, sounded a little like Elmer Fudd now that he'd been stripped of the bombast. Arrogance dies hard though; he gave it another shot, ever the bulldog. "The fact remains, your Honor, that my client deserves full custody and support in the amount..."

Judge Barta cut him off with a curt wave, halfway to his chambers. "Save it for your next client, Mr. Gelder. I have the psychologist's recommendations, all of the financials, and my case law. I'm going to render my decision promptly at three thirty. Court dismissed until then."

Samantha gave me a warm handshake as I sat down beside her and breathed a long sigh. "You were fine, didn't hurt us at all." She looked disdainfully at Gelder's back as he ushered Natalie from the courtroom. "Typical Gelder bullshit." That was the first time I'd heard her swear, coming from a demure professional like her, it carried that much more sting. Alone in the courtroom, we sat and watched them leave, Natalie was whispering furiously down to her lawyer, clearly pissed, spitting her words all over his silver pompadour.

I gathered my briefcase and stood to leave, helped Samantha with her bulging brief. "What do you think? How's it going to shake out?"

She held up a finger and left my side briefly to confer with the bailiff. Came back and smiled. "I'm somewhat optimistic." I knew what was coming, Samantha was "hanging the black crepe." We did it all the time in medicine, to deflect false hopes and unrealistic expectations. "But, you know, anything can happen. And probably will." She gave me an evil grin, the kind conceited girls give to nerds who are fumbling around, trying to ask for a date. "But I will say this. The judge was *pissed!*" I opened the door for her, scanned the hallway for Natalie. Not around, must be spewing in the parking lot, I thought, with an inward sense of elation.

"We'll have to see how that translates into a verdict." She gave me a wave and ran to her car. "See you after lunch. Got to call my boyfriend."

I waved in return, alone with my thoughts. An interesting day, to be sure. I couldn't say I was looking forward to three-thirty that afternoon, just anxious to get it over with.

I found my car fifteen minutes later, lost in a sea of identical sedans, near the western edge of the huge parking lot. Natalie was waiting for me, arms crossed as she leaned against my Nissan, smug smile in place.

I gave her a warm smile in return. So this was how she wanted it? I thought. One last go around. I was ready. Bring it on, I said to myself. Bring it on.

I walked to my door, kept my tone just this side of mocking. "So, Natalie, looks like your little trick didn't work. Pity Gelder can't float your bullshit past this judge."

She stayed where she was, blocking my entrance. I stood my ground, a few feet away. "You're not going to win, Steven. I'm not going to let that happen."

I folded my arms, bone-tired of Natalie and her constant need for confrontation. Tired of all of her crap. "This isn't a game, Natalie. There are lives at stake." I moved to open my door, she blocked my way.

"You're nothing but a loser, Steven. Always have been." The tired old insults, brought back out of storage one last time, I thought with calm detachment. "I'll never let you have Zachary."

I pushed her away from my door, willing myself to stay calm, realizing all at once that she might have been trying to provoke me to violence. Probably even had her shitheel lawyer taping us somewhere. "Excuse me, Natalie. I need to get into my car." She stayed where she was. I kept my voice low, expression neutral, even as I was starting to boil. "What *is* your problem, Natalie?"

She smiled at that, her tone corrosive enough to etch steel. "*You* have the problem, Steven." She tapped my forehead. I looked around the parking lot, searching for a five-foot-three turd in a black Armani suit armed with a camcorder. Wanted to swipe at her hand, get in my car and leave her standing there. She wouldn't move. "Right there in that tiny paranoid brain of yours." I examined her placid face; gave her the same repulsed yet interested attention I gave the laminated hookworms in our first-year Parasitology class. "You threw away our marriage because you can't think straight, Steven. Can't get beyond your own sickness."

I took a step forward, discretion forgotten, proper demeanor a distant memory. "Don't give me that shit, Natalie. Not with all that blood on your hands." She took a quick step to the side, clearly surprised by my venom. I leaned closer, a foot or two from her face. "You fucking cunt. Had to have just one more orgasm, one more scalp for your collection." I moved an inch or two closer, heedless of the parade of people heading to their cars a few feet away. "Never gave a goddamned thought about our son, about our marriage. You blew up our life, just so you could feel good about yourself." I was so mad I was afraid I'd completely lose control; do something I'd regret, hurt my chances in court; lose my son for good. I felt for my keys, stared stolidly into her hateful face. "You threw it away. Just so you could feel somebody else's dick inside you." I shoved her aside, climbed in my car. Felt suddenly exhausted, ashamed of myself for losing it like that. Turned back to her as I started the car, my voice choked with emotion. "Do yourself some good, Natalie. Think about someone else for the first time in your life. Think about Zachary. Think about your future and change psychiatrists. Get some *real* therapy before it's too late."

The judge came in at precisely three-thirty. Samantha exuded calm professionalism, Gelder and Natalie looked like feuding spouses, and I was a wreck. I knew intellectually that the worst that could happen would be the status quo; every other weekend and the same level of support. Not good, but I'd keep fighting for Zach and what passed for justice in Orange County Divorce/Kangaroo Court. Still, the emotional, optimistic side of my brain was turning cartwheels, anticipating a wonderful change in my life, in Zachary's, and Pops' lives too. Barta took his time, clearly enjoying his time in the spotlight. He looked more comfortable, almost compassionate, I wondered at the time if he had taken a sitz bath, gotten some relief from his swollen and itchy hemorrhoids.

Barta looked in turn at both tables and began his speech. "You have each been represented by very able counsel. The facts were clearly presented and I commend each of you, counselors." *Get to the point, Mr. Burns,* I wanted to scream. "My ruling is this: Custody of the minor child, Zachary Jacob Adler, age eight, shall be shared on the following basis. Two consecutive weeks at the father's residence, Dr. Adler for the record, and two consecutive weeks at the mother's residence, Dr. Bogner for the record." I wanted to hug Samantha. She laid a hand on my shoulder, motioned for me to calm down. The judge swiveled his chair, consulted his computer a second or two, rotated back toward us and went on with his ruling. "As for the matter of support. I find a great disparity in the two party's income and expenses, so the court orders that Mrs. Bogner." He looked down at their table, an apologetic smile on his desiccated, apple-doll face. "I'm sorry, ma'am, I meant Dr. Bogner, shall pay to Dr. Adler the sum of two thousand dollars per month, one thousand dollars each for child support and spousal support, payable in two equal installments due the first and the fifteenth of each month." He then straightened his short pile of papers, stowed his reading glasses in a pocket buried deep in his black robe and stood to leave. "The court reporter will have copies of my order for both counselors, close of business tomorrow."

The bailiff stood behind me, shouted, "Court is now recessed. Remain seated."

I couldn't restrain myself any longer. We won! I stood and hugged Samantha; she looked ready to cry, from surprise as much as happiness for Zach and me, I was sure. The other side?

They didn't look so happy. I watched Natalie slam another whispered tirade against Gelder's pompadour, hear her hiss, "We're going to appeal. Right, Raul?" He tried to ignore her. Big mistake in my experience. She moved even closer, this time her voice could have been heard outside, in the parking lot. "Right, Raul?" She tugged at his black wool sleeve. "Answer me, you weasel. I paid you forty-five thousand dollars." I thought she was going to hit him, secretly hoped she would.

Fresh from our parking lot brawl, I decided to exit this insanity as soon as possible, didn't want Natalie's tirade to bring me down. Not likely, I laughed inwardly, as I was now on top of the world. My two guys living with me, less strain on the old budget, and, most importantly, the chance to make a real difference in Zachary's life. I couldn't wait to get to my car to call Pops with the good news. All things considered, this had turned into a truly magical day!

Chapter 30

TWO YEARS LATER

Zachary had his birthday at my new house just one week ago. He'd turned the big one oh, had at least two dozen of his closest friends over, and we had a blowout. Pops was in charge of the barbecue, I had lifeguard duty, and Zach was the star of the show, doing double back flips off the diving board, scaring his dad and grandpa half to death.

Natalie even put in an appearance, briefly dropping by to hand Zach his present, a new ten-speed bike. She and I had a fairly sedate conversation in the kitchen, put aside our differences at least for this special occasion. We'd had more than a few battles in court over the last year; I'd prevailed more often than not, largely because Zachary had turned around his school performance living with me, hadn't gotten into trouble, even made the honor roll at the Country Day School for the last two quarters straight. I knew all along that all he needed was consistency, support, and attention. Pops made sure he was well taken care of during the day, and I worked with him every night, not just with his homework, but with life issues as well. He had become terribly depressed during the first three months after the breakup. I'd had several pep talks with him during his weekends with me. One memorable time a few months in comes to mind: he'd come home with a terrible report card, slunk around the house avoiding me until I cornered him and we sat down to talk.

This was the worst time for Zachary, midway through his last quarter of third grade. I had been called to see his teachers three times in April and May, a few months before the trial. His homeroom teacher told me he was lying about his homework; not just the-dog-ate-my-work kind of innocent lies, either. Zach was telling her that he "never got the assignment," or that he "didn't have to do it, because my dad told me so." She was as concerned as I, worried that she might have to keep him back in third grade come June. I knew he couldn't take that kind of humiliation, not after the ruination of his life after the breakup. I was afraid he'd never recover. This was an extremely bright, very sensitive boy, one who hated any kind of teasing, of which he'd had plenty after our divorce. He'd already called himself "dummy" on the weekends I had him home. I knew I'd have to straighten this out and fast.

First thing on our next Friday night together, I sat him down on the sofa and went over his grades. He sat across from me, head hanging, downcast eyes, barely able to speak. I pulled the grade card from my pocket and went through it line by line. I'm not the kind of parent who believes that elementary school grades, good or bad, will determine a child's entire future, that poor grades will condemn a kid to a life as a busboy or that good grades in second grade merit early enrollment to Stanford. I was, however, more than a little worried about Zachary's attitude. That concerned me to a tremendous degree, as I didn't want my son to give up on himself.

I got to his math score, Arithmetic One, a "U." "What happened here, son?"

"I don't know. I don't like the class, I guess."

I'd talked to his teacher, knew the real reason, that he hadn't done his homework. I had decided in advance to tackle this one head on. "How about, after dinner, we do your homework together?" I looked over at him and he continued to stare at the floor, his voice nearly lost in the folds of his clothes.

"Okay."

The next subject, Art, he'd gotten a "C," up from a "U" the previous quarter. I knew he loved to draw and had more than a little talent, wanted at all costs to accentuate this small bit of positive results, give him a reason to try. So, I'd made him empty his backpack in the den. He had a pile of papers spread out on the sofa and I asked him to show me some of his artwork. He rummaged through a few line drawings and came up with a full-color watercolor of the tide pools at rockpile in Laguna Beach. His drawing, although simply rendered, captured the subtle shadings of gray and blue as well as the multicolored green water perfectly. I tried looking into his eyes after admiring his work; he kept them focused on the carpet. "This is really good, son." I pointed out the highlights of color he had accomplished, the composition, and background; he seemed to brighten slightly, looking into my eyes for the first time as I pointed to the constellation of rocks he'd captured.

He sounded tentative, disbelieving of my admiration; it nearly broke my heart. "You like it, Dad? Really?"

I came over to the sofa and sat next to him. "Of course I do." I put an arm around him, pulled him close. "I'm very proud of you, son. You know that, don't you?"

He looked up at me with a look that nearly stopped me in my tracks, one filled with such sadness and crushing defeat that I wanted to reach over and somehow magically heal his soul, resurrect my confident and funny little boy. He started to cry softly, his head on my chest. "Why would anybody be proud of me?"

That devastating question, his quiet tears, were the defining moment in this horrible ordeal we'd been dragged through.

Here was my son, previously carefree, happy, and secure, reduced to a shell of doubt and self-perceived failure. I hugged him tighter, tried to make sense of how far we'd fallen, how much this had damaged him. I took his chin in my hand, wiped his tears, and said, "Mom and I are both very proud of you, Zach. You're so smart, so talented, you're just going through a rough time." He started sobbing openly now, his chest shaking against mine. I had clearly struck a nerve, needed to find out what was really bothering him. I forced myself to stay positive, even as I fought a rising panic. "What is it, son? What's the matter?" I knew from counseling that Natalie had been riding him particularly hard lately, complaining to me nonstop about Zach's schoolwork, about his "laziness." I had a very good idea about where the root of his problem lay. "Is it Mom, honey?"

That unleashed a fresh torrent of tears; he was too upset to reply, but his body language told the story. We sat there like that for ten minutes until he calmed enough to tell me, again, that he felt nothing he did was ever good enough for her, that she would always expect more, expect him to be perfect at all times. He told me through his sobs that he was trying, that he wanted so much to please her, but always felt like she was disappointed, like he'd "never be any good" in her eyes. This from a seven-year-old. I was reeling; more convinced than ever that we had to find a way out of this. I knew, after nine years with Natalie that she wasn't about to change, her perfectionism and absolute need for control had served her purposes too well for her to do anything differently, even as her sick and dangerous attitudes were destroying Zachary. She might as well try to change her height, as firmly entrenched as she was, in that destructive pattern.

Thanks to Olivia, we found Zachary's salvation in therapy and in our new custody arrangement. It took months of hard work to see any progress, but slowly, very slowly, I noticed a difference. He was more diligent with his class work, more energetic, worlds more positive. Pops had been a great influence on him, helping to hone his golf game, teaching him to exercise and take care of his body; in short, helping Zachary to believe in himself again. I look back on those dark days and shudder with fear at what might have been, what could have happened to my son. Thanks to God, all I had to do on his tenth birthday was look out my back window. I could, at long last, face the future with an ear-to-ear smile on my face. I had my son back.

Chapter 31

FOUR MONTHS LATER

Tuesday morning, mid-July, and I was back at work smack dab in the middle of the dog days of summer. I had a dozen new interns to birddog, we were swamped, and to make matters worse, we were seeing a huge influx of trauma: watercraft and motorcycle accidents, baseball injuries, hang-gliding crashes, and especially car wrecks. This week alone, we'd already had six major crunches from the Laguna Canyon Road, the two-lane highway that was the only route to Laguna Beach from the inland cities. A treacherous stretch of road notorious for high speed, head-on crashes.

I was working with an intern from USC, a truly gifted young woman who'd graduated top in her class, teaching her the finer points of a plastic repair of a lip laceration when Barbara Manning came up behind me and tapped me on the shoulder. She put a hand on my arm and whispered in my ear, "Steven. Your dad's on the phone. He sounded upset."

My heart sank; my thoughts immediately went out to Zach and Pops as I turned away from the intern and walked toward the nurse's station. I had just left them safe and sound at my new place two hours ago. Dad told me Zach was going to have some friends over to swim. What could have happened in just two hours? I willed myself to stay calm, this could be about anything, I reminded myself, yet the fact remained, Dad had never called me at work before.

I picked up the phone, heard Dad's voice, and knew immediately it was going to be terrible news. "Steven. It's Zachary." My heart stopped. I couldn't breathe. I found a chair to sit in, nearly fell on the floor, and waited for the worst. My dad was crying, on the edge of hysteria. "Zach . . . Hit his head . . . Really hard."

I didn't know what to say, couldn't force the words out. I sat there with tears rolling down my cheeks, unable to process Pops' message. It felt like minutes had passed before I was able to speak; my training must have taken over, because the "father side" of me was freaking out, a screaming, incoherent mess, unable to articulate anything, unable to make sense of this burgeoning nightmare. I choked out the words I needed to speak in a voice I didn't recognize. "What happened, Dad?" My guts were turning to liquid, I feared the worst. Dad never got upset. Not like this.

"I'm sorry, Steven. I was outside watching him . . ."

"You don't need to apologize, Pops. It was an accident." I had to keep him calm, had to settle Dad; Zachary needed him now. I couldn't afford to show my fear, even though it was strong enough to strangle my heart. "I need to know how hard he hit. How is he now?"

Dad dropped the phone, I could hear murmured questions, Zachary's weak voice in reply. Rustling noises on the phone, Dad's frantic voice. "He says he feels sick to his stomach."

Shit, shit, *shit*. I was in full panic mode now. He'd really hit his head hard. Zachary had a serious closed head injury, nausea and sleepiness a definite bad sign. I stifled a scream and did my best to get Dad to do the right thing. I felt there was no more time to get any history of the accident; Zachary needed immediate help. Heard myself shouting. "Call an ambulance. Right now, Dad. Tell them to take him here. Understand?"

Pops was crying harder now, his breath ragged on the phone, but his voice was steady, I knew I could count on him to do the right thing. "Shouldn't they take him someplace closer, son?" He dropped the phone again, I could hear him calling to Zach. When he came back on, his voice was raw with panic. "He just threw up, Steven. What should I *do?*"

"Hang up and call 911. Tell them you have a boy with a serious head injury and that the trauma team will be waiting for him at UCI." I hung up the phone with an overwhelming, paralyzing sense of dread. My son was laying on our pool deck with God-knows-what going on in his head and I sat here twelve miles away, freaking out, ready to jump out of my skin.

Barbara had been sitting right beside me the entire time I was talking to Dad. She knew without asking that this was a serious, potentially life-threatening injury, and she simply took over.

She draped her arms around me and whispered, "Go back to your office, Steven. We'll set up for him." I shook my head, started to get out of the chair, ready to open Trauma One. She wouldn't stand for it, motioning frantically to George Gomez to help me back to the office. I stood on legs that refused to work; George draped an arm over my shoulder and led me down the corridor, his eyes filled with tears.

I looked back at my team with the strangest feeling of disorientation, disconnection from reality, that I'd ever had. Barbara was ordering a stat consult with Don DeMaio, the chief of Neurosurgery, who acknowledged a few seconds later that he'd be down personally in five minutes. She set up a CT of Zach's brain and had the lab stand by for type and cross and a full electrolyte panel. I stood there in the hallway, felt as it I were hovering above an accident scene, watching these people talk about someone else, inwardly feeling a sense of detached pride in a job well done, even while they talked about my mortally wounded son.

I heard Barbara make a last call to the OR as she calmly had them set aside the Neuro room for "A Grade I, possibly Grade II closed head trauma. Five minutes out." George led me down the deserted corridor as Barbara ran to the radio room for an update. Time had an elastic quality that I'd never experienced; it felt as if I'd gotten the call from Pops a year ago; it had actually been less than ten minutes. Three lifetimes ago.

As George opened the door, I heard Barbara shout, "ETA one minute. Let's get ready." I collapsed against my desk, my mind absolutely useless as I heard Barbara once again, greeting the Neuro surgeon, "Don, I'm glad you're here. Steven's boy is really bad. Medics said he's unconscious."

George closed the door, led me to my chair, and helped me sit. He tried to cover the noise I could hear from down the hall with his upbeat chatter. He wanted me to remember that "God would take care of Zachary. That He wouldn't let anything happen to my boy." George told me that "God heals all wounds." Said "Our God is a good God, He will watch over us all the days of our lives."

I wanted so much to believe George's comforting words. I'd have given my life to believe it. I knew my faith was weak; hell, it was nonexistent. I'd never even believed in God. That morning I wanted, needed to believe that God would save my little boy. Yet, I felt like a fraud whenever I prayed. Watching George, listening to his heartfelt prayer, I fell back on science, as usual. Put my son's life in DeMaio's hands, knew that he was under the care of an excellent Neuro surgeon, the best trauma nurses in the county and they'd do their best to pull him through.

George took me in his arms, this huge pro wrestler, intimidating force of law and order in the Department, and we wept like babies. He asked me to pray with him. I didn't know what to say, had never actually learned a formal prayer. George knew instinctively what to do. He led me to the carpet, knelt beside me, and began. "Heavenly Father. We ask You in Steven's hour of need to watch over his son, Zachary. Protect him, nourish him, and guide his doctors and nurses so that they may deliver Your healing power. In Your Son's precious name, we ask this. Amen."

Barbara knocked on the door ten minutes later and came in, smiled at me, and mouthed a "thank you" to George. She walked over to me, grabbed my arm, and said, "Come, Steven. Zachary's asking for you,"

I stood on wobbly legs, nearly ran for the door as Barbara guided me toward the hall. "Then he's all right? He's going to be okay?" We made it halfway down the hall, when I heard the commotion in Trauma One. Turned to her in an all-out panic. "What are they doing? What's happening to my son? You said he was conscious."

Barbara looked at me with tears flowing down her cheeks, her voice quiet, reassuring. "He is, Steven. DeMaio said he's Grade II." I nearly died. Zachary was practically in a coma, halfway down the coma scale to brain death. This was not happening. God, no, this couldn't be happening. I picked up my pace, desperate to see my son; heartsick that this may be my last chance to talk to him. Barbara supported me as we came into the room, her voice seemingly coming from Mars. "They're just getting him ready for his CT. You can talk to him."

The small group of nurses and techs parted and let me through to Zach's bed. He was lying there with his eyes closed, still as a sculpture. I took a reflexive look at his monitors: blood pressure, heart rate and rhythm, and oxygen saturation all within normal limits. As I stepped closer, Zach opened his eyes and my heart took flight. I reached out and stroked his hair. "Hi, honey. Daddy's here."

Zach started to cry and I lost it, nearly jumped into his bed, wanted more than anything in the world to hold him tight, heal his terrible wounds. I reined myself in as quickly as I could, didn't need him to feel my terror; didn't want to add to his panic. He whispered through his tears, "Am I going to be okay, Daddy?"

313

I held his hand while Barbara stood beside me, her arm around my shoulder. My words sounded false, even to me. "Of course, son." I nodded toward DeMaio, who stood at the end of the bed, an expectant look on his face. "You have the best nurses and doctors in the whole world taking care of you, Zach."

He turned his eyes to me, wincing in pain as his head scraped against the plastic restraint device. His voice was as I'd remembered from his earliest childhood, pleading, helpless, a panicky tone that pierced my soul. "I'm not going to have an operation, am I, Dad?" He started to cry again, as I rested my palm on his cheek. "I don't want to have a operation." My son was consumed with fear, I felt completely helpless. "I don't want to, Dad."

DeMaio stepped in and looked down at Zachary, his voice kind but firm, his right palm on my son's chest. "We're going to take you over, get some pictures of your head and then we'll decide, son." He tweaked Zach's toes through the sheet. "Does that sound okay, Zachary?"

Zach nodded, and a second later they wheeled his gurney out of Trauma One. I leaned over and gave him a quick kiss, felt my heart shattering into a million pieces. "I'm going upstairs with you, honey. Don't worry."

He blinked back his tears, tried to put on a brave face. "Where's Mommy? Isn't she coming?"

I had nearly forgotten to call her. Cursed myself inwardly for being so thoughtless. George Gomez signaled from the doorway, indicated that he'd just talked to her, mouthed that she *"was on her way."* I nodded my thanks and leaned down to Zachary. "She's on her way, buddy." The radiology crew was anxious to get him upstairs, so I stepped aside and let them go.

A few moments later, DeMaio took me aside, led me to an unused room down the hall. He told me to sit on the gurney. I was trying to prepare myself for the worst, had been through Hell more than once with this man and knew how bad it could get. He folded his arms and tried for a reassuring smile. His words, however, told the real story. He told me that Zachary had hit his left temple on the pool coping, probably had an expanding hematoma of the temporal lobe. His words lacerated my soul; I was suddenly glad to be sitting down. I'd known in my gut that this was what he had; still, to hear the cold, clinical truth nearly put me under. DeMaio went on to describe Zach's exam findings. He told me his pupils were reactive and equal, that his level of consciousness had drifted between Grades I and II, and that his sensation had been intact. He took a deep breath, seemed to be struggling with the last bit of truth. I waited him out, even as my heart threatened to break through my ribs. DeMaio glanced down at his notes. "Steven, he has a left hemiplegia." This couldn't be. My son was paralyzed? *No. Please God, no,* I prayed silently. He had seemed fine, was talking normally, was alert. How could he be paralyzed? DeMaio pulled no punches; ever the straight shooter, even with a good friend's kid. "It could be only temporary, this happens a lot with subdurals." He looked down at me; at a crossroads that I'd known all along was coming. "We'll have to do burr holes, evacuate his clot. I just wanted you and Natalie to be aware." He turned and acknowledged Barbara, who told him the OR was standing by, turned again to face me. "We'll need your consent. You know the risks and possible complications." He held out the form I'd seen a million times, the form that gave him permission to cut my little boy's head open, take out a clot, and hope for the best. The form that gave him permission to try and save Zach's life. Yes, I did know the complications; permanent paralysis, blindness, inability to speak, swallow, or breathe on his own, irreversible coma. Death. Yes, goddamn it to hell, I *did* know the risks. I knew that Zachary's life, my life would never be the same, regardless of his outcome.

I took the form in my shaking hands, managed to scrawl my signature even though I could hardly focus on the line. DeMaio nodded quietly and bid me to join Zach in the Radiology department while he got his team ready.

I found my way to Radiology on the second floor and took a seat where I'd never been before. A position that I'd have a lot of familiarity with over the next few weeks. The Other Side. The family's reserved seating in Hell. The waiting room. I sat there in the cheap little plastic chair, staring at the clock, imagining what my boy was going through; the loud noises, the huge machine, imagining even worse, what was going on inside his skull. How big was the clot, where was it located? How hard would it be for DeMaio to get it out? I sat there in abject misery for a half-hour until Natalie rushed in the door, still in her bloodstained scrubs and a flimsy cover gown, frantically searching the waiting room for my face. I stood and walked over to her, held out my arms. She stood in the hallway, two yards away with her arms folded, sounded eerily calm. "Where is he? Are they finished with him yet? How is he, Steven?"

I led her to the row of chairs farthest from the door, sat her down, and repeated DeMaio's diagnosis, leaving nothing out. She sat in stony silence, a single tear rolling down her cheek, face white as her cover gown. "What did Don say about his prognosis?"

I swallowed my guilt, even as I could feel it coming off in waves from Natalie's angry face, knew I needed to stay focused and get through this burgeoning nightmare for Zachary. "He doesn't know, Natalie. He wants to see the films first."

She turned away from me, her back rigid, not even touching the chair. "This wouldn't have happened . . ."

I turned her to face me, summoned up the last vestige of calm I possessed. "It was an accident, Natalie. My father was watching him like a hawk."

She brushed off my hand, her voice diamond hard. "Don't blame your father, Steven. *You* let this happen to my child."

I didn't want to fight, didn't have any spare energy, couldn't believe she was acting like this. "Okay, Natalie. Just calm down and concentrate on Zachary, would you?"

She turned away and angrily opened her purse, grabbed a pack of cigarettes and flipped open a silver lighter. I pulled her hand down and pointed to the no-smoking sign over the door. She started to light it anyway, her way of showing defiance in the face of our awful reality, when DeMaio came into the room.

We stood as one, he came over and kissed Natalie's cheek, murmured his condolences. I stood there with my heart in my shoes, prepared for the worst. He looked at me and told me what I knew was coming. "He has an epidural hematoma. Frontal-parietal, predominately right of midline, with a leftward shift of the ventricles." He was telling me that Zach's brain had bounced around in his skull from the blow on the left side, ramming against the inside of his skull on the right side, probably tearing an artery or a vein, causing an expanding blood clot. The expansion of the blood had increased the pressure on his right hemisphere, shifted his brain to the left side, ultimately causing his paralysis. DeMaio read my next question with a look into my eyes. "It's something we can fix. Usually. But I can't predict his outcome. I'll have to get in there and see." With that he left for the OR as they wheeled Zachary's gurney past the waiting room.

He was sleeping on his back, covered to the neck in blankets, his cervical collar gone as the CT had apparently ruled out a neck fracture. Natalie rushed to the litter and kissed him on the cheek. "Mommy's here, Zachy." She took his hand in hers and spoke louder, almost shouting, her voice crackling with fear now. "Open your eyes, Zach. Mommy's here."

I moved beside her and kissed Zachary on the cheek, wondering if that would be the last time I'd see my precious son alive.

The transport team gently pushed us to the side and rushed our unconscious son through the double doors. We stood there in the hallway, alone in our devastation as they prepped Zach for surgery.

Chapter 32

If the Radiology reception room was Purgatory, then the Surgery waiting room was the Seventh Ring of Hell. I had never been on this side of the fence, never felt the paralyzing anxiety of those left behind, never wondered if I'd ever see my loved one the same way again. I took a seat as far away from Natalie as I could manage, just didn't want to hear any more of her guilt trip. I was feeling enough on my own, without her vicious, unrelenting prompting and probing. Besides, I had major unresolved issues with her as it was, didn't need to waste any energy plowing those furrows again.

Pops came in a half-hour into our vigil, walked over to Natalie, and put an arm around her shoulders. He murmured something in her ear that made her melt in his arms, crying freely, unashamed to be in such a state. Pops comforted her for the better part of ten minutes, walking over to me only when she nodded that she would be all right by herself.

He came to my corner of the waiting room and sat by my side. Gave me the saddest look I'd ever seen on his face, far worse than the morning Mom died. His voice was a hoarse whisper, it was clear he'd been crying all morning. "Forgive me, son." His voice caught and he stopped to wipe a tear with an angry swipe of his sleeve. "I shoulda told him. Shoulda told him not to do that."

I blew my nose with a wadded-up tissue Barbara had pressed in my hand downstairs. "Pops, what happened? How did he . . ." I couldn't force the words out, couldn't stand to picture my son falling so hard.

Pops took my hand, leaned closer, and said, "Please say it, Stevie. Say you forgive me."

I leaned down and kissed his head. "You're talking crazy, Pops. You didn't do anything wrong."

That seemed to calm him a bit. He bit his lip, took a deep breath, and told me what happened. He said Zachary had skipped breakfast, ran out to the pool before he'd had a chance to clean up. Pops was watching through the kitchen window while Zach ran across the decking and jumped into the deep end, just as he'd done at his birthday party a few months ago.

Dad had apparently cleaned up, was setting up a lawn chair to watch Zach's dives when he took a really long sprint, approached the deck, and slipped in a pool of water. Pops broke down and sobbed as I pictured in my mind the horrible sight of Zachary's head impacting the cement coping. Dad composed himself after a hard-fought struggle and said that Zach slipped into the water and had to be pulled out. He was too modest to admit that it was he, deathly afraid of the water as he was, who'd jumped in and pulled him out. I hugged him with all my strength and said, "Don't you ever apologize again, Dad." I pulled away and met his red-rimmed eyes. "Promise?"

He nodded weakly and we settled in for an interminable wait. The waiting room was less than ten feet from OR Ten, the neuro room, separated only by a pair of doors down a short hallway. I sat there with Pops in the nearly deserted room and listened to the unmistakable whine of the Stryker saw as DeMaio started his craniotomy. I can hardly explain the effect that sound had on me that morning, except to say it was the most frightening, piercing noise I'd ever heard; screaming demons from another world. The thoughts running through my mind that awful Tuesday scare me to this day, almost four years later. I tried everything to blot it out, turned on the TV as loud as I could, talked to Dad until I was practically shouting; nothing helped erase that terrible shrieking. I go to sleep all these years later; sometimes hear it in my sleep, waking in a cold sweat, calling Zachary's name.

I sat next to Pops for the next three hours, hoping, praying that he'd be all right. The sounds of the Stryker stopped eventually and I was soon afflicted by the worst possible dread. Much worse than the fear of the unknown, the crushing anxiety that comes with knowing too much, knowing first hand what can, and often does, go wrong in this kind of surgery. I ran through all of the known risks, obsessively calculating probabilities, and the consequences for my son's future. I went through the most horrific complications, willing my mind to reject them out of hand as being too rare, too devastating. I looked over at Natalie. She was sitting bolt upright, staring across the room at a candy machine, her features still, as if carved from a block of marble.

After three and a half hours of constant agony, DeMaio came through the doorway. I was like any parent of a sick child, hyper alert to his body language, was he smiling? Did he look worried or discouraged? Exhausted? I stood to meet him, Natalie rushed over as Pops took my hand. DeMaio's expression gave me nothing; he looked tired, drawn. I thought I was going to faint. After a few seconds or a few hours, DeMaio took my hand, reached over and threw an arm around Natalie. "Zachary had a tear in his sagittal sinus. We got the bleeding stopped without too much trouble and he's resting in the recovery room."

I shook his hand again, tears of relief welling in my eyes. "Then he's all right? He made it through okay?"

DeMaio looked from Natalie to me and took his time, sending my adrenals into overdrive again. "Yes and no." His words fell like thirty-kilo weights around my shoulders; this was more than I could take. "He should be all right in the long run, but . . ."

Natalie nearly fainted. Pops caught her and helped her into the chair. She looked up at the Neuro surgeon and asked through pale lips, "Is he still paralyzed, Don?"

He shook his head, to our great relief. "No, we just had a little trouble with his rhythm and his BP." He looked over at me and I nodded, knew that expanding blood clots on the brain could and often did cause heart irregularities and low blood pressure. As long as he's intact, I thought, I could handle anything. He sensed our relief and continued, his tone one of professional concern. "He's stable. We'll keep him in ICU a day or two, of course, then see how he does on the ward. If he does well, he could go home by Friday."

Oh, thank you, God! I prayed silently. My heart beating for what seemed like the first time all day. "When can we see him?"

DeMaio ran a hand over his face; fatigue and stress clear in his eyes. "I'll tell them you'll be in recovery in ten minutes. How's that?"

I grabbed his hand and gave it another shake. "Thank you so much, Don. From the bottom of my heart."

He leaned over to kiss Natalie's cheek, turned to me and said, "He's a good, strong, healthy young boy. He should do pretty well with this." A few seconds later, he gave a tired wave and left the room.

We got to see him for a few minutes in the recovery room. The nurses cut us a lot of slack as we were both "family" at UCI. We were able to hold his hand, kiss him, and watch him briefly open his eyes. Enough to send my spirits soaring. I knew he had a long road ahead; still, he was alive and apparently well, all things considered. I couldn't ask for anything more.

That night in the ICU was my first all-nighter with a patient since internship. I watched every blip of his monitor, every respiration, every spike of his blood pressure, all the time willing him to keep going, to keep fighting. They extubated him at around five o'clock and it was uncanny. He opened his eyes, looked around and said, "I'm thirsty." That was it. A four-hour, critical operation, six hours in the ICU, major head trauma, and he was back. Alert, thirsty, and cranky. He knew what had happened, wanted to know if PaPa was mad at him, and wanted to know when he could go swimming again. DeMaio said these young kids usually did well, and thank God, our son was living proof. They did neuro checks on him every half hour, gave him the very best of care, and a day and a half later he was transferred upstairs to the fifth floor, Surgery.

The protocol was much more relaxed upstairs, so we took turns sleeping and staying in his room. Pops had the day shift while I went home for the first time in two days to shower and change clothes. Natalie went to her office to arrange her schedule and call coverage. I was due back at three to relieve Dad.

I walked in the room, and Dad and Zachary were playing poker. Zach with his stockinet head dressing, black eyes, and swollen face, Dad with his borrowed scrubs. They looked like a couple of escapees from the psych ward. I walked over, put an arm on my dad's shoulder. "Hey, what're you two doing?"

Zach smiled and reached out his hand. I shook his right, dropped it and then asked him to squeeze with his left hand. He gave me an irritated look. "Jeez, Dad. Doctor DeMaio was just here. Said I was almost good to go. Just about back to normal."

I looked over at my dad and elbowed him in the ribs. "So, Zachary, when have you ever been normal?"

He stuck out his tongue and lay down his cards: two pairs. Kings over tens. Pops was elated. "Stevie, did you see that? Our little Zachary has the touch."

"Don't give him any ideas, Dad. He's going to be a doc like his parents. I don't want him ruining his life in Vegas."

Zachary gave me a serious look, his voice steady, eyes boring into mine. "That's right, Dad. I'm going to be a surgeon." He looked over at my dad. "Like Dr. DeMaio."

I was crushed. Just like that, I'd been overthrown by a more glamorous specialty.

I had the night shift; Natalie had come and gone, with her mother who'd flown out from Florida. While they were in the room with Zachary, I took the opportunity to go down to the Department and catch up on my paperwork, since I hated administrative stuff only slightly less than I hated being around Natalie at this time in my life.

I settled in for the night with Zachary at eight, just as the last visitors cleared out. The nurses had set up a cot for me to sleep in; unfortunately it was only about five feet long, a full fifteen inches too short for me. No matter, the chair was fine, not the first time I'd spent the night that way. Zachary looked a little off to me. I checked his chart at the nurse's station, found his vitals and nurses notes, scanned DeMaio's latest, and found nothing out of the ordinary. I returned to the room a minute or two later, chalking his appearance up to stress and fatigue. God knows he'd been through enough lately.

I went over and kissed him good night, asked if he needed anything; he shook his head and went back to sleep. Nine o'clock and he was already zonked out. Strange, he'd had so much energy before, even right after they'd extubated him, I thought. I decided to read a few journals in my chair, keep a close eye on him, just in case.

I was awakened by the night nurse a couple of hours later, while she was doing her every-two-hour neuro checks. She was swinging her flashlight across Zach's field of vision, doing the strength check as she asked him, "Where are you tonight, Zach?"

My son sat up and answered, clear as a bell, "Knott's Berry Farm. The log ride."

The nurse laughed and patted his hand. Asked again and he got it right that time. She next asked him what day it was, he got it right the first time. A minute or two after the nurse had left, he peered across the gloomy room and said, "Daddy?"

I was out of my chair like a shot. "Right here, son. Do you need something?"

His voice was a little hoarse. "I need to pee."

I helped him to the bathroom, stood beside him while he did his business, held him close. "All right there, pal?"

He looked up at me and smiled, a drunken grin I'd not seen before. Must be the meds, I thought, either that or he's deep into a post-concussive syndrome. Finished with his business, I helped him back to bed, noticed that he was a little unsteadier, almost shuffling his feet, and that he needed a lot more support than he had even the second day in the ICU. I put him back to bed and he looked up at me in the pale light of the bathroom fixture, his voice a hoarse whisper. "Daddy. I don't want another operation." He tugged at my sleeve, his expression one of naked fear. "Don't let them operate again." His tone shattered my soul. "I'll die if they do."

My stomach lurched; I had to sit on the bedside chair before I fainted. I didn't want to alarm him, but all of us in medicine had heard this sort of thing from critically ill patients. We learned very early on in training to pay attention, as it was often a sign of precognition. All at once I was terrified, absolutely in a panic about his new symptoms: his confusion, his lethargy, his dysequilibrium. I tucked him in a little tighter, gave him a kiss, and mustered up all the courage I could, feeling like a scared boy inside as I reassured him. "You're going to be fine, son. Just wait and see."

I left his room for a second to check his monitors at the nurse's station. Everything looked normal. I spent a few minutes with the nurses, asked about his other neuro checks; they told me he was "a little off, but not too bad."

A minute or two later, I walked back to his room, through the door, and almost died on the spot. Zachary was exhibiting full-blown decerebrate posturing. His hands and feet were turned inward, toward his body, he was shaking from head to toe, and I was stuck. Immobilized with fear in the doorway, screaming at the top of my lungs for Don DeMaio.

The nurses ran as a group to his room; one of them peeled off and ran for the phones. I stood at my son's bedside, trying desperately to calm his posturing, trying with every fiber of my strength to will my son away from the edge. From slipping into what I knew was the next stage in this terrifying downward spiral: brain death.

Chapter 33

There was no time to notify anyone in-House, not at three-o'clock in the morning. DeMaio had to be called in from home. His senior resident, Stan Johnson, thank God, was at Zachary's bedside in less than five minutes. He'd had Mannitol, a powerful diuretic medicine, hanging in an effort to calm Zach's brain swelling in an instant, was feverishly going through a neuro check so that he could give DeMaio an accurate assessment over the phone. I sat in the corner of the room, watching with mounting horror, as Johnson was unable to get Zach to respond, not to shouted verbal commands, not even to painful stimuli. He ran to the nurse's station a few minutes into his exam and I could hear the phrase I'd been dreading since his accident; Zach's right pupil was non-reactive. He'd had so much swelling that his brain stem, the very center of life's functions, was in grave danger of complete shutdown.

DeMaio had just arrived, according to Johnson, who came back into the room a few minutes later with a scribbled consent asking my permission for a repeat frontal craniotomy, possible craniectomy. I choked down a surge of bile as I attempted to still my hand for the consent signature. They wanted to remove a piece of Zach's skull to relieve his swelling; that was how bad it had gotten. I didn't know whether to scream or cry as I watched them race down the hallway, my critically ill son strapped to a gurney. Zachary's last words hit me again with the force of a heart attack as the elevators opened, swallowing my son into the OR suite. No parent alive *ever* wants to hear their child tell them they're going to die.

Three-thirty and I was alone in the surgical waiting room. Again. I paced up and down the tiny room, making laps around the formation of plastic seats, my thoughts on a single obsessive track. Bargaining. Even as I knew I had no right, no claim on His time, I promised God that He could have me there and then. That I would sacrifice myself in that room any way He chose if He'd just spare my Zachary. He was so young, so innocent. I had lived my life, made my mistakes, and had no more to give than my life. I begged God to take me, pleaded with Him to spare my son, even though I'd not talked to Him often enough; I promised my life, I begged Him to please hear my voice.

Fifteen minutes into my ordeal, Barbara Manning appeared at the doorway dressed in a flowing white cover gown. She stood in the gloom of the waiting room, backlit by the hallway lights, as if she were God's answer from Heaven. She walked into the room straight into my arms. Her voice was sweet and soft in my ears, as if in a dream."I heard about him downstairs." She kissed my cheek, led me, on rubbery legs, to a chair. "I'm so very sorry, Steven. He doesn't deserve this trouble."

I held her hand, clinging to her for dear life. I sat there numb, my whole world imploding. He had done so well, I thought, out of the ICU in thirty-six hours, joking with Dad just yesterday, and now this. Try as I might, I couldn't make sense of it, couldn't even find a medical reason for it. His CT scans had been progressively better. I'd checked them personally every day with the NeuroRadiologist; no signs of a re-bleed, brain swelling receding. Every day he'd gotten better. How could this be happening?

Ten minutes later, DeMaio came out of surgery, flicked the lights on in the waiting room, and I ran across the room to him, still holding Barbara's hand. He had to have good news, I thought, with a surge of hope. This was all a mistake, just an anomaly, Zach wasn't really that sick after all. We could all go home in a day or two. Good as new.

One look at DeMaio's face in the harsh fluorescent lights and I knew. I knew Zachary was in real trouble. DeMaio didn't mince words. He put a hand on my shoulder. I wanted to swat it away, it was the same gesture I'd made hundreds of times while delivering horrendous news in the waiting room downstairs. Barbara felt it too, she tightened her grip on my hand, slipped an arm around my waist. DeMaio nearly killed me with his words. "Steven, I'm sorry, he has an opening pressure of seventy."

Oh . . . My . . . Dear . . . God! My little boy. My son. His intracranial pressure was seven times normal. His brain was being squeezed literally to death, trapped by his skull with nowhere to expand, no way to escape the crushing pressures. No other way to see it, DeMaio had just handed Zachary a death sentence.

I collapsed into Barbara's arms, couldn't hear what DeMaio was saying after that, could barely see him standing a foot in front of me. I nodded dumbly, my muscles incapable of motion, my brain unable to process anything except Zachary's impending death. No, God, not him, I screamed to myself. Please, God, not my son. I'm begging You.

I watched Barbara nod, adrift in Hell, a thousand miles away from her side. DeMaio held his hand on my shoulder, said something incomprehensible, and he was gone, through the doors to try his best for Zachary. Barbara led me back to our seats, and I laid my head on her shoulder, crying like a baby while she stroked my hair. After a few moments, she turned her head toward me and relayed, in a halting voice, choked with tears, what DeMaio had said. He was going to re-do Zachary's flap, enlarge the bony opening in his skull to help with his swelling. He'd told me that his chances of survival were less than twenty percent. And his chance of surviving without a significant deficit was less than ten percent. The news was so bad that I had an impossible time processing it. I was unable to speak, sobbing uncontrollably, managing only to say, "Dad" and "Natalie." Barbara nodded, reached into my pants pocket and pulled out my wallet. She leaned over to ask if it were all right for her to leave for a little while to call them. I nodded to her, tried to focus on her face through a torrent of tears, gave up, and closed my eyes against the searing pain.

I wake up crying at night, even all these years later; a vivid memory of what it felt like that Friday morning at UCI tearing at my sleep. I remember an ache deep in my soul, an absolute emptiness that made me feel as if my insides had been hollowed out, leaving only my heart and lungs. Leaving me barely functioning on a primitive, animalistic level. My brain was inoperative; I felt as if I had to will my heart to keep beating, as if I had to force my diaphragm to contract, to physically force my lungs to operate, to take in air.

I sat in that chair for five hours, rocking back and forth, clinging to Barbara, sobbing, unable to make a coherent sound. I felt myself at the edge of an abyss, light and insubstantial as a breath, ready to fall, an inch or two away from the end of my unspeakable pain. At the same time, I felt an eternity away from normalcy, from holding my son in my arms again. Please, God, I prayed, Just Let Me Hold Him One More Time.

I turned to Barbara, murmured that "I'd take Zachary any way I could, just let them release him so I could take him home." I could deal with him paralyzed, I could deal with him being unable to speak or see. I could handle him in a wheelchair, a walker, anything. I held her hand until I was afraid I was hurting her. I pleaded with her, "Please, Barbara, don't let them send him home in a box."

Pops sat two chairs down, struck mute by his own crushing grief. Natalie paced in the hall, murmuring in her cell phone nonstop, processing her terror the best way she could. And we waited. For a total of six and a half hours.

DeMaio appeared through the double doors, exhausted, pale, but with a half-smile on his face, an expression that I clung to as to a lifeboat. "He's in recovery." He shook my hand, gave Natalie a hug. "We didn't have to do a craniectomy, his pressure moderated a little bit with the Mannitol, but he's still one sick kid." He ran a hand through his hair, acknowledged Pops with a nod, and leaned over to kiss Barbara's cheek. He led us to a quiet corner of the waiting room and motioned for us to find a seat, clearly ready to divulge the rest. "He's going to have a very rough two or three weeks ahead, I'm not going to lie about that." He looked me in the eye, his tone as miserable as I'd ever heard it. "He probably is not going to be intact neurologically. The swelling was too . . ."

I grabbed for his sleeve. "But he's going to make it, isn't he, Don? I mean, he's not going to . . ."

He took his time and I sat there with the weight of the world on my shoulders as he took a deep breath, looked over at Natalie. "Steven, Natalie, I'm going to level with you. This kind of injury is very unpredictable. I've seen the whole spectrum of outcomes, from mild deficit to . . ." He didn't need to finish, we all saw it in his eyes, heard it in his voice. He cleared his throat; I watched his Adam's apple travel up and down his neck as he harnessed his emotions before continuing. "We're going to be as aggressive as hell with Zach. He has an ICP monitor in now. We'll have a double team of nurses in the unit." He placed a hand on each of our shoulders. "We'll do everything, folks. You know we will." And then he left, shoulders slumped, clearly exhausted.

We sat in silence, lost in our collective misery. People came and went in a blur of motion as the hospital came alive. The harried sounds of a productive Friday washed over us; frantic announcements on the P.A. system, alarm bells, gurneys wobbling down the hall. Lost as we were that terrible Friday morning, we might as well have been in a dungeon, deep under the Tower of London.

A minute or two later, Pops came back from the restroom, waving frantically. "Steven, Natalie. I saw him." He pointed toward the end of the hallway and the ICU. "They just wheeled him by me, headed to the ICU."

We ran as a pack down the long hall, arriving just as the door closed behind his gurney. A minute or two later, the charge nurse, Stephanie Walters, came out and told us it would be fifteen or twenty minutes before we could come in. They needed to settle Zachary in and adjust his monitors. Barbara waved to her friend Stephanie, walked over and whispered a few words. The door closed behind the charge nurse and Barbara came up to me, held my hand. "I'm going to transfer up here for a few days. Help out with Zach." I was overwhelmed. I knew she was due to go on vacation, in fact it started today, she had been so excited about taking her girls to Hawaii for the first time. My initial reaction was stunned gratitude, disbelief that someone would do such a wonderful thing. My second reaction was that I couldn't allow her do this to her children.

"I can't let you, Barbara." I looked into her eyes. It was clear from her expression that I was going to lose this argument. I gave it my best try, citing her daughters' disappointment, her missed flight, the expense of another ticket later on. She wouldn't hear any of it, shooting down each and every one of my objections. Inside, I was ecstatic, ready to fight like a wolverine for my son with the best nurse in the hospital at his bedside.

She sealed the argument by saying, "I'm going to get time-and-a-half, the girls will have more to shop with, and I'm in charge downstairs, so we can go to Hawaii anytime we want." She kissed my cheek. "So, it's settled." We shook on it and waited to be let into the unit.

An hour of anxious pacing later, we settled back into the familiar, harrowing routine of monitor watching, obsessive inquiries about his frequent neuro checks, followed by questions about what the results foretold for his recovery. DeMaio had put Zach into a drug-induced coma, using a powerful hypnotic drug that anesthesiologists used to begin their anesthesia. This was done to put the brain at rest and help reduce the traumatic effects of swelling. Studies had shown that sedative comas dramatically improved results in the long term. That was my fervent hope as we went into day three of our vigil. Zachary had a brand-new monitor for me to birddog, the Intra Cranial Pressure monitor, or "bolt." This was a telemetry device that measured, in real time, the pressure of the intracranial fluid circulating between the right and left hemispheres of Zach's brain. It gave us an idea of the progress or lack of improvement in his brain swelling. Zach's pressures had receded somewhat, but were still perilously high at around twenty-five to thirty. DeMaio tried to put on a positive face for us, but I knew he was worried. I remembered the nights I'd spent sweating over patients in Zachary's position when I was still in Surgery. Three days in, the clock was ticking and we were running out of options. Try as I might to avoid becoming depressed, it seemed to me at the time that my prayers hadn't seemed to matter much as I sat there and worried late into Monday night.

Pops came in around ten, late for him, as he usually took the early morning shift. He looked exhausted. I was worried about him; a week without sleep and killer stress could put anyone down and he was seventy-five.

I took a break as Pops settled in; left the ICU, and stopped at the end of the hall, stood by the window, staring at the lights strung along Chapman, watched people living their lives, running around without a care in the world. I hated every one of them for a second or two. I took stock of our situation as life went on fifty feet below me. I had done my praying, had tried to strike a bargain with God, really pleaded with Him and still, my son was the same. Perilously close to death. I was ready to give up on God, abandon prayer altogether. It simply hadn't worked; Zach was no better. I felt a quick stab of guilt; after all, God and I were strangers. I didn't even believe, so why should He help my son? I knew in my heart that night that Zach was paying the price for my cynicism and doubt.

I took a few moments to compose myself, gave it one more shot and said a silent prayer for Zach before returning to his room. Looking back on that Monday night many long and difficult years later, it *is* clear to me that Zachary turned a corner. A tiny one, but a significant, noticeable, turn for the better nonetheless. I saw it first in his ICP monitor. As I've said, I had been birddogging that screen for the better part of seventy-two hours; either I or Barbara would get the nurse, have her administer a bolus of Zachary's sedative and watch anxiously as the monitor settled back from fifty or sixty to thirty or forty. Until Monday night. Almost as I returned to his room, we noticed that his monitor stayed in the low teens. For the first time. Without bolusing his medication. We looked at each other and shrugged, unwilling to put too much into it at the time, but overjoyed at the results and the definite, objective improvement we were witnessing.

The trend continued for the next thirty-six hours; his pressure stood at ten when DeMaio and his crew came in for rounds on Wednesday morning. He looked at the bedside chart, checked Zach's previous tracings, scratched his head, showed the record to his senior resident, Stan Johnson, who gave me a bemused smile and the decision was made. It was time to extubate Zachary. DeMaio shook his head, came over to Barbara, Pops and me, and whispered, "I don't believe in God. Never have. But I've seen this too many times in my career to have any other explanation for you." He looked slightly embarrassed, as if he'd been humbled by an even stronger power than our shared deity: science and medicine. "I think we've just witnessed a miracle, Steven." He shook his head. "Nothing else explains Zachary's improvement."

Pops gave me a grin that I'll carry in my memory to my grave: full of overarching joy, unlimited love, and gratitude to God. Barbara hugged me and I couldn't stop laughing, great, rolling, nearly hysterical laughter, as Pops joined our circle of relieved hysterics.

A few minutes later, we collected ourselves as best we could and stood quietly in the corner as Respiratory removed Zachary's tube. There was no dramatic awakening, no sitting up and waving to the folks. Just a quiet sigh and a collective relief of tension from those of us standing anxiously by his bedside. The techs fussed over him for a few minutes, got his oxygen mask in place and adjusted the settings. The nurses came in next, did their neuro checks, and left us alone with Zachary. Clearly on his way back. At long last.

I walked to stand by his right side, Barbara next to me, her hand in mine, Pops stroking Zachary's face from his post on the left side of the bed. I looked down at my bruised and battered son and thanked God, again, for saving his life, for seeing him through this unspeakable ordeal. I didn't see the swollen, black eyes, the hideous machinery screwed into his skull, the yards and yards of stockinet dressing obscuring his head. I saw only the future. For the first time in more than two weeks, I could see myself holding my son, hear his laughter, feel his hand in mine. I could see his whole precious life unfolding before me. We stood there, frozen in place, our breath mingling with Zach's, paying silent homage to God, to the miracle of a restored life for the next thirty minutes.

A moment later, sobbing loudly, Natalie rushed in, took a place near Dad, and smothered Zachary with kisses. My eyes were dry; I'd cried more in the last fourteen days than I thought I could in ten lifetimes. I felt, for the first time, at peace with my new reality, with Zachary's state of health. Whatever the outcome, he was alive, and that was all that mattered. While I was saying my third or fiftieth silent prayer of thanks of the morning, Zachary opened his eyes, looked directly into mine, and my heart began to soar. He tried to talk, oxygen mask fogging with his muffled words.

I took a quick look at his oxygen saturation to make sure it was okay to remove his mask, noticed with relief that it stood at a healthy ninety-eight. I gently moved the mask aside and bent to my son, left ear an inch from his mouth. His whispered voice was a gift from Heaven. "How long have I been here, Daddy?" I stroked his face, ready to give him the whole story, about his accident on Tuesday two weeks ago, about the two surgeries, all of it. I launched into an explanation of his awful fall, and he stopped me with a gratifyingly strong grip on my sleeve. An instant later, he looked around the room, gave Natalie and Pops weak smiles and said, "No, Dad. I meant how long have I been back in ICU?" I nearly jumped to the ceiling. He was back. He was asking not about the last two weeks, but about the last five days, which meant his short-term memory was intact. I didn't dare hope for anything else, hearing his voice, listening to his complete comprehension of his situation was much more than I'd expected. I knew with all my heart that anything else would be a bonus.

All four of us leaned over and kissed him, a group hug of shared elation. I looked into his eyes a moment later, realized he looked tired and replaced his oxygen mask to let him rest, afraid that he would overtax himself. He promptly reached up with his right hand and removed it, gave me a stern look. A classic Adler scowl that told me all I'd needed to know. Zachary, our precious son, treasured grandson, was on his way. We looked at each other that morning in ICU and passed along an unspoken sentiment, one re-born soul to another: We had *indeed* witnessed a miracle.

Chapter 34

omecoming day. The day we'd been praying for, hoping for, and, for the last frantic twenty-four hours, running all over town preparing for. We were going to have the biggest blowout Breakers Drive, Newport Beach, had ever seen. Pops took charge of the food, gathering requests from the twenty kids whom Zach had invited, each and every one of whom had come to see him at UCI in the two days prior to his discharge. I was amazed at the loyalty and camaraderie my son engendered in his pals. I'd thought they would be squeamish, turn away, or worse, abandon him because he was "different." Not even close; virtually his whole class came by to offer encouragement, jokes and his favorite, double-double cheeseburgers from *In-N-Out*. No surprise, then, that Pops had reported that he "had the food situation handled." This after only an hour's work. He told me then that the little portable *In-N-Out* restaurant truck, basically a scaled-down version of their drive ins, would be parked outside our house from eleven till four, all you can eat and drink. Pops was a genius. I asked if he'd like to help with the decorations and pool area; he told me no, that he wanted to take a nap. I had to laugh. He was tired, no doubt from punching in all seven of those numbers.

No matter, Barbara and her girls and I managed to pull everything together in less than a day. Three trips to Kinko's, four to the party store, and five to various cake and grocery stores, and we were ready.

Natalie and I wheeled him down the ramp at UCI at exactly eleven in the morning, two and a half weeks and a lifetime of worry since he'd hit his head. He was still a little unsteady on his legs, still had about a forty percent left-sided weakness, but his spirit was stronger than ever. He'd learned a great lesson about life in the hospital, realized who his true friends were and how important they were to him. Several of his tough-guy sixth grade buddies were in his room late at night sobbing in the corner, unable to look at their friend in that deplorable condition. Zach told me a few nights ago that he'd "never, ever take anything for granted again." I had to second that one with the hardest high-five I could muster. We had all changed, all gone through Hell, and come out intact in all the ways that counted, spiritually if not physically. I couldn't change the fact that we were not back together as a family, but there was no doubt at all that we stood strongly united behind Zachary.

The traffic was mercifully light and after only a half-hour of the most pleasant drive I can remember, we drove up to the house. Zachary started laughing, tears of joy running down his cheeks. He shouted and pointed to the little white *In-N-Out* truck, blue awning proudly unfurled in our drive, proclaiming it "bitchen." He slugged my arm when he read the giant sign over our driveway. *"Welcome home, Zach. Do NOT do this again. Ever!"*

I was nearly as happy as I'd ever been, second only to the morning he was born, as I waved to his friends on our lawn, all thirty-one of them, lined up to welcome him home, dressed in their swimsuits and shorts, Silly-String canisters at the ready to christen the moment. I went around the front of the car and helped him out, grabbed his tripod cane from the back seat, and gave him my arm. He refused with a smile, said, "I can handle it, Dad."

He took his time, reveling in the attention as we were bombarded with Silly-String, raucous laughter, and abundant love. The moment I'd been praying for over the past two weeks had arrived, in the same instant that I knew, without a doubt, the true meaning of life: Family, Health, and Happiness. Nothing else matters.

The party was a hit; neighbors sent their kids, DeMaio and his three boys came by to swim, even my residents showed up, drank all my beer, and kept changing the music to hip hop. I thought Zach and his friends would be upset, tried to change it back to classic rock. My son came over to my chair and set me straight after my second attempt to change the music, leaned down, whispered in my ear, "Dad, leave it on the other stuff. Nobody wants to listen to your dinosaur rock." He gave me an intense stare. "Trust me."

Barbara even got me up on the dance floor, a rented piece of hardwood, spread out on the lawn next to the pool. I was proud and a little surprised by my performance, as no one got hurt and nobody but my son and his friends laughed openly. My residents seemed to be suppressing laughs, though, coughing and fake-sneezing to cover their hilarity, but on second thought, it could have been allergies for all I knew.

The party broke up at around ten. Zach got his legs wet and was begging me to let him go in all the way. Luckily his surgeon was standing next to me, and DeMaio said that he'd have to wait a week or two, let his scalp heal a little more. Other than that, Zach was on top of the world, reveling in his home, happy to be surrounded by so many people who loved him.

I even saw him talking to a girl, someone I hadn't met yet. They were huddled at the shallow end of the pool, sharing a chaise lounge, deep in conversation, oblivious to the glorious party a few feet away. I watched them from the patio, transfixed by the transition Zachary had gone through. He had started to show an interest in girls just before his accident, but, like most dads, I deluded myself into thinking that I could delay "the talk" for a few more years, told myself my son was still too young. While I was sure their talk was purely innocent, I was still struck by Zach's sudden maturity and willingness to reach out to his friends. Surprised and proud. My boy had grown up in the last month, especially, it seemed, in the past two weeks or so.

I couldn't restrain myself a minute longer, had to go over and find out who this young lady was who had obviously caught my son's eye. I tried to be cool about it, sashayed over with Barbara, tried to make it look as if I were just wandering over because the dance floor was located near his chair. Zach didn't buy it for a second. I could see him clam up; whispers and laughs with his friend, a quick nod in my direction, and I knew I was busted.

No matter, I walked right up, stuck out my hand and said, "Hi. I don't think we've met." She was adorable, curly blond hair, green eyes, a spray of freckles over her nose. We shook hands and she gave me an embarrassed smile. "I'm Zachary's father, Steven."

She giggled, Zach looked mortified. She looked from Zach to me, and said, "I'm Sarah Fox. I met Zachary in the hospital."

This was news to me, thought I'd seen all of his friends and visitors, wondered when he'd have time to meet someone so cute and so nice. Had to find out, nosy father that I am. "You're too young to be a nurse. Are you . . . ?"

Her tone was measured, confident, I was immediately impressed by her poise and obvious intelligence. "No, sir, I'm a volunteer. In the ICU."

Zachary had clearly had enough; I noticed his blush even in the dim light of the Tiki torches. "Dad, she's a candy striper, O-KAY?" A serious note of finality in his voice. To hammer his point home, he gave me the look I'd seen many times before, the one I'd given my parents in similar situations, the *"get lost, will you?"* look.

I could take a hint. I waved and said my good-byes, inwardly pleased that Zachary's first female friend was so committed and mature. A definite stroke of good luck.

An hour after we said good-bye to the guests, I went into his room to help him dress for bed. He was getting used to his disability a little at a time, never complained, even when it took him several extra minutes and multiple attempts to do things he hadn't even thought about before. I helped him pull over his pajama top, snugged his bottoms around his waist, and sat on his bed, gave him a quick once over. "You've gotten skinny, son." I pulled the sheets up to his chin, ran a gentle hand over his surgical buzz cut. "Gonna have to fatten you up. PaPa's going to have to fire up the grill again."

Zachary looked up at me with the look I'd first seen that day so many lifetimes ago, when we slept together in his baby room at Natalie's house: complete and utter contentment. He put his right hand on my cheek and said, "I love you more than anything, Dad."

I hadn't cried since that Monday night, over a week ago, thought I was completely cried out. But I couldn't help it, here was my little boy, back home where he belonged, if not as good as new, as good as I could ever have hoped. I had died a little with his every setback, found strength and the courage to hope with every small step forward, even discovered my faith over the past fortnight. I had started the month like most of us, preoccupied with putting food on the table, mundane events that sometimes took on monstrous proportions: minor crises at work, bad traffic, any number of daily annoyances that form the background noise of our lives. I ended this month with a hard-earned appreciation for the truly big things, the vital things about life: the people you love, the people who love you back. Most importantly, I'd learned a new appreciation for how precious our children are to us. They are so resilient, yet so fragile. They are the reason we go to work every day, the reason we stay up at night, sick with worry, the reason we save for the future, the reason we fear the darkness, and the reason we marry. Hopefully forever.

I kissed my son's stubbly scalp, the most wonderful feeling in the world and whispered in his ear, "You are everything to me, Zachary. I love you, too. Welcome home, son."

Chapter 35

Zachary started rehabilitation the very next week. He'd gone to DeMaio's office for staple removal and another CT scan, yet another anxious moment of waiting for me. DeMaio came to our exam room an hour after we'd come in and apologized for being late, said Zach's scan "was good, just a thin residual and no re-bleed" He meant that my son had just a tiny amount of old blood that was being reabsorbed by his system, but hadn't reac-cumulated any new clots. Definitely good news.

Zach was then put through his paces with a full neuro exam, and I really noticed, for the first time, how serious his deficit was. He had trouble balancing on his right foot, had difficulty extending and flexing his arm and leg on the left, and stumbled badly when DeMaio asked him to climb stairs without his cane. DeMaio looked at me after his nurse took Zach to the hallway, to be weighed and measured, anxiety on his face. "He's a little bet-ter, Steven. I'm still concerned about his hemiplegia."

I had not, for even an instant, complained or felt resentful that Zach had not come home "perfect." I was simply overjoyed to have him home at all, so DeMaio's words, although discomforting, were

343

not as depressing to me as I would have thought just a few weeks ago. I opened the exam room door, took a peek down the hall to make sure Zachary wouldn't overhear. "Is he going to get better from that standpoint, Don?"

DeMaio wrote a note while I looked around his exam room, at the brightly colored anatomical charts, the standing plastic model of the spine, and the cross-sectioned brain, resting serenely on the medication cabinet. At length he looked up, his tone somber. "That's hard to say, Steven."

I stared at his model of the brain, my thoughts on a few weeks ago, on the terrible fragility of life, on the miracle we'd witnessed. "I understand, Don. I'm not being greedy, not at all, I just wanted to know what to expect. What to tell Zach when he starts asking questions."

DeMaio put aside his chart, sat on the exam table across from me, lab-coat crinkling on the paper cover. "Having said that, I will say he's a very strong kid and I've seen several boys his age make really astounding progress." As DeMaio finished his comment, Zach came in with a Tootsie Roll pop and a note for DeMaio. The surgeon scanned it, ruffled Zach's half-inch scalp hair, and looked me in the eye. "If anyone can do it, Zach here can."

Zach hopped over to sit beside me, a quizzical look on his face. "Zach can do what, Dad?"

I laid a hand on his knee. "Zach can do anything he wants." I nodded to DeMaio. Right, Don?"

He stood and gave Zachary a wide smile. "Absolutely. Without a doubt, Zach." With that, he left us alone.

I helped Zach gather his things and we found our way to the car, headed south again, to physical therapy at Pacific Rehabilitation Services in Corona Del Mar.

Pacific Rehab looked a lot like my L.A. Fitness gym across from Bloomingdale's at Newport Center; state-of-the-art treadmills, weight machines, running track, and a four-lane lap pool.

Everything but the juice bar and racquetball courts. I was impressed; Zach was a little intimidated, I could tell because he became quiet, tentative, as I held the door for him. We'd talked about this important step in his recovery, of course, but the reality had only hit him when we arrived.

I led him to the reception desk where a perky twenty-something girl greeted us. "Hi, I'm Tracy." She shook my hand, gave Zach a warm smile, and came around the desk, shook his as well. "And you must be Zachary Adler."

Zachary gave her a shy smile in return, studiously avoiding staring at her pretty, freckled face. "I actually like Zach better." I thought I saw him blush as the petite receptionist rested a hand on his arm and winked at him.

"Zach it is, then. Let me show you around." She led us on a whirlwind tour of the twenty-two thousand-square-foot space. Showed Zach what he'd be doing "to help your arm and leg get better." She demonstrated the various Nautilus and Cybex machines, gave him a tour of the pool and locker rooms, and lastly took him to the sauna where she said he could relax after his workouts. Zachary had been very active before the accident and had gone with me a few times to L.A. Fitness, but this was his first time alone with the machines, and I could tell he was a little reluctant. Tracy caught his mood immediately and smiled as Zach tried a bench press. Her voice and manner impressed me as totally professional, rare in someone so young, I thought. "I'm going to be your therapist for the next six months or so . . ."

Zachary gave me a pained look, clearly disappointed that his therapy would take so long, understandably impatient as he was to get back into the mainstream of life. I put a hand on his shoulder and said, "Pops is going to be here every day with you, he'll be here to help Tracy set up and get you back in shape."

Tracy leaned over and looked directly in his eyes. Her voice was soothing; her demeanor belied her young age and apparent lack of experience. She moved her right hand to her scalp, parted her long, blond hair mid way back, and pointed to a thin, white scar running from the top of her right ear nearly to the left. "See, we have a lot in common, Zach."

Zachary craned his neck to take a closer look. "No way?"

She fluffed her hair back in place. "Hells yeah." She put her hands on her hips, gave him a challenging look. "I had my surgery less than two years ago." Zach stared at her open-mouthed. "I came in here using a walker, now I snowboard, play tennis, water ski, everything I used to, before . . ."

Zachary was beaming; hope restored, confidence building, it was clear from his upright posture and grim determination. "You're not putting me on, are you, Tracy?"

She leaned closer, his twenty-something partner in crime. "I'm not going to shine you on, Zach. It was a hell of a lot of work, and took longer than I ever thought it would, but look at me now. You didn't believe I was worse off than you when I came here, did you?"

He gave her the look of the recently converted, clearly ready to get started. "No way. No way in hell."

He caught my look, gave an apologetic grin and they were off, headed for the locker room and the first step in Zachary's journey.

Chapter 36

SIX MONTHS LATER

It was my forty-fourth birthday, and Pops and Zachary had cooked up something special. They had made a date for us to play Shadow Hills in Laguna Niguel, a new public course that I'd been dying to try. Zachary was over the moon with excitement; his limp had improved to the point that he hardly needed a cane anymore, only when walking over rough terrain or occasionally when he was tired and had to navigate stairs. His arm strength, as far as I could tell, was lagging behind quite a bit. He still needed help with things he'd had absolutely no trouble with before, like slinging his backpack over his shoulders, handling grocery bags; still had problems doing pushups at therapy, according to Dad. Not that I was worried or complaining, of course. I was thrilled that he felt well enough to tackle a full round of golf. It didn't seem like seven months since his accident; every day had been so precious to me, to everybody in the Adler family. We had made a real effort to eat all of our meals together, Pops, Zach, and I, and we couldn't get enough of Zachary's laughter and his good-natured insults, at my expense, of course. His memory seemed fine; his teachers reported that he was back on the honor roll, seemed to have no trouble reading or with math, so we were indeed extremely blessed.

The first hole, Zach and Pops took their time, lining up their respective tee shots just so, taking into account the wind strength and direction, uneven terrain, even the weight of their golf balls; all in all, making fools of themselves. They were like a couple of kids, having the time of their lives. Pops hit his usual, a nice two hundred-twenty-yard drive down the center of the fairway. Zach seemed to have a little trouble with his, but still managed to knock it directly down the middle, landing about seventy yards behind Dad's ball.

I came up and took my usual three or four practice swings, trying to tune out the catcalls and whistles from the dolts in the other cart. I could hear my son saying, "White tees. White tees." Pops was no better, laughing like a stoned teenager at everything Zach said. The pressure was on. I didn't want to duplicate the Riverside fiasco and dribble my shot down to the women's tee. I was more than a little worried, as it had been nine months or so since I'd played. We'd been so focused on Zach's rehab that golf had obviously taken a back seat to everything else. I took a few seconds between my practice swings to take a look around. The course was located on a bluff, about two miles from the coast. The morning fog had receded far enough so that Catalina Island was clearly visible, seemingly floating over the horizon to the northwest, and the shoreline shone as if freshly scrubbed. The course was immaculately groomed, lined on either side by forty-foot cypress and date palms. One of the prettiest courses I'd played, certainly the most expensive, four hundred a round including carts. What the hell, I thought, money is nothing compared with spending an afternoon with my guys. Besides, considering what happened a few months ago, I'd have given everything I'd ever owned to play golf with my son.

It was clear from the clowns in the other cart that my practice time was up and it was time to perform. Pops was yelling for a one-stroke penalty for noncontinuous play; Zach was laughing beside my dad until his eyes filled with tears. I squared my shoulders, took a long, slow, backswing, and connected. Like I'd never hit one before. I experienced golfer's nirvana, that unmistakable sensation when club-head meets ball and you feel almost nothing. The tremendous momentum generated by your swing is transmitted instantly and seamlessly to the target and you can almost see the impact side of the ball cave in as it's launched off the tee. I jerked my head up, just in time to see my shot sail over Dad's, landing a good thirty yards past his. The first time I'd ever out-driven Pops. I felt like a kid. Wanted to dance around their stupid cart, making faces, strutting like Bill Murray in *Caddyshack.*

I looked over at the other cart. They gave me nothing, simply undid the parking brake and sailed off down the path. No "Great shot, Dad," no "Way to go, Stevie." Nothing. Sore losers, I thought, as I followed in their wake.

The second shot is one I'll remember the rest of my life. Zachary was away, about one hundred eighty yards from the pin, with a forty- or fifty-foot tall date palm blocking his path to the green. I expected him to take the safe route and skirt around the tree, even if it meant a bogey, because I knew he didn't have the arm strength and hand/eye coordination necessary to make that shot. Not yet.

As he jumped out of the cart, I noticed immediately that something was different with him. He took a five iron from his bag, did a couple of limbering up exercises and seemed utterly smooth, catlike in his movements, none of the stiff back and awkward carrying angle he'd had since the accident. He carried his left arm with a totally natural posture, almost like before, I thought, with a puzzled grin. I didn't dare hope, couldn't be disappointed, but still, he looked really good. He didn't limp, didn't even hesitate as he negotiated the ten feet or so on the downward-sloping fairway. He approached his ball with an infectious confidence. Squared his shoulders, took a last look at the pin, and hit his shot. A monster, straight as a laser, that cleared the tree with at least ten feet to spare. I ran out of my cart, as did Pops, and we stood beside each other, open-mouthed, as Zach's shot hit the green ten yards past the pin, bit with top spin, and rolled backward to a stop three feet from the hole. I looked at Pops; he didn't say a word. He didn't have to. His astonishment and absolute joy were mine as well.

A beaming Zachary sauntered up to us, grabbed Pops in a tight embrace, and whispered, "Thank you, PaPa. For everything."

Pops slapped him on the back and laughed, his smile an absolute wonder to behold. "You did all the work, Zach. Your old PaPa just pushed you in the right direction, is all."

They turned to me, these two, whom I loved more than anyone alive, and sang, badly off-key, but in perfect unison, "Happy Birthday, Dad. Zach's back."

I stood that day on the edge of America, facing the glittering Pacific, surrounded by timeless beauty, by more love than I'd imagined existed, and gave thanks to God, once again, for saving my son. He'd made it through emotional trials and physical pain worse than anyone should have to endure, yet I had no doubt that he'd become a better person for it. We all had.

I took two steps forward and embraced my perfect son. Zachary Adler, My Miracle Child.

* * * * * * * *

Acknowledgments

My Dear Readers,

Writing is the ultimate solo act, but nothing is created in a vacuum. Writing *Six PM Sunday* was a revelation for me, a journey to the very essence of love and life that at times was emotional and harrowing, at other times incredibly fulfilling. I would like to take sole credit for all of the errors and omissions contained in my novel and praise the following wonderful people for the very best portions of *Six PM Sunday*.

I feel blessed to have had the following cast of characters behind me every step of the way.

For early and invaluable assistance in shaping the manuscript, I would like to thank: Charlotte Boe, Ph.D., Gerard Boe, Ph.D., Andrew Deppe, Julie Johnson, Susan Ward, Stephen Weiser, J.D., Mark Weichert, M.D., Jamie Ziggler, Susie Brusig, R.N., Victoria McKinney, R.N., Leslie Albert, R.N., and last but certainly not least, Angela Throith-Fraser, R.N. You are the best support group any author could ever wish for. Thank you for your insight, advice, and criticism.

To: Joel Gotler, President, Intellectual Property Group, Los Angeles. Thank you for your sustaining faith in my abilities and for your invaluable help in shaping and focusing *Six PM Sunday*.

To: The graphic designers at 1106 Design, who are responsible for the wonderful cover art and typesetting style you've enjoyed while reading *Six PM Sunday*.

Finally to Shirlee Sandborg, I give my undying gratitude. My agent, confidante, great friend, amateur psychiatrist, and harshest critic, I owe everything that *Six PM Sunday* is and everything it may become. You are the reason I continue to pursue my dream.

David Colgrove is a practicing surgeon,
living in Southern California and Nice, France.
Six PM Sunday is his third novel.
He is also the author of *Left Back* and *Paris Homicide*.

Contact him at his website:
davidcolgrove.com